Murder
in the Redbrush

A Fire Marshal Jon Novel

by

D. E. Eifler

DORRANCE
PUBLISHING CO
EST. 1920
PITTSBURGH, PENNSYLVANIA 15238

Dorrance Publishing Co
585 Alpha Drive
Pittsburgh, PA 15238
Visit our website at *www.dorrancebookstore.com*

ISBN: 978-1-4809-4638-5
eISBN: 978-1-4809-4615-6

INTRODUCTION

In the southwestern portion of Jackson County Ohio is an area called the Redbrush. If one were to draw a line from the city of Jackson, which is the county seat of Jackson County, down to the village of Minford in Scioto County and east to the village of South Webster, which also is in Scioto County and then northeast to the Village of Oak Hill in Jackson County and back north to Jackson, this would be the area of the Redbrush. The Redbrush name came from the era of the old iron furnaces that were scattered over these hills during the mid to late 1800s. These old stone furnaces can still be found on the hillsides throughout the area. Charcoal was needed to make the iron. It was an important ingredient. The charcoal was made by cutting down trees and burning them in furnaces that smoldered for a long time producing the charcoal. Timber for charcoal making was cut on the hillsides and created large open areas that were barren. The first thing to grow back was the sumac trees. These trees grow very fast. In the fall, when the leaves change colors, the sumac turns a bright red color. Thus, the name Redbrush.

CHAPTER 1

The phone was ringing. He rolled over and reached for it. It wasn't on the stand. He found it on the floor next to her jeans. *Where was she?* he wondered. She wasn't in bed. He answered the phone.

"Hello."

"This is Jackson County Sheriff's Office; we got a house fire out on Glen Cozy Road with a body in it. Dave wants you to come out there."

"Okay. Where at?"

"1877 Glen Cozy," said the female dispatcher.

He knew if Dave wanted him out there that it was important. They had been friends for a long time. Before he went to work for the fire marshal, he and Dave had worked together at the sheriff's office. He had been the only detective when he left to join the fire marshal. Dave took his place as the SO's only detective. Dave Jeffers had worked at the sheriff's office for seven years. He was a good investigator. He was a very big and strong man who had worked hard with his hands as a mechanic for years before he became interested in police work. He was a natural at the job. He was also a compassionate man. He treated people right. He was the only person he knew who could send someone to prison and when he dropped the person off at the pen the person would shake his hand and thank him for sending him there. That was because he treated everyone with respect. He had never heard him raise his voice to a law breaker or anyone else.

"Okay, I'll head that way shortly," he told the radio dispatcher.

He got up and put on his pants and went and opened the bathroom door. "Excuse me," he said as he observed the young blond lady in his bathtub. She was shaving her long legs with his razor. She pulled the shower curtain closed.

"I got to go to a fire," he said.

"I'll walk to work and get someone to take me to get my car after work," she said.

He then remembered they had left her car at the disco after dancing till the place closed at 1:00 A.M. He pulled the shower curtain aside and gave her a kiss on the lips. It was the first time he had seen her without her clothes like this. It was totally dark in the house when they undressed for bed, about four hours ago. They had known each other for several years, but this was the first time they had been together in this way. They hung around with the same bunch of people, and every Saturday night, they all met at the disco. She had to work the day shift at the plant. He usually had Sundays off, unless he got called out like just happened.

"Help yourself to the kitchen; there's cereal and bacon and eggs," he said as he finished dressing.

"I'm still full from stopping at the diner after we left the disco," she replied.

"Okay, I'll call you this evening," he said after slipping his Smith and Wesson Model 19 snub nosed revolver in its holster through his belt loop and headed for the car.

Jon Hamer had been an investigator for the State Fire Marshal for one year now. He had been a deputy sheriff for seven years, with a one-year interruption as a city police officer. He had liked being a foot patrol officer for the city, but he preferred the county and rural law enforcement. About four years ago, he had joined the local volunteer fire department and found out that he really liked firefighting as much as he liked being a cop. Now he had the best of both jobs: investigating fires. He had really lucked into the job. He was eating lunch in the kitchen of the county jail one day and the fire marshal, as most fire investigators were called, came in and got a plate and filled it from the big stove in the kitchen and sat down to eat. He had known the old fire marshal, Bob, for eight years now. He knew that Bob was thinking about retiring. That day in the jail kitchen, Bob told him that he would recommend him for his replacement, as he was leaving in three months. It didn't take Jon but a minute to say yes. He liked being a deputy sheriff, but the pay was poor, and he knew that the state job paid a lot more. Bob got on the phone after eating and called his boss and told him he found his replacement and arranged for an application to be mailed to Jon.

Three months later, Jon went to Columbus and was sworn in and issued a car: a 1978 Plymouth Fury with a hundred thousand miles on it. He had to furnish his own gun, so he traded in his Colt Python .357 magnum for the Model 19, which was also a .357, but with a two-inch barrel. The Python was just too big and heavy to carry concealed. The Python had served him well as a deputy sheriff. In 1980, there were not many cops carrying automatics yet. He only knew one: his old friend, J.O. from Lawrence County, who carried a Colt 1911 like the military used.

He spent six months in training. He would attend classes at the Fire Academy for two weeks and then go out and work with an experienced investigator for four weeks. In all he worked with four different investigators during his training period. They were all different, and he learned from each one. When at the academy, he stayed in the dorms the students stayed in. It was like staying in a fire house in a city fire department with about twelve beds per dorm room and a common shower down the hall. When out in the field working with an investigator, he stayed in a motel and they sent him all over the southern part of the state to work with different investigators.

Now he was on his own. The day the Chief of the Arson Bureau told him his training was over he would never forget. The chief said, "It's like we're setting you up in business down there in southern Ohio. You won't have much supervision, as it's only me and the assistant chief to look after all twenty-two of you investigators. That's why you were picked for the job. You know how to work without supervision. As long as I don't get any complaints, I'll leave you alone to do your job."

The chief was true to his word. He had not seen him for two months. He talked to him on the phone about once every two weeks. The assistant chief traveled around the state, doing polygraph exams for the different investigators and spending a little time with each of them. He had yet to spend a day with him. He had got to know him during his training period and found him to be a nice guy. He was old enough to be his dad and had retired from a city fire department and then went to work for the state.

Each fire investigator for the State Fire Marshal had from three to six counties that he was responsible for, depending on the size of the counties, the fire activity in the counties, and the amount of involvement of the local authorities in investigating fires. The big cities like Columbus and Cleveland had their own fire investigators in their fire departments or police departments.

Mostly the State Fire Marshal assisted and worked for the smaller counties and cities and villages. John Hamer's headquarters county was Jackson County. He didn't have an office anywhere. He did his reports and made his phone calls from home. His office equipment consisted of a portable manual type-writer and a two-drawer file cabinet. He conducted business in firehouses, sheriff's offices, and police stations in whatever jurisdiction he might be investigating a fire in.

After leaving the house, Jon stopped and got a cup of coffee and headed out past the lake and turned onto Glen Cozy Road. Fire Marshals drove un-marked cars and did not use lights and sirens. He didn't even have a red light to set on his dash. Didn't need one. His job was to figure out what caused the fire. Not put it out.

He had to park at the bottom of the driveway, as the drive was crowded with fire trucks. When he got to the top of the drive, he saw a marked sheriff's car. It was Dave. Even though he worked in plain clothes and was a detective, he preferred to drive a marked car. He noticed that the firefighters were rolling up their hoses and getting ready to go back to the station.

"Hey Jonny," said Dave Jeffers. He was sitting in his car drinking a can of pop. "Haven't seen you for a while; where you been keeping yourself?"

"Down in Lawrence County," Jon replied. "You know how that place is… fires every day. Arrested me a real fire bug."

"What'd he set on fire? A couple bales of hay?" Dave said, referring to the big round bales that farmers were using now. They left them sit outside instead of putting them in a barn.

"Well, that's how he said he got started out a couple of years ago, but he got tired of them and started doing barns and then old houses."

"You get a confession?" replied Dave.

"Yeah, J.O. and I got him to talk. Two houses, six barns and he don't re-member how many hay bale fires."

"Them farmers need to quit parking all those big hay bales in one place so close to the road, so the fire bugs can't get to them so easy," said Dave.

"Yeah, I know, but they say they can't get to them when the snows real deep if they put them back away from the road."

"Get in the front seat, and I'll tell you what we got here," said Dave.

Jon went around and got in the front seat of the cruiser. Dave kept his front seat cleaned off so he could use it to talk to people. So many cops had all their stuff sitting on the front seat and they had to put the witnesses in the back seat, which made them feel more like a prisoner.

A firefighter came up to the car and knocked on the window, and Jon rolled it down. He noticed it was a young lady. She had a pot of coffee and offered to fill his cup. He thanked her. There weren't many female firefighters around, just like there weren't many female cops around. When he was doing his training, he had to go to some of the bigger cities, and he met a couple of female firefighters. The first time he was standing at the urinal in a fire station taking a leak, a lady in uniform walked in and smiled and went in a stall. When he got done at the urinal, he turned around and saw that she was sitting on the throne and hadn't even shut the stall door.

"A lady lives here by herself. They found a body in the living room, but its burned really bad, so we're waiting on the coroner," Dave explained.

Jon looked up at the fire scene. It was a trailer. The metal roof had been peeled off by the firefighters and was laying in the front yard so they could get to the fire. The wall studs were mostly burned up, so he guessed that the floor probably wasn't in very good shape. They were ten miles from the fire station, so there wasn't much saving to be done on trailers in this neck of the woods.

"What do ya know about her?" Jon asked Dave.

"She's in her early eighties, lives alone, doesn't drive. Her niece and nephew live down the road next place; I been talking to them. They watch after her and take her to town when she needs to go, and today they would have taken her to church with them if this hadn't happened. Her name is Inez Burton."

"Who reported the fire?" Jon asked.

"Guy up the road about a quarter mile; said he woke up to go the bathroom and saw a glow in the sky and looked out and knew it was the old lady's place, so he called the fire department. He got in his car and drove down and told the niece and nephew and then came up here and this whole end of the place was burning." Dave pointed to the right end of the trailer. "Time the fire department got here the place was burning from one end to the other."

"You know the woman?" Jon asked Dave. In a small county like this, cops like Dave knew a lot of the folks; both good and bad folks.

"No, don't know her. Met the niece and nephew once. He's some kind of a preacher that travels around a lot, and they keep some foster kids at their house. Seem like good people. Was there once to back up a deputy on a call.

One of the foster kids was throwing a fit and tore his bedroom all up. Got him calmed down, and the preacher said they would take care of it."

"They have a lot of trouble like that?" Jon said.

"Nope, that's the only call we've ever had there."

"Looks like the coroners here, Jonny," said Dave.

"I hope he's sober this time." Jon replied referring to the fact that the old doc usually had a strong odor of alcohol on his breath whenever he came out at night on a call. In recent years, he didn't come out much at night.

"That ain't Doc Carter; he don't come out anymore. Got him an investigator to help him. Good lookin', too."

Jon saw a black Ford pickup go slowly past the cruiser and park behind a fire truck. The door opened, and a tall, young woman in tight jeans and cowboy boots got out and looked around. Looked to be in her early twenties.

"That's the doc's granddaughter," said Dave. "Just got out of nursing school and got a job at the hospital. Doc Carter got the county to hire her to help him so he doesn't have to go out at night anymore since no one else wants the coroner's job. She's a good looker, all right."

"Yeah, I reckon she is. She from around here?"

"Chillicothe," said Dave. "Her dad's a big shot at the paper mill up there. Come on, and I'll let you meet her."

They got out and walked up the hill to the pickup. Jon noticed some loose hay in the bed of it. He knew the doc had horses and cattle on his farm.

"Liz, this is the Fire Marshal."

Jon extended his hand and took hers. "I'm Jon Hamer, the fire investigator; glad to meet you."

"Glad to meet you, Jon," she said with a nice smile. "This is my first fire death, so you'll have to show me around. I've been on a couple suicides with Dave."

Jon looked down at her cowboy boots. They had mud on them. "Looks like you're dressed for the occasion," he said. "Doc always wore his best pair of shoes when he came out, till we got him a pair of fire boots."

"I was just doing chores when I got the call. I got to be at the hospital at eight for my shift,, but I can call in that I'll be late if need be," she said as she pulled a bag out from behind the seat of the truck.

"I got to get my shovel and camera, and I'll be back up," Jon said to Liz and Dave.

By the time he got back up to the trailer, Liz was taking pictures of the body. It was laying on a couple of two by six floor joists that were heavily charred. Most of the trailer floor was burned through. He would have to walk on the ground beneath the trailer, which put him about waist high to the top of the floor joists.

"I'm goin' to go talk to the neighbors while you do your thing," said Dave as he turned to go back down the hill. Jon knew Dave didn't like the burned ones. He didn't mind dead bodies, but he said he couldn't stand the smell of the burned ones. It smelled too much like barbequed chicken, he said.

Liz had on a pair of rubber gloves. Jon handed her a surgical mask and put one on. He put on a pair of light rubber gloves and then a pair of leather firefighter gloves over them. The leather would keep him from getting cut, and the rubber would keep him from getting body fluids on his hands. He also wore three-quarter-length rubber fire boots, the kind similar to waders that fishermen wear. He had on an old canvas fire coat that some fire chief had given him. The state didn't provide any kind of protective clothing.

"Do we know who we think it is?" Liz Carter said to Jon.

"An elderly female lived here by herself," the fire marshal told her.

He then started clearing the fire debris off the body with his gloved hand, gently.

"Looks to be face down," Jon said as he worked slowly.

"Where's her legs and arms?" Liz asked.

"They're burned off; they may have fallen down in the crawl space. We'll see if we can find them later; I'm going to roll her over with my shovel." He placed the shovel beneath the main part of the body and rolled it over. Beneath was unburned clothing that appeared to be a night gown. He pulled a plastic bag out of his pocket and placed some of the clothing in it to keep for identification and also to send to the lab to test for accelerants. The State Fire Marshal had one of the best forensic laboratories in the country.

"Can you come in here and determine sex?" he said to Liz. She got down and crawled under the trailer and came up between the floor joists with black all over her face and shirt.

Jon pointed and said, "This is the head. It appears to be intact; sometimes it explodes from the heat, but it didn't happen here." He was referring to the fact that often in a hot fire the fluid in the head expanded and caused the skull to explode. An inexperienced investigator might think that the head had been crushed with a weapon.

Liz started looking at the other end of the body. He had to give her credit. She didn't mind getting right in there. Doc never did this. He always waited till the body got to the funeral home to examine it.

She placed her gloved hand on the pubic area and poked around and said, "Appears to be female. I don't see any male sex organ. Can we peel the rest of this clothing off the breast area?"

Jon carefully removed the remaining night gown material. "You have to be careful; sometimes the stomach area will burst open and spray you with body fluids," he warned. He had learned that the hard way.

At that point, Liz moved back some. When he had the clothing off, she looked and commented that she could identify female breasts.

Jon rolled the body back over on its stomach and said to Liz," I always ask Doc if it's okay for me to cut some of the flesh off so it can be tested for presence of flammable liquids."

"Go ahead," she said, giving him a look that suggested he was kind of strange.

He pulled an old pocket knife out of his coat pocket, opened it, and sliced off some meat on the back of the body and placed it in a plastic bag. "Would you mind taking a picture of me doing this for the record, please?" he said to her.

He heard her camera click a couple of times.

"So, if gasoline was poured on the body, your lab could find it?" she asked Jon.

"Usually, but not always. Sometimes it all burns up."

A couple of firemen brought a back board and a black body bag.

Jon said, "I'll need a couple of you guys to help me get the body in the bag." He then instructed them on how to put rubber gloves under their leather gloves and to pull their face shields down and wear surgical masks. He told them to throw away their leather gloves after handling the body. He knew the chief wouldn't like that as they cost thirty bucks apiece, but they would be soaked with body fluids.

After loading the body in the undertaker's car, they all gathered around a fire truck and washed off with a booster line from the fire truck and a pump can with bleach water in it. Everyone tossed their gloves back into the crawl space of the home, where they had found what was left of the feet and hands.

He could smell some vomit on the coroner investigator's breath. She had disappeared for a little while as they were bagging the body.

"Where do you think the fire started?" Liz asked as she was washing her hands. She then took her ball cap off and undid the pony tail and let her long, wavy dark hair lay on her shoulders.

"Probably in the living room, where we found the body," the fire marshal told her. "I'll be doing a fire scene investigation, but I don't expect to find much with this much damage; that's why I'd like to ask you to have an autopsy done. The body may tell us some things that the fire scene can't tell us."

"I'll have to ask Grampa; he already told me we only have enough money in the budget for one more autopsy, and we still got three months to go before the fiscal year is over," she said, referring to her boss, the coroner, who everyone called Doc.

By then Dave had joined them and the three of them sat on the tailgate of Liz's truck. Jon said," I never like it when an older person or couple dies in a fire like this. Too often it can be a robbery that went bad. You remember that time that old guy was robbed over at Jim Town, don't you, Dave? Beat him up real bad. Didn't set the place on fire, but if they had we probably never would have known what happened."

"Yeah, you're right, Jonny. Too many murders covered up by arson. Hope the Doc can see to let you have an autopsy done."

Both Jon and Dave knew that Doc was hard to convince. He always wanted a smoking gun. It was a money thing. The county commissioners only gave him so much money to operate on each year.

CHAPTER 2

It was Monday morning. Jon Hamer had spent all of Sunday morning doing the fire scene investigation. He didn't find much. It was apparent that the fire started in the living room area where the body was found, but that was all he could tell. He couldn't even eliminate accidental causes. Now he was on his way to the Sheriff's Office in Jackson with the report that he had typed up Sunday evening after he had taken a nap.

Like most sheriff's offices in southern Ohio, this one was in an old building next to the courthouse in the center of the county seat. It was built right after the Civil War. The jail cells were in the rear two story section. The front, two-story section housed the offices. Up until the present sheriff took office two years ago, the sheriff had lived in the upstairs of the front section, but this was no longer the case. The current sheriff had preferred to live on his farm, so he converted the upstairs into more office space for his staff. Besides, the building was not in very good shape. The jail itself was secure. The first floor contained a large cell area for the general male population. It held about twenty prisoners. There was also a holding cell which was called the drunk tank. Persons who were intoxicated were placed there to sober up. It lacked the comforts of the cell area. No mattresses. No shower. Every morning after the drunks had been taken to court or moved into the main cell, the tank was hosed out and disinfected.

When one entered into the Sheriff's Office through it's only unlocked door, on the side facing the courthouse, you were in a small lobby that contained the radio room. Everyone who came into the building came in this way. The public. Officers with prisoners. Employees. Behind the plexiglass window of the radio room was the dispatcher. There was a radio console. The counter beneath the plexiglass window had a twelve-inch gap between the counter top and the bottom of the glass, so that things could be passed back and forth and prisoners being booked into the jail could lay their personal property. The dispatcher did the booking. The officer bringing in the prisoner searched the prisoner and took them back to the drunk tank. It was highly likely that someone sitting in the small lobby waiting to see the Sheriff about something would witness a prisoner being booked. This might consist of foul language on the part of the prisoner and sometimes a physical struggle with the officer. In a modern jail, there would be separate entrances so that the public was not exposed to the prisoners being brought in.

Jackson County was a nice place to live and work. It lacked a lot of the things of the larger cities, but it made up for that in the friendliness of the people and the slower pace of things. There were only twenty-seven thousand people living in the county. Up until two years ago, there were no fast food restaurants. Now they had a McDonald's in Jackson. Jackson was the county seat. Most of the businesses in town were in the downtown section of Jackson. It wasn't like some of the other places like Chillicothe where things were starting to move out into the edge of town. Jackson and Wellston were the two main cities. Jackson was a couple thousand people larger than Wellston. Oak Hill in the southern part of the county was a small village of about two thousand people.

"Hey, Fire Marshal Jon, what are doin'?" said Rose the dispatcher on duty.

"Came in to see Dave about that fire we had yesterday."

"He's up in his office," Rose said. She had worked there over ten years and knew as many of the people in the county of twenty-seven thousand as the deputies that worked there did.

Jon went through the jail kitchen and got a cup of coffee. The smell of breakfast was still present. Bacon, eggs, toast or homemade biscuits. Day shift deputies were allowed to eat breakfast and lunch in the jail kitchen. Lunch was the best meal served.

Mille the cook was on the phone, ordering groceries from the market across town to be delivered. She offered him a biscuit, but he declined.

Upstairs in what used to be a bedroom, he found Dave in his office. He was sitting at his desk, typing a report on an electric typewriter. He had a McDonald's cup on his desk. He never drank coffee. He always drank Coke.

"Get any sleep, Dave?" he asked.

"No, got called out at four this morning on a rape out on Roy Road. Don't think it was a rape. Think that boss of yours could come down and run the victim on a polygraph?"

"Yeah, he probably could; he's never been down to see me since they turned me loose down here. I'll give him a call later and see."

Often the victim of a rape was asked to take a lie detector test, especially if the officer investigating doubted their truthfulness. Some rapes were not rapes and were actually consensual. A deputy did not want to send someone to prison for something that did not happen as the victim said it happened.

"What'd you find out at the fire scene after I left yesterday?" Dave said, still typing.

"Not much. I can't tell what caused it just where it started at. Did we get an autopsy report from that pretty young lady?"

"I just got off the phone with Liz. She said she talked Doc into it and even a dental record I.D. I got to go out to the dentist's office after a bit and get the records and mail them to the morgue in Columbus. And Liz asked me to have you come out to the hospital today to talk to her. I think she likes you."

"Maybe I'll go out about noon and eat hospital food with her. What does she do out there?"

"ICU nurse," Dave said, using some white out to correct a mistake on his typing.

"You find out anything in the neighborhood yesterday?"

"Not really. Did learn that the old lady was legally blind for years until about six months ago. She had her cataracts removed so she could see again."

"You got a gut feeling about this?" Jon asked Dave as Jon was reading through the witness statements that Dave had taken at the scene.

"No, but there's a guy that lives down the road about a quarter mile, who's got some brothers that are in a lot of trouble. Folks said two of the brothers been hanging out at his house a lot lately. All three of them cut timber. The one that lives there is the youngest and has a woman with him. He's never been arrested, but the other two have."

"Who are they?"

"Brown's. One that lives there is Wesley and the other two are Dave and Pee Wee."

"Yeah, I know Pee Wee and Dave; they been in jail here a lot for fightin'. Drink a lot. Go down to the Swamps and Blackfork a lot," Jon remembered from when he used to work in the jail. "That's them; they been in the Gallia County and Lawrence County Jails a lot more than ours."

The Swamps was a bar just across the Jackson County line in Gallia County. There was another watering hole at Blackfork, just across the county line into Lawrence County. Gallia, Lawrence, and Jackson Counties all came together just south of Oak Hill, a village in southern Jackson County. Glen Cozy Road, where this fire happened, was ten miles west of Oak Hill. Oak Hill and Madison and Jefferson Townships that surround it were all dry. Didn't have any bars or carryouts.

"What's the plan, then?" Jon asked Dave.

"I gotta go get the dental records and mail them to the morgue. How about you go back out there and talk to the guy who discovered the fire again? He was pretty upset when I talked to him."

Jon headed back down to the fire scene after stopping at the K and L Restaurant on the south edge of town for breakfast. It was the favorite eating place for the cops, as they gave fifty percent off to them and a couple deputies wives worked there. He decided to drive down Four Mile Pike instead of State Route 93 to Oak Hill and out. It was shorter this way.

When he got to the home of the guy that reported the fire, he was let in by his wife, who said that her husband was in bed as he worked late, but he wanted to be got up anyway as he had firewood to cut today.

The witness introduced himself as Ed Kyger. Jon asked him to repeat his statement. Jon had his statement on his clipboard and read it as Ed repeated himself, almost to the T.

Then something unusual happened. Ed's wife said to him, "Honey, why don't you tell him about what you and I talked about last night?"

"I work at the post office in Portsmouth, and I get off work at 1:00 A.M. I was pretty sleepy as I was driving home Saturday night, but when I went by this lady's house, I think I saw a truck parked in her driveway. It was green."

"You're not sure?" Jon asked.

"Well, it's like I was on automatic pilot as I was driving the last few miles to home," the witness said. "I know I saw this truck there, but I'm not sure if it was that night or the night before." He went on to describe it as about a late sixties Chevrolet Pickup truck with a wooden flatbed built on to it to replace the original bed.

"Have you ever seen that truck parked in her drive before?" Jon asked.

"No, never; there never is any vehicles parked at her place, except for her niece or nephew who looks after her."

"Have you ever seen that truck before?"

Ed hesitated and looked at his wife and she gave him a nod." Yeah, I seen it parked down at that house down the road yonder where the Brown kid lives with his girlfriend."

"Do you know Wesley Brown, the guy that lives there?"

"Just see him when I go by there sometimes, but he has a white car; the truck's not his, I don't think."

"Do you know who owns or drives the truck, Ed?"

"No, I don't; I'm sorry I'm not much help. I never saw anyone driving it, but I seen it parked at Brown's house before."

After leaving Ed's house, Jon went down to Wes Brown's and asked him about the truck, and he said that he never seen any truck like that and didn't know who it belonged to. When asked about his two brothers, Dave and Pee Wee, he said that he hadn't seen them for about two months.

Jon knew he should talk to some more people in the neighborhood to see if anyone else had seen the truck at the fire scene or at Brown's house. But it was 11:00 A.M. and he was anxious to meet with that new coroner's investigator at the hospital, so he headed for town and the hospital.

He found her in the cafeteria, eating her lunch, and asked if he could join her. He got a tray and went through the line and got a cheeseburger and fries and a chocolate milk. She was wearing a white nurse's dress. Her dark hair was braided in a French curl on the back of her head. He expected her to be wearing one of those nurse's caps, but she wasn't. Boy she looked good.

"So, how are you today, Miss Coroner Investigator?" he said in a flirty kind of way.

"I'm fine, Mr. Fire Marshal," she said back in a kind of flirty way.

"Did you catch up on your sleep?" he asked her in a concerning way.

"Yes, did you?"

"Yes, Dave said you wanted to talk to me," he replied.

"Well," she said, "I'm kind of new at this investigation stuff, so I wondered if I could kind of tag along with you guys and see how you do it?"

"Sure," he told her, "but we do most of our work on day shift, but not always. Do you always work days here?"

"I've got the next four days off and then I go on midnight shift for twelve days."

"I wanted to thank you for getting us an autopsy," he told her.

"Well, it wasn't easy, but I did it. I talked Grampa into it."

"I appreciate it. Your job is actually more like that of a law enforcement officer," Jon told her.

"Actually, I took some police science classes when I was in nursing school. I've always been kind of interested in police work, but my parents wanted me to go into nursing as they didn't think I could get a job in police work unless I went to the big city."

"Where did you go to school?" he said.

"Hocking College."

"Same here. Police Science class of '73."

She looked at her watch and said, "I've got to get back to my floor. I'll give you my phone number; it's the same as Grampa's. You probably already have it."

"I've got it," he said. "I'll call you tomorrow morning, and we'll meet at the Sheriff's Office and go from there. If I don't call before eight o'clock, then I got called out on another fire."

"Sounds interesting; I'll see you tomorrow then." She walked out of the cafeteria. He couldn't help but watch until she disappeared. Nice legs in those white hose. Really nice.

CHAPTER 3

On Tuesday morning, Jon called Dave. Dave was going to be tied up, as Jon's boss, whom he had contacted for Dave, was coming down to run Dave's rape victim on the polygraph. Joe, the boss, was going to spend the night so that he could ride with Jon on Wednesday.

Jon made arrangements to meet Liz at the fire station instead of the Sheriff's Office, as it was closer to the area the fire occurred in.

She was wearing Western jeans, cowboy boots (no mud this time), and a Western blouse. Her dark hair was down. She got in his car, and they headed out to the fire scene, and he told her about the truck on the way.

They started the day by visiting the victim's niece and nephew, who assured them that this pickup truck should not be at the victim's house. When asked if they knew the truck, they both replied that they had seen it on occasion at the Brown residence down the road. By noon they had four statements from persons who had seen the truck at the Brown residence. Two of those four persons had seen Dave and Pee Wee Brown, whom they knew, driving the truck in the neighborhood as late as the week before the fire.

They went into Oak Hill to the coffee shop for lunch.

"Have you ever had a Jackson County veal sandwich?" Jon asked Liz.

"No," she replied.

They each ordered one with pickles, mustard, and ketchup. It was a big, round, thin, breaded veal, deep fired and on a sandwich bun. The veal was twice the size of the bun.

"Wow," she said, "it's really good."

"So, how did you get this job helping your Grampa?" he asked her as they ate.

"Well, I got the job at the hospital first, and then Grampa asked me if I would like to be his investigator. He would like to retire, but no other doctors want the job. The county commissioners didn't have the money to pay me, so Grampa took a fifty percent cut in pay so I could get paid. He wanted to take more, but if he did they would cancel his health insurance and he needs that. So, I get a salary and paid mileage. If it works out the Sheriff is supposed to make me a Special Deputy so I can carry a gun if I want to. If this happens I'll have to go through the basic police academy at Rio Grande."

He thought about that a minute and said, "If you get commissioned, you don't have to take the class for a year and I can teach you to shoot so you can carry and one of the firearms instructors at the city police department can certify you if you can qualify and pass the written use of force test."

"I don't know anything about pistols, but I've shot a rifle and a shotgun hunting with my dad and brother," she volunteered.

"You'll catch on. Main thing is you're not afraid of guns like a lot of young ladies."

"So, it kind of looks like something might be suspicious about this fire," Liz said as she was struggling with her veal.

"This truck doesn't make sense. I just wish the guy could remember what night for sure that he saw it there. No doubt he saw it, but his uncertainty about what night would not go good in court."

They sat there and talked for about an hour and then got in the car to head back out to the fire area to find out more about these three brothers and the truck. He called in on the radio before they took off to see if there were any messages. Rose said that Gallia County was wanting him on a fire on Back Hill Road down below the Swamps a few miles.

"You wanna go, or you want me to drop you at the fire station where your truck is?" he said to Liz.

"I'll go," she said. "I don't have to do barn chores during the week. Grampa has a hired hand. I just do them on weekends."

The Swamps is just what the name says: it is a swamp. The road that runs through it is a state highway that was built on an old raised railroad bed called the CH and D Railroad. They drove down through the swamps and the community of Gallia and to Back Hill Road. The fire was still burning in the basement when they got there. It was an old house that had been a summer home or hunting cabin for the last twenty years. There are a lot of these in this area, owned by people living in Columbus or further north in Ohio.

"Hi, Chief, what's going on down here?" Jon said when they pulled into the yard. There was nothing left but the basement. The fire chief was a young man in his early twenties. This was Jon's first fire with this little fire department near the town of Gallia. It was a fairly new fire department. For years, this area of Gallia County did not have fire protection.

"No electric to the place, they used LP gas for lights and the frig and wood to heat. No running water in the house. Guy down the road has a key and checks the place every two weeks. He was here a week ago to mow the lawn, and everything was all right then. Out of town owner like most of the summer places and hunting cabins around here." The fire chief told them.

"Got the owners name and address," said the marshal to the chief of the fire department.

"Yeah, here's a copy of my report. We're out of water and the basement is going to be too hot to dig around in until tomorrow sometime." The chief was ready to take his men and trucks back to the station. "If you need some help digging it out, give me a call and I'll bring a couple guys down," the chief added.

"Okay, I'll take some pictures and come back in a couple days to sift around in the basement. Maybe I can get the owner to come down and we can determine if anything is missing from the place. Hate to find a body in there so we gotta make sure." He added, "This is Liz; she's the new coroner's investigator for Jackson County."

"Heard you had a woman killed up there the other side of Oak Hill over the weekend. Know what happened?"

"No, not yet; Jon told him. "We're still working on it."

On the way back to the fire station, Jon and Liz talked mostly about her Grampa, Doc, who had been coroner forever. Doc was her paternal grandfather. She was living at his place, a place she had often visited while growing up and where she spent her summers. She had a horse there that her Grampa got her when she was thirteen years old. He also learned that after getting her LPN at Hocking she moved back home to Chillicothe and worked in a doctor's office while attending Ohio University Chillicothe where she got her RN degree. He dropped her off at her truck telling her he had to go to the SO to meet his boss and that he would probably spend the next day with his boss so she wouldn't be able to work with him.

When Jon got to the SO, Joe, his boss was still doing a polygraph exam on Dave's rape victim, so he and Dave sat and talked about the fire. Dave's phone rang.

"It's for you, Jonny," Dave said after talking to the dispatcher. "Line two."

"Hamer," he answered.

"Hi, its Rita," said the caller. He had forgot about Rita. His friend. He then remembered Saturday night. *How did that happen?* he thought. They had been friends for years and never a spark between them. Then all of a sudden. Could be because they were each on the rebound. She from a year-long engagement that broke up. He from an eight-month fling with woman up at Wellston that he didn't really like that much. She was one of those that liked cops just because they were cops. He met her when he still was a uniformed deputy. After he got the job at the FM and quit wearing the uniform she seemed to have lost interest.

"Hey Rita, how you doin'?" he answered.

"Startin' midnight shift at the plant tonight. Won't be at the disco Saturday night. Have to go in at 11:00 P.M. You goin'?" she asked.

"Yeah, I'll be there as usual if nothin' comes up."

"Want to get together some evening this week?" she asked.

"Uh, I'd like to, but I'm not sure. Workin' on this fatal fire. I'll call you."

Rita lived with her mother. But now there was this Liz. He couldn't get his mind off her. What was he going to do? He wasn't going to have two women at one time. He couldn't do that even if he had the time. Wasn't right.

Just as he hung up the phone it rang again so he answered it. The dispatcher said it was for him on line three. It was Liz. She had just got the results of the autopsy. Positive ID on the lady who lived there. No carbon monoxide in the blood which meant she was dead before the fire.

"What killed her?" he asked Liz.

"Skull crushed by a blunt instrument, the medical examiner said."

All the counties in southern Ohio had their autopsies done in either Columbus or Cincinnati as there were no qualified doctors or facilities in the smaller counties to perform autopsies. He thanked Liz for letting them know and getting the autopsy done.

"We got a murder, Dave," he said.

"I heard you talking. Dead before the fire. What caused the death?"

"Blunt trauma to the skull, according to Liz. Pathologist is sure that's what happened," he replied to Dave, who was straightening up his desk. It always had bags of evidence sitting on it and several case file folders that he was working on. Dave was always working on burglaries. A lot of them were daytime jobs while people were at work. Used to be house burglaries only happened at night when people were away from home overnight, but now this new trend of daylight jobs.

"We gotta find that truck. You and the new coroner investigator could go out there at night and sit and watch Browns house to see if it shows up, but I don't think you'd get much watchin' done." Dave smiled and started to chuckle.

Jon hadn't told Dave about spending the night with Rita. They didn't have any secrets from each other, but he wasn't going to open that can of worms. He'd never hear the last of it from Dave. Dave always had more than one woman on the string at one time. Jon knew that there were a couple of deputies that met their girlfriends out on backroads when they were on duty. Dave wasn't like that.

An old white haired man came into Dave's Office with a long strip of paper in his hands that looked like it had marks on it from an EKG machine, but Jon knew it was the strip from the polygraph.

"Hi Jonny," said Joe, the Assistant Chief and Polygraphist for the Arson Bureau. He had the stub of an unlit cigar in his mouth. "You behavin' down here? Dave says you may have a murder."

"Looks like we do. Dead before the fire."

"That's going to keep you busy," Joe said in his very rough voice. The first time Jon met this guy, he was kind of intimidated, but as he got to know him during his training period he found him to be a very nice and caring person. He regarded all twenty-two of the investigators as "my men" and would stand up for them and argue on their behalf to the chief when he felt it was necessary. He spent thirty years on the Columbus Fire Department. He was never an officer. He had done every job that a firefighter could do from hoseman to EMT to chief's driver to academy instructor. He had never done investigations, but the chief hired him as his assistant and sent him to New York to polygraph school. He was considered one of the best polygraphists in the state.

"Well, Dave, I think your young lady in there is lying. I think that if you and I go in there and talk nice to her, she'll admit that she made up the rape story," Joe said.

"Let's give it a try then," Dave said.

"Don't take off, Jonny. I'm spending the night and going to ride with you tomorrow. The boss told me to spend the day with you. You better call him and tell him about this murder. How about getting me a room somewhere for the night."

"That won't be hard, there's only two motels in Jackson," Jonny replied. He got out the phone book as Dave and Joe were going back to the interview room.

Forty-five minutes later, they were all three sitting in Dave's Office. The young lady had admitted she wasn't raped. It was consensual and she thought she might get pregnant and her husband would find out about her having a quickie with a guy at work when they were alone in the break room.

"Got you a room at the Cedar Hill," Jon told Joe.

"How about we meet for supper about six, unless you got a date tonight."

"Okay, I'll pick you up at the motel and we'll go down to Oak Hill to the Highway Grill."

"I was hopin' you'd say that. Haven't been there for a couple of years."

Jon had to stop and wash his car and clean it out before he went home. He didn't want the chief to think he didn't take good care of it even if it was startin' to rust out and had over a hundred thousand miles on it. He was up on the list for a new one the next time they bought a bunch of cars.

Jon didn't have a place of his own. He housesat. People paid him to live in their houses when they were gone. He had just moved into a place in Jackson on High Street that he would stay in until the following May when the folks came back from Florida. Then he would spend the summer in about five different houses while people were on vacation. It kept the burglars away having a cop staying in your house.

He and Joe had a good dinner that evening and sat and talked for over an hour after they finished supper. He took Joe back to his motel and they agreed to meet at the K and L at eight in the morning for breakfast and then go down to Gallia and dig out the fire scene where that weekend home burned. It wasn't a high priority and he could shove it on the back burner and work the murder, but he didn't want to end up finding a dead body in there a few weeks later when he got time to dig it out so he might as well get it done. Anyway, the owner had told him when he called him that he was going to be down there all day so he needed to talk to him, too.

Dave Jeffers was working late in his office that evening. He had just helped an evening shift deputy interview a burglary suspect and get a confession out of him and now he was typing up a supplement on that. He heard a light knock on his open office door and looked up from his typewriter and there stood Liz Carter.

"Hi Liz. What brings you to our modern correctional facility." Dave said, referring to the over one-hundred-year-old county jail.

"Oh, just thought I'd stop and talk about the murder case," she said.

"Well, we appreciate you getting the Doc to have an autopsy done."

"It wasn't easy. Actually, what he said was, 'Is this another one of that Dave Jeffers and Jon Hamer's suspicions?' And I said that yes, you guys asked for it, but that I agreed that it should be done," Liz replied.

"You know one time we had to have one dug up because Doc wouldn't autopsy it and a year later we got information that indicated it was a homicide. It cost the county a lot more having to have the body exhumed."

"Was it a murder?" Liz asked Dave.

"Oh, yeah, and we solved it, too. Jon Hamer and I. That was back when Jon was a deputy."

"Tell me about this fire marshal?" Liz asked.

"You mean Jon?" Dave asked her.

"Yeah."

"Well, what you want to know?"

"Everything," she said.

"Well, that could take a while, but I'll give you the short version. Jon started working here at the SO when he was nineteen years old. He was a dispatcher and a jailor. About a year later he got put in uniform as a deputy. When I came to work here in '75, Jon was my training officer. In the three months that I trained with him we arrested ten persons for burglary. Three of them were involved in a big ring that was doing jobs in Jackson, Vinton and Meigs Counties. I learned a lot working with him. When the detective we had back then quit, the Sheriff made Jon the detective. I worked a lot with him over the next few years. We solved a lot of crime including three murders. Well, Jon got interested in firefighting when he joined one of the volunteer departments. He also helped the old fire marshal solve some arson cases. When Bob, the fire marshal, decided to retire, he asked Jon if he wanted the job. Jon took it. I don't think it was so much for the pay raise he got as it was for the fact that it was a combination of fire service and law enforcement and he liked them both."

"So, how long you been the detective?" she asked Dave.

"When Jon left for the fire marshal job the Sheriff made me detective. A little over a year now. I know Jon Hamer suggested it to the sheriff."

"Grampa said that Jon Hamer's a lady's man," Liz said.

Dave laughed. "Now I don't want to be getting' into Jon's personal life."

"Well, does he have a girlfriend?"

"No, not right now he doesn't," Dave answered.

"Does he drink?" she asked.

"Yes, he does. He's not a drunk if that's what you're asking. You see, Jon's like me. He works a lot of hours on the job. He doesn't have a lot of time for going out. On Saturday nights, you'll usually find him at one of the two watering holes in the county that has disco dancing. He hangs out with a small group of folks. Some of them work in police work. They meet every Saturday night at one of these places."

"Does he date much?" she asked.

Dave smiled and Liz blushed.

"Well, yeah, but he ain't never had a relationship that lasted more than a year. It's mostly because he doesn't have much time. Now he likes to hunt and fish. He does a lot of hiking and when he takes a vacation he goes over in West Virginia in the mountains and fishes and hikes."

"Does he ride horses?

"Not very often. So, why all the questions?"

"Just curious," she answered.

"Sounds to me like he might have caught your interest."

"You won't tell him I asked will you, please," Liz said as she smiled.

"No, I won't. Wouldn't want his head to get too big."

"Thanks, Dave. I really appreciate it," she said as she got up to leave.

CHAPTER 4

He was having another one of those dreams. He was chasing a guy down an alley. There was a glow from a fire burning behind him. He was getting closer to the guy, about fifty feet when all of a sudden, the guy stopped dead and turned around and pointed a pistol at him. Then the phone rang. He looked at the clock: 2:00 A.M. He reached for the phone and answered. It was the Jackson Co SO. They had a cabin fire at Lake Jackson down by Oak Hill. A deputy was on the scene and said it was suspicious and wanted him to come out. Okay he would be there. Then he remembered about his boss, Joe. He had to meet him in the Morning. Should he call him and see if he wanted to go on this fire with him. He wasn't sure what to do. He got dressed and thought about it. I won't bother him. It's hard to tell where he has to go after he leaves here tomorrow. Could call the pretty coroner investigator. She's still on her days off from the hospital.

The phone rang six or seven times and then a very sleepy woman's voice answered, "Hello."

"This is Jon," he said. "You want to go on a fire with me down at Lake Jackson?"

"Yeah, I guess, of course, sure I do; I was sound asleep." He could picture her in a sexy nightie, no not her, she was more like a tee shirt woman.

"Okay, I'll come by and pick you up," he told her.

He headed down Franklin Valley Road. Her Grampa had a big farm three miles or so south of town. As he pulled into the driveway he saw her coming down off the porch carrying two cups of coffee. She got in and handed him one. "Black, didn't know how you took it," she said.

"Thanks, no place open this late to get a cup" he said, taking the mug and sitting it in his cup holder as he turned the car around. She sure smelled good.

"Hope I didn't wake up the doc when I called."

"No, when I'm here he unplugs the phone in his room so he doesn't get bothered," she said.

They cut across Antioch Road toward Oak Hill and then turned off onto a side road that went down the hill to a bunch of cabins along the lake. Lake Jackson was a state park. On this side of the lake were a lot of cabins. On the other side was a campground, beach and picnic area. There were the remains of an old iron furnace near the boat ramp. It had been called Jefferson Furnace. Some of cabins were permanent residences, but most were weekend places. There were three fire trucks and a sheriff's car at the scene. He didn't see any smoke or even smell any. He couldn't tell from here which cabin had burned. Maybe this one didn't burn bad. He saw the fire chief talking to the deputy sheriff. It was the deputy that took his place when he left the SO. He had met him, but didn't know him well. Jones was his name. Probably Welsh. A lot of Welsh folks around here. Jones, Evans, Lewis, Davis. Real good people.

"Hey, Chief, hey, deputy, this is Doc Carters investigator. She's hanging out learnin' some things," he said as he approached the sheriff's car they were leaning on.

"Hi, I'm Liz," she said as she shook their hands.

The fire chief explained that when they arrived the fire was coming out the window of a rear bedroom and the front door was standing open and apparently had been forced open. It was a weekend cabin.

"Could have been the person who reported the fire that kicked in the door, thinking someone was inside, you know how that is," the chief told them.

"Who called it in?" asked Jon.

"Don't know. Person called the SO and said a house was on fire on Sunset Lane and then hung up. No name or phone number," the deputy responded.

"Let's take a look inside," Jon said as they all four walked toward the front door. It was apparent the door had been kicked in. The door jamb was busted where the dead bolt broke through it. There was no fire damage in the front of the house, just smoke. When they got to the bedroom it was obvious that this is where the fire started. They had put a good stop on it. The bed was burned up pretty much. Probably where the fire started, Jon thought, as he looked around. Usually the area with the most fire damage was where the fire started. But not always.

"Hey, Chief," hollered some fireman from outside, "the owners here."

The chief and Jon went outside and met the owner who said his name was Evan Lawdermilk from Wellston. Jon took him inside and asked him to look around and see if anything was not right.

"Where's the T.V.?" the owner said.

Jon looked at the fire chief and he shrugged his head. They went over to the entertainment center and shined their lights around. The antennae wire had been cut.

"Better take a good look around," Jon told the owner.

When they were done, they had a list from the owner of the T.V., eight track cassette/stereo/radio, an old double barrel twelve-gauge shotgun that hung over the fireplace. It had an old wire twist barrel. Maybe the burglar would shoot it with smokeless powder ammo and blow himself up. Old wire twist barreled shotguns could not take the pressure of smokeless powder. They were designed for black powder.

They dug through the debris in the bedroom and determined the fire started on the bed. He took some samples to test for accelerants, but he doubted they would find anything. There were a bunch of clothes hangers on the bed. The owner said they shouldn't have been there. They had been in the closet. Looks like someone piled some clothes on the bed and set it on fire. This was often the case when a woman set a fire to get back at her man for something, but Jon didn't think this was the case here after he spent some time talking to the owner. This was probably a burglary covered up by a fire.

He found Liz talking to the lady firefighter who had filled his coffee cup Sunday morning. They were talking about horses.

"You ready to go?" he said to Liz after looking at his pocket watch. It was almost 6:00 A.M.

On the way back to Liz's place, Jon told her that he had to spend the day with his boss and they were going to go back to the house fire at Gallia and she could go if she wanted to. She declined saying that she had chores to do and had to go buy some hay from a neighbor and truck it back home. The hired hand was spending the day doing fall brush hogging.

He stopped by the house and changed clothes before meeting Joe. He got to thinking that with the fire set to cover up the burglary last night and the murder of the lady, the fire at Gallia may be a burglary, too. That's three fires in three days in a ten-mile radius of Oak Hill.

CHAPTER 5

Jon and Joe got to Gallia about nine that morning. Gallia was just a little crossroads town. He told Joe about the cabin fire at the lake on the way down the highway. There were two firemen waiting with a brush truck to help them dig. The property owner was there, too. The only thing they could do was ask him about things he had in the house that someone would want to steal. Things that would not completely burn up in the fire. The owner would have to tell them what part of the house the things were in and they would dig through the debris and see if they could find the remains of the things. Most burglars were interested in T.V.s and small appliances, tools, chainsaws, and especially guns. They seemed to sell good.

Fortunately, the house had a tin roof on it and the fire department had already pulled it off the debris that was left in the basement. This was better than a slate roof which made for heavy shoveling. The shovel was the fire investigators most important hand tool.

They finished by noon and determined that there were two chain saws, a circular saw, a tool box full of tools and a T.V. missing from the house.

Joe told him that he needed to find out what all was in the lady's house that died that could have been stolen and do the same thing they just did at the house at Gallia. He suggested that there might be a connection between the homicide and the fires set to cover the burglaries. Joe had to head out after lunch at the coffee shop to drive to Georgetown for a polygraph tomorrow.

Jon drove up Franklin Valley Road and stopped by the Carter Farm. Liz was unloading bales of hay into a barn.

"Need some help?" he asked her.

"Sure, I'll throw them off the wagon and you can stack them in the barn." she said.

It was a good workout. Better than shoveling out a fire scene. While they worked, he asked her if she wanted to go back to the fatal fire scene with him the next day to talk to the niece and nephew again and see if they could figure if anything was missing. After they got the hay stacked Liz asked him to stay for supper. He talked to Doc while she cooked. They talked about some old cases that they had been on together and Doc started talking about the first murder he had back in 1935 when he was first elected coroner. It was interesting. He had a coroner's jury impaneled to consider the evidence and rule on the cause of death. Back then the sheriff only had two deputies. No radios in their cars. The doc continued to tell the story of that old murder as they ate. Steak, mashed potatoes, coleslaw, homemade rolls. This gal could cook pretty good.

She walked out in the yard with him after supper. "What time you want to meet tomorrow to go back to the fire scene?" she said.

"I'll pick you up about eight. Wear old clothes. We'll be getting dirty."

"I'm taking a weeks' vacation, so I won't be going on midnights till a week from tomorrow night," she replied, "Got a lot of things to do around the farm, matter of fact it would be better if I met you in Oak Hill in the morning, so I can pick up a load of feed at the mill when we're done."

"Okay we'll meet at the fire station at eight-thirty. See you tomorrow."

On the way home, he got to thinking about this woman. She was about four years younger than him. That made her about twenty-three. Sure, was nice. Good lookin'. Good cook he had learned. Smart, too. Filled out the tight jeans good, too. Nice butt. Not real big in the boobs department, but he was an ass man anyways. Seemed to work pretty hard too. Helpin' take care of that farm and workin' eight hours a day at the hospital. He'd seen Doc out on the tractor earlier in the summer pulling the baler while some kids loaded the wagon. He had to be close to eighty. Now he remembered. It must have been her he saw last summer pulling a wagon load of hay bales with a tractor on Franklin Valley Road. Yeah it had to be. Dark hair blowin' in the breeze.

Then he got to thinkin' about the murder Doc had told them about. He thought it would have been neat to have been a deputy back then when they didn't have radios. He'd heard the old sheriff talk about how it had been back then. You had to stop at a country store or someone's house and call into the office or the telephone operator and see if anyone was looking for you. Back then they didn't patrol. They just went out when they got a call.

No phone calls that night so Jon got some sleep. He had gone to bed at nine and got up at seven. When he got to the fire station in Oak Hill Liz was there already. She was talking to that lady firefighter about horses again.

"I'm Pam Davis," the redheaded fire woman said, extending her hand to shake his as he approached them in front of the station. "My husband and I have a farm out on Five Points in Madison Township."

"Glad to meet you," he replied. "Your husband on the fire department, too."

"He used to be, but he took a job down at the Gavin Power Plant so he had to quit so he would have time to work the farm."

"You good with a shovel? Want to help us?" he joked.

"No, thanks," she said. "I've heard how you like to shovel these fires. I gotta go home and shovel out barn stalls except I'll be using a Bobcat."

He looked at Liz and said, "We better go get started so you can get your farm work done today and I need to spend this afternoon typing reports."

They stopped at the niece and nephews house and talked to them about what all the aunt had in her house. She had about everything and it took them awhile to make a list and draw a sketch showing where she kept things. She didn't have much of a T.V., just a little portable since she was almost blind for several years.

"There's something I got to thinking about after you were here the other day talking about the green truck and the Browns. My aunt had the Browns sister work for her for a couple of years until she got her sight back about six months ago. She came in three days a week and did housework and helped her clean. My aunt was teaching her how to make quilts." the niece said as they were finishing the sketch.

"Had the Brown brothers ever been to her house?" Jon asked.

"Sometimes one of them would drop the girl off in the morning and some-times one would pick her up and sometimes, she would walk down to Wesley Browns house. She stayed there sometimes."

"Looks like we have a connection between these Browns and our victim," Liz said as they drove up the driveway to the fire scene.

"Looks that way," he agreed.

It was hard to sort out things in the fire debris, mostly because most of it had fallen down into the crawl space. They couldn't find the remains of the old foot treadle type of Singer Sewing machine that was supposed to be in the living room. They couldn't find the T.V., but it was so small that they may have missed it in the debris. That was about all they could tell. She didn't own any tools or guns or anything like that that most thieves were looking for.

They ate at the coffee shop again. Liz wanted another veal. He did, too.

"You got a boyfriend?" he said as they were eating.

"Not anymore," she answered.

"How come not anymore?" he replied.

"We broke up after I decided to move down here."

"How come?" he asked.

"I'd rather not talk about it. It hasn't been that long ago." She then grew quiet and they didn't say much for the rest of lunch.

He dropped her off at her truck and headed home to do reports. He got his evidence packaged and mailed to the Arson Lab in Columbus. He called Dave. They agreed that the next day, Friday they would look for the Brown brother's sister and talk to her. She was supposed to be living with her parents out on Slithering Ridge.

They found her at her parents in a rundown place on Slithering Ridge about five miles from where the fatal fire occurred. She was busting up big chunks of coal in the yard with a sledge hammer. They sat in the yard and talked. She hadn't been back to the lady's house since she got her eyesight back. No, her brothers had never been in the house that she knew of. Did she know where Pee Wee and Dave were? No, hadn't seen them for over a month. What were they driving? Dave's old green truck with a wooden bed. Did she have any idea who would do in the lady? No. She was a nice woman and treated her right when she worked for her.

"So, you teachin' that Liz how to investigate?" Dave asked Jon as they were headed back to the SO in Dave's car.

"She don't mind gettin' dirty at a fire. Got invited in for dinner with her and Doc the other evening. I helped her unload some bales of hay."

"I heard she had some doctor for a boyfriend up at Chillicothe," Dave said.

"I don't know, told me she broke up with her boyfriend before she moved down here. You know how doctors are always trying to put the make on the nurses."

"Yeah, don't give us country boys a chance, them doctors."

"Well, we ain't got too many doctors down here at our little hospital so maybe I got a chance," Jon said.

"What do ya mean you got a chance?"

"Well, she's friendly to me and asked me in for supper, and you know I get along good with her grandpa."

"Everyone gets along good with Doc," said Dave. "He delivered most folks our age."

They decided they weren't going to work on this case over the weekend. Let it rest awhile and see what happened. Hope there weren't any more fires over the weekend. Jon wanted to go to the disco Saturday night and he knew that Dave had a woman he was seeing. Dave never went to the disco. He really never went anyplace but to work. He worked at least sixty hours every week and usually worked on Saturdays and Sundays. He had a lot of other cases to work on besides this fire. That was the trouble with being the only detective in a small department.

Jon walked into the Lounge Saturday night. He looked forward to this every Saturday. Getting together with friends to disco dance. There were only two places in Jackson County to dance, The Lounge in Jackson and the Stage Coach Inn at Wellston. They alternated between each place every week. He saw his friends at their usual table. Jess was there with his new woman. Couldn't remember her name. Jess was a deputy sheriff. He knew that Rita wouldn't be there as she was on the night shift at the plant. Kathy and her husband Denny were there. She was a clerk at an insurance office in Oak Hill and he worked at one of the refractories near Oak Hill. There was Cheryl from up at Wellston. Looks like she didn't have a date. She was a dispatcher for the Wellston PD.

He greeted everyone. There was a lady that he didn't know. He put out his hand. "I'm Jon."

"I'm Amy, Cheryl's friend. I live at McArthur. I set desk at the Vinton County SO on the evening shift, I'm off tonight."

"Oh, I've heard you on the radio," Jon said, "and always wondered what you looked like. You got a nice voice and you're just as good lookin' as I could tell you were from your voice."

"Thank you," she said, "but how do you tell what someone looks like from their voice?"

"Comes from years of listenin' on the police radio. Used to be when we shared frequencies with a lot more counties you got to hear a lot of different radio operators and it was fun to wonder what they looked like and then someday when you met them you found out. Never been disappointed."

The server came around and Jon ordered a Miller Lite. Everyone else already had drinks. The DJ wouldn't start playing for another thirty minutes. They all talked. Once the music started Jon had a hard time hearing people talk.

He noticed two lovely ladies come in and take a seat at a small table over in the corner. Looked kind of like Liz. He kept looking and finally decided that it was her. Didn't know the lady with her. She looked to be probably about ten years older than Liz.

The lights went dim and the music started. They all went on the floor together and danced to a fast song. The next song was a slow one and Jon ended up with Amy. She was a good dancer. He always tried to keep a respectable distance when slow dancing with someone that he didn't know well, but Amy pulled him close. The next dance was YMCA, his favorite and they all danced it making the signs of the letters YMCA with their arms over their heads.

Things slowed down and everyone took a break except for Kathy and Denny. They continued to slow dance. Jon got into a conversation with Amy and Cheryl about what each had done for summer vacation over the summer that ended just a month ago. Jon had gone to the beach with the girl he had recently broke up with. Amy went with her parents to Chicago to see her older brother and his wife and kids. Cheryl had spent a week backpacking on the Appalachian Trail in Virginia.

Jon already decided that he was going to ask Liz to dance. He had been keeping an eye on her, but she didn't see him. The two girls had gotten up and danced to YMCA and then sat back down and talked. He walked over to their table and said, "Hi, Liz, how you doin'?" She looked up kind of surprised and replied," Jon, good to see you, this is my nursing supervisor from work Karen."

"Glad to meet you, Karen."

"Jon's the fire marshal I told you about," Liz said as she turned back to Karen.

"I've heard a lot about you, Jon."

"I hope it's all been good," said Jon.

"Oh, it was," Karen said, smiling. He could see Liz was kind of blushing.

"Sit down with us," said Liz.

"I'm with a bunch of friends over there" he said, pointing in the direction of his table. "Maybe you two would like to join us."

The two ladies looked at each other for a second and then both nodded yes.

Jon took them over and introduced them to everyone and got two chairs from a nearby table and everyone made room.

Jess said, "I been wanting to meet you, but I haven't had any coroner cases. I saw you on a tractor one day down on Franklin Valley Road." At this point, Jess's girlfriend punched him lightly on the shoulder.

Jess's new woman reminded Jess," You're taken, honey." Everybody laughed.

Jess said to Karen, "I think we met. Don't you work at the hospital?"

"We both do," replied Karen.

"I think you took care of my mom about a year ago," Jess said to Karen.

"I remember you now. She's a real sweetie and your dad is so nice. I had your dad for a teacher in high school."

"Yeah," said Jess, "I think everyone that went to Jackson had him for a teacher."

The DJ was taking a break so it was easier for Jon to carry on a conversation with the others.

After the DJ came back they all danced continuously for the next hour. Fast mostly, but some slow dances. Tavares Disco Inferno, Cool and the Gang Ladies Night, September by Earth Wind and Fire. Since there were more girls than guys, the guys took turns dancing with the different girls. They worked up a sweat.

Jon finally found himself with Liz in his arms dancing to Easy. She didn't snuggle up close like Amy, but he could tell that she was relaxed.

During the next break, Jon found himself sitting between Amy and Liz and carrying on a conversation with both of them. Amy was getting a little tipsy. He noticed that Liz was drinking soda. Amy had her hand on his inner thigh. He hoped that Liz couldn't see it so he scooted his chair up closer to the table.

The place closed at one. They usually went out to the K and L for something to eat after they left. He asked Liz if she wanted to go. She declined saying that Karen had to be at work at seven in the morning. He walked Liz to her truck after Karen had drove off.

"You wanna go for a drive? There's a full moon tonight," he blurted out.

"What about Amy?" she said. "Aren't you with her?"

"No, don't even know her. Just met her tonight. She came with Cheryl. They're friends."

"Oh, I just thought you and she looked pretty friendly."

"That was her, not me, she had a little too much to drink. Not my kind of woman anyway," Jon replied, hoping he was saying the right things.

"So, if I did want to go for a drive with you, how late are you going to keep me out?"

"Not too long; there's a place I'd like to show you out at Lake Katherine. You ever been to Lake Katherine?"

"I took a hike out there once a couple years ago with my Grampa and my dad," she said.

"So, let's drive out and I'll show you my favorite place."

"Okay, but I'm driving. You been drinking."

"Okay," he said, even though he'd only had two beers in four hours.

He had to tell her which way to go, out Route 35 and up to Rock Run Road where they parked. They took a trail off to the side. The moon was shining. He took her hand. "There's a big cliff that drops off out here above the lake," he told her.

When they got out to the edge of the cliff they sat down on a rock. The moon was reflected off the lake below them.

"This place reminds me of a painting of some mountain lake with all the trees surrounding it on the steep hillsides and the rock cliffs," Jon said.

"It's beautiful," Liz replied. "Can you canoe on the lake?"

"Yeah, but you have to get a reservation from the manager. It's a State Nature Preserve and they limit the number of people who can go out on the lake each day so it doesn't get crowded. It's hard to fish from the shore because of the steep hills and cliffs."

"Wow," was all that she could say. "Wow."

"I know the manager. He lives in the big cabin passed the gate where we parked at. He's got a canoe down below his place. All I gotta do is call him and I can use it anytime. We can give it a try sometime if you want to."

"Wow," she said again, "that'd be neat."

"I didn't mean to be prying when I asked you the other day if you had a boyfriend. I just figured you probably did as pretty as you are."

"That's all right. I met this guy when I worked at a doctor's office in Chillicothe. He was a doctor in the clinic and he also worked at an ER at a hospital in Columbus. We dated about a year, but he was always working so we didn't get to go out a lot. When I moved down here he never would drive down here to see me, but I kept driving back home to see him. I felt like it was a one-way street so I told him it was going to be over if he didn't start coming down to see me. He said he didn't have time so we broke up. Two weeks later one of my friends called me and told me he was seeing a lady doctor at a hospital in Columbus. I kind of think he may have been seeing her before we broke up. That's why he didn't have any time."

"Sorry, sounded like it was hard to let go," he said as he took her hand in his.

"Not as much for me as for my mom. She was hoping we would end up getting married and living happily ever after."

They turned and looked at each other. Their faces were just inches apart. Their lips met. It was a long and passionate kiss. "Wow," she said.

"Are you talking about the lake or the kiss?" he said to her.

"The kiss, do it again." They did.

"I like your friends. You hang out at the lounge a lot?"

"We rotate back and forth between there and the Stage Coach in Wellston every Saturday. There's a few others that weren't there tonight," he explained.

"Can I join your group? I really haven't made many friends here yet," she asked.

"Sure. I think we better be getting back to town. You ready?"

"Okay, let's go, promise me you'll bring me here to canoe."

"We could do it tomorrow afternoon. I'll call and make sure the canoe is available."

They talked on the way back to town. She liked to trail ride horses, something he had not done much of. He liked to fish, something she had not done much of. They sat in her truck and talked some more before he got out.

CHAPTER 6

He was having that dream again. Chasing someone down the alley, flames in the background, the guy turns a corner and he turns too and the guy is standing there with a revolver pointed at him. Then the phone rings. He looks at the clock. Its 7:00 A.M. I suppose it's another fire. No one else would be calling him at this early hour.

"Hello," he answered.

"Hi," she said.

"Who's this?" he said.

"Who do you think?" she said.

"Well, it's not some police or fire dispatcher, or I would be hearing radio noise in the background. It's not my mom because I know her voice and it's probably not someone calling to confess to being a serial arsonist so it must be some lovely young lady named Liz."

"You want to go horseback riding this afternoon?" she said.

"Well, I haven't been on a horse since I was in high school."

"I'll bring you a gentle one."

"Where we goin'?" he asked her.

"Cooper Hollow. We can ride on the forest roads down there." Cooper Hollow was a state wildlife area east of Oak Hill. He had squirrel hunted there a lot and knew there weren't any horse trails.

"Okay, what time?" he asked.

"Do you go to church?" she replied.

"Not very often; sometimes, once in a while."

"I'm going to early church so why don't you come down to the farm about ten thirty."

"Okay, I'll be there."

"See you later." She hung up.

He didn't have any cowboy boots. He always wore Wellingtons with steel toes, even to dance in. That's what he would wear. I bet she'll wear a cowboy hat, too. Don't have one of them either. Maybe I should wear my fire helmet in case I fall off or hit a low tree limb.

He pulled in to the driveway at exactly ten thirty. She and Doc were loading a horse into a double trailer behind her truck. He didn't know what to do so he just watched. There was another horse already in the trailer. They both had saddles on them.

"You know how to ride, Jon?" Doc said.

"Not really," he replied.

"Well, Liz will teach you. She's been riding since she was four years old."

Liz smiled. "I had a good teacher Grampa."

"Your gramma was a good rider, too. She taught you more than I did," Doc said.

Jon had known Doc about eight years and he was a widow when he first met him.

"Let's go," Liz said. "See you this evening, Grampa."

"Be careful," Doc said.

She was wearing a white cowboy hat and jeans and a plaid Western shirt and her dirty cowboy boots.

"Looks like it might rain," he said as she turned left onto Camba Road.

"I brought rain gear; its rolled up and tied on behind the saddles."

They went up Route 93 aways and then turned across Evans Road toward the CH and D Road.

"Where you go to church?" he asked her.

"Presbyterian in Oak Hill."

"You Welsh?' he asked her.

"My mom was, she was a Lewis. She grew up out in Madison Township. Her and daddy met at 4H Camp. She went to Oak Hill Schools and daddy went to Jackson Schools. Daddy was Methodist, but he converted to Presbyterian when they got married so that's why I'm Presbyterian."

"When I go, I go to Franklin Valley Methodist where your Grampa goes," he told her.

They soon pulled off the CH and D road into a parking area and unloaded the horses.

"This one's for you." she said, handing him the reins. "His name is Biscuit; mine's name is Triscuit."

"Do they ever get their names mixed up?" he asked.

"No, but I do sometimes. They're both the same age so they've been together a long time."

He noticed she had saddle bags and a western style canteen on her horse. She also had a lever action carbine in a scabbard.

"What kind a gun you got?" he asked her.

"A .22. Grampa won't let me go without it."

"That's good. I got a little snub nose .38 in an ankle holster on. Never know who you might run across out here on these back roads."

They mounted up and she gave him a short course on how to handle the horse. She told him to follow her and they started up a gravel road. It was unlikely they would meet any cars on Sunday as hunting was not allowed on Sunday and that's what most people came to Cooper Hollow to do. At night, they came here to park and smoke dope.

They talked as they headed up the hill. When they got to the top they went back a dead-end road that he was familiar with, as there were a couple fishing ponds back there. When they got to the first pond she called a halt and they dismounted and tied the horses to separate trees. She got her saddle bags off her horse.

"You hungry?" she said.

"Yeah, I skipped breakfast."

"I have chicken salad sandwiches, chips, and apples."

She got out two metal cups and poured from her canteen. "Lemonade," she said.

"I hear thunder; looks pretty dark to the west," Jon said to Liz.

She got up and fetched raincoats from behind the horses' saddles and they put them on. She then unrolled a tarp and they covered up with it and continued to eat as it started to rain, slowly at first, but gradually getting harder.

The rain lasted about a half hour and then let up. They put things away and left their raincoats on and mounted back up.

They rode back out onto the gravel road and headed across the ridge.

"Did your doctor friend ride with you?" he asked Liz.

"No, he said he was allergic to horses."

"If you go out this old service road up here, there is an old hunting cabin that people kind of take turns using if the weather turns bad. It's got a stove and usually some dry firewood."

They turned out the old road and went about a half mile to the cabin. Someone kept it in good repair, but it was never locked. Obviously, the dopers didn't know about it yet or it would be torn up.

"This is it," he said. It was still raining. They tied their horses to a couple small sapling trees in the grassy yard and went inside. There was one big room with an iron stove against the back wall and a pile of firewood and kindling. A rough wooden table with two benches set in the middle of the room with a candle lantern on it. There was a kitchen counter and some cabinets, but no plumbing. The other room had two pairs of crude wooden bunks, but no mattresses. The place was really clean.

"I'm going to get a fire going," he told Liz. They hung up their raincoats. He found some matches in a coffee can in the cabinet. Soon he had the stove going.

"How did you know about this place?" Liz asked.

"Came across it when I was squirrel hunting a few years ago. Some people I know come back here and stay the night and run their fox hounds."

They sat on the bench in front of the stove and leaned back against the table. The heat felt good as the rain was cold.

"My pants are wet," Liz told him and she got up and went into the bedroom. He didn't know what to expect. He had visions of her in panties. She came out wearing her raincoat and carrying her jeans and cowboy boots. She hung the jeans by the stove to dry and sat back down beside him.

He looked down at her bare feet. "You got nice feet," he said.

"They're cold," she said and stretched them out toward the stove. He got up and opened the stove door and put some more wood in.

"It'll be getting dark in about three hours and it's still pouring the rain down," Jon said.

"Yeah," she said. "Good day for horse riding." They both laughed.

"We could spend the night here."

"I don't think that'd be a good idea. Grandpa would have your buddies at the sheriff's office out looking for us."

"Right, I shouldn't have said that, I mean I didn't mean it in a bad way, I'm a gentleman you know and you're a lady, right?'

"Thank you," she said. "That's very kind."

He was wondering what kind of undies she had on under her raincoat. Maybe she didn't wear panties. Some women didn't. Well, he wasn't going to look and see. If he just happened to get a glimpse that was something else. But he wasn't going to try to.

An hour later, the rain let up and she put her pants back on and they put on their raincoats and got on the horses and headed back toward the truck and trailer. It was almost dark when they started loading the horses up.

"Thanks for going with me," she said.

"I enjoyed it. We could go up to Richland State Forest sometime and ride. There are trails up there."

"Where's that at?" she replied as she was turning off Camba Road onto Franklin Valley.

"Up by Wellston. Half of it is in Vinton County. There's an old stone iron making furnace in the middle of the place."

"Grampa told me about the old iron furnaces. He used to be the company doctor for one in Jackson, but it blew up," he said.

"I think that was Globe Furnace," Jon said. "It was across from the Manpower Training School."

He helped her unload the horses and brush them and feed them.

"Your carbine's soaked. You want me to take it home and clean it for you?"

"I'd like that very much," she told him with a smile.

"Well, I got to be going, I got to work in the morning. You're still on vacation."

"I have a lot of work to do around here, but I'd still like to help you work on that case if you don't mind," she said as he put his arms around her waist and pulled her close to him.

They looked in each other's eyes for a minute and then started laughing and ended up in a real lip lock.

Chapter 7

Monday morning was a nice fall morning. The trees were beginning to change a little as October was approaching. Jon got up early and took a walk around town. He needed to do this every day, but he was so busy. He could smell the smoke from the foundry. He didn't mind it at all. It meant that folks were working. There was only one foundry left in Jackson. He walked down High Street and took a break and sat and watched the train crews moving railroad cars around. The DT&I had a shop on Athens Street that repaired railroad cars. It was simply called the Car Shops by everyone. It was a big employer, but lately some of the employees had been transferred to another shop in Michigan. Rumor was that the shops may be closing.

He got to the sheriff's office at eight-thirty. Dave was typing. He handed Jon a sheet of paper. It was a copy of the typed radio log from the radio room.

"We got a lead," Dave said.

Jon looked at the log sheet. Halfway down was a yellow highlighted paragraph stating that a female had called in and said that Dave and Pee Wee Brown had killed the woman out on Glen Cozy Road and they had taken a T.V., sewing machine and a jar of money. It said that Judy Brown had the T.V. The woman refused to give her name.

"Who's Judy Brown?" Jon asked Dave.

"Probably a sister, there's ten or eleven of those Brown kids in that family."

"We gonna find her today?"

"Yeah, let me call Hugh Dorr down at Scioto County SO. A bunch of those Browns live down around Portsmouth. Maybe he knows her." Dave said as he picked up the phone and punched in the numbers.

Dave put the phone on speaker.

"Scioto County Sheriff's Office," said a female voice.

"Is Hugh there?" Dave asked.

"Just a minute, please."

"Dorr, what can I do for you?" a gruff voice answered. Reminded him of Joe, Jon's boss. Everyone knew Hugh. He was chief deputy sheriff at Scioto County. He had retired from Portsmouth PD before going to work for the sheriff.

"It's Dave up at Jackson County."

"What you up to, Dave?"

"Got us a murder up here." Dave said and went on to tell him about the lady dying in the fire.

"I heard about that," Hugh said.

"You know a Judy Brown?" Dave asked Hugh.

"Is she one of them Brown's from out on Slithering Ridge?"

"Yeah, that bunch of critters."

"She used to be married to Dave Brown. She was a Foulton. Big family from around South Webster. Same kind of trouble as the Brown's."

"You know where we can find her?" Dave asked.

"She's right here in our jail. Just started serving a thirty-day sentence for DWI." DWI stands for driving while intoxicated. Same as OMVI. Operating a motor vehicle intoxicated. The state highway patrol said OMVI. Deputy Sheriff's called it DWI.

"That's darn nice of you to do that for us, Hugh. If we come down there, can we talk to her. I got the fire marshal on here with me."

"Hey, Jon, haven't seen you in a while."

"Been wanting to get down your way," Jon said. "Now I got a good reason."

"Come on down. I'll be here all day. Fried chicken in the jail today if you get here in time."

"We'll be down this morning," Dave said.

"Okay, see you after a while," Hugh said as he hung up the phone.

"You had breakfast, Jon. I'm hungry. Let's go through McDonald's."

They drove down the Appalachian Highway to Route 23 and took 23 south to Portsmouth. Dave drove no less than seventy miles per hour in the fifty-five limit that was imposed after the gas shortage a few years ago. Jon knew that was one of the reasons Dave drove a marked car. Didn't have to worry about getting stopped by the staties. The App as it was called was a four-lane highway that stretched across southern Ohio from Belpre to Cincinnati. It wasn't completely finished yet. There were still sections of two lane road here and there.

The Scioto County Jail and Sheriff's Office was on the third floor of the court-house in the middle of downtown Portsmouth. They went in the basement entrance and took the elevator up. Hugh wasn't in his office. The jailer said he was in court with a prisoner. He showed them to an interview room and went to get the Brown girl. He returned a few minutes later with a female jailer and a Slim blond girl about five foot seven tall and wearing orange jail clothes. The female jailer pulled out a chair and motioned for her to sat across from Dave and Jon.

Dave introduced them. "Judy, my name is Dave Jeffers, and I'm a deputy sheriff with the Jackson County Sheriff and this is Jon Hamer who is an in-vestigator for the State Fire Marshal's Office. We would like to ask you some questions about a case that we are working on."

"Okay," she said. "Am I in any kind of trouble?" One of the first things folks always asked.

"Not if you are truthful with us and tell us what you know about this case."

"Okay.

"Judy, do you know Dave Brown?" Dave asked her.

"I was married to him for three years. We're divorced."

"Do you know where he is now?"

"No, he's been cutting timber over at South Webster for some guy that has a sawmill out there."

"When was the last time you saw Dave?" he asked her as he looked directly into her eyes.

"It was a couple days before I came here to serve my sentence. I got here yesterday. He came to my house one night this week about 4:00 A.M. with his brother Pee Wee. Pee Wee didn't come in."

"Did Dave give you anything?"

She hesitated a bit. "I don't want to get in any trouble over this."

"You won't as long as you are truthful," Dave assured her.

"Okay. He knew I didn't have a T.V., so he brought this little portable T.V. in the house and said I could have it."

"Did he say where he got it?"

"No, but I suppose he stole it or you wouldn't be here," she said, shaking her head back and forth like she had been through this before with Dave, her ex.

"Where is the T.V. now, Judy?" Dave asked her.

"It's at my apartment in New Boston." New Boston was a town just east of Portsmouth.

"Can we have it to see if it's the one that we think is stolen? If it's not, you'll get it back. If it is, we will have to keep it."

"Yeah, if it's stolen, I don't want it, the SOB, I should have known better than to take it."

Dave asked her, "Is anyone living at your apartment now?"

"No, my little girl is staying with my mom."

Jon asked, "Where is the key to your place?"

"In my personal property envelope. They took my stuff when I came in yesterday."

"Excuse me a minute." Jon left the room and went down the hallway. He found Hugh in his office. He explained that they needed to get the T.V. from Judy's place.

"Just take her with you to get it and then bring her back here," Hugh said. "She won't try to take off on you. Just have her back before supper time."

Jon went back in the interview room. Dave had Judy writing out a statement about what she had told them.

Jon said, "Hugh said we could take Judy over to her place to get the T.V. and bring her back here before supper. Is that all right with you, Judy?"

"Yeah, but it's almost lunch."

"Yeah, and today is fried chicken. We'll go through McDonald's. You'll have to give us a consent to search your apartment." He said as he pulled a form out of his clipboard and started filling it out, asking Judy what her address was and telling her that all they were interested in was the T.V. and that she had the right to refuse to let them search her apartment.

After getting Judy's key out of the property room, they put her in the back seat of the cruiser and drove through McDonalds and Jon bought everyone a Big Mack and a large Coke. When they got to Judy's apartment she let them in. It wasn't what Jon had expected. It was very clean and modestly furnished. He expected it to be a mess.

The T.V. was on a stand table. "Don't anyone touch it," Dave said as he took a couple photos of it. He went out to his car and returned with a brown paper grocery bag. It was a little black and white thing. He put in down in the bag after he put rubber gloves on.

"Is this the T.V. Dave gave you a couple days ago?" Jon asked Judy.

"Yeah, that's it."

"Okay, we're ready to take you back to the jail," Dave told her. "We thank you for your help. You know that you may have to testify in court about this."

"I really don't want to. Dave'll kill me when he finds out."

"Hopefully he'll be in jail before you get out," Dave told her.

"Who'd he steal it from?" Judy asked.

"An old lady down at Oak Hill" was all that Dave told her.

After they returned Judy to the jail. Dave and John headed up Route 140 to South Webster and cut across Jackson Furnace Road to Oak Hill to visit the victim's niece and nephew to see if they could ID the T.V.

Dave put his rubber gloves on and carefully took the T.V. out of the sack in the living room of the niece and nephews after telling them not to touch it as there might be fingerprints on it. They looked it over closely.

"It's hers," the niece said.

"Is there anything about it that can help you say for sure its hers?" Dave asked.

"Well, no, I just know it's hers cause it looks like hers." she said, looking at her husband who was shaking his head in agreement.

"Do you know where it was purchased?" Jon asked.

"No," the nephew said," she brought it with her when she moved her from Kansas about seven years ago."

Jon and Dave decided to stop by Wesley Browns house and see if he would give them a consent to search his house. Wesley wasn't there, but his woman was. They told her they were looking for a stolen sewing machine and asked if she would sign a consent to search. She said she didn't have a sewing machine and she didn't have anything to hide so they could search all they wanted to. Nothing was found. They were also looking for a jar of money, but they didn't tell her that, but they didn't really know what kind of a jar of money they were looking for. The niece and nephew said that they didn't know their aunt to keep a jar of money. Just a few dollars in her purse.

"Well, all we got right now is possession of stolen property," Dave said as he drove up Route 93 going back to Jackson.

"We need more than this," Jon agreed.

"I'll take the T.V. to BCI tomorrow and have it dusted for prints. Dave's prints are on file as many times as he has been arrested for drunk and fighting. Pee Wee's, too."

"We need to find that sewing machine before they get rid of it if they haven't already," Jon said as they were parking behind the Jackson County Jail.

"I'll bet it's in the family somewhere. There's a bunch of Browns and a bunch of Foulton's and probably one of them has it. They may have sold it to someone in their family. We got a lot of people to talk to. It's too early to make a move on Dave or Pee Wee, but the word's out now that we're looking at them," Dave said.

"If you'll take the T.V. to BCI I'll start talking to the Browns tomorrow," Jon said. BCI is the Bureau of Criminal Investigation and Identification in London, Ohio. It is operated by the State Attorney General to assist local law enforcement in criminal investigations. They have crime scene investigators around the state that are similar to Fire Marshal's in that they work out of their homes and cover several counties assisting local law enforcement. They also have the Crime Lab that processes physical evidence.

They went in the jail kitchen and Jon got a cup of coffee and Dave got a glass of Kool Aid from the frig. Mille gave them each a piece of fresh baked sheet cake with chocolate icing that she had made for the prisoners' supper. They sat at the kitchen table eating and talking.

"What are you guys doin' in my kitchen this time of day?" said the Sheriff as he sat down at the table with his own big piece of cake on a plate.

"Takin' a break, Chuck," Dave answered.

"Good cake, Chuck," said Jon. Chuck Gunther was in the last year of his first term as sheriff. No one called him Sheriff. Everyone knew him as Chuck. He had started back in the fifties as a deputy when the office only had two deputies. Now they had ten. Jon had worked for him when he was Chief Deputy Sheriff and then after he got elected Sheriff. Chuck was an easy person to work for. That was sometimes a problem because he had a couple of lazy deputies that took advantage of his good nature.

"You guys doin' any good on that fire?" Chuck asked.

Dave told Chuck about the T.V.

"Sounds like you're getting a good start. You guys be careful with the Brown's, they can hurt you. Their old man took a shot at me when I was a young deputy. Only thing saved me was the gun jammed after he missed on the first shot. I got it away from him and backhanded him a good one and put the cuffs on him."

Jon remembered the first time he had ever seen Chuck backhand someone. Matter of fact, it was the first time he had ever seen anyone back hand someone except for maybe John Wayne. Jon was sitting the desk when he first started at the SO. A highway patrolman brought in a drunk driver and the guy was cussing up a storm and the trooper didn't do anything to shut him up. Chuck was back in his office. He came out and told the guy to shut up. The drunk called Chuck some kind of name and all of a sudden Chuck swung his left arm across and hit the guy in the face with the back of his hand and knocked him across the room where he hit the wall and collapsed on the floor. Chuck went back in his office. The statie didn't know what to do. Pretty soon the guy got up and emptied his pockets and didn't say another word.

Chuck was a short man with a big belly and grey hair. He was strong though. He had farmed all his life. You had to have a second job if you were a deputy sheriff because it didn't pay much. The bad guys didn't realize how strong he was and thought they could shove him around. Chuck was a church going man and he didn't allow cussin' in the office. The deputies all respected it. It was mostly because of the women who worked there that Chuck didn't allow it. Dot the secretary was very church goin' and Chucks wife helped Mille out in the kitchen. Of course, the prisoners knew better to cuss at the cooks. They were fed good and knew if they weren't nice to them they all would get put on bread and water. Chuck was in the Navy in the Second War. He said that if bread and water was alright for sailors sent to the brig then it was all right for prisoners in his jail if they misbehaved.

CHAPTER 8

On Tuesday morning, Jon called Liz and asked her if she wanted to go along and help him look for the sewing machine. He told her about the T.V. and she told him she had gotten the written autopsy report. He picked her up at the farm and they headed down toward Slithering Ridge.

"You still on vacation?' he asked her.

"The rest of the week. I cut and split firewood with Grampa all day yesterday. We had a load of logs delivered to the farm. Once we get it all cut and split we'll have enough to last all winter with what we had left over from last year."

"I never seen a woman do man's work like you do," he said. "You put me to shame. I don't get near the exercise you get. I try to walk a couple miles every morning or evening, but that's about the extent of it."

"I like the farm. I grew up in Chillicothe, but spending the summers at my grandparents was fun. I learned how to work. In the winter, we came down every Saturday and I rode my horse and cleaned his stall."

They got to the Brown home place on Slithering Ridge. Old man Brown was working on an old pickup truck in the yard. Jon asked him if they could look through his house for the sewing machine.

"I knew you'd be out here sooner or later nosin' around. You tryin' to pin something on my boys they didn't do. Hell, no, I won't let you in my house. You tell that Chuck Gunther that he'd be dead today if my gun hadn't jambed on me."

Jon replied, "We can get a search warrant and come back."

"You go get one and come back. You won't find nothin'. I ain't never liked the law since that Chuck Gunther sent me to prison back in fifty-seven. Now you can be leavin' and not comin' back unless you got one of them search things with you."

Jon knew he had no choice but to leave. He hated to back down from someone like this, but he had no choice. The law was the law. And they didn't have probable cause to get a search warrant.

"He's not very nice, is he?" Liz said as they drove out the ridge road.

"No, he's not and the thing of it is we don't have probable cause to get a search warrant so we won't be searchin' his place."

"What was he talkin' about, the Sheriff?" Liz asked.

"He took a shot at Chuck years ago and missed then his gun jammed and Chuck took it away from him. I didn't know the Sheriff sent him to prison. I suppose that's what he sent him up for."

"That reminds me, when you going to teach me to shoot?"

"We can start this weekend if you want to. You got a gun?"

"Grampa said I could use his .45 he carried when he was in the National Guard."

"You might not like it; it'll kick a lot," he told her.

"Where we goin' to shoot at?"

"Well, we could go out to the Farmer Sportsman club and use their range, but there might be other people there shooting. You got anyplace on your farm we could use?"

"Out back of the barn in the hillside is a place where we dig dirt out for filling ground hog holes. That's where I shoot my .22 at."

"That'd be good enough," he said, "we don't need any more than thirty-five feet. Any shootin' further than that and you need a shotgun or a rifle."

They found two more of the Brown sisters living on out Slithering Ridge. They each consented to letting them search their homes. Their husbands were all at work cutting timber. Seemed like this whole family cut timber. Nothing found but at the one sisters house Liz was attracted to a lamp that was a glass goose and she commented on how nice it is. The girl said that actually her brother Pee Wee had just given it to her a couple days ago.

"Do you mind if we take that with us to show to some folks?" Jon asked.

"No, I don't mind, but I want it back. I think you're barkin' up the wrong tree if you think my brothers killed that woman. Our sister worked for her you know."

They went by the niece and nephews house again. The niece said her husband was gone on a preaching tour in Kentucky. She looked over the lamp and said she had never seen it in her aunt's house.

As they were leaving Liz asked him if they were going to take the lamp back to the sister.

"No, I think I'll hang onto it for a few days. You know we had those other two fires and then we might check some burglary reports to see if it belongs to someone. If them Brown brothers had it then it's probably stolen from somewhere."

"It's pretty," Liz commented.

"It'd look good sittin' on Dave's desk for a few days," Jon laughed.

"He needs to get rid of all those beer cans in plastic bags he's got on his desk," Liz said, laughing.

"Let me tell you a little story about that," Jon said. "Me and Dave were workin' on a bunch of fires out around Limerick last year. Same kind of deal as this. Fires set to cover up burglaries. Well, we were supposed to be workin' on those fires one morning, but when I got in the SO Dave said they had a woman report her car stolen from her house in McKiterick Heights the night before and about six in the morning someone found the car burned up on the road that goes from Firebrick over to Blackfork. Well, Dave said the woman that had the car stolen had two guys livin' with her and he figured they were the ones that took the car out there and burned it so she could collect the insurance. So, Dave had a deputy out lookin' for them guys to bring them in and he wanted me to help him talk to them. In the meantime, we got another call on a new fire out at Limerick so I went out there and it was an old farmhouse that burned down. There was a beer can layin' in the yard so I picked it up and put it in a bag and when I got back in Dave's office I tossed it on his desk. Well, a deputy brings these two guys in that we want to talk to about burning the car so we get one of them in Dave's office and start talkin' to him and he was pretty nervous. We started accusin' him of doin' the car and he puts his hands up in the air and says, 'I might as well tell ya. You got me.' Then he pointed to the beer can in the plastic bag that I had just brought in. 'That's my beer can. I threw it in the ditch after we set the car on fire. It's got my fingerprints all over it.' He then gave us a complete statement on how they took the car down there and the woman followed them and watched them set it on fire and brought them back home and she reported it stolen."

Liz laughed, "You're kiddin' me. The can wasn't even from the car fire."

"No. I hadn't even been down to the car fire yet. The car was still sittin' down there smoldering."

"Wow, that's funny," Liz laughed some more.

On Wednesday, Jon got called on a fire in Athens County by the OSP, which is what they called the Ohio State Highway Patrol. The highway patrol is strictly a traffic agency. They only have jurisdiction on public roads and state of Ohio property. This call was for a fire at the roadside rest on US 50 about halfway between Athens and Coolville. He knew the place. It set off the highway on the old two lane highway. It was in a nice grove of trees and had a nice picnic area and an older restroom with pit toilets. It was hardly visible from the main highway because of the trees. This made it a popular place for persons to meet for sexual activity. Local people who knew this stayed away from the place. Travelers often found that they were interrupting the plans for some sexual activity between two adults of the same sex, usually males. They made a mental note to never stop there again. Jon could never figure out why the OSP didn't do anything about what went on there. There was a similar problem at a roadside rest up near Columbus and the county Sheriff did an undercover sting and made a bunch of arrests. The place still had a stigma about it so no one stopped there anymore so they closed the place down and demolished the restrooms.

When he got there, he found that the wooden restroom was destroyed by fire. The fire was out and the fire department was no longer there. There was a single highway patrolman there.

"I'm Jon Hamer, Fire Marshal," he said to the young patrolman.

"I'm waiting for the district investigator from the Jackson Post to get here and I'll turn it over to him," the patrolman said.

"Who reported the fire?" Jon asked, looking around for any houses. He saw one about six hundred yards away and up on a slight hill.

"Passing truck driver on the CB. I heard him on my CB. I was over toward Guysville and got here before the fire department. The men's restroom side was burning. No one around. I waited for the fire department. They came from Coolville."

"Any ideas," Jon asked.

The patrolman shrugged his head.

Jon went in the men's side. The burn pattern pointed to the back corner. There he found a fifty-five-gallon drum on its side. A trash can lid was laying on the concrete floor beside it. One of those with a flapper on it. From the looks of the fire debris it was apparent that the trash can had been laying there during the burning of the fire. It was not knocked over by the fire department. There was no electric wiring in this corner of the place. He got his camera and to took some pictures.

"Looks like someone took the lid off the trash can and laid it on its side and lit the trash on fire," Jon told the officer.

"You think they used gasoline?" the patrolman asked.

"Nothing to indicate it," Jon replied.

"I went up to the house over there and no one was at home," said the patrolman.

"Well, when is your investigator going to get here?" he asked the patrolman.

"Be a while. He was at Lucasville when they got ahold of him."

Jon knew what he was probably doing at Lucasville. Investigating some crime at the Maximum-Security State Prison there.

"I live in Jackson. I'll drop my report off at the Jackson Post next week," Jon said as he got back in his car. The Jackson Post of the Highway Patrol was the district headquarters as well as the Jackson Post. A Lt. ran the Post and a Captain along with his staff officers ran the district headquarters. Jon knew the Captain as well as the Post Lt. The Captain was a nice guy if you didn't work for him. If you worked for him, you better watch yourself. He was all spit and polish and military like.

When he got to Guysville, he went to the service station and used the payphone to call the office in Reynoldsburg and talk to the chief. He told the chief about the fire at the rest area and what kind of activity went on there. The chief said to leave it to the patrol to investigate. It was probably a good thing the place burned down. Make that stretch of highway safer for travelers. People could stop at the gas station in Guysville and pee and get a soda pop. Be good for the local economy.

On the way back home, Jon stopped at the Wellston Fire Department to loaf a while. One of the old investigators had told him that you needed to stop and visit once in a while. Not just when they called you on a fire, but you needed to be sociable. It made sense. He liked talking firefighting anyway.

That night was a Jackson County Firefighters Association meeting at the Coalton Fire Department. This was a good opportunity for a fire marshal to meet several fire chiefs, officers and firefighters at one time. The meeting started at seven. The Coalton Fire Station was small with barely enough room for its two trucks and one van. When he got there at six thirty the trucks were parked across the street and chairs set up in the truck bays. All of the counties in his response district had similar monthly meetings.

Half the meeting time was taken up by two candidates for county courthouse jobs in the upcoming November general election. The rest of the time was spent in socializing and eating various snacks.

It was ten o'clock by the time Jon got home. He had already decided to take Friday off. Fire Marshals did not get paid overtime so he already had more than fifty hours in this week so he would take compensative time off on Friday.

CHAPTER 9

The phone by the bed rang. Jon looked at the clock. It was seven AM. He hoped it wasn't another fire to go on. He was looking forward to the day off. Maybe even a three-day weekend if he was lucky.

"Hello," he answered.

"Hi, Jon, its Liz."

"Oh Hi, how you doin'?" he answered.

"Fine, wanted to see if you were working on our case today," she said.

"No, takin' the day off on comp time."

"Oh, sorry, you probably wanted to sleep in."

"No. You wanna have your first pistol class tomorrow?" he asked her, trying not to talk like he had just woken from a sound sleep.

"Yeah, that sounds neat. I found some ammo that Grampa had out in the garage."

"I got some targets. What time you want to get started?"

"Come out about eight for breakfast. It's supposed to be nice tomorrow," she said.

"You want to go with us tomorrow evening to dance at the Stage Coach?"

"Okay."

"When you go back to work?"

"Tuesday night at 11:00 P.M." she said, sounding as if she wasn't looking forward to it.

"Okay, I'll see you in the morning then."

"Bye," she said sweetly.

After breakfast on Saturday, Jon and Liz sat on the back porch and he gave her an hour lecture on the gun she had and how it worked and how to hold it and about safety. It was an old Remington Rand model made during the Second World War. He could tell that she was anxious to go out and shoot, but this safety stuff was important as well as knowing how the weapon functioned.

They walked out to the hillside and he fastened targets to a couple old fence posts that someone had obviously put in the ground for that purpose as you could see the bullet holes in them.

"Who's been doing all the shooting?" he asked Liz.

"I come out here and shoot my .22 rifle a lot," she said. "I bring Grampa's beer cans and shoot at them on top the fence posts."

"Okay," he said as he unholstered his revolver and unloaded it, putting the rounds in his pants pocket, "I'm going to show you how to hold your pistol with both hands. Whenever possible you want to shoot with both hands as it is more accurate."

He held the grip in his right hand and then extended his left hand out and cupped it around his right hand. "Now you want to have your right elbow bent just slightly and you shove forward with your right arm and you pull backward on your left arm. This steadies the gun in your hands. Now you try it with your gun."

She brought her pistol up and did what he had showed her to do. She locked her right elbow so he took hold of it and showed her how to unlock the elbow just a little. He took hold of her right wrist and shoved forward with it. He then cupped his hand around her left hand and pulled back on it. She smelled good. He then let go and she held the gun steady.

"Okay, now holster the gun and pull it out and do the two hand hold again."

She got it right this time so he had her practice it about a dozen times.

He pulled two sets of ear plugs out of his pocket and gave her one set to put in her ears.

"All right, take one of the charged magazines out of your pocket and put it in the gun like we did back at the house."

She did.

"Now pull the slide back and release it. The gun is now ready to fire. Keep it pointed down range and set the safety on it."

He checked and made sure the safety was on. "Now place the gun back in your holster."

She did as he said. "Now when I say holster ready position, I want you to place your hand on the gun, but don't remove it from the holster. Just keep a good grip on it in the holster."

She did this. "Now bring the weapon up out of the holster and click off the safety with your right thumb, keeping it pointed downrange, taking your time, no hurry."

"At the same time, you are bringing your left arm up to cup your left hand around your right hand as we practiced."

She did this.

"Now point the gun at the target using the sights like we practiced back at the house."

She aimed the gun.

"Now pull the trigger and fire one round and hold the gun in the high ready position like I showed you at the house."

BLAM, the gun went off and she kind of leaned back at the recoil.

"Place the safety back on using your right thumb and holster the weapon," he instructed. "Now let's go look at the target." They were shooting from fifteen feet.

There was a big hole in the target about four inches above the bull's eye ring.

"Good shot," he told her as she smiled.

"It sure does kick a lot," she said.

"Don't pay any attention to the kick. Don't anticipate it. If you do you won't get good hits."

"All right, let's go back to the line and do it again and again."

They kept it up. One round at a time. She had two magazines. Her fingers started getting sore from reloading the mags. They shot two fifty round boxes of ammo before they took a break. She was shooting a good tight group from two to four inches directly above the bull's eye.

"How am I doing?" she asked him.

"Real good. You have an advantage over most women who try to shoot a .45. You have strong arms so you can handle the recoil and the heavy gun."

At one in the afternoon they quit and went back to his car and cleaned her gun on the hood of the car. He showed her how to take it apart and clean it good. By the time they were done, they both smelled like Hoppes Number Nine cleaning solvent.

She was going to go inside and fix lunch when he heard three beeps coming from the radio in his car. "Jackson County to all units. Report from a trucker on CB of a highway patrolman having trouble with two subjects on a traffic stop at the store just south of Camba Road on 93."

Car three answered. "Responding from McKitterick Heights."

Jon knew that there was only one deputy out today. McKitterick Heights was eight miles away. Jon was just two miles away. There should be at least two highway patrolmen out on a Saturday. "I gotta go," he told Liz.

She had heard the call. "I'm going with you," she said.

"No, you better stay here." But she got in the front seat anyways. He started the car and swung around in the drive way and headed down Franklin Valley Road. "FM47 responding from Franklin Valley School House," he said into the radio mic as they passed the school house and started up Camba Road.

"Jackson County to all units be advised OSP unit responding from the post."

"Oak Hill Unit Two responding from Oak Hill" they heard on the radio along with the roar of the Oak Hill Cruisers engine roaring.

As they came down Camba Road to Route 93 Jon could see the lights flashing on a OSP car sitting in the gravel lot of the store. A coal truck was stopped about two hundred yards down the highway. The trucker was standing in the road holding what looked like a club.

"You stay in the car unless I wave for you to get out," Jon told Liz as they slid into the lot. He could see two guys standing over a patrolman who was laying on the ground. A skinny guy was kicking the officer. A fat guy was bent over the officer.

Jon jumped out of the car and drew his revolver. He could see that the fat guy was trying to get the officers revolver out of its holster. He stopped just behind the patrol car and knelt on one knee and aimed his pistol at the guys. "Stop or I'll blow your heads off," he hollered as he fired a round about a foot over the skinny guy's head. They both looked at him. He cocked his gun with his left thumb. The fat guy was starting to rise with the officer's gun in his hand. "Drop the fuckin' gun, or I'll kill you," Jon hollered. The guy hesitated a second and dropped the gun.

"Both of you. Put your hands on your heads." They complied. "Fatso, turn toward the store and take three steps. Now turn away from me and get down on your knees and keep your hands on your head." He could hear a siren coming from Oak Hill.

"Skinny you put your cotton pickin' hands back on your head and turn away from me. Now take three steps and get down on your knees before I shoot you."

Skinny complied. The Oak Hill Officer screeched to a stop and the cop jumped out with his shotgun aimed at the skinny guy. "Call for a squad," Jon told the Oak Hill officer who had a walkie talkie.

The deputy sheriff arrived. "Bob," Jon said to the Oak Hill Officer, "put your shotgun back in your car and you cuff them while me and the deputy cover you."

Bob moved in and cuffed the skinny one. The deputy tossed Bob another set of cuffs and Bob cuffed the other one. A highway patrol car pulled in and started checking the officer on the ground. "He's breathing, but hurt," the patrolman said.

Jon holstered his pistol and motioned for Liz to get out of the car. "There's a blanket on my back seat. Could you take care of the officer till the squad gets here?" She went over and covered the patrolman up and checked his pulse, using her wristwatch.

Jon went over and helped Bob put the skinny guy in the Oak Hill car after searching him. He then helped the deputy search and put the fat guy in the sheriff's car. By then the squad arrived from Oak Hill. Within thirty-five minutes, there were three more OSP units on the scene, a sergeant, the post commander who was a Lt. and the Captain that ran the District.

Jon walked over to the little store and asked to use the phone. He called Joe, his assistant chief and told him what had happened. Joe told him to give a verbal statement to the patrol and tell them that he would bring them a typed statement sometime on Monday. Joe said he didn't know what the procedure at the SFM was for handling this kind of thing as it had never happened since he had been working there and there was no written policy that he knew of.

Jon went back outside and set in the OSP Lt's car and told him what happened and told him what his boss had told him to do. The Lt. said their district investigator would be handling the investigation and would probably want to talk to him. He thanked him for helping. The patrolman was on his way to the hospital.

Liz was leaning against his car. He went over to her. She gave him a big hug and said, "I was scared to death."

"You did good," Jon told her. "Let's get out of here before more brass gets here. They may want to talk to you, but it can wait until Monday."

When they got back to Liz and Doc's farm Jon asked Liz if he could have one of Docs cans of beer. She went inside and came out with a Blue Ribbon and they sat on the front porch swing while he drank it.

Jon looked at his pocket watch. It was 4:00 P.M. "We still going to the disco tonight?" he asked Liz.

"I guess, but how do you just walk away from something like that and then go out for the night?"

"You get used to it. This kind of stuff doesn't happen every day, but it's just part of the job."

"You want another beer?"

"No. I'll drink a few tonight. You want to meet up there or do you want to ride up with me?"

"I'll meet you there. I got to do the chores."

"You want some help?"

"No," she said. "You've done enough for the day. I'll see you in Wellston tonight." She gave him a light kiss on the lips and went back in the house.

Jon walked into the Stage Coach Inn at Wellston about eight thirty Saturday evening. He stopped just inside the dance hall door and looked around. There was his bunch. They had two tables shoved together. Kathy and Denny. Cheryl and her friend Amy. Jess and his new woman. Jimmy George who was assistant fire chief at Wellston. Eric Potter who worked at the Stove Plant, a foundry at Jackson. There was Rita. No. He forgot all about her. He didn't see Liz. He remembered that she had chores to do and would be late. What was he going to do about Rita? He had to go to the bathroom, so he turned around and went into the men's room and sat down in a stall. He should have called Rita a couple times this week. In all the years he had known her, she had never called him except for the one time after they spent the night together a couple weeks ago. She always told him that her momma had told her she should never call a guy socially as he would think she was pursuing him. One time he asked her, "What if you were pursuing him?"

"Don't worry, Jon Hamer, I'm not pursuing you." He really valued her friendship over the years and he didn't want it to end. Now he wished he wouldn't have slept with her. He went into the dance hall and greeted everyone at the table and sat down beside Rita.

"Heard about your savin' that statie this morning," Jess said. "We been talking about it."

"We heard the Colonel is going to give you a medal," said Cheryl the WPD dispatcher. She was referring to the superintendent of the State Highway Patrol.

"Yeah, sure," Jon said. "Anyone know how the patrolman is getting along?" he said as he looked at Jess.

"He's in the hospital with a bad concussion and some broken ribs," said Jess. He turned and faced Rita. "How you doin', girl?"

"Good, guess you been pretty busy."

"Yeah, a lot goin' on. Haven't had much time to do anything."

He ordered him a Miller Lite. They all talked about his escapade saving the patrolman until the lights dimmed and the music started.

As usual, the DJ started off with YMCA and the whole table got up and danced. The place was crowded tonight. The next song was slow and Jon turned around and he was in Rita's arms.

"I was hoping you would have called me this week," she said.

"Sorry, I should have, but I been busy."

"I heard you were hangin' out with a nurse."

"We're workin' together on that murder at Oak Hill. She's the coroner's new investigator."

"Heard she was with you today when you helped that patrolman," Rita said.

"Yeah, we were working," he lied.

Rita had her head on his chest as they danced. She wasn't very tall.

He was on the lookout for Liz. He drank three beers. One more than he usually drank in one evening and it was only a quarter till ten. It seemed like the stress from the day's events were starting to catch up with him and he had to unwind. Then there was Rita and Liz. He had danced one more time with Rita. Right now, the girls were all out there dancing a fast one together and the guys were at the table talking.

Then he saw her. Liz. She had her friend and boss Karen with her. They were headed toward their table. There appeared to be a guy with them, about forty years old and wearing a sport coat and a tie.

Liz was wearing jeans, but Karen had a tight short skirt on. "Hi everyone," Liz said. "Are Karen and I the only gals here tonight?"

"No." Jon pointed to the dance floor. "The rest are out there dancin'."

"This is John Gillespie, we call him Doctor John, he's a radiologist at the hospital and you all remember Karen."

The guys all got up and shook John's hand.

"Come on, Jess," Jon said, "we got to find some more chairs." They returned shortly with three chairs they had found in the banquet room next door. By then the girls were back from dancing and introductions were taking place again. Jon found himself sitting between Liz and Rita. He wondered who Doctor John was with. Liz or Karen. Maybe both. He soon found out when a slow number started and John asked Karen to dance.

"Karen and John have been seeing each other for a couple of months," Liz told Jon. "Have you recovered from all the excitement today?"

"Yeah, how about you?" he replied.

"I rode up with Karen and John, and I was telling them about it. I hope that was all right."

"Sure. No problem." They included Rita in their conversation and the three of them got up and danced a fast song together.

Doctor John was funny. When the DJ was on break and they could all hear better he told a couple of funny stories. One was about when he was in the Navy and he was being transferred from a carrier to a destroyer on a bosuns chair and he got dunked in the South China Sea and lost his shoes.

The next slow dance Rita asked Jon and they danced together. "Is that your nurse friend?" Rita asked. He could detect the jealousy in her voice.

"Well, yeah, she's my friend like you're my friend, but we also work together."

"I kind of thought we were more than friends after the other night," Rita replied, still jealously.

"We are. You're a special kind of friend. We have been for a long time."

"I should have taken Momma's advice about not pursuing guys," Rita remarked.

"You're not pursuing me. You never call me. That's pursuing," Jon said laughing.

"I called you once," she said. The number was over and Rita excused herself to go to the ladies' room.

Jon ordered another beer and finally asked Liz to slow dance. He had lost track of how many he had drank. It couldn't have been that many. He hadn't been drunk for over a year. He used to get that way about once a month. It helped with the stress of the job.

"Where's Rita?" Cheryl asked as they were all sitting around the table. Kathy and Denny were the only one of their bunch still dancing.

"Last I knew she went to the restroom," Jon replied.

"I better go check on her, Cheryl said. She came back a few minutes later and said she couldn't find her and that she had looked around the dance hall and didn't see here anywhere.

"Maybe she left," someone said.

"I'll go out in the parking lot and see if her car is here," Jon said. He felt responsible.

He walked around outside and checked down Broadway Street both ways, but couldn't find her dark blue Nova.

"She must have left," he said after he got back to the table. "Her car's not out there."

"I'll wait about a half hour and call her house and see if she's home," Cheryl said. "That's not like her to leave without saying anything."

"Karen and John are ready to leave. I want to stay. Could you take me home, Jon?" Liz said into his ear. She had figured out that he couldn't hear good when the music was loud.

"Either that or you got to take me home. I've had a couple too many beers. Where's your truck?'

"At home. Karen and John picked me up," Liz said.

"Turn right here and go up Broadway Hill and down 93. I wanna see if Rita's car is at her house. Cheryl didn't get an answer when she called her house." Liz was driving his car. He drove his state car about everywhere he went so they could get ahold of him on the radio. The boss told him to unless he left the state of Ohio.

"Slow down through here," he told Liz. "It's one of these houses on Morton Street." They were just coming into Jackson. "There it is, there's her car. She's okay. Take me home."

"I don't know where you live."

"Turn next at the light and keep going until I tell you to turn. Be careful as you go by the Crown and Bridge Inn. Be drunks leaving there about now," he said, referring to the two most notorious beer joints in Jackson.

"Go right up here at the Wye. Now go up to the flashing lite and turn left onto High Street."

"Okay, here it is on the right. Go in that driveway," he said, pointing to the big, two-story white house.

"You can drive my car home. I'll get someone to bring me out in the morning to get it," he told Liz.

"I need to go to the restroom first," she said.

"Okay, come on in."

"Wow, this is nice," she said as they entered the big living room.

"It's not mine," he said.

"Whose is it then?" she said.

"Some people who spend the winter in Florida. There's a little restroom back behind the kitchen."

He laid down on the couch and started getting dizzy.

CHAPTER 10

He woke up on the couch and looked at the grandfather's clock. It was seven in the morning. He set up. There was a girl with dark black hair, wearing tight jeans asleep in the Lazy Boy. It was Liz. He got up and went back through the kitchen to the bathroom and then got a drink of water from the kitchen sink. He went back in the living room. She was awake.

"I thought you were driving my car home."

"I called Grampa and told him I was staying at Karen's place and gave him the number here. He won't know the difference."

"I'll run you out to the farm," he said, running his hands through his hair. "I didn't do anything I shouldn't have last night, did I?"

"Like what?"

"Like try to put the make on you."

"No. You fell asleep as soon as you got on the couch. I sat there and watched you sleep and finally I dozed off."

"I could make you breakfast," he said.

"I don't eat till I get the chores done first, and I've got to do them this morning and then go to church. You want to go to church with me?"

He thought a minute. "Okay, what time does it start? And only if you let me help you do your chores."

"Eleven o'clock. We better get going. You want to bring some church clothes?"

"I've got a bag in my car trunk. Have to. Never know when I'll have to stay overnight somewhere," he said as he was checking his pockets for his car keys. Then he saw them laying on the coffee table.

They got the feeding done and as he was taking a shower, Liz was fixing breakfast. Doc had already left for his church. He was gone when they got there. Liz said he always went to the cemetery by the church and sat at his wife's grave for about an hour before Sunday School started. Jon put on a tie and sport coat. He knew the Presbyterians were pretty big about dressing for church. While he ate, she got ready for church. She looked great wearing a skirt that came down below her knees and a white blouse.

"Wow, you clean up good. I forgot to tell you that you looked good last night," he complimented her.

"Karen and John like to dress up when they go out."

"Can I use your phone. I got to call the SO and see if they been looking for me for any fires."

"There's one in the living room."

The Oak Hill Presbyterian Church was an old cut stone building in the center of town. He had been there before. He had a hard time with the Welsh Hymns since he was raised in a Baptist Church. As they went in they were greeted by Jean Johns and her husband Joe. He knew them both. Jean worked in the village hall and Joe worked at the county prosecutor's office. They were really nice people.

They sat toward the middle of the church. "This was my Gramma and Grampy Jones' pew," Liz told him. "They moved to Florida about ten years ago."

He liked the service. The preacher gave a good talk. He was an old Welshman and was known for giving talks to groups on Welsh heritage. Jon knew him from the Highway Grill. He ate there a lot and he always got up and went behind the counter and got a coffee pot and went around the room filling patrons' cups and talking to them.

When they left the church, Jon called the SO on his radio to see if there was any traffic for him. The dispatcher said for him to call FM2 at his convenience. FM2 was Joe, the assistant chief. He decided to wait until that evening to call him.

As they were driving back to the farm, Liz said, "Can I ask you something Jon?"

"Sure."

"When you shot at those guys yesterday were you trying to hit one of them?"

"No, if I was trying to him one of them I would have hit him. That was a warning shot to get their attention hoping that they would stop what they were doing. Most departments don't allow warning shots."

"Does yours?" she asked.

"We don't even have a firearms policy."

"I was watching the whole thing. Would you have had time to shoot that guy if he had not dropped the gun?"

"Oh, yeah, I had the hammer back so my shot would be more accurate," he told her, referring to his double action revolver. Firing it when it was cocked was much more accurate than firing it in what was called double action mode. This meant you had a longer and harder trigger pull because you were causing the cylinder to turn and the hammer to come all the way back. Firing single action with the hammer already back did not involve turning the cylinder. All you were doing when you pulled the trigger was dropping the hammer on the primer of the cartridge. It was very smooth.

After he dropped Liz off Jon went home and called Rita. They talked for about an hour and she seemed to be all right. Nothing was said about Liz. Rita apologized for leaving without telling anyone. Then he called Joe, his boss. Joe said he had to come to the office Monday morning to talk to the attorney for Commerce. The Department of Commerce oversees the State Fire Marshal's Office. "What does he want?" Jon asked Joe.

"The Director has a friend at the Patrol Headquarters in Columbus and he has been talking to her about their firearms policy," Joe replied. The director is the head of Commerce. Jon met her once when he got sworn in. He couldn't remember her name. All he could remember was that they went to a big tall building in downtown Columbus and it was the first time he had been in a building over six stories tall.

"Am I in trouble?" he asked Joe.

"No. They don't know what to do as they have never had anything like this happen before and they don't have any SOP."

"I got to get my statement typed and dropped off at the Patrol Post."

"Bring the original with you," Joe said, "I'll be there when you talk to the guy. Don't worry about it."

Jon then got ahold of Dave and told him that he was dropping off a lamp at the SO in the morning and that he had called the owners of the cabin at Lake Jackson and the one at Gallia to have the owners come in and look at it to see if it was theirs. Dave said he would take care of it if the folks came in to look at it.

"I just hope that patrolman is okay," Jon said.

"They transferred him to OSU Hospital, I heard.," Dave said.

"That's good. He'll get good care there. Our little hospital just doesn't have the staff for stuff like that."

"Okay, I'll see you Tuesday, and maybe we can get back to work on our murder."

"All right," Dave said as he hung up the phone.

It took Jon an hour and a half to drive to Reynoldsburg to the Fire Marshal's Office on Monday. It was in a new building called the State Fire Academy. It sat between a big outdoor movie theater and the State Department of Agriculture. There was a big training grounds out back for firefighting classes.

"Hi, Debbie," he said to the secretary as he walked into the little suite that housed the Arson Bureau.

"Hi, Jonny. Haven't seen you in a long time. The chief wants me to take your picture and hang it on his wall so he'll remember what you look like."

"That's funny; where is the chief?"

"He's up near Toledo. They got a big fire up there at a mall."

"Hey, Jonny, give Debbie your statement so she can make copies and take over to the attorney in the corner to read before we meet," Joe said from his desk in his little office. "Let's go down to the cafeteria and get a cup of coffee before we get started."

They sat at a table in the cafeteria and drank some coffee and Joe assured him this was no big deal. The big deal was that they had no firearms policy and Joe hoped that they didn't try to put one together in a hurry and not do it right.

The meeting took place in the Fire Marshal's Office, but he wasn't there. The Fire Marshal was the top dog at the SFM. He was a retired chief of some big city fire department. Jon had met him a couple of times. There were two men seated in the office as Jon and Joe went in. One introduced himself as Jack Conkle, Deputy Director of Commerce. The other introduced himself as Mohammed somebody, legal counsel for commerce. Mohammed sat at the Fire Marshal's desk. The rest of them sat at chairs in front of the big desk that had several old brass fire hose nozzles sitting on it. There was a picture on the wall of Governor Rhodes and another one of a woman who he thought looked like the Director of Commerce.

"Jon, I read your statement and I must say that what you did was very commendable. You saved that patrolman's life," the lawyer said.

"Thank you," Jon said. He thought about calling him Mo, but then thought he probably better not.

"The problem we have here is the warning shot," Mohammed said. "Most departments prohibit them in their SOP's."

"Yes, I'm aware of that," Jon replied, "but as you read in my statement, I had a clear view of where my shot was going and it was an open field with a hillside at the end of it. It is doubtful that the bullet would have traveled as far as the hillside."

"What did they tell you in basic police school about warning shots?" the attorney said.

"I don't recall it ever being discussed," Jon was trying to remember." That was eight years ago, when I took the course."

"We are going to have to have some kind of a review of this. The Director has selected Mr. Conkle here to do it. He will get copies of the patrols reports when they are available."

"I've been in this kind of a situation before," Jon replied. "I've always chose to hesitate for a second and try an alternate means of resolving the situation instead of using deadly force. Hesitating can get you killed, but so far it hasn't gotten me killed. I could have shot both of those guys and it would have been justified, but I didn't. Then you would be investigating a real shooting with dead bodies." Jon wanted to ask this guy what kind of experience he had in these things. Like if he had ever been a cop and been in situations like this.

Joe gave him the look, like be careful what you say.

"I can assure you that the next time something like this happens we will have a policy in place," Mohammed said.

"You were a deputy sheriff, Jon," Mr. Conkle said. "What was the firearms policy at your sheriff's office about warning shots?"

"They were not allowed," Jon said.

"Have you ever fired a warning shot before?" the assistant director asked.

"I'm not going to answer that question, that has nothing to do with what happened Saturday," Jon answered.

"We can compel you to answer questions," the lawyer said.

Joe got up and said. "Guys, this is not an official hearing. I think we need to stop here. You get your investigation done and if you want to have a hearing then fine, but I'm telling my man here to not answer any more questions."

"Let me remind you, chief," Mr. Conkle said, "you are a part of management here and it is not your place to advise your employee."

"I don't care about management. This man is my man, and I look out for my men. Come on, Jon, we got work to do." Jon had always heard that Joe would go to bat for his men. He had just experienced it firsthand.

Jon and Joe went to Joes office and Joe closed the door. "Don't worry about this, Jonny. We don't have a union here like we had at the fire department, but you have rights."

"Thanks for sticking up for me in there, Joe. I hope you don't get in any trouble over it."

"I've been around a lot longer than that young whipper snapper lawyer in there. They don't have a leg to stand on. They have no policy. Don't you worry about this. If they have a hearing I'll get you a lawyer. And it won't cost you anything."

"I appreciate it, Chief," Jon said.

"Now, you get back down south and solve that murder you got down there and I'll take care of this. The chief is on your side, too. We talked about this on the phone last night. He told me to look out for you."

As Jon drove back down Route 23 he couldn't help but think about this thing. I supposed they would rather I shot the guys he thought. Don't make since. No since in killing someone if you don't have to. He remembered then a lecture he heard an FBI agent make at a seminar at Chillicothe about how the FBI investigated police shootings and how an officer could be charged with denying someone their right to a trial by killing them. It had scared him. He wondered how many cops had been killed because they hesitated because they were thinking about that kind of stuff happening to them.

When he got back to Jackson he went to the SO and found Dave who had some good news. The guy who owned the house that burned at Gallia had looked at the Swan Lamp and said it was definitely from his house. He told Dave about what had happened at the SFM Office that morning.

"You did the right thing," Dave said. "I would have done the same thing."

"We need to find that truck, Dave," Jon said, referring to the green truck that the Brown brothers drove.

"Yeah, I know. It might have some evidence in it. I can't help you for a couple of days. I got a jury trial on a burglary."

"I'll start looking for it tomorrow," Jon said as he left Dave's office.

That evening about eight Jon was watching T.V. Dallas was on. He liked it. He didn't watch cop shows anymore. JR Ewing's wife had just found out that he was having an affair. He felt sorry for Sue Ellen. She was a nice lady, but JR was definitely driving her to drinking.

The doorbell rang. He opened the front door. It was Liz. She had her nursing uniform on.

"Come in," he said.

"I don't usually call on guys," she said kind of awkwardly, "but I couldn't remember your phone number."

"I been to the office at Reynoldsburg today," he told her.

"That's what I was wondering about. How did it go?"

He gave her a rundown of what all was said.

"Some investigator from the highway patrol came out to the farm today and took a recorded statement from me," Liz said.

"I hate for you to get drug into this thing."

"I just hope you don't get in any trouble," she said.

"I won't," Jon assured her.

"He asked me how many times you shot. I told him once. Then he wanted to know what I was doing with you. I told him you told me not to go with you, but I got in anyway."

"You on your way to work?" he asked her.

"Go in at eleven."

"You can watch Dallas with me, if you want to."

"Okay. I haven't watched it for a few weeks, so I don't know what's going on."

"Sue Ellen just found out that JR is having an affair," he said.

"Poor woman," Liz said.

Somehow the conversation turned to Saturday night at the Disco. Liz asked if he had talked to Rita.

"Yeah, I called her I think it was last night."

"I hope you don't mind if I ask," Liz said, "but are you and her like girl-friend and boyfriend?"

"No, we've been friends for years. We've been through a lot together. All of us in our little group. We lost a good friend last January."

"You mean the officer who was killed at Oak Hill?"

"Yeah, we were all good friends," he responded. "Rita helped me through it. I helped her through it. Not long after Jim was killed Rita and the guy she was engaged to broke up. I think it had a lot to do with what we were going through."

"I didn't know Jim," Liz said. "I was still living with my parents in Chillicothe when he was killed. My gramma knew him. She taught him at Oak Hill High School."

"I guess that is the way it is in small towns. Everyone knows everyone. My Grampa seems to know everyone. Well, I guess he delivered about everyone. I can't remember what happened exactly to Jim."

Jon explained, "He stopped a car for speeding. The guy was wanted for parole violation. Jim was sitting in his car running the guy's name when the dispatcher came back and said he was wanted. The guy must have heard it because he got out of his car and pulled a pistol out as Jim was getting out of his cruiser, and he shot Jim."

"I heard it was a big funeral."

"A solid line of cars from the Presbyterian Church out to C and M Cemetery. Reverend Evans did a good job."

"Is this your first night back to work?" Jon asked Liz.

"Yeah. The first night is rough. I stay up all day after I get off and then eat supper about four thirty and pack my lunch, take a shower, lay my clothes out, and go to bed and sleep until ten and then go to work."

"You look nice in your nurse's dress. How come you don't wear one of those little white caps?"

"The younger nurses don't wear them much. Just the older ladies." She yawned.

"I'm goin' to make some popcorn. Be right back."

When he came back in the living room, Liz was stretched out on the couch asleep. He sat down and looked at her legs for a while and then got a quilt and covered her up. He would wake her up about ten.

Jon decided to type some on reports so he went into the den and started going through his notes. At ten he woke Liz up and presented her with a cup of fresh coffee. When she was ready to leave, he walked to the door with her and they stood there. "Can I kiss you?" he asked.

She didn't reply, but their lips met. It was a passionate kiss that lasted a long time. He moved his hands down her back and gripped her butt. He pulled her close. She was breathing heavily and he was excited. She pulled away and smiled. "Wow," she said. "I better get going to work." Out the door she went.

Jon stayed up late typing and catching up on a lot of reports that he had been putting off. He knew he wouldn't be able to go to sleep after that passionate moment with Liz. This could be getting serious. He knew he needed to take it slow. Sex too soon in a serious relationship could cause one to be more in lust than in love. Besides, Liz might be one of those women who didn't believe in sex when one was not married to her partner. There were still some women like that even after the so called sexual revolution of the sixties and the seventies. He had never heard her utter a cuss word. She didn't smoke or drink alcohol. She went to church and he had seen a Bible laying on the console of her pickup truck. He had never had a serious relationship with a woman that did not involve sex. Of course, he had had some not so serious relationships with women that involved sex. It seemed like it was just something that was expected as part of the relationship. He didn't know what to think. One thing he knew was that he really liked Liz. His feelings for her were different than those he had for Rita. He should never have slept with Rita. It could ruin their friendship and he didn't want that to happen.

The phone rang. Jon looked at the clock. Six thirty.

"Hello," he answered.

"This is Gallia County SO. We got a deputy out on a fire near Center Point. It's a house. Not occupied. Can you respond?"

"Yeah, where is it?"

"Gallia Centerpoint Road, a mile off Route 233."

"Okay, I'll be there in about forty-five minutes."

He went through McDonalds and got an Egg McMuffin and a coffee to go. He headed down to Oak Hill to take 233 out to Gallia and then across toward Centerpoint. Not far from the other fire they had down there where the Swan Lamp was stolen from. He forgot to tell Liz that the lamp was stolen.

When he arrived at the scene there was only a deputy sheriff there. The house sat very close to the road and was completely burned down and was still smoldering. There was no basement.

"Where's the fire department?" he asked the deputy.

"They didn't get called. A guy going to work called it in and said it was burned down. When I got here there were no flames. Just hot coals like it is now. I was at Rio Grande when I got the call."

This happened frequently in the rural areas. A place would burn in the middle of the night when no one was out and about and no one knew about it until morning. Some that burned in remote places were not discovered for several days after they burned. There were still some places out in these parts that had no fire department. Blackfork over in Lawrence County was one of them. If a place caught on fire they just stood there and watched it burn. No fire department to call. It was like that in Jackson County for a long time. In the last ten years, Jon had seen three new fire departments established in the rural areas that had no fire protection.

The deputy gave Jon the name and address and phone number of the owner. He had gotten it from a guy down the road that looked after the place. It was another weekend home that belonged to a doctor in Columbus. There was no sense in calling the fire department out to put water on the place. It would cool off by tomorrow and he could go through the debris. Same drill as the other house down the road. Check to see if anything is missing and no bodies. That was all you could do. He got out his camera and took some pictures.

"You talk to the neighbors?" he asked the deputy.

"I've talked to everyone up and down the road. No one saw anything."

"Okay, I'm going to Oak Hill and call this doctor and see what he has to say and find out when he can come down and help us determine if anything is missing."

"Okay, thanks for coming out, let me know if you find out anything interesting," the deputy said as he got back into his car.

Jon went to the Village Hall in Oak Hill and used the phone. He got ahold of the doctor at his office. The doctor said he couldn't come down until Saturday so they made an appointment to meet at the scene Saturday morning. Jon learned that it was a hunting place that was shared by several doctors and other professional persons from the Columbus area. The doctor was going to contact them all and try to determine who was the last person to use the place.

CHAPTER 11

Jon decided to spend the rest of the day on Tuesday trying to find out where the green truck was at on the murder investigation.

He went down to South Webster to see an old guy who sold insurance from an office in his house on Jackson Furnace Road. He had visited this man before when he was looking for someone as the guy seemed to know about everyone in the area. He was able to get a complete family history on the Brown family from him. All the brothers and sisters and aunts and uncles and where eveyone lived at.

He didn't get much help from anyone. No one seemed to know where Pee Wee and Dave were at. Most acknowledged that the two ran around in the green Chevy truck, but no one had seen them in it for a few weeks. Some of those on the list lived in Portsmouth, so that would have to wait until Wednesday as Tuesday was about done.

He stopped at the fire station in Oak Hill and called Rita. She was going to work at midnight at the plant. He offered to buy her supper if she met him at the K and L at five o'clock. She agreed. He had a key to the Oak Hill Fire Station as he did several of the stations in the area. He used their facilities to make phone calls and to meet people for interviews. The Oak Hill PD was in the village hall, but it wasn't a very good place for doing interviews or making phone calls as there was little privacy.

He and Rita had a good supper and since he hadn't been getting in his daily walks lately they decided to walk the streets of Jackson for a couple of hours and get some exercise. They walked all over town, leaving their cars at the restaurant. Rita had to go to the restroom so they stopped at his house and took a break.

They were sitting on the couch drinking ice water when Rita asked, "Jon, did you like the night we spent together a few weeks ago?"

"Yeah, I did, but I didn't start out the evening with that in mind."

"Neither did I. I guess it just happened. I missed my period last week."

"Oh." He said, "I thought you were on the pill."

"I quit taking them when Roger and I broke up."

"You think you're pregnant?" he asked, wishing more than ever now that they had never done it.

"I don't know. I've never been late before, ever."

"Have you told anyone else?"

"No, I wanted you to be the first to know. I don't want you to think I planned this or anything."

"I know you didn't. We just got carried away that night. I won't let you down."

"I know, but I hope I'm not. I'm not ready to have a baby yet. And I don't want you to feel trapped."

"Let's finish our walk," Jon said. They left the house and held hands as they walked back across town. They didn't talk anymore about their predicament. They stopped a couple times to talk to people they knew.

Jon leaned over and put his forearms on Rita's car door window ledge as she fastened her seatbelt. "Don't worry," he told her. "Everything will be all right."

He gave her a peck on the cheek and watched her drive off. What a mess, he thought as he drove back home. If she was he would have to marry her. Abortion was not an option. Rita was Catholic, but then he thought, he didn't think that Catholics used birth control pills. Well, I guess a lot of them probably did. He had never thought much about the abortion business, but he knew he could not be a partner to that kind of thing. Not if it was his kid.

He went home and got a can of beer out of the frig and took a swig. The phone rang. It was Liz. "I thought you slept all evening?" he asked. It was almost seven thirty.

"I laid down this afternoon and took a nap and now I'm all messed up," she said.

He told her that had he known that he would have taken her with him today as he was working on the murder and it would have kept her awake.

"Is it all right if I stop by your place on my way to work?" she asked.

He really didn't feel like company with what he had on his mind, but he couldn't say no.

"Okay, I'll be here. Come on by."

The doorbell rang as Jon was opening his third can of beer. He went to the door and let Liz in. She was dressed in her nurse's dress and white hose.

"Can I get you something to drink?" he asked.

"Do you have any Sprite?"

"I think so; let me check." He returned with a can of Sprite and opened it for her.

"How is the investigation going?" she asked.

"I've been trying to find the green truck, but no good so far. Another fire of similar circumstances down at Gallia not far from the other one. Probably a burglary, too. And that swan lamp was identified as coming from that weekend house that burned down near Gallia."

"That's interesting. Can I go with you tomorrow? Maybe it will keep me awake so that I can sleep in the evening."

"Sure, I'll pick you up at your place about eight. We may be going to Portsmouth to look for the truck."

She kicked her shoes off and swung her feet up on the couch and laid her calves across his knees and stretched out on the couch. "I'll bet you can give a good foot massage," she asked.

"I'll try," he said, and started massaging one of her feet through her hose. He looked at her. She was smiling. "What's so funny?"

"I've never had a guy do this before. I'm really kind of shy about these things."

"Well, maybe we can *unshy* you. Take your hose off. I've got some lotion that will really sooth your feet."

She got up and went in the bathroom and came back with bare legs. He opened the bottle of lotion and she laid down again. He began putting the lotion on her feet and working it in. He could feel her relaxing. He then started working on her calves. She made some kind of pleasant noise. Her dress was pulled up halfway to her crotch. He wanted to massage her thighs, but he thought he had better stop there, so he worked his way back down to her feet. By now she was asleep. He gently got up and she rolled over with her back toward the coffee table. He put the quilt over her. He then slipped underneath the quilt and placed his arm around her. It was kind of crowded, and he was afraid that if he fell asleep he would roll off on the floor. He dozed some and when the grandfather clock struck ten he woke her. She turned over, almost shoving him off on the floor. They kissed several times. He knew that if he did not stop now she would be late for work, so he got up and went to the kitchen to make her some coffee.

Jon didn't sleep well that night. He thought about Liz and he thought about Rita.

If Rita was pregnant, then he would have to marry her. That was all there was to it. He didn't love her. He could learn to love her. A lot of people had married this way and stayed married until death did them part. She was a good woman. A year younger than him. She worked hard at the plant. She had been there five years. She would be a good mom. They had no secrets. Except maybe his feelings for Liz.

But his feelings for Liz were different. He was attracted to her in a different kind of way. They weren't in too deep yet. That was good. He didn't want to hurt her. He better back off a bit on her until he found out what was going to happen to him and Rita.

The phone rang at 8:00 A.M. as Jon was eating his breakfast. He had taken an early walk around town. It was his boss, Joe.

"Jonny, we gotta send you up to Marietta. You know the guy we had up there quit a few weeks ago," the chief told him.

"Yeah, I know," he said.

"Well, Harrys been covering it, but our guy in the St. Clairsville district is off sick and will be for a couple of months so Harry has to cover all the way up to Steubenville."

"Okay, anything going on up there?" Jon asked.

"We got a call yesterday from the Marietta Fire Department. Someone is trying to burn the county fairgrounds down. They've been working on it. They can't get much help from their PD so you need to go up there and help them. Be prepared to stay a few days."

"What about this murder?"

"You got a good man there in Dave. Tell him you'll be back as soon as you can."

"Okay, I'll head up there today and see what I can do for them."

Maybe this would be good to chill things with Liz and get away from this mess. He always liked getting away to other places and working for a while. He called Liz and told her he would be gone for a few days. He stopped by Rita's house. She lived with her mom, but Mom was at work. Rita was on night shift. They drank some coffee and visited and he told her she ought to go to the doctor next week and see what's going on. She said she planned to.

CHAPTER 12

It took Jon an hour and a half to drive to Marietta. Eighty-five miles. He knew some of the folks at the fire department as he had done a couple of fires there when he was in training with Harry, the Cambridge District Fire Investigator. As he passed the road side rest where he had been on the fire last week he saw a bulldozer shoving down the rest of the restroom.

Marietta was a nice, small city. It was a river town like Gallipolis and Ironton and Portsmouth. The population was about sixteen thousand. That was over twice that of Jackson's seven thousand persons. It had a paid fire department unlike Jackson's volunteer department. There were four stations in the city. The downtown area was like Jackson's with a lot of stores and a lot of bars. A lot more bars than in Jackson. But it was slowly starting to change. They were building some big stores out on the edge of the city going up the Ohio River. There was a lot of history in Marietta, like Chillicothe. Marietta had been the first settlement in Ohio. Chillicothe had been the first capital of the state.

He found the fire chief, Gene Bohl, in his office. "Hi, Chief," he said, "the boss sent me up here to help you, said you had a bit of a problem."

"Yes, Jon, I'll get the Inspector in here to tell you what's going on," Gene said as he picked up the phone and announced on the intercom. "Inspector come to the chief's office; Inspector come to the chief's office."

Captain Aaron Jensen had risen through the ranks of the Fire Department. His primary duties as an Inspector were fire safety inspections of buildings. He was also the departments only investigator, although the chief was also an investigator who had taught Aaron the ropes of investigation. The chief would be retiring in a couple of years and Aaron would probably take the assistant chief's test which would put him second in command and make him the training officer. He would still be involved in investigations if he wanted to.

In a couple of minutes a big feller wearing Captains bars came in the office carrying some file folders. "Hey, Jon, you remember me, Aaron Jensen?"

"Hey, Aaron, they sent me up here to help you out."

The chief leaned back in his chair and lit up his pipe. Aaron lit a cigarette.

Aaron said, "About six weeks ago, we started having some small fires at the fairgrounds here in the city. The first two were dugouts at the baseball fields. The next two were ticket booths at the entrance gates. Then we had a storage shed with mowing equipment in it burn. Last Saturday night they set a two-story building on fire at the 4H Horse Arena. It had a concession stand on the first floor and a judging window on the second floor with an office. It burned down. All the fires have been on Friday or Saturday nights. We had a witness on the second dugout fire who was parked with his girlfriend and he saw a flash of fire and saw a guy standing in front of the burning dugout throwing some kind of flammable liquid on it. He was too far away to get a description."

"What time of night?" Jon asked.

"Between eleven and three," the inspector said. "The problem is we got a small trailer court in the fairgrounds where people spend the summer, but they leave their campers there all year round. We got boats and campers stored in some of the barns for the winter. There is a roller-skating rink that is crowded every Friday, Saturday and Sunday. Then the horse barn where people keep their horses year-round. Some of horse people are starting to move their horses elsewhere. The place is fenced in, but there are three entrance gates, but they are all unlocked all the time because so much goes on there all the time."

"You have any suspects?" Jon asked.

"No. We can't get any help from the PD. They are shorthanded as it is. I didn't bother you guys with it because it was just little fires to begin with, but it seems to be getting bigger."

"You say you've had a fire there every weekend for six weeks?"

"Yeah, either Friday or Saturday night."

After going through the reports for each fire Jon found that only two of the fires happened on Friday nights, the rest being on Saturday nights. He and

Aaron spent the rest of the day going to all the fire scenes. The fairgrounds were very large. It was bordered by Front Street on the east, the Muskingum River on the west, a large public boat ramp on the north, and a golf driving range on the south. On the north-east corner outside the fence were several apartment buildings.

On Thursday, they spent the day talking to people who worked in the fair grounds at the skating rink and over at the golf driving range. They went to the horse barns and talked to some of the horse owners. No one had any ideas or had seen any suspicious persons. Everyone was concerned. Jon told Aaron that it was highly likely that the suspects may be coming from either the skating rink or the apartment buildings on Pennsylvania Avenue.

On Friday morning, Aaron told Jon that he had gotten a call from the chief deputy sheriff who said that the Sheriff had been to a fair board meeting Thursday night and had told the board that he would offer his departments assistance in the investigation.

Aaron scheduled a meeting Friday afternoon with the chief deputy sheriff.

Aaron introduced Jon to the chief deputy. "Jon, this is Bill Malone, Bill, this is Jon Hamer of the State Fire Marshal's office." They all shook hands and sat down Bill asked Aaron to give him a run down on the fires and what had been done.

"What do you think Jon?" Bill asked.

"Well, there have been fires every weekend for six weeks straight. This might be a good case for catching someone in the act. If we could put together a stakeout, we might catch them. Unfortunately the state fire marshal can only offer you my services. They aren't too big on stakeouts as they usually are time consuming and not very productive."

"I think I could supply about three persons, how about you Aaron?" Bill said.

"Myself and the fire chief."

"We have the night vision stuff and radios for everyone. I can't put anything together for tonight, but we could shoot for Saturday night," Bill said. "I agree that it would be a good chance to catch them in the act as they have a definite pattern. I'd hate to have a fire tonight though and miss the opportunity to catch them."

"I was thinking that maybe Aaron and I can spend some time in the fairgrounds tonight scoping out how we are going to do things on Saturday night and if anything happened tonight we would be close by," Jon replied.

"Okay, we'll meet here at the SO Saturday at 10:00 P.M. and go over the plan and make assignments. I think we should have a couple guys roving the grounds undercover and the rest of us can be hiding in places where we can see a lot of area," Bill stated.

Aaron and Jon decided to meet back at the FD that night at nine to snoop around the fairgrounds. Jon returned to the Holiday Inn where he was staying. He called the doctor he was supposed to meet at Gallia the next day and made arrangements to meet him the following Saturday. He then tried to get some sleep.

Jon and Aaron sat in the car in front of the roller rink for about an hour watching people go inside. Most were junior high school age kids, a few who may be in senior high and some adults. Jon went in the roller rink for a while and kind of looked over the crowd and didn't see anyone interesting. He had heard some of the older investigators talking about being able to spot a fire bug in a crowd that was watching a fire, but he had not yet acquired that skill.

They then walked back to the horse barn, but no one was around there. They drove up to the boat ramp. No cars there. "Let's leave the car parked here and walk over toward those apartment buildings and see if we can find a place where we can get a good view of those buildings. I just got a feeling our problem is coming from there," Jon told his partner.

Aaron had a walkie talkie that he could call the PD and FD on. Jon didn't have one. They walked across a small field and into some tall pine trees and found a place that allowed them to stay concealed and watch Pennsylvania Ave. They laid down in the grass and looked toward the apartment buildings. They laid there about a half hour, whispering to each other.

Jon thought he noticed a movement behind them. He turned around and looked. Nothing. He turned his attention back to the apartments. He had a pair of binoculars. They were all right at night as long as you were looking at something that was lit up and the apartments and street were lit up. Then he noticed the movement behind them again and he thought he saw someone. He told Aaron that someone was behind them. Jon got up and walked about fifteen feet and saw movement behind a big pine tree. He turned on his flashlight and walked around the tree and there was a guy standing there. He was tall and had on thick glasses. He had a towel in his hands and was holding it close to his stomach. It looked like the towel was wrapped around something.

He shined the light in the guy's eyes and asked him what he was doing. The guy acted like he was going to vomit and both Jon and Aaron stepped back a couple of feet and the guy threw the towel down and started to run away. Right away Jon and Aaron could smell gasoline and saw some plastic bottles laying on the ground.

"Call for help," Jon said to Aaron.

Jon took off after the guy and they went out of the pines and up Pennsylvania Avenue, toward the apartments. He knew he could not catch him. He was not a runner. The only person he every had caught in a foot pursuit he caught because the guy jumped across a small creek and landed in mud and sank up to his knees.

The guy went between two apartment buildings and headed up the hill to Muskingum Drive. By the time Jon got up to Muskingum Drive, he was gone. He looked both ways on the street and saw no one. He figured he probably went up through the brushy hillside toward the hospital. Jon was out of breath and he stumbled and almost fell down. His revolver fell out of the holster and bounced on its rubber grips across the street just as a police car was pulling up. Aaron must have got ahold of the cops.

The cop, who Jon knew, got out of his car and picked up Jon's gun and handed it to him. "You lose something, Jon?" He grinned. "What's going on?"

Jon gave him the scoop on the guy and told him he probably went up over the hill toward the hospital. Jon walked back down toward the pine trees and found Aaron. He went and got his car and photographed the towel and three plastic bottles of gasoline and then packaged them for evidence.

An officer arrived with a dog and the dog sniffed the towel, but he didn't like the smell of the gasoline, so he didn't find the guys scent.

There were reports from the hospital that the suspect crossed through their parking lot, but he could not be found. They gave up the search about 1:00 A.M. Jon and Aaron went to the PD and looked at some mug shot books. Aaron found one that looked like the guy. Jon agreed. Sure looked like him. They got his last known address and decided to go get some sleep and go see the guy in the morning.

On Saturday morning, they ran the guy down. He was staying at a mission shelter outside of town a couple of miles. They went there. The lady that ran the place was very nice. "I know for sure that he was here all night last night," she said. "I was here all evening and did not leave. We had three other residents. None of them left."

Aaron told Jon, "I know this lady. She wouldn't lie and she runs a good place here and doesn't put up with any nonsense from any of their clients."

She loaned them her office and they talked to the guy. He sure looked the part, but not as much in person as he did in the mug shot book. He said that he did not leave the shelter all night. They concluded that they had the wrong person.

"That's something they taught us in investigation school, Aaron," Jon said, "Eye witnesses can be wrong. Now I see how wrong they can be. I thought for sure it was him from the mug shot, but it isn't."

"I agree. It's not him. Okay, we'll do the stake out tonight. He probably won't be out though. We spooked him," Aaron said.

"You're probably right," Jon agreed.

They all met at the SO Saturday night and discussed their plan. They were all in place by 11:00 P.M. They had two deputies on roving patrol on foot inside the fair grounds. They wore dark fatigues. They each had a little flashing lite on their hats that could only be seen through a night vision device. Everyone had night vision optics like they used in Vietnam. The rest of them were hidden in places around the fairgrounds, where they had a good field of view. If they saw anything moving, they would radio the roving patrol to check it out. Everyone had a walkie talkie with an ear piece. Aaron was back over underneath the pines watching the apartment buildings. Jon was in the top of a two-story building that housed the controls for the water wells. The city's water wells were located in the part of the fair grounds that contained the ball diamonds.

About midnight a car came down the road and parked just passed where Jon was stationed. He was sitting at the top of the steps that went up the outside of the building. He had a key to go inside, but he couldn't see very good through the windows so he moved out to the porch. No one got out of the car. He reported it to the roving patrol. Pretty soon he could see them moving in and they crept up behind the car. They sat there by the car about twenty minutes and then moved out. "Just a man and woman screwin'," they reported to everyone. The radio frequency they were on was private and no one else could hear them. There were a few comments from certain members of the team.

Nothing happened the rest of the night. They called it off at about four thirty. Jon, Aaron and the chief deputy decided that Monday evening they would start going door to door as they all felt that the suspect probably lived in one of the apartment buildings or a house on Muskingum Drive.

Everyone caught up on their sleep on Sunday. Jon made a phone call to Rita and they talked for an hour. She had a doctor's appointment on Tuesday. She reported on Saturday nights activities at the lounge. Liz and Karen and the doctor were there. The doctor was quite a funny story teller. Jon wanted to ask Rita who Liz danced with, but he thought he better not.

On Monday at about 5:00 P.M., Jon, Aaron, and Bill met at the SO. Bill and Aaron would team up and take one apartment building and then start on the houses on Muskingum Drive. Jon would go door to door at the other two apartment houses. They each had a photo of the guy who wasn't the guy to show to people explaining that they were looking for a similar looking subject.

They had been banging on doors for about an hour when Bill called Jon on the radio and said to meet at the main gate to the fairgrounds. They pulled their cars close to each other, driver's door to driver's door as cops do when they meet to talk.

"We got lucky," Bill said. "At one of the houses on Muskingum Drive, some guys told us the guy is Rod Quincey and that he lives in one of the apartment buildings. He doesn't have a car. He rides a bike everywhere and he runs a lot. They said he has been in trouble before."

"Sounds good," Jon said.

"We're going down to the jail and see if they have a picture of him. How about you trying to find out what building and what apartment he lives in? We'll be back shortly," Bill said.

Jon headed back to the apartments and went to the resident manager's office. When he told her the guy's name, she told him what apartment he lived in. It was on the second floor with an outside entrance. He took a look. There was a bike chained to the railing of the balcony and lights on in the apartment.

The three investigators met again in a half hour. Aaron handed Jon a picture. Jon looked at it. "That's him, I'm sure this time, I hope," Jon said. "I found his apartment. His bike is on the porch and the lights are on."

"Let's go see if he's home," Bill said.

"I'll take the back of the building in case he tries to go out the window," Jon told Bill and Aaron.

Jon went to the back. He could hear Bill and Aaron banging on the door. He looked up at the window and saw a man come to the window and look out. When the man saw Jon, he went back deeper in the apartment.

"He just showed himself at the window," Jon said on the walkie talkie.

"He won't come to the door?" Bill answered.

"Try to talk him out," Jon replied on the radio. "Tell him we'll watch his place and get a search warrant."

After about ten minutes of talk through the door, Bill called and said he let them in.

Jon went around and up the steps and into the apartment. Sitting on the couch was the guy that almost stepped on him and Aaron on Friday night.

"I know why you're here," the guy said. "I set the fires." Bill was sitting on a chair by the couch.

"Are you Rod Quincey?" Bill asked.

"Yes," the suspect said.

"I'm going to advise you of your rights," Bill said and proceeded to read off the suspects rights and asked him if he wanted to waive his rights and talk at this time.

"Yeah. You got me. I did it."

"Tell us what you did, Rod," Aaron asked. "Start with the first fire," Bill said.

Rod began to tell about all the fires at the fairgrounds starting with the baseball dugouts and ending with the horse judging stand and then telling that he had went out Friday night to set another fire and he saw a Police Car go through the boat ramp so he decided to go back home and that is when he about stepped on "you guys."

"Where did you get your gasoline?" Jon asked Rod.

"In the closet in my bedroom on the top shelf is a gas can."

Jon went to his car and got a consent to search and explained it to the suspect. Rod signed it. Jon and Aaron went to the closet and found a five-gallon gas can about half full.

"Where are the clothes you had on last night?" Jon asked.

"In the dumpster down the street," he said.

They spent about an hour in Rod's apartment and then called for a marked car to take him to the SO where Aaron and Jon would take a formal statement from him and then place him in the jail. Jon would search the dumpster for the suspects clothes. Aaron called the fire station and arranged for an engine company to help him.

They couldn't find any clothing in the trash that smelled like gasoline. On Tuesday morning Rod was arraigned in Municipal Court where bail was set that he could not post. Bill, Aaron and Jon met with the Sheriff and the Fire Chief on Tuesday and briefed them. They would do a joint news release. Jon went to the motel and packed his bags and headed back to Jackson. He was glad this was over. It was a fast-paced investigation and put a stop to some serious fire setting in the city.

Jon called his boss Joe when he stopped in Guysville to take a pee break and told him what had happened. "Well, Jonny you may be the first fire marshal to catch someone in the act in the last thirty years or so," Joe said.

"Don't tell anyone that he about stepped on us." Jon laughed.

When Jon got home he went to bed. It was four in the afternoon. He hadn't had much sleep all weekend. He felt like he used to feel when he was on midnight shift.

CHAPTER 13

He was awakened by the ringing of the doorbell. It was dark. He looked at the clock. It was 9:00 P.M. Jon pulled on his pants and went to the door. It was Rita. Oh, my gosh, I forgot she was going to the doctor today. Well, I guess I'm going to find out who I am going to be spending the rest of my life with, he thought.

They hugged. Rita was crying. Not loud crying. Just tears. They held each other for a long time. They sat down on the couch.

"So, what did the doctor say?" Jon asked.

"I am."

"Pregnant?"

"Yes," she said, still wiping year from her face.

"When do you want to get married?" he said.

"That's not funny."

"We want our kid to have a mother and a father, don't we?"

"We can't get married."

"Why not?"

"We're just two friends who got in trouble, that's all."

"We got in trouble, so we got to make it right."

"But we don't love each other," she said.

"We can."

"How do you know if we can?" she said.

"Because it happens all the time. People like us get married because of this sort of thing and they live happily ever after."

She started to cry again. "I didn't want this to happen."

"Neither did I, but it did and now we got to do the right thing," Jon said. "We can't undo it."

"I'm glad you don't want me to have an abortion."

"Of course, I don't. Have you told your mom?"

"No, I can't. She'll be mad. The same thing happened to her and dad and they never got along with each other."

"Are you working tonight?" He changed the subject.

"Yes. Just give me some time to think about this. I don't know what I want to do."

"Okay. Have you had supper? I haven't."

"I'm not hungry," she said.

"You got to eat and take care of yourself. I'll call and order subs and go get them. You want your usual?"

"Okay. I need to use the bathroom."

"You can use the big one off the master bedroom down the hall." He said as he picked up the phone.

She didn't come out of the bathroom before he left to go get the subs. When he got back, she was sitting on the couch. After they ate they played checkers on the dining room table. She didn't like to lose. She didn't lose very often. He walked her to her car when she left for work. "I'm not going to work tomorrow. I worked all weekend. Why don't you come over here tomorrow when you get off work and sleep some, and then we'll hang out tomorrow."

"Okay, I'll go home now and get a change of clothes for tomorrow and leave Mom a note, telling her I'm going shopping all day."

"I'll leave the door unlocked. I'm going to try to sleep in. Just come on in."

"Okay."

In the morning, he was awakened by Rita getting into bed with him. He rolled over. Her hair was wet and she was wearing one of his tee shirts. He smiled. "Does this mean we're getting married?" he asked her.

"No. It means I want held." And she turned her back on him. He put his arm around her waist. Her stomach was flat and firm. In a couple months, it would not be. Something about pregnant women always had turned him on. Her hair smelled good. He knew that she got very dirty at the plant. She sanded fiberglass hoods and fenders for trucks. Big trucks.

He wanted to move his hand down her leg, but he didn't. He could feel her panties. He didn't think she was here for sex. She just needed him. He held her tight and went back to sleep as soon as she started to snore.

He woke up about ten. She was still sleeping. He walked into the kitchen in his underwear and put on a pot of coffee and started to fry bacon. He ate his and put her plate in the oven on warm. He got dressed and went out and walked about two miles. It was nice to not have to work after that big weekend. He would have a lot of reports to type on that case. He would have to mail copies to the prosecutor in Washington County for the Marietta case. He would do that tomorrow.

When he got back home Rita was sitting at the kitchen table eating her breakfast. He noticed his shirt pulled up halfway above her knees.

"Thanks for breakfast," she said.

"See what you got to look forward to," he said, smiling at her.

"I can do the dishes," she said as he started running water in the sink.

"Do you work tonight?"

"No. I'm off until Sunday evening at three."

"Let's go for a hike today, like we used to do." He said. When they first met, they used to hike a lot. Neither of them were dating anyone at the time. Then she started dating Roger and he didn't like her to hike with him so they quit. Then they got engaged. They came to the disco and sat with the rest of the crowd, but she never danced with anyone but Roger.

"Okay." She got up and brought her plate over to the sink. He turned and gave her a hug. "I'm going to get dressed," she said.

They drove up 93 into Vinton County and then went east to Lake Hope. This was one of their favorite places. A beautiful lake surrounded by hills. They had packed a lunch and Jon carried it in a backpack. They took the trail that circled the lake. It was a beautiful day. They stopped at a picnic shelter and built a fire in the fireplace and ate lunch. They didn't talk about what they had created. They saw deer and wild turkey. Lake Hope was surrounded by Zaleski State Forest. It was the first real day off that Jon had taken in several weeks.

Jon hadn't thought much about Liz. Too many other things to think about. He knew he had been having strong feelings toward her, but now he was suppressing them. He had to do the right thing by Rita. He needed to go out and give Liz another shooting class. She needed several more so she could pass her qualification shoot with a certified instructor. Then she could get her Special Deputy commission from the Sheriff and start carrying a weapon when she did coroner investigator work. Within a year, she would have to take the basic police officers course down at Rio Grande. It was a long class. Five evenings a week from six till ten and sometimes eight hours on Saturdays.

Rita went home after they returned from their day at the lake. Jon decided to call Liz about ten that evening as she would be getting ready for work then. She answered on the first ring.

"Hey, Liz. You wanna shoot again in the morning after you get off work?"

"Hi, Jon. Sure. When did you get back?"

"Day before yesterday," he said, and he told her about the arrest they had made in Marietta.

"Come out about eight in the morning and we'll have breakfast before we shoot," she said.

"Okay, see you in the morning."

He felt kind of guilty doing this. But, this was part of the job, kind of part of the job.

They had been shooting all morning. Liz was doing pretty good. She wasn't anticipating the recoil which caused a person to flinch. Her grip was good. They had just started learning how to switch magazines while shooting. He loaded three rounds in each of her two mags and when she emptied the first one she dropped it out and put in the new one and shot three more rounds. She was kind of clumsy with it, but everyone was. It just took practice. He told her to practice with empty mags in her spare time.

"I won't be having much spare time the next two weeks," she said. "Our hired hand is going on vacation so I'll be doing chores during the week as well as weekends."

"Take your gun to work with you and practice there."

"I don't think that would be a good idea," she said.

They were eating lunch in the kitchen when the phone rang. Liz answered it. "It's for you, Jon," she said, handing him the phone.

"I figured I'd find you there," Dave said. "You been spending a lot of time out there."

"Liz is learning to shoot."

"Ya I'll bet that ain't the only thing you're teaching her."

"So, what's goin' on?"

"We got another one of those phone calls from somebody who won't give their name. Said Dave and Pee Wee got into a big fight down at Portsmouth and one of them rammed someone's car with that pickup truck. It ruined the truck and the car. It was in the city," Dave told him.

"Okay, I'll go down there and see if they still got the truck and check it out. Where's Dave and Pee Wee?"

"Don't know if they got arrested or not."

Dave told Liz what was going on and asked her if she wanted to go along. "I don't think I better," she said, "you might be gone all evening and I have to get some sleep, so I can work tonight."

Jon drove to Portsmouth to the Police Department. The brothers had spent the night in jail and were released on their own recognizance. The truck was at a junk yard at West Portsmouth. Jon went out there to look at it. He figured he probably had better get a search warrant, but he could look in the windows without one and take pictures of the truck. At the junk yard the operator told him that Dave Brown had come out the day before and signed the title over to him instead of paying the tow bill. This solved the problem of the search warrant. The junk yard operator gave him consent to search.

The first thing he did was to dust for prints. He got one really good print off the inside rearview mirror. He got some partials off the steering wheel. He got two more good ones off the dash and the glove compartment door.

There were a lot of beer cans on the floor and in the bed. He gathered up twelve cans. He wasn't going to take them all, too many. He would have them checked for prints at BCI. They could do a better job than he could. Behind the seat, he found a tire tool. He remembered about the pathologists saying the victim's skull was crushed with a blunt instrument. He couldn't see much of anything on the thing, but he bagged it to take to the lab.

He knew that evidence could be checked into the BCI lab at night and on weekends, but they didn't do any testing except during normal working hours. There was a communications person who also was an evidence room tech on duty at all hours. BCI had a radio room just like a police department. He decided to head straight for London to drop off the evidence. If he didn't then he might never get it there for several days if he got called on fires. It was 5:00 P.M. and a three-hour drive up 23 and across 56 to London.

Even though this was a murder case Jon knew that it would be a long time before the results came back. They had not heard anything about the T.V. they had sent there to be processed. This was the hard part, waiting.

He got home at midnight from his trip to BCI.

Thursday morning Jon called Dave at the SO and told him what he had found in the truck. Dave said that he was going to set up a meeting for them with Joe Johns, the Prosecutor's Investigator to give him the reports they had made so far and discuss the case. That told Jon what he was going to do all day Thursday. He had to get everything caught up on the murder. He had to do the reports to send to Marietta. He usually spent about one day in five doing reports. Reports had to be in the SFM office within thirty days of a fire investigation. He mailed them in. He also mailed in his thirty-five-millimeter film to the office and they had it developed and sent him prints and they put the negatives and one set of prints in the office file. Every fire had to have a sketch drawn also.

At noon Jon took a walk and went to the little beer joint at the corner of Broadway and Pearl Streets and got a veal and a beer. This was a men's only place. It was full of men on their lunch breaks. He sat at the bar. The owner was too busy to talk. One of the local funeral directors came in and sat beside him. He knew him because he worked on the PD and SO car radios as sort of a hobby. He was a friend of law enforcement. He told him he had been called out overnight on a suicide in Wellston. He said he got to meet Docs new helper and was impressed not only by her beauty but her work.

At five o'clock he called Rita and asked her if she wanted to go out to eat supper. He picked her up and they went out on the Chillicothe Pike to Gadler's Restaurant. As they ate he told Rita the story about the time these three boys from Columbus had broken into Gadler's. He was still at the SO and he got called out to the restaurant about eight in the morning. Someone had broken the glass out of the front door and went inside. They had made some sandwiches in the kitchen and stole a bunch of candy bars.

A couple hours later he was sitting desk at the SO, so the dispatcher could take a break when he got a call from a Jackson PD unit. "I think I got the yahoos that broke into your restaurant last night. I'll bring them up the jail." It was Sgt Graisden. He was a character. A good small town cop. Pretty soon he came in the jail with three boys, who looked to be about twelve or thirteen years old. The sergeant put a paper bag on the counter and reached inside and pulled out a couple of candy bars. "They were walkin' down Bridge Street and I knew they weren't local or they would be in school so I stopped and talked to them and each of them's pockets was full of candy bars. I'll leave them with you. They told me they ran away from home in Columbus a couple days ago."

Jon got confessions from them and put them upstairs in the juvenile section of the jail. He filed charges through the prosecutor's office, but he knew they would be tried in Franklin County as juveniles had to be tried in the county that they lived in. They were in jail three days before their parents came and got them.

Rita always liked to hear his stories like that. He never told her anything about a current case he was working on, but it was good to have someone outside law enforcement to talk to.

"You thought anymore about what we are going to do?" he asked her.

"Yeah, a lot of women raise a kid on their own without a man in the house. I've got my mom. She'll come around after she gets used to it."

"But it's better to have a husband. I want to be a part of this, too, you know."

Rita smiled and took his hand in hers. "I'm glad you do and you still can be. We can all three do things together and you can help babysit when I'm at work so Mom doesn't have to do it all."

"I still think we should get married, Jon said.

"We've got time to figure it out," Rita said. "I won't start showing for a couple of months and I'm not telling anyone till then."

"We could live together, a lot of people are doing that these days," Jon told her.

"I know, but I'm Catholic; you know that, it wouldn't be right."

"Well, whatever it's going to be, I'll take care of you and the baby."

"I know you will, Jon. You're a good man, and I'm glad that you're going to be my baby's father. There's no one else I would rather share this with."

"You just said it, that's why we should get married."

"Let's go," she said. "I need to go for a walk. I'm supposed to get a lot of exercise."

They parked up town and walked several blocks. As they were walking out South Street a firetruck went by with its lights and siren on going straight out

South St. Then another one. He hoped he didn't get called. They stopped and talked to Ned Stark. He was walking his dog. He was the local newspaper editor. Jon hoped he didn't put their names in his weekly column. He usually commented about some of the folks he met on his evening walk around his neighborhood.

Friday Jon and Dave met with the prosecutor's investigator and went over what they had. He told them to keep him up to date with everything so that when it got to the point that they could file charges they would do it, but now there wasn't enough and the latent fingerprint work wasn't done yet. It looked like this case was going to take a while. They all agreed that they needed someone as a witness like someone who the suspects told about what they did to the woman. They needed to find out who was making the phone calls giving them the tips. That person probably would be a good witness or would lead them to a good witness.

Jon was trying to keep a distance from Liz as the felt a responsibility to Rita. Friday evening Liz called to see if he was going to the disco on Saturday and he told her that he was and that it would be in Wellston that night. "Do you care if I stop to see you before I go to work tonight? My sleeping is all messed up. I can't go to sleep after supper like I usually do."

"Sure," he said.

She arrived about eight o'clock.

They were playing a game of checkers when she said, "It was in the newspaper tonight that you and Rita were on a stroll around town the other evening."

"I was hopin' he wouldn't put that in there. I'm going to stay away from his part of town unless I'm by myself."

"Maybe you and I should take a walk over that way. That'll really give him something to write about."

He wasn't too sure how to take her comment. "Rita and I have been walking for years. It's not the first time he's mentioned us."

"I think it's funny. You don't read that kind of stuff in newspapers like the one at Chillicothe."

"That's life in a small town," he said.

"Come on, let's go walk before I have to go to work."

"Okay, but we're staying away from that part of town."

Liz laughed. "Don't want people to think you got two girlfriends?"

"Don't want people to think I got any girlfriends," he said.

"You mean you don't want to have a girlfriend?"

"I think I like having friends that are girls rather than having girlfriends."

She grabbed his hand as they walked. "Do you hold hands with girls that are your friends?"

"Sure."

"Do you rub the feet of girls that are your friends after taking long walks?"

"Sure."

He changed the subject: "How about letting me take your .45 to a friend of mine who works on guns and he'll do some things to it to make it more accurate?"

"Okay, how much will it cost?"

"Not much. Just the cost of a barrel bushing and a couple of springs. He won't charge for the labor."

He noticed that she wasn't dressed for work. When they got back to his house she got a bag out of her car and asked him if she could change for work. She came out of the bathroom carrying her white hose. "Now how about that foot massage," she said. She handed him a bottle of lotion.

She laid down on the couch and put her feet in his lap, and he started working her feet. He could feel a tenseness in her calves so he massaged them real hard. As she had before, she fell asleep. He looked at the clock. It was nine-thirty. He would wake her up a little after ten so she could go to work.

He tickled her feet at ten-fifteen and she woke up. She sat up and started putting her panty hose on. "Turn your head," she said. He did. She finished putting them on. "Okay, you can look."

She went to the bathroom and came back with her hair in a French braid. He walked out to her car with her. She gave him a brief kiss on the lips and got in her car and drove away.

CHAPTER 14

On Saturday morning, Jon went to Gallia County and met with the doctor about his fire. He had a couple of firefighters help him shovel the debris and they couldn't find anything missing. The doctor didn't seem to really care. After the digging he and the doctor talked in his car for a while.

Jon was late getting to the Stage Coach on Saturday night. He had decided to go squirrel hunting late that afternoon down in Cooper Hollow. He got three squirrels so he had to clean them. Not everyone was there. Rita and Cheryl, but not Cheryl's friend from McArthur. Jess and his girlfriend. He worked dayshift all the time. Karen and Liz were there and everyone was listening as Doctor John was telling an obviously funny story. Jimmy George came in after Jon got there. Jon sat down beside Rita and ordered a beer. Apparently, the DJ was late because there was no dancing yet.

When the dancing finally started, everyone got up and started dancing. They worked up a sweat before a slow song was finally played. He was dancing with Rita and he noticed that Liz was with Jimmy. Everyone seemed to be tired so they didn't stay as late as usual. Everyone agreed to meet at the K and L for something to eat when they left at midnight. He wondered if Rita had been drinking her usual rum and Coke or just plain Coke. He guessed just plain Coke for the baby.

When they were leaving the restaurant, Liz asked him if he wanted to go to church with her in the morning. He told her he would call her before nine in the morning if he could go. Rita had left after picking a little at her food, saying she wasn't feeling too good. When Jon got home he called Rita to check on her. "Are you all right, Rita?" he said when she answered the phone.

"My stomach is upset," she said. "I took a couple of Tums, I'll be all right."

"Okay," he said. She thanked him for checking on her and they hung up.

Sunday morning Jon got up at eight and thought about going to church with Liz. He really should go with Rita, but the Catholic service was too different for him. He had gone with Rita a couple times and he went with her once to a wedding at the Catholic Church. He had a hard time with the Catholic hymns.

He finally decided he would go with Liz and called her and said he would be down. She asked if he had eaten yet and as he hadn't she told him breakfast would be ready.

As they ate breakfast in the kitchen Liz asked "Is Rita all right? She seems awfully quiet lately and makes a lot of trips to the bathroom. It's not because she drinks too much because one drink lasts her most of the night."

"She must have something on her mind," Jon replied. "The last time she was quiet like this was after she and Roger broke their engagement."

"She just picked at her food last night."

"I called her after I got home to make sure she was all right. She said her stomach was upset," Jon said.

"That was nice of you," Liz replied.

"That's what friends are for," he told her.

"Well, friend Jon, we better be getting going or we will be late," Liz said as she picked up a basket. "I forgot to tell you that we are having a dinner in the social hall after church."

"Us Baptists call them eatin' meetin's," he said.

"So, you are a Baptist?" she said.

"Yes, my mom was from the hills of West Virginia."

They had a good time at the dinner after services. He hadn't been to one of these church dinners since he left home to go away to college. As he did at the Highway Grill, Reverend Evans got up and got a pot of coffee and a pitcher of iced tea and made the rounds refilling everyone's drinks. When they got back to the farm, Doc was back from church. He told Liz that the SO had called and had a body in a house out on the Beaver Pike that had been dead for some time. Liz changed clothes and left to go on her call. Jon stayed and talked to Doc for a while. He then headed for home. He had in mind to take a nap that afternoon.

As he was coming into Jackson on Main Street, Jon heard on his fire radio the Jackson Fire Department getting toned out for a house fire on Ralph Street with persons trapped. He turned left on Ralph Street and went two blocks and saw a two-story house with smoke coming out the eaves. He pulled up in the yard and a woman was screaming that her baby was inside. Another woman was holding her. He started putting on his turnout gear. He needed an airpack. He listened for the sound of sirens and heard none. The fire station was up town. He saw a neighbor putting a ladder up to the front porch roof. He went up to the woman who was screaming and asked her where her baby was at. She said in the left front room upstairs in bed. He hollered at the guy about to climb the ladder to let him go first. He grabbed his shovel and went up the ladder. The man followed him up the ladder. Jon took his shovel and broke out the window of the bedroom. He told the man to wait on the porch roof for him.

He went in head first so he would be down low. The smoke was heavy and dark. He had his Nomex hood up over his mouth and nose to try to filter the smoke, but he really needed a mask. He had only done this once without a mask and that was in his basic training. They were burning straw in a barrel in an old house and the old instructor wanted everyone to know what it was like to work without a mask so they would appreciate the masks they had.

He kept his face to the floor and crawled to the right following the wall. Feeling as he crawled. There was some fresh air on the floor, but not much. He came to a dresser and then a door. It was a closet. He checked inside it. Nothing. Next, he came to another door. It went into a hallway he thought. He slammed it shut to hold back the smoke and in case the fire flashed and rolled up the stairway. He could tell when he arrived that the fire was burning on the first floor in the rear of the house.

He kept going, around the room, but stopping to sweep across the center of the floor for the child. He came to a crib and raised up and reached inside and felt a baby. He choked on the smoke. The baby was small and he lifted it out and put it on the floor. It started to cough. He was coughing. He knew if he got up on his knees that the smoke would get him so he put the baby on its back and dragged it by both its feet across the floor going around the room until he came to the window. He shoved the baby out the window and someone grabbed it. He stuck his head out the window and two people grabbed him and dragged him out onto the porch roof. He saw a firefighter on the ladder take the baby. He tried to get up on his knees, but he passed out.

Jon woke up. He knew he was in the emergency room of the hospital. He had been there many times on business, but not as a patient. He was on oxygen. His throat was sore. There was a nurse standing there. He thought he knew her. It was Karen. He tried to talk, but his throat was sore. Karen told him not to try to talk. He wanted to say baby, but he couldn't get it out. She must have known what he wanted because she told him the baby was okay. He saw a doctor give Karen a syringe and she inserted the needle in the IV line coming from a bag by the bed. He felt a warm feeling and went to sleep.

He woke up again and he was in a hospital room. He looked up and a nurse was standing there. He remembered Karen. This wasn't Karen. It was Liz. She asked him how he felt. His throat was not as sore. He tried to talk, but it was still hard. He started to cough and she got him a pan. He didn't have an oxygen mask on anymore. He had one of those tubes under his nose that blew oxygen into his nose. He raised up and coughed up a bunch of black stuff and spit it out.

"You breathed a lot of smoke, but no heat," she said. He was relieved to hear that. He knew that was what killed a lot of people. Getting their airway and lungs burned. They sometimes got pneumonia and had a really bad time. He figured if that was the case he wouldn't still be here in this hospital. They would have transferred him to OSU burn center. He was glad of that.

"Can I have a drink?" he said.

"No, you're getting your liquids through your IV. You can suck on this cold cloth for a minute." She placed a wet wash rag to his lips and he sucked on it, but he didn't get much relief.

She gave him a yellow legal pad and a pencil. She told him to write on it instead of trying to talk. He wrote "baby" on it.

"The baby is better off than you are. The doctor said she was face down on the bed and the sheet must have filtered out the smoke. She can cry louder than you can talk. She'll be here a couple of days."

He wrote: How long am I going to be here?

"Until you can talk and eat," Liz said. "Don't try to talk until the doctor says you can. He will check your throat for the swelling to go down."

He saw a clock on the wall. It was almost one o'clock. He looked at the window. It was dark out. He had been here since early this afternoon.

"Rita is out in the waiting room. I'm going to bring her in. She wants to sit with you. Just don't try to talk to her. Use the note pad. If you get sleepy go to sleep. You need to rest."

Liz brought Rita in. She looked at him and took his hand and kissed it. Then she started to cry. Just tears. Not crying loudly. Liz left the room after showing him and Rita how to operate the nurse call thing.

He wrote: How are you doing?

"Scared," she said. "Jess came over to the house and got me and told me what happened and brought me to the hospital."

She pulled up a chair and took his hand in hers and sat there watching him. He went back to sleep.

For three days, he had four breathing treatments a day. On the third day, they started giving him soft foods to eat. He started talking, but it still hurt. On the fourth day, they let him have some visitors. The first was the mother and father and the baby. He got to hold the little baby. She was nine months old.

The next visitor was Reverend Evans. He had prayer with him.

The next visitor was the Mayor. He told him he would be getting an award from the city council. Jon told him that was not necessary as he was doing what any fireman would do.

All this time, Rita did not leave his room. She brought in a checker board and they played checkers. She slept in a big Lazy Boy kind of chair. He tried to get her to go to work, but she would not. Her mother brought her a change of clothes. Liz was there every night from eleven till seven. They brought Rita her meals from the kitchen.

On the fifth day, he was discharged to go home. Rita drove him home. Someone had taken his car to his house. He still had to eat fairly soft foods. Rita stayed all night and all day for two days. She slept on the couch. Then she went back to work on the midnight shift. Liz stopped a couple days to check on him. She listened to his breathing.

On the third day, he was home when Rita got off work in the morning. He told her he wanted to go for a walk. They walked several blocks and came back home and he fell asleep on the couch. They did not talk about their baby. She still got sick at her stomach some when she ate. He was grateful that she was looking out for him.

He went back to the doctor for a checkup after one week and they gave him a breathing test. The doctor said that he could return to work, but he could not inhale any smoke or any kind of vapors from flammable liquids for the next thirty days. That meant no investigating fire scenes for thirty days.

The restrictions the doctor placed on Jon pretty much ruled out doing any fire scene investigations even when the fire was out and there was no smoke. It was a known fact that after the fire was out there were vapors coming off the things that had gotten hot. You couldn't see them and rarely could you smell them, but they were there. That's why firefighters were finally being made to wear their air masks when doing overhaul. Overhaul is the process of finding hidden pockets of fire after the fire is put out.

He called a friend of his who worked at the Atomic Energy Plant at Piketon and asked him if he could get him a respirator and a supply of filters that would take care of his problem. The next morning there was a box sitting on his porch with a respirator and a dozen filters and instructions on how to use it. He wondered why the SFM didn't give them these things to wear. He had heard stories about retired investigators who had developed throat cancer. Next, he called his boss to tell him he could go back to work. "Hey, Chief, it's Jon; I'm cleared to go back to work."

"Good job you did down there," Joe said,

"Thanks."

"You made the front page of the second section of the Columbus paper."

"I made the front page of the only section of the Jackson paper," Jon replied.

"Send in your doctor's slip. I'll talk to the chief. We don't normally have light duty or restricted duty like that, but he might overlook it."

"How come they don't issue filter respirators to us?" Jon asked.

"That's a good question. It would be a good idea, but most of the guys probably wouldn't wear them. Just like the SCBA's. Firefighters didn't like them when they first came out and it took a long time to get them to wear them."

SCBA stood for Self-Contained Breathing Apparatus. It was a bottle of fresh air on your back and a facepiece that gave you fresh breathing air for thirty minutes. The first bottles were heavy steel. Now they had a lighter aluminum bottle, but it was still heavy.

"Don't forget to send in your sick leave paper," Joe reminded him.

"Okay, I'll see you later."

Tomorrow was Saturday so Jon wouldn't have to work till Monday unless he got called out. He called the SO and told Rose at the desk that he was back to work and asked to talk to Dave. "He's out, I'll have him call you when he gets back in. You at home?"

"Yeah, I'll be home all day. Thanks"

His phone rang.

"Is this Jon?"

"Yes," he said.

"This is Aaron Jensen at the Marietta Fire Department. I just wanted to tell you that our firebug just pled guilty today and the judge gave him eight years in prison. No presentence investigation."

"That was fast," Jon said.

"His public defender called the prosecutor and told him that her client wanted to plead to all the charges."

"That's really good. We can close that one out."

"I wanted to thank you for coming up here and staying with us on that. It had a lot of people around that part of town scared. The horses are back at the fairgrounds and everyone is happy on the fair board."

"That's what the SFM is supposed to do for you." Jon replied. "I'll be covering your area for a while until they hire someone."

"You want to consider moving up here and taking the job?"

"I never thought about it. Probably not. I appreciate the invite, though."

Jon spent the rest of Friday reorganizing things in his car. He didn't know what happened to his turnout gear that he was wearing the day of the fire. Hope they didn't cut it off him. Maybe they got it at the Jackson fire station. He drove over to the station and let himself in. It was a volunteer department like all of them in the county. He found his gear hanging up in the apparatus bay. Looks like they must have washed it. He took it out and put it in the trunk.

Dave called about 4:00 P.M. "Sorry I didn't get out to the hospital to see you, but I heard you had good care."

"Thanks for the flowers from the SO," Jon said.

"So, you had your own personal nurse I heard and then your friend Rita by your side. You doin' both of them gals?"

"No. I don't want any scorned women after me. Like that woman you all got a few years ago out on Mulga Road that burned her ex's house down."

"She was sure scorned," Dave said. "Worse case of scorned woman I ever seen."

"Anything goin' on our murder?" Jon asked.

"I got the latent print work back on the T.V. Had Dave Browns and Judy Browns prints on it. But not Pee Wee's."

"That's good. Hope they hurry up on the stuff I got out of the truck."

"Sheriff wants that truck brought up here. Rangle's Garage is going to go get it and put it in their impound lot and cover it up with a tarp. Sheriff said that since we don't have much of a crime scene we could show a jury the truck."

"I never thought of that," Jon said.

"There's a lot of things that we don't think of that Chuck thinks of. That's why he's the sheriff."

"What's next. I'm back to work."

"Can you do a photo lineup on the truck. Show it to all the witnesses. The guy who discovered the fire and those that have seen Dave and Pee Wee driving it?"

"Yeah, I'll do it next week," Jon said.

"I got a bunch of photos in my desk that you can use to make the photo spread."

"I'll be in Monday to do it."

"Okay, see you Monday."

Jon didn't go to the disco Saturday night. He called Rita and she wasn't feeling good. Liz said she was on night shift still. He was still kind of run down from his ordeal. He decided he would fix supper Saturday evening and invite Rita over to eat. He fixed steak on the outside grill. After they ate they took a good walk around town.

They played three games of checkers. "You want to stay all night?" Jon asked Rita.

"Okay, I brought some church clothes. I was hoping maybe I could stay and then we could go to Mass in the morning."

"I'd like that," Jon said.

"Can we sleep together?" Rita asked.

"If you want to," he replied.

"I do," she said.

She wore one of his t shirts to bed. He always slept in his underwear. He had never worn pajamas since he was a kid. He rubbed her back and she went to sleep. Sometime during the night, they both became aroused and made love. He was gentle with her. He didn't want to hurt the baby.

They slept in and went to eleven o'clock Mass.

"Let's pack our lunch and go out to Lake Katherine," Jon said.

"Can we go canoeing?" Rita asked.

"I'll call Ken and she if we can use his canoe."

They went to his place and changed clothes. He called and got permission to use the canoe from the park manager. They fixed lunch and drove out to the lake. They had canoed on the lake many times.

"I want to steer," Rita said.

"Okay, get in the back." The person in the rear seat of a canoe did the steering. Rita was good at it.

They went to the other end of the lake and beached and had lunch on a big rock. He should have brought his fishing rod.

She was sitting on the rock and he had his head in her lap.

"I really appreciate you staying with me at the hospital," Jon said.

"I thought I was going to lose you," she replied.

"Does that mean we have went to another level above just being good friends?"

She smiled. "It might; it's good to have good friends. You saved my life, you know."

"I think you guys would have probably figured out something if we hadn't come along."

They were talking about how they met. He and his partner at the SO were on patrol years ago, up around Wellston, and decided to drive out the Scenic Highway. It was late on a Saturday night. It really wasn't a scenic highway. Just a narrow gravel road that followed a creek. No houses on it. A lot of places to pull off and park. They had come across a car that had lost control and was teetering on the roadside, about to slide in the creek. There were four people in it. A guy who was driving and three girls. Rita was one of the girls in the back. They tied a rope to the car and to their cruiser, so it would not go into the creek and then broke out the back window of the car and everyone crawled out.

They all had been drinking. They took them to the SO. The guy they charged with DWI. The girls they let call someone to come and get them. About three months later, he was at the Stage Coach with his friends when Rita came over from another table and sat down and thanked him. She told him that she had quit the hard partying and quit hanging around with the crowd that partied hard. He invited her to sit with them that night. She has been with them ever since.

"I never did tell my mom about the car almost going in the creek," she said.

"I'm glad you joined our little group at the disco."

"You keep me out of trouble. That was before I got on at the plant."

"I don't know how you stand that dusty place."

"It pays pretty good for around these parts," she said.

"It pays better than being a deputy sheriff," he said.

"Do you mean that?" she said.

"Most of the guys at the SO could get food stamps if they wanted to. Their wives work. They work an extra job. I used to paint houses to make ends meet."

"That needs to change," Rita said.

"Yes, it does. That's why I left. I took a three thousand dollar a year raise when I went to work for the state."

"We could make it all right together, couldn't we, Jon? I mean, financially?"

"Yeah, we could. You'd have to go back to work after about a year. I can pick up some fire service teaching jobs to help out."

"I get three months paid maternity leave," she said.

He didn't want to bring up the subject of getting married, not yet, again. They got back in the canoe and went around the shore line and back to the dock.

That night Rita went back to her house.

CHAPTER 15

On Monday morning, Jon went to Dave's office and put together a photo lineup of the green truck and other trucks that were similar. He made a list of the persons he need to show it to. He called Liz and asked her if she wanted to go along. She did so he said he would pick her up. If they got done in time they would do some more shooting.

"So, what are we doing?" Liz asked as she got into his car.

"We're going to show folks a photo lineup of pickup trucks, including our suspect's vehicle, and see if they can identify the suspect vehicle. We want to place the vehicle at the fire scene and we want to place the suspects in the vehicle at various times in the area. We know we can't place them in it at the fire scene." He handed her the photo lineup. Six photos.

The first stop was the neighbor who discovered the fire. He picked out the green truck that belonged to the Browns. Next was the victim's niece and nephew who said it was the same truck they had seen at the Brown residence down the road. Then there were four persons who said that they had definitely seen Dave and Pee Wee Brown in the truck on the roads and at the Wesley Brown house. This was all circumstantial evidence that was like a puzzle going together. This took all morning.

They ate lunch at the coffee shop. Veal again. They talked about the case. "Do you have enough to make arrests yet?" Liz asked.

"No, not yet. We need more. What we really need is some one or two people that they told what they did to the victim," Jon explained. "All we really got right now is Dave Brown disposing of stolen property. It's enough probable cause for Burglary and the Homicide, but not enough for a conviction. Prosecutors want enough for a conviction before they file charges. We don't have that yet."

"How are you going to get it?"

"Keep working on it. Good, old fashioned detective work. Beatin' the bushes," Jon said.

"Are we going to shoot this afternoon?"

"If you want to."

"Sure."

They shot until four o'clock. She was getting better. He started her on multiple targets. When they finished, she cleaned her gun as he had taught her to do. He then took it with him and dropped it off at the gunsmiths to have some accuracy work done on it.

On the way back to Jackson, Jon saw Dave's cruisier setting at the K and L. Dave always ate supper there. He stopped and ate with him and told him about the successful photo lineup. A detective from the Jackson PD came in and sat down with them. He said that one of his informants told him that there was a guy who had told him that he was hired to burn down the old truck stop building out on Chillicothe Pike. Jon remembered the fire, it had happened about three months ago while he was off to the Northwest Ohio Arson Seminar. Another investigator was sent in to investigate it. The guy from Marietta who had just resigned.

"I'll get a copy of the report from the SFM office," Jon said. "The Jackson Fire Chief told me that our guy ruled it accidental."

"What's the guy's name who is supposed to have done it?" Dave asked the detective.

"Doug Denny." The detective said," He's a local doper about twenty years old. He lives over on Athens Street. When you want him, call me and I'll get him and bring him in to you."

"Can you change the cause on a fire?" Dave asked Jon.

"If you got the evidence. If you for instance find indisputable evidence at the scene that it is an arson, not just a difference in opinions, three months is a long time for an accelerant to survive if one was used. A confession corroborated by physical evidence would be ideal. We can work on it and see what happens."

"Well, we're kind of on hold on the murder until we get the lab results back on the things you found in the truck. How about an accelerant on that fire?" Dave asked.

"I took samples, but haven't got the results back yet. It's passed due. I'll check tomorrow when I call to get a copy of this fire at the truck stop."

"You know more crime gets solved over a cup of coffee or a meal than any other reason," Dave said, looking at the detective and then at Jon. "The Sheriff told me about a murder they had down below Oak Hill back in the fifties. They had a suspect, but couldn't put him at the scene. One morning they were having coffee in the jail kitchen and a highway patrolman was sitting at the table. They were discussing the murder and the patrolman was listening. When he heard the name of the suspect, he said 'I know him. I stopped him for speeding and gave him a written warning notice one night right down there where you're taking about this thing happening'. The patrolman then went out to his car and came back in with his warning book and leafed through it and found the notice copy. It was the same night and just an hour before the body was discovered. They got the guy in and destroyed his alibi and got a confession."

"Wow," the detective said. "Them old guys knew how to do it."

"They talked more with each other than we do today. We do a lot, but not enough. We need to start having some kind of intelligence get togethers about once a month. Not just this county, but a bunch of counties. Eat and talk," Dave said.

"Sounds like a good project for you to work on Dave," Jon said.

"I got enough to do," Dave said.

"I might get the chief to let me set something like that up," the detective said.

On Tuesday, Jon called in and got one of the girls in the office to send him a copy of the truck stop fire. Then he talked to the lab. They had just finished the samples on the murder case. Nothing found on any of the samples he had taken. Now he could not even prove that the fire was intentionally set.

On Tuesday afternoon Jon decided to go fishing. He called out to Lake Katherine to see if the canoe was available and took his walkie talkie with him. He had a good day. Caught several bass and turned them all back in. He never put in for vacation time for things like this. He could put in for compensative time off as he had enough overtime built up, but he didn't like to fool with the paper work. Besides, he could never get all his comp time back. After six months if you didn't take it you lost it and you could not get paid for it. He was strictly salary. He knew his boss didn't care. He knew that the chief carried a fishing pole in his car everywhere he went and fished whenever he wanted to.

The next day Jon went to the post office and checked his mail. He got the report on the truck stop fire. He also got the BCI report on the things from the Browns truck. They found some prints that matched. He took them to the SO and found Dave in his office and opened his mail.

"Good news, Dave, got the BCI report on the stuff from the truck," Jon said. "Two matching prints from the truck dash on Dave Brown. Two matching prints on the glove box door for Pee Wee Brown. One matching print for Dave on the beer cans and two for Pee Wee on the beer cans."

"What about the tire iron?" Dave asked.

"That's the good part. They found blood and it is the same blood type as the victims."

"Wow, we're getting there a little bit at a time."

"Let's get all our recent reports to the prosecutor, things we have done since we last met with him, like this stuff and the photo lineup. Then I'll get a meeting set up with Joe Johns for next week and see if we got enough to do anything with." Joe Johns, the Prosecutor's Investigator reviewed all cases that were brought to the prosecutor's office. He then briefed the Prosecutor on them and the Prosecutor decided what needed to be done. Sometimes he let the investigator file charges. Sometimes he took it directly to the Grand Jury for an indictment. Sometimes he told you to do some more work on the case.

"All right, here's the report on the truck stop fire. He said it was accidental. Said water ran down a leak in the roof into an interior partition and caused an electrical short that went up into the attic and burned the roof off."

"I'll call our good friend at the PD and see if he can get this Doug Denny in here this morning," Dave said as he picked up the phone.

Jon went back in the kitchen and got another cup of coffee and a biscuit. If he spent the day working here on this case, he would eat lunch here. "What's for lunch, Mille?" he asked the cook. "Meat loaf, baked potatoes and baked beans and homemade rolls."

"I hope I'm still here for lunch," Jon said.

He and Dave went in to the sheriff's office and briefed Chuck on the recent development on the murder case. He was pleased. He was a good guy to work for. Jon had hated to leave the department and Chuck hated to lose him. He had worked for Chuck as sheriff and when Chuck was chief deputy for the previous sheriff. The phone buzzed and Chuck answered it. "JPD has a guy out there that you wanted to talk to."

Dave's office was set up for interviewing. It was not too big. It had a camera and a recording device. The person being interviewed sat in a chair at the end of Dave's desk and everything was recorded on camera. Dave and Jon introduced themselves to Denny and Dave told him that he was free to leave at any time, that he was not under arrest and he advised him of his rights and asked him if he understood them and wanted to waive them and talk to Jon and Dave.

"Doug," Dave said, "we've been doing some investigating on the fire at the truck stop a few months ago. Several of your friends have given us statements saying that you told them that you were hired to burn the place. Now we would like your cooperation on this. We really want the owner or whoever it was that hired you. You can help yourself by telling us who it was. We can't promise you anything, but things have a way of working themselves out."

Denny looked down at the floor for a minute. "I didn't do it by myself. Another guy asked me to help him burn it and said he would give me two hundred dollars. So, I did."

"Who was he?" Jon asked.

"Rodney Loring."

"Why did he want to burn it?" Dave asked.

"He told me some other guy hired him to do it and he just asked me to help him."

"How did you do it?" Jon asked.

"Rodney picked me up and we went and got a five gallon can of gasoline at SA. We went out to the place. It was about one in the morning. Rodney had a key. We went in and I poured the gas where he showed me. In a room and then down a hallway till we ran out. I sat the can down there and we went down the hall further and Rodney lit a of ball of paper he had rolled up and tossed it down the hall and the place like exploded and we got the hell out of there."

"What kind of gas can was it?" Jon asked.

"It was plastic and it was blue and I left it in the hall."

"Has Rodney paid you?" Dave asked.

"Yeah. Two hundred."

"Doug, we're not going to arrest you right now, but you will eventually get arrested for this. Are you willing to testify in this?" Dave said.

"Yeah, if it will help me out."

"Okay, don't tell anyone you told us about this," Dave told him.

"Okay, you can go now. Don't take off on us, okay?" Jon said.

"All right, thanks," Doug said.

"I know Rodney Loring, he lives over in Vinton County at Dundas. I'll have Vinton County get ahold of him and send him down to see us tomorrow," Dave said.

"I got to get in there and find that gas can. It could still be good evidence if it's covered with debris. I'll need to get a search warrant," Jon said.

"We'll go down to the prosecutors after lunch and get one done up. Let's go see what's to eat in the jail," Dave said.

"Meat loaf and baked beans," Jon said.

"I figured you been in there checking that out."

It took the rest of the afternoon to get the search warrant. By the time they got it, the judge had already left the courthouse for the day and he would not be in the next day. They called him at home and went to his house in Wellston, where he signed it.

Jon called his boss, Joe and told him what was going on with the truck stop fire.

"That's why I keep telling you guys not to put a cause on a fire unless you can prove it. If you can't prove it make it undetermined," Joe said.

"Well, I'm going to have to make our murder undetermined because the lab didn't find any accelerants and I can't tell what caused the fire," Jon told Joe.

"But you have the murder though, the coroners ruling on the cause of death being homicide, the skull crushed by a blunt instrument."

"We meet with the prosecutor on it next week." Jon went on to tell him about the prints in the truck and the blood on the tire tool.

"Keep at it, you'll get them," Joe said, encouraging him.

"I may be down to see you next week. Things have slowed down for me some. The chief is interviewing people for the Marietta job."

Jon and Dave ate at the K and L again that evening. Jon called Rita from the restaurant and asked her if she wanted to go walking. He picked her up at her house and they parked up town and walked all over the place. She had to go to work at eleven.

"You been feelin' all right?" Jon asked her.

Yeah, I feel more like eating than I did last week."

"Haven't told your mom yet?"

"No, I'm not going to until I absolutely have to, even when I start to show I can hide it for a while."

Jon felt a special closeness to Rita, different from what they always had, because they were sharing this special thing.

On Thursday Dave said that Rodney Loring was coming in that morning. Jon lined up a couple firefighters to help him that afternoon dig out the fire scene when they executed the search warrant.

Rodney told them basically the same story about how the fire was set. He said that the boyfriend of the woman who owns the building contacted him and offered him a thousand dollars to burn the place. It wasn't hard to get Rodney to confess. They told him that his flunky helper had told on him and he came clean. He agreed to testify against the guy who hired him. They turned him loose and told him that he would be indicted and arrested sometime in the near future.

Insurance was the obvious motive for the fire. The amount of insurance coverage on the building was far more than the building was worth. The building had been setting empty for three years. Hopefully they could indict the boyfriend and he would tell on his girlfriend and then they would get her. He was going to have to visit the insurance agent and then the bank that was listed as holding the mortgage to see how much was owed on the place and what the owner stood to gain after the insurance paid the claim. The insurance company would pay the mortgage off first. It may already be paid, since three months had gone by and the fire was ruled accidental.

That afternoon, they went out to the fire scene and started digging. The roof was burned off the place over where the fire started at. They shoveled out the room that had the most fire damage. The floor was deeply charred. Jon took some samples to send to the lab. They went down the hallway and Jon's shovel hit something that was stuck to the floor. He pried it up. "Whew, smell that gasoline," he said as he pulled up the blue bottom of a plastic can. He put it in a plastic bag. Now they had corroborated the stories of the two fire setters and had established that the fire was set, both by their testimony and the physical evidence they had found. Three months after the fire. He couldn't believe it.

The fire debris had protected the evidence. If the other investigator would have just shoveled out the place he would have found the same thing.

Another trip to Reynoldsburg that afternoon. He couldn't UPS the samples in because it was obvious it was gasoline and that was prohibited to send by UPS or mail. He made a quick trip to the office to submit the samples to the lab. It was after 7:00 P.M. when he got back home. He planned to spend Friday checking the insurance and the bank and getting his report done. He took a short walk around town before hitting the sack.

Friday was a crisp, fall day. Jon started out at the insurance agent. He had known the man for years.

"Bill, I'm here about the fire at the old truck stop building. The owner and insured is Callie Lions. Have you paid the claim yet?" he asked the agent.

"I think the company has settled, let me get the file," he said and left his office and came back a couple minutes later with a file that he opened on his desk. "They paid two hundred thousand dollars a month ago. That's what it was insured for. No contents coverage since it was vacant."

Jon handed Bill the appropriate form that he had filled out to request information from the agent and relieve him of any civil liability for sharing that information. "Can you give me copies of the proof of loss, the check that was cashed if you have a copy of it and the application for insurance?"

"Sure, let me run the copies." He returned with the copies. "What's going on Jon? The adjuster said that the fire marshal said it was electrical."

"It wasn't me that said that.," Jon said. "I was out of town and another fire marshal did the investigation. Dave at the SO and I just got confessions from two persons that were hired by the insureds boyfriend to set the fire. It may lead back to the owner."

"That's nice to hear. I've got her house, a restaurant, and two rental houses insured."

Jon had prepared a subpoena to take to the bank. Fire Marshal's had the authority to issue subpoenas and to hold formal hearings on investigations and take testimony under oath. The bank would not give him any info without a subpoena.

He introduced himself to a vice president at the bank. "I have a subpoena for all the information on a loan you made to Callie Lions on the truck stop that burned."

"Let me get the file." He came back with a file full of papers.

"The loan was made for sixty thousand dollars and the balance was fifty-five thousand, which the insurance company paid off a month ago. The place was appraised for ninety thousand and it says here that she paid eighty thousand for it."

"Was she behind on her payments?" Jon asked.

He looked through the file. "Never, always on time," the banker said. "Is there some problem?"

"We got a couple of guys who set the place on fire."

"Is Callie involved?" he asked.

"We don't know if she is or not. We're still working on the case."

"She's always been a good customer here."

"Thank you for your help," Jon said as he got up and shook the banker's hand.

Jon spent the rest of the day typing the supplemental reports on this case and getting everything together. He and Dave had decided that when they met with the prosecutor next week on the murder that they would give him this case and ask to indict the two guys who set the fire and the owner's boyfriend.

CHAPTER 16

Saturday morning was a nice fall morning. Jon decided to go squirrel hunting early in the morning. He got two squirrels and took them home and cleaned them and froze them. He called Rita to see if she was going to the disco tonight. She had to work. He called Liz to see if she was going. They were going back to the stage coach. It was Kathy and Denny's fifth wedding anniversary, and they could get food at the stage coach, but they couldn't at the lounge.

He arrived at eight-thirty. There was a big cheese and meat tray on the table and pizza was ordered. Everyone in their group was there. Liz arrived with Karen and Doctor John. They did a lot of dancing. He danced with Liz a lot. The place closed at one. Karen and John had left earlier as usual. Liz had asked Jon if he would take her home. He had told her he would.

Liz asked Jon if he wanted to come in for a while. They sat in the living room and watched a scary movie on the Night Owl station. Suddenly Liz turned to him and embraced him and put a long passionate kiss on his lips and shoved him over onto his back on the couch. She straddled him and her skirt slipped up revealing black panties. She leaned over him and put her lips to his again. It was very passionate and Jon became aroused. However, he did not feel comfortable with the changing feelings he had for Rita. He didn't expect this aggressiveness from Liz. Her breathing became heavy. "We'll wake up your Grampa," Jon said.

"No, he's sound asleep. I went in his room when we got home and unplugged his phone in case we got a coroner call."

They continued their heavy kissing. "You want to make love to me?" Liz said.

"Right here?" he answered.

"We can go to my room. Grampa will never know. "

"I don't think we better," he said.

She got up and pulled her dress down to a more modest level and sat down on the couch and he sat up next to her. "What's wrong?" she said.

"I don't know. You kind of took me by surprise. I didn't expect this."

"I didn't either," she said. "I didn't have this in mind you know, when I asked you in."

"I've just got some personal things going on. I don't think we should do this right now. I mean, you are very attractive and sexy and all those things."

"But you don't like me," she said.

"Of course, I like you. I just can't explain it."

"Is it Rita?" she asked. "I saw how she looked at you while you slept in the hospital."

"Well, maybe, kinda; I don't know. I better go now."

"Okay." They both got up and she walked him to the door.

"I'm sorry," he told her.

"That's all right. I'm a patient person."

Jon didn't go to church Sunday morning, mainly because Liz didn't ask him and Rita probably would not go to mass, but straight to bed when she got home from work. He should just go on his own to Franklin Valley Methodist, but then Doc would probably ask him over to dinner after church and after last night with Liz he didn't think that would be a good idea. He just needed to stay away from her. He felt a tremendous responsibility toward Rita and the baby, but she did not want to get married, but he believed that her feelings toward him were changing. Being around Liz was confusing the situation.

He took a morning walk around town and then called Dave and they agreed to meet at the K and L for lunch. "We have a meeting on Tuesday morning with the prosecutor on our murder case."

"Okay, what time?" Jon said.

"Ten A.M. He has our reports and everything and is reviewing them. I suspect he'll be telling us what more we need to do on it."

"We need another tip from the tipster," Jon said.

"I wish we knew who the tipster was. It would be nice to have a witness," Dave said.

"So, you still hanging out with Doc's helper?" Dave asked Jon.

"Well, we been workin' together and she's joined our disco group. I been teaching her to shoot so she can get qualified and start carrying. I don't like working with someone who isn't carrying. Not only can they not protect themselves, but they can't back you up. I have that problem when I work with inspectors on the city fire departments. Most of them are not law enforcement officers, so I have to protect them as well as myself."

"I thought it was a good reason to just hang out with her," Dave said.

"She's fun to be around. And very kind. She's got me interested in going to church again."

"That won't hurt you none too much. I need to start going again, too. It's just hard to do on this job with the hours you work."

"So, where you gettin' yours at lately?" Jon asked Dave.

"My ex."

"Which ex?"

"The second one."

Frank Willis was the duly elected Prosecuting Attorney of Jackson County. He was finishing the first year of his third four-year term. His father had been prosecutor and then judge. Frank planned to run for judge when the opportune time came along. He was a part-time prosecutor, meaning that he could represent people in civil cases in his own private practice. This was necessary in a small county like this as the prosecutor job didn't pay a whole lot.

He had just finished a two-day jury trial a couple weeks ago in which two burglars were convicted of breaking into a rural school house and stealing food from the cafeteria. This was his third and probably last trial for the year. Most of his cases were settled in plea bargains. He had a part time assistant, as well as a full-time investigator. He didn't take a case to trial if he knew he would not win. When he went to trial he was fully prepared. His investigator had interviewed all the witnesses, both prosecution and defense. The really important or "star" witnesses he interviewed himself and prepared them for their taking the witness stand. He had only lost one jury trial in nine years.

Today he was reviewing a murder case that he knew he could not win in a trial with the evidence that was on his desk at this time. It was a burglary, robbery, murder and was covered up with the crime of arson. He had to do something with the case because of its importance. It was a murder and even though they only had about one murder a year there were no unsolved murders in the county. Some had pled guilty and some had been convicted before a jury.

He had a plan on this one. He had discussed it with his investigator and tomorrow they would discuss it with the detective from the sheriff's office and the fire marshal. He had known both for many years and they were good at their job. He knew that it wasn't their fault that this case was lacking. He knew that if he declined to prosecute at this point that they would continue to work on it. However, he had an idea. It involved a risk that he did not like to take, but he was going to have to take the risk on this one.

On Tuesday morning, Dave and Jon were led into Prosecutor Willis's office by his investigator Joe Johns. They greeted one another and shook hands.

"I've looked over and read all your reports," the prosecutor told them. "Joe and I have discussed it. There is not enough for a conviction."

"We realize that," Dave said.

"I'm going to do something that I don't like to do and that is take a risk and call a bluff. I want to present this to the Grand Jury for an Indictment on Dave Brown for Aggravated Murder with death penalty specs, Robbery, Burglary, Theft and Aggravated Arson. Hopefully he will be inclined to accept a plea deal in which he will have to testify against his brother in exchange for being allowed to plead guilty on one of the Aggravated Felonies, maybe two of them, and the murder will be dropped."

"Them Brown's don't turn on each other very often," Dave said.

"Well, it's the only chance we have unless you come up with something really good."

"Okay, sounds good, Dave said.

"All right with you, Jon?" the prosecutor said.

"Sure; will it be a secret indictment?"

"Yes, it will be. It will be at the next scheduled grand jury. We don't have a date yet."

"We'll keep working on it in the meantime," Dave said.

"Also, on your fire at the truck stop," the prosecutor said, "we'll take it to Grand Jury the same time and indict the two that set the fire and the guy that hired them. Then maybe we can get the boyfriend to tell on the owner for a lesser charge. If he won't take the deal, we won't be able to charge the owner."

As they walked up Main Street, back to the SO, Dave said," We did pretty good. I sure didn't expect any charges on the murder."

"Me neither," Jon agreed.

"Let's go tell the Sheriff; he'll be happy," Dave said.

The Sheriff was indeed happy. He didn't want an unsolved murder. There had never been an unsolved murder in the county as long as he had been sheriff and before that as a deputy going back to the early fifties.

"You guys have done a good job," Chuck said. "I appreciate the time you have given us, Jon. I thought when you left us we wouldn't see you much anymore. I'm glad you're our arson man."

"Thanks, Chuck," Jon said.

"Now my next question to you Jon is: Are you hankering with Doc Carter's new helper?" Chuck grinned.

"You know me better than that," Jon said.

"That's the problem, I know you better than anyone else," Chuck said, laughing.

"I'm teachin' her to shoot. You going to make her a special deputy?"

"That's part of the deal with the Doc and the commissioners. She's from a good Republican family. Might even let her wear a uniform and go on patrol if the deputies will keep their hands off her," the sheriff said.

"I'd say she'd be good at it. You need a female deputy. Be good on sex cases and child abuse. She is a caring person."

"Don't let him fool you, Sheriff," Dave said. "You put her on patrol and Jon might come back to work for you."

"That'd be a good deal," Chuck said with a big grin.

Tuesday evening Jon called Rita. She said she was on a four-day break from work. He asked her if she wanted to come over and spend the night. She said she would like to.

They watched *Dallas* together. Had some popcorn and then played checkers. They took a late evening walk around town. Rita would have a hard time sleeping as she was coming off midnight shift, even though she had stayed up all day.

They slept together after making love. They fell asleep in each other's arms. They had talked on their walk about the baby. He asked her if she had picked out names yet. She said she had not, but she was going to get a book so they could do that together. No one knew their secret yet. He would never tell anyone without Rita's blessing.

He woke up in the middle of the night. He had that dream again. The one about chasing a guy down an alley with fire glowing in the background. He reached for Rita. She wasn't there. Probably couldn't sleep. He went to the living room and she wasn't there. He went back in the bedroom and noticed the bathroom door was closed. He could hear her in there. He knocked on the door. "You all right?" he said.

"No," she said, "I'm having cramps."

"Can I come in?"

"Okay."

She was sitting on the toilet. "Is it bad?"

"Yes," she said as she cringed in pain. It lasted about thirty seconds and then seemed to let up.

"Are you going to the bathroom?" he asked.

"No, that's what I thought it was at first. I'm bleeding some."

"Let me see," he said.

She seemed embarrassed as she got up. There was blood in the toilet. Not a lot, but the water was red.

"You want to go to the hospital?

She cringed from another cramp. He could tell it was pretty bad. She was wearing his tee shirt that had a badge on it and said State Fire Marshal.

"I think I better take you to the emergency room," he told her.

He left and returned with her shoes and his long wool trench coat. She was in too much pain to get dressed. He helped her up after putting the shoes on her feet. He put the coat on her and walked her out to the couch where she sat down. He went and got dressed and went out and started the car.

"Okay, let's go," he told her as he helped her up and she had another cramp that caused her to let out a little cry. He picked her up in his arms and carried her out and put her in the front seat.

At the hospital, he got a wheel chair from the entryway to the ER and put her in it and rolled her into the ER. Liz was setting at the desk. She looked at Rita and said, "My gosh, what's wrong, Rita?"

"She's having bad cramps and bleeding. She's about seven weeks pregnant," he told Liz.

Liz said, "Follow me."

They went down the hall to a room with four beds in it. No one else was there. Liz turned on the lights and they helped her into bed after getting the coat off of her and putting a gown on her.

Another nurse came in. He didn't know her. She lifted Rita's gown and looked between her legs. She looked at Jon and said, "Are you the father?"

Jon looked at Rita and she gave him a look that said no. "I'm her friend," he said.

"I'll get the doctor," Liz said.

He hadn't expected Liz to be there. She was usually in ICU.

The doctor came in and asked Jon to leave while he did an examination. Jon went out in the hallway and sat in a chair. After about ten minutes Liz came out and sat beside him. The doctor came out and walked passed him to the nurses' desk. "She's having a miscarriage. It's nature's way of taking care of things when there is a problem. We gave her a shot for the pain. She'll be having cramps just like when a woman has a baby."

"Can I go in and sit with her?" Jon asked Liz.

"If you want to. How long have you known about her being pregnant?" Liz asked.

"Several weeks. She hasn't told anyone else. She doesn't want her mom to know."

"Who's the dad?' she asked him.

"She made me promise not to tell."

Liz looked at him in a way that he could tell that she suspected that he was the dad. She didn't say anything more. She went to the nurses' station. Jon went in the room and sat down beside Rita. She was kind of groggy. He took her hand in his. Her legs were propped up and a sheet over them. A nurse sat at the foot of the bed keeping an eye on things."

"I'm going to lose the baby, aren't I?" Rita said.

"Probably," Jon replied.

Rita started to sob. She had another bad cramp. She squeezed his hand real hard. He sat there with her for an hour as she went through the ordeal. The cramps seemed to lessen, and Rita went to sleep. The nurse nodded to him to follow her out into the hall. "The worst is over. She lost the baby. I'll get the doctor to examine her. You'll have to sit out here for a while. There's coffee at the nurses' station."

"Thank you," Jon said.

He went to the nurses' station and helped himself to the coffee. The doctor came by and Liz went with him. He sat down in the waiting room. Liz came back and sat down beside him.

"She'll be all right. We'll move her to a room. She'll probably be able to go home later this evening if everything is all right."

"Thanks," he said.

"She'll need someone to be with her for a couple of days after she is discharged. Can her mom watch her?"

"Her mom doesn't know, and I don't think she'll want to tell her. I'll take her to my place and watch after her."

"I'm going to go help move her to a room. I'll come get you when we get her settled."

Jon sat down beside Rita's bed. She was asleep. He sat there for an hour or longer and dozed in the big chair. He heard her stir and he woke up as she woke up. He took her hand in his. She looked at him: "I lost our baby."

"I know. I'm sorry. It couldn't be helped. It's not your fault."

He saw her tears and hugged her and held her for a long time. "I called your mom and told her that you were having some bad stomach pains and that I took you to the ER to get checked out and that they wanted to keep you for a few hours," he told her.

"Thank you. I'm not going to tell her what happened. I really don't want to tell anyone."

"You know how it is in this town. The nurses won't say anything. Liz won't say anything. But it may get out. We'll just wait and see."

"Liz was really nice," Rita said.

A nurse came in and asked Rita if she wanted something to eat. She said she would like some soup if they had it.

A half hour later, Karen came in. Jon looked at her name tag. It said Nursing Supervisor. That meant that she was the head nurse in the whole hospital on the shift. "How are you, Rita? Hi, Jon," Karen said.

"I'm feeling better."

The other nurse came in with soup and juice and crackers.

"After you eat, I need to examine you, and if everything is okay, and you feel like it then you can go home," Karen told Rita.

After Karen examined Rita Jon went back in and sat with her. They talked. "I didn't want it to happen like this," Rita said.

"I know, I didn't either. I was looking forward to having a kid with you."

"You really were, weren't you?"

"Yes, I was. I wanted to take care of you both. I still want to take care of you."

"You're so kind, Jon. We have been through a lot together. I'm glad you're my friend."

An hour later, Karen came in. "You ready to go home?" she asked.

"I think so," Rita said.

"Let's get you up and walk down the hall and back and see how you do."

She was a little unsteady on her feet, but they both walked beside her with their arms through hers.

"I think you're ready. Why don't you get dressed?" Karen said.

"I'm not leaving here wearing that old wool coat with no pants on under it," Rita said.

"I'll go get you a set of my scrubs out of my locker. You can return them the next time we go to the disco," Karen said.

After helping Rita get dressed, Jon and her sat on the side of the bed together. Karen came back in and started talking: "You need to rest for two days and then resume your normal routine. I have made you an appointment with a gynecologist for two weeks here at the doctor's office building. There is a nice doctor who comes down from Chillicothe once a week to see patients. No intercourse until he OK's it. You need to keep busy. A lot of women that go through this get depressed. That's why you should go back to work after two days' rest. You should have someone with you the next two days. You can start walking tomorrow if you feel like it. There will probably be some bleeding for a few days. If it increases call your family doctor."

"Thank you, Karen, you all have been so nice," Rita said.

"I'll get you a wheel chair and Jon can take you home. "

They went to Jon's house. Rita would call her mom and tell her she was all right and that she was going to stay with Jon for a few days as they didn't want her to be alone and her mom had to work.

CHAPTER 17

Jon called his boss and told him that he was going to stay home for the next two days and do reports as he had to take care of a friend who was sick. Joe told him that if they got a call or if he got a call at home to tell them he would be out in two days. This happened often when they were busy. If it was a fatal or something that really needed handled Jon would have to get someone to stay with Rita as he was not on sick leave or vacation.

He put Rita to bed. She went to sleep as they had given her a pain pill before she left the hospital. He laid down on the couch and took a nap for a couple of hours. When he woke up it was dark. He tried to remember what day it was. He decided that it must be Wednesday. It was 9:00 P.M. He went in the bedroom and Rita woke up. "You hungry?" he asked her.

"No, what I really would like to do is take a shower. I haven't had one since yesterday and I really got sweaty when I was having all those terrible cramps."

He helped her out of the bed and into the bathroom. She still appeared to be in pain. "Do you want me to help you?" he asked.

"You can help me step into the tub. I don't think I can step over the side of the tub by myself." She got undressed and he started the water and got it adjusted and helped her into the shower. He went out and sit on the bed until he knew she was finished.

He took her the robe that she had in her travel bag. He helped her dry off and into the robe and back into bed. "I feel much better now," she said. "Let's play checkers."

He got the board and they sat on the bed and played several games. "Do you want me to sleep on the couch?" Jon asked Rita.

"No, I want you to sleep with me and hold me. And I want to thank you for taking such good care of me."

"I'm really sorry about the baby."

"I am, too; I was actually starting to like the idea and was looking forward to sharing our child, even if we didn't get married."

"I wanted to get married. You didn't," he said.

"Now we can be friends again," she said.

"We're more than friends. We're sleeping together."

"I know. I like sleeping with you. Not just the sex, but being together."

"Well, I think it's time to sleep together. I'm going to put these checkers away and take a bath and get in bed with you," he said, bending over to kiss her.

"Okay, I'll be right here."

On Thursday, Jon got up at eight and fixed breakfast and took Rita's to her in bed. He had already eaten, so he sat on the bed while she ate and they talked. He went into the library room and looked through the collection of books and found three that he thought might interest her and took them to her. Then he went back to the library where he had his typewriter set up and started typing. The phone rang. "Jon it's Dave; grand jury is next Tuesday. I got your subpoena here."

"What time?"

"Nine on the murder and ten on the truck stop."

"Which actually means ten on the murder and one on the truck stop," Jon said.

"I know. They never start on time and then they'll bump us around cause some other witness on another case has a dentist appointment."

"Did you get the evidence from BCI?"

"Leaving here in a minute."

"I'll see you Tuesday then. You got any idea where we are going to find Dave Brown?" Jon asked.

"I'll work on it over the weekend. If he knows we are coming, he'll take off for the mountains of Eastern Kentucky and we'll never find him."

"Okay, is Liz testifying?"

"She is going to read the medical examiner's report to the jury and answer any questions they have about it."

"Okay, later."

By Saturday Rita was ready to go for a walk around town. It was raining so they put on rain parkas and took a big umbrella. The leaves were starting to fall, and it made for nice fall walking. They did three blocks, and he forgot about the newspaper editor and they ran into him. He hoped he didn't put them in the paper again. Give someone else some press time.

Liz called on Saturday night. She was going to the disco. She asked to talk to Rita.

"She's really nice," Rita told him. "She asked if I needed anything and how I was feeling."

"Yes, she is a caring person," Jon said.

"Do you think she will tell everyone tonight what happened to me?"

"No, and I don't even think she will tell them that she talked to us. And I don't think Karen will either. Nurses aren't supposed to do that sort of thing."

"That's good; maybe this will be our secret forever."

"It's nothing to be ashamed of, what we did, you know," Jon said.

"I know, I'm not ashamed of it. I just don't like how it ended."

"Me, either."

The weekend went fast. Jon and Rita went to Mass on Sunday, and she went back to work at eleven on Sunday night. They took a longer walk on Sunday. Rita had called her mom the day she got out of the hospital and told her she had a stomach virus and was all right. She decided to go back to her mom's when she got off work Monday morning. Jon was liking having her around all the time.

Monday morning his phone rang. Jon looked at his clock, and it was seven. He answered.

"This is Wellston PD; our fire department is out on Mulga Road on a fatal fire and would like you to respond. The coroner is on the way."

"Okay, how far out of town?"

"About two or three miles."

"I'll be there."

The Wellston Fire Department was volunteer except that it had three paid persons. One was the chief. There was one paid fire fighter at the station at all times. They covered two townships outside the city. Jon went all the way out the Appalachian Highway and turned onto Mulga Road and went back toward town instead of going through town to get there.

He found a one-and-a-half story wood frame house that had significant fire damage to it. He found the chief who told him that there were two children, two girls DOA in one of the back first floor bedrooms. The parents and a four-year-old had gotten out of the upstairs onto the porch roof and jumped. The girls appeared to be about ten to twelve years old.

He went inside and took a look at the girls. They were in two separate beds and covered up. Their faces were smoke stained, but they were not burned. He could tell by looking at the bedroom door that it had been closed during the fire. The door jamb was not burned. If it had been open the jamb would have been charred where the fire came into the room from the living room and there would have been more damage in the bedroom.

He went out into the living room. It appeared that the fire started in this room as it was damaged more than the kitchen and dining room. There was a wood burning stove in the living room. The door on it was open. It looked like it had been open during the fire as there was debris laying on the door itself.

He went upstairs and looked around. The fire had traveled up the stairs and done a number on the two bedrooms up there. He found glass on the porch roof where the parents had escaped. He went outside and found the fire chief. "Chief, get your folks together and find out if that wood burning stove door was open when they went in the house or if one of them did it during overhaul. Where are the parents at?"

"Across the road in the house with the little one," the chief pointed across the blacktop road.

"I'm going over to talk to them. When Liz gets here tell her to go ahead and look at the bodies and photograph them. I'll be back."

"Okay, Jon," the chief said. He heard him hollering at his firefighters to gather around so they could talk.

He hated interviewing parents that had just lost a child. It was sad and very emotional. He found the parents in the living room of the house across the road, the lady was crying in her husband's arms. A little boy about four or five sat on the couch with them.

"I'm Jon Hamer, the fire investigator," he said. "I'm very sorry for what has happened tonight."

"Thank you," the man said.

"I know you want to find out what happened. I need to ask you a few brief questions to help me determine the cause."

"I don't think my wife will be much help, but I can answer your questions," he said.

"Just tell me how you discovered the fire," Jon said.

"The kids went to bed about nine. The two girls are downstairs, and our little boy upstairs in his room. My wife and I stayed up and watched the eleven o'clock news. We then went to bed. I filled the stove in the living room before we went upstairs. I don't know what time it was, but our little boy woke us up and there was thick black smoke coming up the stairs. I shut the bedroom door and broke out the window and put the wife and boy out on the roof, and then I went out and jumped off and I caught the boy when she dropped him, and then I tried to slow her fall. I tried to go back in the house through the back door, but when I opened it there was just too much heat."

"Where did you first see flames?" Jon asked.

"In the living room, before the fire trucks got here. I went across the road to this house and woke them up to call."

"Did you get up any during the night?"

"No," the man answered.

"Have you had any problems with anything electrical or heating?" Jon asked.

"No, we haven't."

"Okay, I'll probably be back with some more questions. There will be someone here from the Red Cross pretty soon to talk to you about getting you a place to stay and clothing."

"Thank you," the man replied.

When Jon got back over to the house, Liz was inside photographing the two kids. "Hey, Liz," he said.

"Hi Jon, not a very good night is it."

"No, these are the worst kind. Can you look down their throats for smoke deposits?"

"Okay." She had her gloves on. She got out a little flashlight and a tongue depressor. Jon put on rubber gloves and helped to open the mouths. "Yes, smoke in the airway," Liz said.

"Now swab the nose."

She swabbed both victims' noses, and they had black soot in them. "Now wait a minute, Fire Marshal Jon," Liz said. "Who's the coroner investigator here, me or you?"

"You said you wanted to learn. Now do you have your stuff to draw blood?"

"Okay, I don't think we are going to need an autopsy here so to save the county some money. How about drawing blood and taking it to the hospital and having them tell you how much carbon monoxide is in it."

"Okay, Mr. Fire Marshal," she said.

"You'll probably do better in the neck," he told her.

After she drew the blood, he said, "Now if you will examine the body for trauma and lividity, I think that will be sufficient. You might want to do that at the funeral home where you have better light."

Lividity is the settling of the blood in a dead body. If a body is laying on its back, then the blood will settle in the back and buttocks. If you find a body that has lividity in the back and buttocks, but the body is face down then it has been moved after lividity set in.

"Okay, Fire Marshal, Jon; anything else?"

"Now, if you want to hang around maybe I can tell you what caused the fire."

"Can I make a suggestion?"

"Yes, you may, if it is in your area of expertise."

"Well, as you can tell, I am now wearing a pair of fire boots, which have a steel toe and insole. I would suggest that you put yours on before you run a nail through your foot."

"Where you did you get those fire boots?" he asked her.

"My friend at the Oak Hill Fire Department gave them to me. They fit nicely."

In the living room, it was apparent from the burn patterns that the fire started on the couch. The chief came in and said that none of his men opened the stove door and that one of his men found it to be open and he gave it a shot of water inside the stove.

The couch was pretty much burned up. No fabric or stuffing left. Some wood framework that was deeply charred. The springs of course were there. The floor beneath the couch was deeply charred. Jon knew that when a couch burned that burning liquid like napalm dripped out beneath it from the foam rubber and burned into the floor.

After removing the debris from the couch, they found two, interesting objects: an ash shovel that is used to clean the ashes out of a wood burning appliance, and a metal poker rod that is used to stir up the fire in a wood burning appliance.

Jon looked at the fire chief. "Are you thinking what I am thinking, Chief?"

"Someone playing in the stove," the chief replied.

"Come on, Liz; let's go over and talk to the parents again."

He introduced Liz to the mother and father. The little boy was not present. "Has your little boy ever opened the stove door, sir?" Jon asked him.

"He has when it's cold, but never when it is hot. He knows to stay away from hot things."

"The stove door was open when the fire started. We found the ash shovel and the poker rod on the couch. There is no doubt the fire started on the couch."

The man started to shed some tears. "Does this get in the paper if that is what happened?"

"No, we will just say that the fire was accidental and it started in the living room. That is all, but we would like to ask your boy if it is all right with you."

The father sent for the boy and sat him on his lap on the couch. "Son," he said to the boy, "these folks would like to talk to you. Daddy would like for you to tell them the truth. I want you to know you are not in any trouble."

Jon nodded to Liz, and she sat down beside the boy and his dad. "Billy, do you help your daddy clean the stove out?"

"I do it for Daddy. I did it for Daddy last night."

"Did you do it while Daddy and Mommy were asleep?" she asked Billy.

"Yeah, I wanted to help Daddy."

Jon said, "I think that will be all. We're really sorry about what happened. I see that the Red Cross lady has been here. Did she help you out?"

"Yes, we are going to spend a couple nights in a motel she is sending us to, and then we will go to my in-laws. The lady gave us vouchers for clothing and personal items at the store."

"Okay, thank you helping us find out what happened," Jon said.

As they walked across the road Jon said to Liz," I didn't mean to put you on the spot back there, but I thought the little boy needed a woman's touch, and you did very well."

"Thank you," she said. "So, the cause is going to be accidental?"

"Unless you find something on the bodies that you don't like. Call me and let me know."

"So, how is Rita? Doing good? Back to work tonight?" Liz asked.

"She's doing well," he answered.

"I'm glad you were there for her."

"I'm glad you were there for her, too," he said.

Jon briefed the fire chief on what he thought happened and asked him to call it accidental and not mention the part about the kid playing in the stove. He needed breakfast so he headed for the K and L.

CHAPTER 18

On Monday morning, after he had breakfast at the K and L, Jon Hamer found Dave in his office at the SO.

"Well, Dave, if we get an indictment tomorrow on Dave Brown, where are we going to find him at?"

"I've had a guy working on that over the weekend. He just called me and told me that the guy is cutting timber with a crew down on Bucklick Road. They work every day from 7:00 A.M. till 4:00 P.M. Dave has been real regular in showing up. There are three of them on the job. We need to drive down there after four this afternoon and check the place out. We'll go there Wednesday morning when they first start to work and grab him."

"Sounds good; you think he'll try to run?"

"No, he never has ran when approached, but he has been known to resist and fight. This is the most trouble he has ever been in, and I wouldn't put it passed him to be carrying a gun. If we get the drop on him, he'll give up."

"Is Pee Wee working with him down there?"

"No, no one seems to have seen him around any lately. Probably in Portsmouth."

"Okay, I'm goin' in the deputy's room and use a typewriter to type up this report on last night's fire and make some phone calls. "

"Here's your subpoena," Dave said as he handed him a paper.

"Thanks."

It took Jon two hours to get the report done and draw the sketch. The phone rang. He answered it. "It's Liz for you on line two," Rose said.

"Hi, Liz."

"I have the lab tests back from this morning. High level of carbon monoxide. I didn't find anything suspicious about the bodies when I examined them."

"Good, I'm just typing my report, so I will close it out."

"I didn't mean to give you a hard time this morning. I've got a lot to learn."

"We all do. Learn something new every day."

"I've got chores to do and then some sleep to catch up on. Still on midnight shift," she said.

"Okay, I'll see you in Grand Jury tomorrow."

"I've never testified in court before."

"Come into the SO at eight in the morning, and Dave and I will explain it to you. It's very informal."

"Okay, see you in the morning."

Jon and Dave drove up Bucklick road about four thirty that afternoon in Jon's car and found the logging site. There was a skidder and loader sitting by the road and a skid road going up in the woods. It looked like a select cut where they cut certain trees that were marked instead of cutting down all the trees as in a clear cut.

"There's no place here to sit and wait for them to come to work without being seen and if we roll in on him as he just gets here he will see us and he can get the draw on us or take off into the woods," Dave said.

"Then we need to get him when he's back in the woods," Jon said.

"We'll have someone drop us off about six in the morning, and you and I will go back up the skid road to where they are cutting and hide in the woods. When they come back in to cut, if Dave is one of them, then when they start sawing we'll sneak up on him. The saws will mask our noise. We should be able to get up close to him before anyone spots us. We'll wear woodland camo's. I'm bringing my carbine."

"I'll have my shotgun. Where we gonna hide the car?"

"Let's drive up the road a piece. There's a barn up there where whoever drops us off can hide behind till we call him to come and help us."

They found a barn a quarter mile up the road. There were no houses in sight.

"Let's go to the K and L and get supper. I got a burglary suspect coming in this evening to talk to me about his activities."

"Liz, Jon said you have never been in grand jury before," Dave said in his office on Tuesday morning.

"No, I haven't," Liz answered

"Well, it's very informal. There is only one attorney and that is the prosecutor, so there is no cross examination. There are twelve jurors, but only eight have to agree to get an indictment. Hearsay evidence is admissible and that is what you will be doing. The prosecutor will ask you to read the medical examiner's report or parts of it that he will have highlighted in order to establish the cause of death. He may ask you some questions. Some of the jurors may ask you some questions. If you feel that the questions are not within your expertise, then you should tell them that."

"Okay, I understand," she said. She was wearing a nice dark business suit type of dress and had a small leather brief case with her.

"You'll do fine. Your job is to establish the cause of death which the medical examiner has done for you. You are in effect relaying this information to the grand jury," Dave explained.

"Let's go in the kitchen and get a cup of coffee before we go over to the courthouse," Dave said.

The Jackson County Courthouse was not a large building. It is three stories tall. The courthouse burned in a fire back in the early fifties and it was rebuilt. The Common Pleas Courtroom is on the second floor and that is where the grand jury meets. The witnesses sit in the hallway until called to testify. Their case was to be the first presented. The judge had to impanel the jury and give them instructions on their duties. He would then retire to his office and the prosecutor would run the show.

The fire chief was the first witness to be called followed by the person who reported the fire. Then the niece of the victim would testify. Dave was next and he was in there the longest. Then Liz and then Jon. It took about an hour.

There was a short break and then the truck stop case was presented. Dave, Jon, and the guy who was originally hired to set the fire were the only witnesses. Jon told about the cause of the fire and the results of the Arson Crime Lab test. He showed some photos and told about the insurance and the bank loan.

Jon and Liz sat in the hallway as Dave testified in the truck stop case. The three of them were going to go to lunch after their cases were presented. The jury voted on each case separately at the conclusion of the testimony in that case. The Prosecutor could not tell the results of the jury's deliberation until the papers had been filed with the clerk at the end of the day. These two cases would be secret indictments and they would not be made known to the public until the arrest warrants were served. Jon was explaining all this to Liz. "So, how is Rita?" Liz asked.

"She's good. I talked to her this morning on the phone."

"Poor girl," Liz said, "does her mother know?"

"No, and I don't think she is ever going to tell her. I don't think she is going to tell anyone."

"You realize that nurses don't talk about patients, don't you?"

"Yes, and Rita knows that."

"You said she broke up with her fiancé several months ago."

"About six months ago."

"That rules him out as the father, then, I suppose," Liz said. "It's not really any of my business anyways."

"I don't think she wants anyone to know."

"But you know."

"I do."

"I've never seen such a close relationship between a man and a woman as you and she have and not being a boyfriend-girlfriend kind of thing."

"It is kind of unique," Jon agreed.

"I don't think I could have that with a man without becoming intimate."

"You never know. You might want to try it sometime."

Jon knew that Liz suspected they were more than friends, but he could not tell her that because of the promise he had made to Rita. He would like to tell her so she would stop her pursuing of him. He liked her and if it wasn't for Rita he would enjoy dating her.

Jon and Dave hung around the SO after they had returned from lunch. At three o'clock, the clerk brought over the indictments with warrants to arrest. They got what they wanted on both cases. They would let someone else make the arrests on the truck stop case. They met with the sheriff.

"I'll take you two down there on Bucklick in the morning and wait down the road. We'll meet here at 5:00 A.M., so you guys can get in place by seven," Chuck said. Chuck liked to do things like this every once in a while. He liked to look after the safety of his guys.

Rita called Jon that evening and asked if she could come over and spend the night. She had two days off from work. They took a long walk around town.

"Did you have a good day?" Rita asked Jon.

"Yep. We made some good progress on some of our cases. You'll read about it in the paper next week."

"Thanks for letting me come over tonight, Jon."

"Anytime. I like the time we spend together."

"I do, too," she said as she took his hand as they walked.

"Let's make popcorn when we get home and watch *Dallas*."

Jon cleaned his shotgun as they watched *Dallas*. He had built it out of an old Remington model 870 receiver and stock. He ordered a twenty-inch barrel for it with changeable chokes and iron sights. He put an extended magazine tube and a sling on it. He experimented with different chokes until he got a good tight pattern at fifty yards with no. 4 buckshot. The trouble with police shotguns was that they had cylinder bore or improved cylinder barrels on them. They were only good out to thirty yards and then the shot spread out too much. He swabbed the barrel with an oily patch and coated the metal receiver and barrel with a coat of oil.

He laid out his woodland camo fatigues and field jacket. He got his bullet proof vest out of the car. He put mink oil on his leather paratrooper boots. "What are you getting ready to do?" Rita asked.

"Going to get a bad guy tomorrow," he said.

"You be careful."

"I will, that's why I'm getting this stuff ready."

They went to bed. "Next week when I go to the doctor, I'm going to ask him to put me back on the pill," Rita said.

"That's good," he said as he held her in his arms. He was looking forward to their intimacy.

At six-fifteen, Chuck dropped off Jon and Dave at the foot of the skid road. They had blackened their faces with burnt cork. Dave had a pair of binoculars. They both had walkie talkies with ear buds. Dave carried an M-1 carbine that he had somehow brought back from his service during the Vietnam War. They walked up the skid road. "I'm going up in the brush right here, where I can see them coming up the skid road. You go up there where they are going to be cutting and hide. When I see them coming, I'll call you and tell you if

Dave is with them. I'll tell you how he is dressed, so you will know for sure who he is."

"Okay, I'll wait till they start their saws before I sneak up on him. The noise will cover up any noise I make, and I can move in faster. I just hope they don't drop a tree on us," Jon said to Dave.

Jon went on up the road to where they had some trees marked to cut. He hid in some brush and sat down and waited. In about twenty minutes, he heard the skidder start up. Dave called on the radio.

"They're coming up the road. Dave is walking with another guy. Dave has a red hard hat on and a green jacket. The other guy has a white hard hat on."

In about five minutes, Jon saw them. The skidder stopped about where Dave was, and the guy got off and all three of them walked toward him carrying chain saws. They each took a tree and started their saws. Dave Brown was about fifty feet from Jon. "I'm going to start sneaking up on him now Dave and when the tree drops I'll surprise him," Jon said into the radio mic. Dave was in the brush about fifty yards away. Jon knew that he would have his carbine sights on Dave Brown and that he could hit him. He had shot a lot with Dave.

As he got to within about ten feet of Brown, one of the other guys saw Jon and put his saw down and made a motion to Brown. Brown turned around and looked at Jon as Jon pointed the shotgun at his chest." Drop the saw and put your hands on your head real slow like Brown, or I'll blow your fuckin' head off." Dave complied.

"Come on down and cuff him, Dave," Jon said into the mic, "and watch those other two guys."

He could hear Dave yell: "You two guys put your saws down and put your hands on your heads until I tell you differently. We're just here for Dave Brown." Jon knew that Chuck was monitoring their traffic and was headed their way now.

Dave laid his carbine down behind Jon and put the cuffs on Brown. He searched him and found a .380 automatic pistol in his pocket.

"All right, Dave, you're under arrest for murder and a whole bunch of other things. Let's go walk out to the road."

By the time they got half way down the hill, Chuck was walking up the hill. The other two guys had started their saws up and were back to cutting. Jon got in the back seat with Brown after putting both his pistol and his shotgun in the trunk. They drove back up Route 139 to the jail.

They placed Dave Brown in the interview room at the jail. Dave advised him of his constitutional rights and asked him if would waive them and talk to them. He flatly refused. He said that he wanted an attorney. That was all there was to it. They could not talk to him.

CHAPTER 19

Jon called Liz and told her about the arrest and the plan they had that Dave Brown would decide to testify against his brother rather than stand trial for an offence that carried the death penalty.

"So, what happens next?" Liz asked.

"We wait. The court appoints him an attorney. There will be discussions between the prosecution and the defense. Hopefully he will have an attorney who would rather plea bargain than go to trial and take a chance on having his client executed."

"When we going to shoot again?" Liz asked him.

"How about this Saturday?"

"Okay, I go on a four-day break starting after my shift tomorrow night. Why don't you come out for breakfast about nine?"

"All right, see you then."

Jon called his boss, Joe and told him about the indictment and arrest on the murder.

"I knew you would do it," Joe said. "I got some good news for you. You're getting a new car next week. It'll be a four-door Jeep Cherokee with four-wheel drive. We got four of them. It is an experiment to see if these kinds of vehicles will work out for us. Each district will get one."

The Arson Bureau had the state divided into four districts: Southeast, Southwest, Northwest and Northeast. Each district had a senior investigator, but he was not a supervisor. His job was to help the other investigators on cases that they needed help on. He was also to coach new investigators.

"Sounds nice. They don't have any more room in them than a full-size car, though," Jon said.

"May have to get you a trailer," Joe said, laughing.

"I've never backed a trailer."

"Well, it will have new radios installed when you pick it up. You'll also get a new walkie talkie and a charger mounted in the car for it."

"What color?" Jon asked.

"I haven't seen them yet, so I don't know."

On Saturday morning, Jon went out to Liz's and had breakfast and they shot all morning. "I think you're ready for your qualification. You'll need two boxes of shells. I'll get a hold of the range officer and set it up for you for some morning about nine o'clock. I'll go with you. I need to shoot, too, for my twice a year qualification, so we'll shoot at the same time."

"Okay."

"Do you like the gun better since I had it worked on?"

"Yes, it seems to be more accurate and the trigger pulls easier."

"I'll get you another mag because you'll need three for your qualification. I'll get you a leather holder for your two mags and a new leather holster. You'll need to break in the holster before you qualify by practicing your draw to loosen up the holster. You can pay me back after I get it."

"Thank you for helping me with this."

"I've enjoyed it."

"Are you going to the disco tonight?" she asked him.

"I think I will; you going?"

"Yes, I'm going out to dinner with Karen and Doctor John first. We're going down to Bob Evans."

"Actually, I'm going out with a friend of Johns. I've never met him. I hope you don't mind."

"I don't have any hold on you, do I?" he replied.

"You could have if you wanted to, but I think you and Rita got something going."

"The things we have been through the last month has seemed to bring us closer together."

"Is Rita going tonight?" Liz asked.

"No, she has to work."

"You want to help me get a load of hay over on Antioch Road?"

"Yeah, I could use a work out."

He helped her hook a wagon behind her truck. "You want to drive?" she said.

"No, I can't back a trailer let alone a farm wagon."

The farmer helped them load the hay on the wagon, so it did not take too long. Unloading took longer because it was just the two of them. They used an elevator which is like a conveyor belt to take it to the second story of the barn. Liz unloaded the wagon onto the elevator and Jon stacked it, but he couldn't keep up and he had a bunch of bales piled up when the elevator stopped. Liz came up and helped him to stack the rest of it.

"I hate to run you off and not feed you after all this work, but I have to get ready to go out to eat. Karen and John and my date will be picking me up."

"I better get out of here then or he will think you got a boyfriend," Jon said.

"I'll tell him you're the hired help."

That night at the Lounge, they had a good crowd at their table. Rita was the only regular that was not there. Liz introduced her date. "This is Bob, Doctor Johns friend. He's a radiologist at the hospital in Gallipolis. Bob this is Jess, Kathy, Denny, Cheryl, Amy, Jimmy, Eric, and Jon." She named everyone around the table. Jon was sitting between Amy and Cheryl. They talked in small groups. Amy and Cheryl wanted to know about the arrest in the murder he and Dave had made. He told them about it. They started dancing at nine. Jimmy and Eric were focused on a couple of young ladies sitting at a small table next to theirs. They kept asking them to dance. Jess was dancing with Cheryl. Jon didn't know why Jess's girlfriend wasn't there. That put Jon with Amy on the slow dances. During break Cheryl said, "I heard that Rita had been sick." Everyone looked at Jon for an answer. Of course, they all knew that he and Rita were good friends.

"She had some kind of stomach virus, had to go to the ER," Jon explained.

"Is she still sick?" Kathy asked.

"No, she's working tonight," Jon answered. He just wondered if the word had gotten out about what really had happened.

The music started again and Amy grabbed Jon and they went to the dance floor. The next song was slow. Amy was really holding him tight. When they sat back down she put her hand on his inner thigh. Liz grabbed him and took him to the dance floor for the next slow dance. "I'm rescuing you from Amy," she said. "You've got more than you can handle with Rita and me."

"Don't make your date mad," he said.

"I won't; besides, he's dancing with Amy."

"Did you all have a good dinner?"

"Yes, very nice, on the way up here Bob pulled a flask out of his jacket pocket and offered me a drink. Of course, I refused. He took a couple swigs."

"Maybe he would be a good match for Amy, she's getting a bit tipsy."

"I noticed where her hand was," Liz said.

"Why are you looking underneath the table?" Jon smiled.

"Just checking," Liz smiled.

When they sat back down Bob had taken his seat and was in conversation with Amy. Jon sat down with Liz. She shrugged her shoulders. "I've never had much luck with doctors," she said.

"Or Fire Marshals," Jon said.

"Too early to tell about that," Liz said.

Amy got up and left the room. Five minutes later Bob got up and left.

"YMCA" played and the rest of them got up and danced.

Jon continued to dance with Liz. It had been over forty-five minutes, and Amy and Bob were still gone.

As they were sitting there, Liz whispered in Jon's ear, "Do you mind taking me home Jon? I'm humiliated, and I don't want to ruin Karen and John's evening."

"Okay. You leave first, and I'll meet you in the lobby in about five minutes."

As they drove down the road, Liz said, "That really pisses me off. The nerve of that guy to do that. I never did like blind dates."

"I've never seen you mad before," Jon said.

"I don't get mad very often," she said. "And I should be mad at you, too, Jon Hamer, Mr. Fire Marshal."

"What for?" he replied.

"You know what for."

"No, I don't."

"You were the father of Rita's baby."

"How do you know that?" he said.

"I just know; I can tell the way you two are."

"I don't know what to say," he replied.

"You don't have to say anything. Just take me home."

He dropped Liz off at the farm. She didn't say a thing as she got out of the car and went inside.

Jon drove home and went to bed.

Jon woke up about seven in the morning. Rita was getting in bed with him. Her hair was wet. "Hi," she said to him.

"How are you?" he said, laying on his back and putting his arm under her neck and drawing her close to him as she placed her head on his chest.

"You know," she said, "we haven't been backpacking since I started dating Roger, and that was over a year and a half ago. Let's go backpacking."

"Where you want to go?" he asked her.

"You know that place you took me down in West Virginia that time along that stream?"

"Cranberry," he said

"Yeah, can we go there?"

"How about Thanksgiving weekend? We can skip the dinner at home and eat by the river. Can you get the time off?" he asked her.

"The plant is shutting down for a week at Thanksgiving for maintenance."

"We'll plan on it then. It may snow a little down there, but not very much. We'll check the weather forecast before we go. If it's going to snow a lot in the mountains, then we we'll have to go somewhere around here like Zaleski Forest."

"Did you go to the disco?"

"Yeah, everyone was there. They asked about you. Heard you were sick. I told them you had a stomach virus and had to go to the ER."

He told her about Liz's date and how he disappeared with Amy.

"What'd she do?" Rita asked.

"Got mad and went home."

"I'm going to sleep. I go back out tonight. Tomorrow I go to the doctor. Maybe we can fool around tomorrow night," she said as she put her hand between his legs.

"Then don't do that; save it for tomorrow night."

She rolled over and went to sleep. He rolled over and put his arms around her.

Monday morning, Jon called Liz and asked her if she could go to the range on Tuesday morning to qualify.

"What time?" she said.

"We gotta be out there at nine."

"Okay, where we going?"

"Farmer Sportsman Club out by Canter's Cave. Meet me at my house at eight-thirty. I got your holster and mags. I'll drop them off at your house in a little bit so you can break in the holster a little bit today so it won't be so stiff."

"I'll probably be out in the barn."

"Okay," he said and hung up. She didn't sound too friendly.

The phone rang before he left the house. It was his boss. "They want you up here on Wednesday for an investigative hearing on the deal where you helped the highway patrol."

"What time?" he asked.

"Ten. I got you a lawyer. I gave him your statement and we got all the stuff the patrol did on their investigation and he has it, too."

"Okay, I'll see you Wednesday."

Jon went to the SO and Dave said that they had the boyfriend in Jail on the indictment on the truck stop fire. He wanted to talk to him before he was arraigned in court. The guy lawyered up and wouldn't talk to them. "Well, maybe the prosecutor can work out a deal with his attorney to get him to turn on his girlfriend," Dave said.

"I hope so or we won't be able to get the woman who was behind the whole thing and ripped off the insurance company," Jon said.

"He may decide to take the rap for her."

"Yeah, he could. Does he have a record?"

"None at all."

"That means he might get probation," Jon said.

"All he would have is a felony conviction and he wouldn't lose his woman."

"Yep."

On the way out to the range on Tuesday, Liz said very little. They both shot at the same time. She shot faster than he as she had a semi-automatic with seven-round mags. He had his six-shot revolver with speed loaders. It took two hours, and Liz did good. As they were leaving Jon asked her if she had ever been to Canters Cave which is a Four H Camp. "No," she said.

"You want to go look around, there's some nice caves?" he asked her.

"Okay, thanks for helping me learn to shoot and bringing me up here today."

"You're welcome."

There was no one at the camp this time of year. They parked at the gate and walked back in. They explored some of the caves and then sat on a picnic table.

"You still upset from Saturday night?" he asked her.

"Kinda."

"You mad at me?" he asked.

"No, not anymore. I can't stay mad at you. I like you. I want to have a relationship with you, but obviously, you're with Rita."

"We can be friends," he said.

"I guess that will have to do then, for now," she answered.

"We better head back to town. It is going to rain."

When they got back to his house, Rita's car was parked in front of the house. "Looks like you have company Jon," Liz said.

"Rita stopped by," he said.

"I'll get going," Liz said, "I don't want to be in the way." She got out of the car and slammed the door and got in her truck and drove away.

That night he and Rita took a walk around town. Her doctor's appointment went well. They talked about their upcoming backpack trip to the mountains. She wasn't jealous of Liz at all. He told her that they had been to the range and she asked no questions.

They went to bed after watching *Dallas*. "I start the pill tomorrow," Rita said as she pressed a condom into his hand. They made love very passionately, more so than they ever had before. In the middle of the night, she gave him another condom after arousing him from his sleep. He had to get up early and drive to Reynoldsburg.

"For the record," the Deputy Director of the Department of Commerce said as the hearing began, "would you please state your name and occupation?" He looked at Jon.

"Jon Hamer, Investigator for the State Fire Marshal."

"How long have you been employed in this position?"

"Fourteen months."

"Before being so employed, how were you employed?" the DD said.

"Seven years as a Deputy Sheriff and one year as a City Police Officer."

"What training have you received in these jobs?"

"Associate degree in Police Science at Hocking College, Basic Police Academy at Buckeye Hills Career Center, all levels of the Arson Investigator Training Class at the Ohio Fire Academy."

"On September 25, 1981, would you describe the event that you were involved in that is the reason for this hearing?" The DD stated.

"I heard a call on my police radio of a Highway Patrolman needing help on State Route 93 just south of Camba Road in Jackson County. I was just two miles from that location, so I responded to the call in my state issued car. On the way, I learned that I was the closest unit to help." He went on to describe everything that happened.

"Are you aware that most law enforcement agencies have a policy that prohibits warning shots to be fired?"

"Yes," Jon stated.

"I have no further questions at this time. Your counsel may now ask you questions," the DD said.

Jon had spent an hour with the attorney that Joe had gotten for him. He seemed to know what he was doing.

"Jon, are you aware of any firearms policy or SOP in place in the Investigation Bureau?" his attorney asked.

"No," Jon answered.

"Were you given any firearms training by the SFM when you were hired?"

"No."

"What were you told about helping other law enforcement officers?"

"I was told if an officer needed help and I was in a position to help that I was to go help."

"If you would not have fired this warning shot, do you think that the suspects would have complied to a verbal command by you?"

"I did give them a verbal command, and they did not comply."

"Do you think you would have been justified in shooting one or both suspects instead of firing a warning shot?" the attorney asked him.

"Yes," he answered.

"Why did you not shoot one or both of them?"

"I really don't want to kill anyone so I gave them another chance to comply by firing the warning shot. It worked, and they are still alive and the patrolman is still alive."

"You told us that there was nothing behind the suspects that your shot could harm. Are you quite sure of that?"

"Yes. I did not see anything, and I know that place well. I have driven by it a thousand times."

"No further questions, Mr. Deputy Director," his attorney stated.

"Do you have any witnesses to call, sir?"

"Yes, I would call Joe Powell, Assistant Chief of the Investigation Bureau." The DD swore in Joe.

"Chief," his attorney said, "does the investigation bureau have any firearms policy or SOP?"

"No."

"Do you know why they do not?"

"When I was hired four years ago, myself and the bureau chief submitted in writing a request to the Fire Marshal to create a policy. I have here in my hand the reply in writing from the Director of Commerce stating that this would have to be done by the departments legal counsel and that at the time they were too busy."

"Have you made other inquiries about this?"

"Yes, I have here two more inquiries, the latest been one year ago, in which I inquired of the Fire Marshal about the policy and the reply in writing that it was in the hands of legal counsel."

"Mr. Powell, prior to your employment here you were employed by the Columbus Fire Department, is that correct.?"

"Yes, for thirty years."

"Did they have a firearms policy in writing for their departments fire and arson investigators?"

"Yes, they did."

"No further questions."

"Do you have any statement to make, sir?" the DD said to his attorney.

"Yes. The gist of this hearing appears to be the firing of the warning shot. In the absence of any policy about this subject, then, this investigator cannot be brought up on charges for something that there is no policy against. This is like charging a person with a crime in which there is no law on record making the act a crime. I ask that the charge be dismissed against this man who at great personal risk saved the life of a Highway Patrolman. Thank you."

"This concludes this hearing. I will consider the issues and render a decision in writing to the investigator and his counsel within fourteen working days," the DD said.

CHAPTER 20

Jon liked his Jeep Cherokee. It was red. It had a six-cylinder engine. The front seat had bucket seats, and they had put a console in it with his fire and police radio and a walkie talkie in a charger. He also had a siren and a blue light that he could put on the dash. By the time he got his gear changed to the Jeep and drove back to Jackson, the work day was over with.

He went out and walked all over town for two hours and ended up at the Corner Bar, where he got a beer and two veal sandwiches. When he got home, he went to bed early. At nine o'clock, the phone rang. It was the Marietta PD. The Fire Department wanted him on a fire on the west side of town. He told them he would be there in an hour and a half. It was exactly eighty-five miles from the Jackson County Courthouse to the Washington County Courthouse in Marietta. Jon could drive seventy miles an hour on the four-lane portion of the Appalachian Highway. The two-lane section between Athens and Coolville he would have to slow down to fifty-five or sixty.

When he got to the fire scene, he found that there was still one fire truck on the scene. He found Aaron Jensen, the inspector, waiting on him. It looked like a big, two-story, wood-frame house. There was no visible fire damage from the outside unless it was in the rear. "What ya got tonight Aaron?" Jon asked.

"Well, we have two separate fires: one in the attic and one in the basement. We also got the cap on the chimney that was blown off, and it went through the window of the house on the lower side and landed on a stair landing. We have three witnesses, neighbors, in those houses there." He pointed to three separate houses. "They each heard an explosion and came out on their porches about the same time and looked around. It was dark. About 7:00 P.M. After a couple of minutes, they saw a man coming out the front door and across the porch. One of the witnesses, the one up there on the corner," he pointed to the house on the corner, "yelled at the guy and called him by name and asked him what the big explosion was and the guy said he didn't hear an explosion and got in his van and left."

"The witness knew him," Jon asked.

"All three witnesses knew him. He owns the building. They also said he was carrying what looked like a black garbage bag."

"Was anyone home?"

"Not that we know of. There are three apartments, two down and one up. Only one of the first-floor apartments was occupied and the lady is at work over town. She's a dispatcher at the cab stand. She came over and then went back to work. "

"Where did the witnesses see the fire at?"

"They didn't see any fire when they heard the explosion and saw the guy. About fifteen minutes later the guy in the house on the corner came out on his porch and saw a glow in the attic window."

"Let's look at the fire," Jon said.

Aaron took him around back and downstairs into the basement. There was a couch in the basement that was burned about halfway up. There was also a gas hot water heater in the small basement room. He was taking photos as he looked things over.

They then went to the second-floor apartment and up into the attic where there had been some fire on the floor. It looked like a flammable liquid as there was nothing else in the attic to burn. "There is something in the second-floor bathroom I want you to see," Aaron said. They went down the stairs to the second floor and into the bathroom. Aaron pointed to a gas space heater sitting there that had apparently been pulled out away from the wall and the vent pipe removed. The pipe was laying on the floor. "This is how we found this. We can't figure out the explosion that blew off the chimney cap. The cap is big and heavy. I'll show it to you when we go back outside."

"Okay," Jon said, "the first thing I got to do is take samples from the attic floor and the couch in the basement and then we'll try to figure out the explosion. Was the gas on?"

"Yes, we shut it off," Aaron said.

"Has the owner been around since you got here?" Jon asked.

"No."

Jon got his evidence collecting stuff and took samples of the attic floor boards and the material on the couch in the basement. Neither fire was very bad. He looked at the chimney cap that they had removed from the neighbor's house. It was big and heavy. He took photos of it and the broken window of the neighbor's house. As he was placing the evidence in his car a big man approached him. "I own this house," he said. "What happened?"

"It caught on fire." Jon said. "Could you sit in the front seat of my car so I can get some information for my report?"

He got the basic info that he needed: owner, occupant, insurance etc.

"The fire happened at 7:00 P.M. Where were you at?"

"I was at work. I am a janitor at an office over town," the big man said.

"Were you here at this house this evening?"

"I got a phone call at about six thirty from someone who didn't tell me their name and they said there was a gas leak at the house so I drove over in my van and went inside the empty first floor apartment and did not smell anything so I went back to work."

"Did you talk to anyone while you were here?" Jon asked him.

"No, I did not."

"Did you hear an explosion?"

"No, I did not."

"Would you give me consent to search your van?" Jon asked him.

He read him the consent form and the man signed it. Jon opened the back of the van and looked around inside of it. It had nice carpet on the floor and nice seats. He got down and sniffed the carpet. About two feet from the back door, he smelled gasoline on the carpet. He got his knife out and cut a piece of the carpet up and smelled it again. Gasoline. "What are you doin' to my carpet?" the guy said to him.

"I'm takin' a piece for evidence," Jon said.

"You're ruinin' my van," he said.

"Too late; you done gave me consent," Jon said.

"Okay, you can go now, sir," he told the owner.

"Let's go inside and see if we can figure out this explosion," he told Aaron. They went in the basement, and he looked at the base of the chimney. The hot water heater was vented into it. It ran on natural gas. There was no cleanout in the chimney so he took a hammer and a chisel and removed a couple of bricks from the chimney. He reached back inside and grabbed a hand full of dirt and pulled it out and smelled it and held it to Aaron's nose.

"Gasoline," Aaron said. He bagged the dirt for evidence.

"I think he took that pipe out in the upstairs bathroom and poured gasoline down the chimney. He lit the other two fires, but I don't know in what order he did these things. The hot water tank in the basement probably lit off the gasoline in the chimney and that blew the cap off." He told Aaron what the guy had said about getting the call about the gas leak and coming over and going in the house. "I think he intended for it to look like a natural gas explosion," Jon told Aaron.

"Let's go look at the occupied apartment on the first floor," Jon said.

"Look at that," Aaron said as they went into a bedroom. He pointed to the wall. There had been a mortar plug in the chimney and it was blown out. There were pieces of mortar on the bed and they found the plug on the other side of the bed where it had hit the opposite wall. "No wonder it blew that chimney cap off."

It was now four in the morning. "We got more work to do, not here at the house. Did you get witness statements from the folks that saw him leave the house?" Jon asked Aaron.

"Yes."

"We didn't find any jug or anything that he carried the gasoline in, so he probably had a gas can in the plastic garbage bag the witnesses saw him carrying. We need to go to his place of employment and look for it. Let's get some sleep first and get started about ten in the morning."

"I'll meet you at the fire station at ten," Aaron said.

Jon went to the Holiday Inn and got him a room.

Jon Hamer and Aaron Jensen went to the office where their suspect worked as an evening janitor. They learned that he worked alone after they closed at 5:00 P.M. and had a key. They asked if they could look around the office, which was just three rooms on the first floor. They found nothing. As they were getting ready to leave Aaron said," Let's go back in the alley and check the trash."

"That's a good idea," Jon said.

Aaron took the lid off the trash can, and on top was a black plastic garbage bag. He opened it, and the smell of gasoline was strong. Inside of the bag were four, one-allon bleach bottles that smelled of gasoline.

"We hit the jackpot here," Jon said. "I'm glad you thought of this Aaron."

Jon put rubber gloves on and carefully put his initials and the date on each jug and sealed them tight. "I'll take these to the labs to be checked for latent prints and verify the gasoline," he told Aaron.

"Now we go to the insurance agent and see what we can find," Jon said.

The agent knew Aaron and was very helpful. The house was over-insured and for replacement cost, meaning if it was destroyed the insurance company would pay what it cost to replace it, but only if it was rebuilt. If it was not rebuilt, they would only pay actual cash value. They would have to pay the mortgage off also.

"Let's go back to the station so I can type out a subpoena for the bank," Jon said.

Jon and Aaron walked down the street from the fire station to a large, three-story bank building and went inside and introduced themselves. They were soon shown into an office of a gentleman, who was a vice president of the bank. Aaron knew the banker and introduced him to Jon.

"I'm very familiar with this account," the banker said. "We just filed fore-closure proceedings, and I can give you a copy of that. He is behind nine months in payments."

Jon gave the VP the subpoena and explained that it was just a formality to protect them both under the Privacy Act.

"Let's go back to the fire scene and walk through and see if we missed any-thing," Jon said as they left the bank. "I want to get some outside pictures in day light, also."

They walked through the house and looked around again. The lady who lived in the one apartment was there. She told him that a friend of hers was in her apartment at the time of the fire and got scared and took off. She gave them his name and told were to find him.

"Are you Bill Green?" Jon asked the man sitting at the bar stool in the little beer joint in the one hundred block of Front Street.

"Yeah, who are you?" Bill said.

"We're fire investigators. We heard you were at the house on the west side last night when it caught fire. Can you tell us about it?"

"Yeah, yeah, I was drunk, and I went over there and Marge wasn't home, so I just went in and laid down on the bed and went to sleep. I don't know when this happened, but I heard a loud noise and I woke up and fire shot out of the wall and went right over the bed about a foot above me and then it just sucked itself back in the wall. Man, I was scared and I just got up and went out the door and took off running and went down on Maple Street to a bar and got me another drink."

"Did you see anyone around when you left the house?" Aaron asked.

"No."

"Did you see any fire anywhere else other than coming out of the wall?"

"No, it scared the shit out of me."

As they walked down Front Street Aaron started laughing. "I bet that did scare the shit out of that guy."

"Yeah, and it makes us a better case of aggravated arson with someone actually in the house. That guy will be a good witness if he's sober when he takes the stand."

They went back to the fire station. "I'm going to use your typewriter and type my report up now, so you'll have a copy to take to the prosecutor. Can you get your police involved and have them bring this guy in and try to get a confession out of him?"

"I'll see what I can do," Aaron said.

"Regardless of whether he confesses or not, we got a good case on him. Get statements from all your firefighters that were there that night."

"They already made out their statements. They found the two separate fires and that is documented in their statements. "

"Tomorrow I am going to take the evidence to the Arson Lab. You should take your reports to the prosecutor and ask him to take the case to the Grand Jury," Jon told Aaron. "There's no need to wait for the lab test results. We have three witnesses. We smelled the gasoline. If they find his prints on the jugs that will be good, but we can do all right without them."

On Friday, Jon left Marietta and drove up Interstate 77 and down I-70 to Reynoldsburg and dropped off his evidence at the Lab. He got home at 5:00 P.M. He hoped for a quiet weekend. This was a pretty good case in Marietta. It was not often that you had witnesses to the crime of arson. It was usually done under cover of darkness. This guy just did it a little too early in the evening when people where still up.

On Saturday, Jon called Rita and asked her to bring her backpacking things over and they would start packing for their Thanksgiving Weekend trip. She knew what all to bring. She had been doing this for several years and they had been on about four short overnight trips together. They would not take a tent because the area they were going in had three-sided wooden backpack shelters about every three or four miles. He had freeze dried food that he always kept around for these trips. They went to the grocery and got some other things that they would need. So far, the weather forecast for the mountains was not predicting any snow and an overnight low of twenty degrees.

"You want to do something different tonight Jon instead of going dancing?" Rita asked.

"We could. What you want to do?" he replied.

"Let's go roller skating."

"Okay, but let's go out to dinner first."

"I'll go home and change clothes after we're done packing."

"And I'll pick you up at your house."

"That sounds like a real date."

"It is a real date."

They went to Kentucky Fried Chicken to eat and then to the roller rink and skated for three hours. He fell down four times. Rita didn't fall down. She was a good skater. They had done this once before and he remembered how good she was. She could skate backwards, something that he could not do.

After they left the roller rink, Rita asked," Can I spend the night with you tonight?"

"Sure," he answered.

"I left some good clothes in your closet. We could go to Mass in the morning."

"Okay. I'd like that."

Their lovemaking that night was more passionate than ever. They couldn't get enough of each other. They repeated themselves again at six in the morning. Doggone, he thought to himself. All these years we been hanging out together and we been missing out on the best part. On the other hand, they became very good friends before they became lovers. Maybe that was what made it so good.

After Mass, they went out to Lake Katherine and took a hike. Then they went back to his place and took a nap. "You want to get married yet?" Jon asked her as they lay in bed together, naked and breathing heavily after making love again.

"Why are you asking me that?"

"Just checking. Want you to know that I still feel the same as I did when you were pregnant."

"That's sweet of you, but no not now."

"I'm glad we've taken our relationship to a higher level," Jon said.

On Monday, Jon got called on a fire down in Lawrence County. It was a house fire. No one was hurt. The fire chief thought that there were two points of origin. Usually two points of origin means the fire was set because accidental fires don't usually start in two separate places. Arsonists often set fires in two or more places to try to burn the place down. Jon was quite sure that what happened in this fire was that it started in a trash can in the kitchen and the fire rolled across the living room ceiling and caught a wreath made out of grapevines on fire that hung on the wall above a couch. The wreath dropped on the couch and caught it on fire making it look like the couch was also a point of origin. Jon thought that it was just as important to keep an innocent person from being accused of arson as it was to catch someone who set a fire.

Monday, after noon, Jon got a call from Aaron at Marietta who said that they were having Grand Jury on Tuesday and they were going to squeeze in the arson case. There would be a subpoena waiting on him in the clerk's office at the courthouse. The case was scheduled for three thirty in the afternoon.

On Tuesday morning, Jon got an unexpected visit from Liz when he answered the door bell as he was getting ready to go to work. She had apparently just gotten off work as she had her nursing clothes on. "Hi Liz," he said when he answered the door.

"Hi Jon, can I come in?" she asked.

"Sure," he said as he was finishing buttoning his shirt.

"I just thought I'd stop and visit. Haven't seen you for a while."

"It's good to see you," he said.

"Grampa just got appointed acting Coroner in Vinton County. Their coroner resigned and no one wants the job. He's giving me seventy five percent of his pay and making me the acting coroner's investigator."

"Pretty soon you'll be investigator for all the coroners in these parts."

"The week after Thanksgiving, I'm going to a Homicide Seminar in Columbus. Grampa's sending me. I'm taking a weeks' vacation from the hospital."

"Did you go to the disco Saturday?" he asked her.

"Yes. Had a good time. Amy wasn't there. I'd say she was off with that doctor from Gallipolis somewhere. Karen apologized to me for what happened that night; so did Doctor John."

"That's good."

"And I got sworn in as a special deputy sheriff, and the sheriff wants me to work in plain clothes helping Dave especially on cases in which women are the victims of violent crime. He's going to send me to a weeklong seminar on sex offenses. I'm going to run out of vacation and won't be able to go to the beach next summer."

"You're fitting right into law enforcement."

"My mom's afraid I'm going to quit nursing and be a cop. After I get through my basic police training next winter, I might just do that."

Jon went in the bedroom and got a tie and came out and tied it. "I've to go to court in Marietta this afternoon," he told Liz.

"Well, I better go home and brush my horses," Liz said as she got up and left.

Jon stopped at the post office and got his mail. In the envelope from the SFM office was a flyer on a homicide seminar in Columbus with a note written on it from his boss: *Please plan to attend this seminar*. He looked at the dates. It was the week after Thanksgiving. There of course could not be two homicide seminars in Columbus going on at the same time. Well, he thought, I guess I know who I'll be sitting with.

The Grand Jury in Marietta didn't take long, but they were an hour behind schedule. It was he and Aaron and one of the persons who saw the guy come out of the house that testified. He was back home by seven that evening. He called Rita and asked her if she wanted to come over and watch *Dallas*. She said she would pick up a pizza on her way over.

"Next Thursday morning, we leave for the mountains." Jon told Rita as they ate pizza in the living room.

"I know. I can hardly wait. Is the weather forecast still good?"

"Yep. No snow and a low of twenty at night. Unseasonably warm for this time of year down there."

"Are you going to fish any?"

"Takin' my pole. Some fresh trout would taste good. Just got to be careful I don't fall in the water. Be pretty cold."

"I have to work tonight. Wish I didn't. I'd like to spend the night with you."

"Come over when you get off work. I'd like to sleep in tomorrow. I got to take some comp time off," Jon told her.

"Okay, that sounds fun. You don't mind me waking you up in the morning, do you?"

"Depends on why you're waking me up," he said, smiling.

On Thursday morning, Jon and Rita left at eight for their drive to the mountains. The weather was nice, and it took them five hours to get to their destination atop a mountain east of the town of Richwood. The sky was clear. They parked at the trail head and put on their backpacks and hiked down the trail. It was actually a forest service road that was closed to vehicles. Bikes and horses were allowed. This time of year, it got little use. There was only one other vehicle parked at the trailhead.

They walked three miles before coming down along the South Fork of the Cranberry River. They passed the first camp shelter and continued for another two miles to the second shelter. It was vacant. It set at the forks of the North and South Forks of the Cranberry River. The river level was good and you could hear the water distinctly from the camp shelter. By the time they got their packs unloaded and their beds made in the shelter, it was almost dark. They built a fire in the fire ring in front of the open shelter and fixed their supper. It was nice to sit there in front of the fire and listen to the water in the river.

They slept in the next morning because it was cold and they didn't want to get out of their warm sleeping bags. They did not have bags that were compatible and would zip together. There was something about the smell of bacon frying on an open fire out in the woods like this. Jon fished for two hours and caught two nice trout that they would fry for supper. They had brought potatoes to fry also and along with freeze dried corn in butter it made for a nice supper.

They spent all day Saturday hiking different trails, making a loop hike of about eight miles. They found some really nice water falls on creeks that tumbled down off the mountain into the river.

That evening it started to snow as they were finishing their supper. Not heavy snow. The shelter had an overhang on it so that they could sit in front of the campfire and not get wet. It quit snowing about ten o'clock with about an inch on the ground. The sky cleared and the full moon came out and it was really pretty.

"This is really pretty," Rita said as they lay in their sleeping bags and looked at the snow under the full moon.

"Yes, it is," Jon agreed. They fell asleep while holding gloved hands.

The snow melted off as they hiked out on Sunday morning. It warmed up so much that they had to take their parkas off as they were starting to sweat.

Jon arrived at the huge hotel on the Eastside of Columbus at eight on Monday morning for the Homicide Seminar that he was attending. He got his room and headed to the big conference center to register. He looked around for Liz, but did not see her so he found himself a seat. About five minutes before the event started, Liz sat down beside him. "I should have come up last night instead of driving up this morning. I didn't leave early enough," she said.

"You could have stayed at your parents in Chillicothe and drove back and forth every day," he said.

"I thought you were going to show me the town." She winked at him.

"I like to spend my time going to hardware and sporting goods stores when I am out of town overnight. It keeps me out of trouble, but can be just as expensive as partying. Maybe we can find a good tack shop that would interest you," he told her.

"What room you in?" she asked.

He showed her his key: 204.

She showed him her key: 206.

"I wonder if we have a connecting door?" she said.

"I definitely have to go to a hardware store. Get a hammer and some nails and nail the door shut." He laughed.

CHAPTER 21

Class was over at four thirty. "I'm taking you out to eat this evening. Be ready to go by six. We're going down to German Village," Liz told him as they left the seminar room.

"Can we stop at a hardware store afterwards?" Jon asked her.

"There won't be any open at that hour."

"Okay, I'll be ready."

Jon went to his room and set the alarm for five fifty and went to sleep. When Liz knocked on his door, he was ready to go. "I'm driving," she said.

"How come?" he asked.

"Because you'll probably want to drink," she said as they walked out to the parking lot and got in her truck.

"I'm glad you cleaned the hay out of the bed," he said. "I wouldn't want people to think we were a couple of farmers come to experience the city life."

"I am a farmer. Actually, I didn't clean it out. It blew out on the way up here."

He noticed that she was dressed in a Western skirt and blouse and wore nice cowboy boots.

"If you're planning on going square dancing let me tell you that I don't know how to."

"I thought we'd go to one of those western places that has a mechanical bull and you could ride it," Liz said.

They ate sausage and German potato salad. They each had a cream puff for desert. "How'd you learn your away around the big city so well? I've been down here a couple of times, but I couldn't find my way like you did."

"When I was at Hocking once a month, some friends and I would come up here to eat out and dance," she said.

"You didn't go to Athens to party?" he said, referring to all the bars in downtown Athens that caused Ohio University to be called the number one party college in the nation.

"No, we didn't like that crowd. Did you?"

"No, never been to a bar in Athens. We went out to Club Thirty-Three. It was more to our liking."

"I was there once. I liked it."

They left German Village and Liz drove east on Main Street. She pulled into a big parking lot that was about half full of cars.

"What's this?" he asked her.

"A place to dance. They have a mechanical bull," she said.

"Oh, I never seen one of those things."

"You'll like riding it."

They went inside. The place was about half full, probably because it was Monday. He saw the bull in the center of the big dance hall. There was a band on stage playing. They got a table and ordered. He got a Miller Lite, his third for the evening. She got pop as usual. Liz got up and went to the bull and handed the guy some money and got on. It didn't throw her.

"Now it's your turn," she said and led him down to the bull and handed the guy some money.

"I don't know about this," he said. He got on and the thing started up slowly but speeded up. It threw him off.

They went back to their table. "Did you tell that guy to crank the thing up?" he accused her.

"No, but I told him you were an experienced rider." She laughed. "Come on, let's dance."

They danced several fast songs. He hadn't danced to a live band for several years. They didn't slow dance. Jon didn't ask her to and she didn't ask him to. They had fun. They left about eleven and drove back to the motel.

"Did you have a good time?" Liz asked him.

"Yes, very much," he said.

"You want to do this every night this week?"

"I don't know about every night. I don't want to fall asleep in class. We gotta be in there at eight."

The next morning, Jon could hardly get out of bed. His back was messed up. He had a hard time getting dressed. He called Liz. "I'll be right there," she said.

He unlocked the door, so she could get in his room. She handed him a bottle of aspirin. "Take two of these three times a day." She looked at her watch. "Take off your shirt, and I'll make an ice pack. You have time before class." She took his ice bucket and went to find ice.

After lunch, they came back to his room, and Liz made up another ice pack and put it on his lower back until it was time for class to start again.

That evening they had dinner in his room and she gave him a deep muscle massage of his lower back.

"This was all my fault," Liz said. "I shouldn't have put you on that thing."

"No, I shouldn't have gotten on it."

"Do you mind if I go down to the lounge here in the motel? They have disco. I'll get you plenty of ice and you can put it on your back for fifteen minutes every hour."

"No. Go ahead. No need for you to sit around and do nothing," he told her. They had the room doors open between their rooms. She went and changed clothes and came back with a bucket of ice and told him she would check on him later.

About ten-thirty, Liz came back. "How you doing?" she asked him.

"I got up to go to the bathroom a couple of times," he said.

"You just need a few days of bed rest. The hard part is sitting in class all day."

"Yeah, I know. Did you have fun tonight?"

"Yes, I sat with some people from the seminar. We danced."

"I'm jealous. I laid in bed all night and you partied." He smiled.

"I'm going to bed. Did you take your aspirin?"

"No, not yet."

She brought him a glass of water and opened the aspirin and gave him two.

"Thank you, nurse; you may now retire to your quarters," he said.

"Good night."

Jon felt better when he awoke in the morning. Liz came in his room wearing a robe and gave him a glass of water and two aspirins. "I'm going after some more ice. You get up and move around and see if you are any better."

"Yes, nurse," he said. By the time she was back, he had his pants on and found that he could move better than the day before.

"Lay on your stomach, so I can put this ice pack on," she said.

"Yes, nurse."

"You want to get better or not?"

"No, I like lying in bed all evening while you go out and have fun."

"Actually, I met this nice coroner investigator from down around Cincinnati. We had a good time dancing."

"If you had a boyfriend back home, I would tell on you."

"He wants to have dinner together this evening. I told him I would let him know at lunch."

"Well do it, take the young man to the Bull Ridin' place, too."

"He's not really a young man. He's older than you."

"I'm only twenty-seven."

"He's probably thirty-five," she said.

"You know, I never did ask you how old you are Nurse Liz."

"I will be twenty-three on my next birthday." She took the ice pack off and worked her knuckles into his tight muscles.

"That hurts," he said.

"Your back muscles are tight. You really need some muscle relaxer pills."

"And you don't have any in your kit?"

"You have to have a prescription to get them."

"All right. That's enough. Let's go get breakfast."

It was nine in the evening. Jon was lying in bed on an ice pack. He heard Liz come in next door. She came into his room. "You doing any better?" she said.

"I think so. I'll be ready to visit a hardware store tomorrow evening. How was your date?"

"All right, till we went dancing."

"I suppose you put him on the bull."

"No, he asked me if I minded that he was married."

"And did you?" he asked her.

"Of course, I minded. I told him to bring me back to the motel."

"Did he have a ring on?"

"No. I just don't do any good with guys."

"You'll find the right guy. What's the hurry anyway? You're young."

"I'm not wanting to get married. I just want a steady guy to go with. A guy like you."

"I don't know what to say. Go get us some more ice and a couple cans of pop, and we'll watch a movie together."

She came back with pop, ice, and chips. He was flipping through the channels. "Have you seen *Poseidon Adventure?*" he asked her.

"Once, when it came out."

"It starts in twenty minutes."

"Okay, I'm going to take a shower."

She came back in and laid down on the other bed in his room as the movie was starting. She had on a white robe. He wondered what was on beneath it, if anything. He remembered the night at her place when she wanted to have sex. Gosh, this could be dangerous, he thought.

When he woke up, Jon looked at the clock. It was one in the morning. He looked over and Liz was asleep on the other bed. He got up and went into her room and got the blanket off her bed and went and covered her up and turned the T.V. off and went back to sleep.

In the morning, Jon's back was much better. He woke up Liz after he had taken a shower and ordered breakfast brought to the room.

"Thanks for letting me sleep with you," Liz said.

"You didn't sleep with me," he said.

"I suppose that's the closest I'll ever get to it."

He shook his head. "My back is much better. If we would have had sex, it would have set me back two days."

"You think so?" she smiled.

"I think so. How long has it been since you had any?"

"That's not a nice question to ask a lady," she said.

"Why not? We don't seem to have any secrets, do we?"

"It's none of your business anyways."

"I know. I shouldn't have said that."

"We got one more night in this place," Jon said to Liz as they took their seats in the seminar after lunch.

"They have a DJ in the lounge here tonight. You feel like going?"

"I can't dance, but I'll chaperone you," he said as he looked at the schedule for the day. "You better pay attention to this next speaker. Say's here he's the coroner down at Cincinnati."

They had supper in the restaurant at the motel and then went outside and walked a couple of laps around the parking lot to loosen up Jon's back. They went to the lounge at nine when they heard the music starting to play. There wasn't a single person at this seminar that Jon knew. Usually at these sorts of things, there were a few people from the southeastern part of the state. He had been talking to a guy who was a Homicide Detective in Toledo. He came in with a very attractive lady and asked if they could sit with he and Liz. "This is my wife, June; she drove down this afternoon to spend the night," he said as he introduced himself to Liz and Jon.

"Pleased to meet you. I'm Jon, and this is my friend, Liz. We're from Jackson County. Liz is the coroner's investigator, and I'm a fire investigator."

"I work in the county coroner's office as a forensic chemist," June said, "That's how Ed and I met ten years ago."

"How interesting," Liz said. "My grandpa is the coroner. He has been for over forty years. No one else wants the job, and he's getting old so he hired me to be his investigator."

"That's neat," Ed said. "I bet things are a lot different in the smaller counties."

"Yes, we don't do our autopsies. We send them to Franklin County," Liz told them.

"How long have you been doing this, Liz?" June asked.

"About four months. I'm a nurse at the local hospital. Jon here has been teaching me about investigating. We're working on a murder case right now that was covered up with an Arson."

"Any arrest yet?" Ed asked.

Liz looked at Jon and he nodded for her to explain. "We arrested one of two brothers who did it. We're hoping that he will agree to testify against his brother instead of standing trial for the death penalty."

"How was the victim killed?" Ed asked.

"Hit in the head with a blunt instrument. Jon found it later," Liz said.

"It was a tire tool. I found the truck they drove. It had been in a wreck and was in a junkyard. took the tire tool to BCI and they found blood the same type as the lady victims blood," Jon said.

"Any fingerprints?" June asked.

"Not on the tire tool. But on beer cans and the dash of the truck from both suspects," Jon replied.

"Sounds like good, old fashioned police work. Hittin' the streets and talking to people," Ed said.

"We call it beatin' the bushes down in Appalachia," Jon said, laughing.

"Do you folks like to dance?" June asked.

"We do, but Jon's back is out on him. He got on a mechanical bull Monday night and it threw him off," Liz told them.

"You put me on that thing," Jon said, looking at Liz.

"Come on, Liz, you can fast dance with us," June said, and the three of them took to the dance floor.

Ed told them about a couple of cases that he had worked on in Toledo. Their fire department had their own Fire Marshal's office and did their own investigations. The police department helped them especially on homicides.

"Okay, Liz," Jon said, "I think I can slow dance." He got up and led her to the dance floor. "Are you enjoying the evening?" he asked her.

"Yes. Very much. I'm glad you decided to dance with me."

"Are you going to the disco this Saturday?" he asked her.

"I think I will. Are you?"

"Probably."

"Will you dance with me?"

"Probably."

"What do you mean, probably?"

"Of course, you know that I will," he answered.

They called it a night at eleven. They would be on their way home by three tomorrow afternoon.

He watched the eleven o'clock news on channel ten. The door between their rooms was still open. He could hear the shower running in Liz's room. She came in his room wearing a night shirt that stopped just above her knees and had a horse on the front of it. She sat down and started brushing her long, dark, and wet hair.

"Liz," he said to her, "are you trying to tempt me?"

"No."

"Well, you are. Sitting there in that horse shirt with your legs crossed and combing your hair."

"I'm sorry," she said," I didn't know you thought I was that sexy."

"Yes, I certainly do, and there is only so much a man can take."

"Do you want me to go back to my room?"

"No," he said and threw her a pillow. "Just put this on your lap to cover your legs."

"Why, Fire Marshal Jon, that is the best compliment you have ever paid me."

"I'm just going to have to help you find a boyfriend."

"No blind dates," she said, still brushing her hair. "You know I thought we had something going between us after we first met. That night you took me out to Lake Katherine. By the way, we never have went canoeing. The walks we took."

"I am very attracted to you, Liz. From the first time I saw you that Sunday morning. But then this thing happened with Rita. And, yes, you got it figured out right. What I'm going to tell you I want you to promise not to tell Rita or anyone else."

"I promise."

"I'm the one that got Rita knocked up. It was a one-night thing. We went to the disco together, and she drove me home. I had too much to drink. I invited her inside, and it just happened. Three weeks later, she told me she was pregnant. I knew I had to do the right thing by her and the baby. I asked her to marry me, and she refused. So, we started spending more time together and became closer to each other."

"Do you love her?" she asked.

"No, and she doesn't love me, but I believe that we would have grown to love each other like a lot of other people who get caught in the same circumstances."

"I commend you for wanting to take responsibility for her and the baby."

"It was the right thing to do."

"I've not told anyone what I thought was going on, and I haven't told anyone that Rita was pregnant."

"I know you haven't. You're a good person. You don't gossip."

"So, is there still a chance for us?"

"I don't know. Right now, we can be friends. Rita is not a jealous kind of person."

"I'll take what I can get," she said. "Are you going to tell Rita that we hung out together up here this week?"

"Yes. She won't mind."

She got up and walked over to the bed and gave him a light kiss on the lips." I'm going to bed. See you in the morning. I'm glad we had this talk."

"Good night," he said. "Sleep well."

On Saturday morning, Jon took a walk around town and stopped at the diner on Broadway for breakfast. He walked up by the courthouse and saw Dave's car parked behind the jail, so he went in to see him. He was sitting in the kitchen, eating a biscuit and drinking orange juice." You have a nice vacation up there in the big city, Jonny?" Dave asked.

"Yeah. It was a good school."

"You're walkin' kind of stiff. Liz told me she was going, too. I suppose she wore you out."

"No, she put me on one of those mechanical bulls and it threw me off and messed up my back for a couple of days."

"Of course, Liz nursed you back to good health."

"Well, she knew what to do."

"The question is: Did you know what to do with her?"

"Now is not the time to get involved with Liz. She is tempting, though."

"We got what we wanted on our murder," Dave said.

"What?" Jon asked.

"Tuesday the Grand Jury meets again. Same jurors so we all don't have to repeat our testimony. Dave Brown is going to tell them what happened."

"What's the deal?"

"He pleads to manslaughter and aggravated robbery. Both first-degree felonies. Gets the max. Ten to twenty-five on both counts. Consecutive sentence."

"Well, that's not bad, considering we didn't stand much of a chance of convicting him anyways."

"Yeah. The victim's family don't like it very well. The prosecutor tried to explain it to them."

"What time Tuesday?"

"Ten o'clock."

"How we going to arrest Pee Wee?"

"I've had my man working on it." Dave said, referring to some informant, someone he gave a break to at one time. "He's staying back out on the ridge with his parents. He don't come out during the daytime at all. Not even to go to the outhouse. Shits in a bucket. At night, a guy by name of Kenny McKowan picks him up in a light blue '67 Chevy Bel Air four-door. Beater kind of car. They drive the back roads and drink and smoke weed. They find someone parked along the road, and they stop and rob them. Take their weed, beer and money. No one has reported it as most of them are underage drinkers, in possession of drugs and don't want to get in trouble."

"They using a weapon?"

"Pee Wee's got a pistol. The other guy sits in the car."

"So, what's the plan?"

"You and me gonna get an old pickup truck from Rangle's Garage and a six pack of Blue Ribbon and go out on the ridge and pull off the road and sit and wait for them to come by, and we'll nab him."

"We gonna have back up?"

"There'll be a marked unit down at Monroe Hollow and Route 140 hidden. We'll have a walkie talkie, but I don't know if it will reach that far. Hope it does."

"When we doin' this?"

"Tuesday night about nine. The word could be out about him going to get indicted. Dave has visitors you know and he could tell them and they could tell Pee Wee."

"When they sentencing Dave?" Jon asked.

"Wednesday morning. I hope we can get him Tuesday night."

"Okay, sounds good. What are we dressin' up like?"

"A couple of timber cutters."

"I don't have a chain saw."

"Don't need one. Bring your shotgun."

"Sounds fun. At least we're not using dirt bikes."

Dave started laughing. A couple years ago, they were having brush fires on Slithering Ridge every afternoon right after the kids got home from school. They found out they were using dirt bikes and setting fires back in the woods. Dave and Jon borrowed a couple of bikes and went out there just before the school buses dropped the kids off. When they heard the dirt bikes take off into the woods, they took off to try to catch them. Jon was going around a curve in a trail and suddenly laid it on its side. He had gotten the foot peg caught in some barbed wire. Dave caught up with them just as they were stopped and setting a fire. He got both of them. They made them ride home to their parents' house, where they called for a truck to come and get the bikes and cited the kids into juvenile court. Hadn't been anymore such fires on the ridge since then.

"Yeah, and I'm goin' to drive the old truck just to be on the safe side."

"Okay. You're the boss. I'll be here Tuesday morning. You going to tell Liz what we're doin'?"

"Yeah. She's coming in here Monday morning, and we're going to talk about how we're going to handle sexual assaults. The Sheriff's adopting a new policy. Liz is going to be helping us. She has a friend out at the hospital that's going to go through the academy next winter too and help us as a special deputy."

"That's probably Karen. She's nice. More your age than Liz is."

"What's that supposed to mean?" Dave said.

"Time for you to find a new woman."

"I got more than I can handle the way it is. See you Tuesday. I got work to do."

"See ya," Jon said as he left and resumed his Saturday morning walk. Jackson was always busy on Saturday mornings. A lot of folks came to town to shop and get groceries and go to the feed mill. He visited with several persons he knew as he walked around the town.

CHAPTER 22

On Tuesday morning before Grand Jury, Dave and Jon met with the prosecutor. The prosecutor explained what was going to happen: "Dave Brown is going to go in and testify to the Grand Jury that he and Pee Wee were drinking that night at their brother Wesley's house. Wesley and his wife had gone to bed, and Pee Wee and Dave decided to go break into the victim's house. They thought that she was blind as their sister had worked for her. They drove up to the trailer, and Pee Wee pried the door open with a tire tool and they went inside and took the T.V. and the sewing machine. They went back in, and Dave got a large pickle jar full of change. The victim came down the hallway and recognized them and called them by name and asked them what they were doing. Pee Wee hit her in the head with the tire tool. She fell on the floor. They went out to the truck, and Pee Wee got a can of gas out of the truck and went back inside and set the fire. They went to Portsmouth and gave the T.V. to Judy Brown. They took the sewing machine down to the Oho River and threw it in. They spent the change on beer and gasoline."

"Makes sense," Dave said.

"Is Dave going to have to testify in the trial of Pee Wee?" Jon asked.

"Yes, that is part of the deal. If he doesn't, we will oppose his parole when he comes up in about eighteen years. We have also reserved the right to charge him with Aggravated Arson and Aggravated Burglary if he doesn't testify. That would add two more ten to twenty-five consecutive sentences to his time."

"Tell us when you're ready for him and we'll go get him and bring him over from the jail," Dave told the prosecutor, referring to their new witness, Dave Brown.

Tuesday evening, Jon and Dave met at the SO. The Grand Jury had indicted Pee Wee Brown for Aggravated Murder with Death Penalty Specs, Agg. Robbery, Agg. Burglary, Agg. Arson and Abuse of a Corpse. They had the warrant. They had an old '63 Chevy pickup truck that was pretty rough-looking. Jess was their backup who would be in a marked car down the road about three miles. Jon had his shotgun.

They drove the old truck out to Slithering Ridge and pulled off the road about a quarter mile down the road from Brown's parents' house and onto a frequently used place where people parked. Jon opened two cans of Blue Ribbon and poured out the beer and threw the empty cans on the ground beside the truck. He thought about sipping on one, but then thought he better not in case they had trouble. Besides it was warm. It came from the evidence room at the SO. It was scheduled for disposal.

They hadn't been sitting there twenty minutes, when a car came down the road toward them. It stopped beside them on the road. It was a light blue, four-door Bel Air. Jon had his window rolled down. Dave said," That's the car."

The guy on the passenger side of the car had his window down and yelled at them. "You guys got any money?"

Jon got out and looked at the guy. It was Pee Wee Brown. "No, but we got some beer." Jon said and reached into the bed of the truck and pulled out his shotgun and jacked a round into the chamber and pointed it at Pee Wee and said: "Both of you put your hands on your heads." He could hear Dave getting out of the truck on the driver's side.

The guy driving the car punched the gas down and the car lurched forward. Jon shot out the right front tire and jacked another round in the gun and shot out the right rear tire. The car swerved to the right and went down over an embankment. Jon put his shotgun inside the truck cab and grabbed his flashlight. He heard Dave calling for backup.

Jon went down over the embankment with his revolver in his right hand, supported by the wrist of his left hand in which he held his Maglite. He got down to the car. It had hit a big tree. He shined his light inside and the driver was slumped over the wheel with blood running down his face. He didn't see Pee Wee. He shined his light in the back seat. He was gone.

"Pee Wee took off," Jon yelled to Dave, who was coming down the bank.

Jon saw leaves that had been disturbed on the other side of the car, indicating the suspect went that way through the woods. He started to follow the trail. He got about fifty feet from the car and heard a sound to his left. He turned coming up with his revolver and flashlight. There was Pee Wee pointing a pistol at him. They both fired. Pee Wee fell. Jon felt a sharp sting in his left side. He thought about firing another round, but Dave was there and went up to Pee Wee and took his pistol and threw it up the hillside. He then cuffed him in back. Pee Wee was moaning. Jon found it difficult to breath so he sat down. Dave came up to him. "You hit?" he said.

"I don't know."

"Lay down," Dave said as he unzipped Jon's coat. He took a knife out of his pocked and cut his shirt.

"Yeah, you're hit. Lay back down."

Dave took a handkerchief out of his pocket and started poking it in Jon's chest. Jon screamed. Dave got on the walkie and called for a squad and more backup. "Them Brown's will all be down here in a minute." He took off his coat and covered Jon with it. "I'm goin' to check the driver and go get your shotgun." He took Jon's handcuffs.

Dave came back a few minutes and said, "The driver is starting to come around. I cuffed both hands to the steering wheel." They could hear a siren. Dave got on the walkie to Jess. "Stand by at our truck. We're down over the hill. FM is hurt as well as both suspects. If anyone other than law enforcement or EMS shows up, don't let them come down here. There may be some people show up to cause us some trouble."

"Okay, where you at?" Jess came back on the radio.

"About a half mile east of Gieke Ridge," Dave told him.

Jon was having a hard time breathing. It hurt to breath. He could see the blue lights of Jess's car. They could hear a couple other vehicles pull up on the road. They heard Jess rack a round in his shotgun and say, "Don't anyone go down over that hill, you hear?"

"You got my boy down there?" a man said.

"Who's your boy?" Jess said.

"Pee Wee Brown." the man said.

"I don't know," Jess told him.

There were more sirens.

"I'm sending two EMT's down," Jess said on the radio.

A man and a woman came down, carrying a bag. "We're from South Webster Fire we heard the call and came out. We're closer than Oak Hill."

Dave told them what he thought happened to Jon. He pointed to Pee Wee. The woman started to work on Jon and put him on oxygen. The man went and checked Pee Wee and came back and said he was dead. "There's a driver in the car," Dave said. He's bleeding from the head." The man went to check him.

"I'm sending two firemen down with a litter," Jess said on the radio. "There's several guys up here that look like they're up to no good."

"I'll be up to help you," Dave said. "You'll be all right, Jonny." He said as he started up the hill carrying Jon's shotgun.

Two firemen came down and helped the lady put Jon on a backboard and onto a Stokes Basket. They carried Jon up the hill. Jon looked and could see Dave and Jess standing between them and four or five guys. A police car from Oak Hill arrived and Dave asked the officer to go down over the hill and help with the other victims.

They put Jon in a squad. The EMT lady and a fireman were in the back with him. The squad took off down the road with siren going. Jon was having a hard time breathing. The ride was crooked and rough. "We're going to Huntington. That's the closest place that can deal with what you got," the EMT lady said to Jon. 'If we take you to a local hospital, they'll send you somewhere else. I'm a paramedic. I was a nurse in Vietnam. You've been shot in the lung. I know it hurts to breath. I'm going to start an IV and give you something for the pain. You may go to sleep. You'll be all right."

Jon woke up in a hospital room. He looked around. No one was with him. It didn't look like the hospital back home. He felt groggy. Pretty soon a nurse came in. He didn't know her. "How are you feeling?" she asked.

"Not very good. Where am I?"

"Huntington, West Virginia," she said.

"What happened?" he said.

"You had surgery. There was a bullet in your right lung. The surgeon removed it. You have a drain tube in your chest. I'm going to give you something for the pain."

He felt a warm sensation and then went to sleep.

When he woke up, there were two, young ladies sitting in the room, carrying on a conversation. Rita and Liz. "Hi, Jon, how are you?" Rita said.

Liz grabbed a little pan and held it to his mouth as he threw up. "Is that your answer to Rita's question?" she said.

He looked at them both and said, "We need to quit meeting in hospitals. I got to pee," he said.

Liz handed him a pee bottle. "You know how to use one of these?"

"You hold the bottle Liz and I'll hold his thingy," Rita said.

"No, I'll hold his thing," Liz said, laughing.

"All right, send me a real nurse," Jon said.

Liz placed the bottle in his hand and Rita raised the sheet. Jon took the thing and put it between his legs. "That feels better," he said as he handed the bottle to them. Neither one of them was anxious to take it. Liz finally did and went in the restroom and flushed the toilet.

A nurse came in. "The doctor wants you up and walking."

"This is nurse Liz and her capable aide," Jon said.

"I know. We have already talked about you. I have to go with you the first few times till you get your legs back. Come on, girls, let's get him out of bed."

It hurt, but they helped him get his feet on the floor and with Liz on one side and Rita on the other and the nurse pushing his IV stand along behind them they walked down the hall aways and back to the room. They got him back in bed and hooked the oxygen back up.

"How long am I going to be here?" Jon asked.

"Probably about a week. It's up to the doctor," the nurse said as she left the room.

"Well, how long have you girls been here?" Jon asked.

Rita looked at the clock. It was twelve o'clock. Jon looked outside. It was daylight. It must be noon then he thought.

"We got here at six this morning," Rita said.

"Well, you all don't have to stay here, you know," Jon said.

"We're taking turns. We're both going to leave about five and in the morning Liz is going to drive down and spend the day. The next day I'll come down in the morning and spend the day. We're both on night shift," Rita said.

Liz smiled in agreement.

"Have you all talked to Dave?" he asked.

"Yes. He came to the hospital back home and got me and we went over to the plant and told Rita. He told us what happened."

"What about the guy driving the truck?" Jon asked.

"He's in the hospital back home, under guard. He'll be all right."

"The other guy is dead?" Jon asked.

The two girls looked at each other and then both shook their heads in agreement.

"I'm sorry," Liz said.

"It must have been awful," Rita said.

"It wasn't much fun," he said.

The doctor came in at three. "I'm Doctor Avery," he said. "I did your surgery. I want to look at your incision."

"Can my friends stay?" Jon asked.

"Sure," the doctor said as he began taking the dressing off.

Jon looked down at it. It was about six inches long and stitched. There was a drain tube coming out and hooked to a bag.

"Looks good. You'll probably be here about a week. You are getting antibiotics to prevent infection. I would say the bullet was a .22 caliber. I gave it to an investigator who came to get it."

"Okay. Thanks for taking care of me so good."

"That's what we're here for," he said, smiling. "You have had a traumatic experience. You will be visited by a psychologist every day. I would encourage you to talk with him about your experience. These things can manifest themselves in different ways with different persons."

"Okay, you're the doc."

"I'll send the nurse in to put a new dressing on. I'll check on you tomorrow."

At ten the next morning, Liz came to sit with Jon. She brought him some flowers. She brought him a book from the library about the Battle of The Bulge. He had told her that he liked to read history of the Second World War. "Thank you," Jon said to Liz. "You two don't really have to come down here every day."

"Yes, we do. You're seventy miles from home. No one else is going to be able to visit you regularly, and we care about you."

"So, you and Rita seem to be pretty good friends," he said.

"Yes, we have something in common: you."

"I don't deserve such good friends."

"Well, you've got us, whether you like it or not."

"There's supposed to be a shrink come talk to me sometime today. I guess they think I've had a bad experience."

"It's good that they brought you here. You probably wouldn't have gotten that kind of treatment back home."

"I know, they got a looney bin here. My dad was here back in the sixties."

"You've never talked about your family, Jon."

"My dad had problems from the Second World War. He had several nervous breakdowns. He's been gone for five years now. Mom is still living. We don't have much of a relationship. She probably doesn't even know I'm here."

"You want to call her?"

"No."

The phone rang and Liz answered it. "It's for you, Jon," she said, handing him the receiver.

"Hello, this is Jon."

This is Herb Honesty. I'm an Investigator for BCI. We are doing the investigation on the incident you were involved in at the request of the Jackson Co Sheriff. How are you doing?"

"Sore."

"I would like to take your statement. We want to wrap this up and take it to the County Prosecutor for review. He may take it to the Grand Jury for review. I don't know what his procedure is on these kind of things, but most prosecutors are starting to do the Grand Jury review."

"Well, I don't feel up to it yet. Call me back in a couple of days, and I'll let you know. Do you have my guns?"

"Just your revolver. We'll do ballistics on it."

"Okay, call me in a couple of days."

"That was BCI," he told Liz "they're doing the investigation. The Prosecutor will probably take it to the Grand Jury. I'll probably get in trouble with the SFM for shooting at a moving car. That is prohibited in most firearms policies, except that we still don't have a firearms policy."

"Has anyone from your office talked to you?" she asked.

"My boss called this morning, and I talked to him. He told me not to worry about things."

"I brought a checkerboard," she said as she removed the box from a bag and started setting it up on his table. "Have you walked this morning?"

"Once," he answered.

"Well, let's go for a walk down the hall. The nurse said I could take you."

They walked down the hall. He had to sit down in a chair at the end of the hall before starting back.

"Would you call Rita and ask her to bring me a set of sweats to wear? I hate these gowns."

"Okay, I'll call her when I get back home this evening."

They went back to his room and played checkers until the psychologist came to visit him. It was getting late so Liz decided to drive home.

The psychologist was a lady in her mid-thirties. She told Jon that she had counseled a lot of law enforcement officers that had been involved in shooting incidents. They talked for an hour, and she said she would be back the next day. The surgeon came and checked his incision again and gave him a good report.

The BCI Agent came to interview Jon on Friday morning. He gave him a full account of what happened on tape recording. The agent said in his opinion it was what they called "a good shooting" and that the only trouble might be administrative with him shooting the tires on the car.

Jon was able to get up and walk the halls by himself. He no longer had an IV or oxygen. Rita and Liz continued to take turns spending the day with him.

On Sunday, the doctor told Jon that he could be discharged on Monday. The drain would remain in, and he would need to come back in seven days for a checkup and to probably have it removed. Rita was there with him at the time. "I don't have to work tonight. I'll just stay down here tonight and take you home in the morning."

"You going to get a motel room?" he asked her.

"I'll see if they will let me sleep in a big chair in here tonight."

Rita went to a store and got him a new pair of jeans, shirt, and underwear. She drove him up Route 93 and took him to his house. That afternoon Dave stopped by. They talked about what they had been through and Jon thanked Dave for taking good care of him out there that night, "even if you stuck your snot rag in my side."

"That's all I had; I guess I'm going to have to get a first aid kit to carry when we work together," Dave said.

"The prosecutor wants to know if you feel up to coming to Grand Jury this Friday. He would like to get this thing over with."

"Yeah, I can do it. I want to get it over with, too," Jon replied. "You'll have to come and get me. I can't drive till the doctor clears me. I see him Monday."

"Your car's got a bunch of parking tickets on it sitting behind the jail."

"How about taking them down to the police station and seeing if they will tear them up."

"I'll try," Dave said, "but this new mayor has made a couple of deputies pay their tickets here lately."

There were four parking places behind the jail reserved for sheriff's cars, and sometimes deputies parked their personal vehicles in them when they weren't needed for cruisers. The new mayor was on a kick and had his meter maid putting tickets on their cars.

After Dave left, Rita said, "I have to work midnights the rest of the week. Liz is off for four days, so she is going to come stay with you. I'll stay with you in the daytime."

"You all right with Liz staying here all night?" Jon asked Rita.

"Yeah, you're the one I don't trust," she said, smiling.

"I'll behave."

"I don't know. Maybe we should ask Liz what she thinks," she said, laughing.

"Would you mind walking up to the courthouse and getting my car and bringing it over here before the Mayor has it towed?" Jon asked her, getting the keys out of his pocket.

"Okay, but I got to get some sleep so I can go to work tonight."

"You can take a nap here when you get back. What time is Liz getting here?"

"About nine," Rita said.

"People in this neighborhood are going to talk about me having too many females staying overnight. There might be some kind of city ordinance against it. That mayor's liable to have me arrested."

"Maybe Liz could get a sign for the door of her truck that says Home Nursing Service," Rita responded.

"Yeah, I'm surprised you two hadn't thought of that already."

CHAPTER 23

At nine o'clock, the doorbell rang. Jon was on the couch, watching T.V. "Come in," he hollered.

"It's time to change shifts," Liz said as she came in carrying her nurse bag. "Where's Rita?"

"In bed; go ahead and wake her up. She wanted up at nine."

Liz and Rita came out of the bedroom and Liz said, "Stretch out on the couch, Jon, so I can check your incision and drain." She checked his blood pressure and temperature first.

Rita said, "I'm going to go home and take a shower and get ready for work. I'll be back in the morning about eight."

"Thanks," Jon said.

"See you in the morning," Liz said.

After Rita left, Liz said, "You really got it made having two, young women taking care of you."

"The neighbors are going to be talking," he said.

"I'll bet they are. I better pull the drapes or they'll be looking in."

"You want the couch or the bed?" he said. "You can take a bedroom upstairs if you want."

"I don't know," she said. "I better take the couch. I just got off midnights and I'll have a hard time sleeping."

"You two really don't need to stay with me like this," Jon said.

"Oh, we don't mind sharing you at all," she said.

"Does your grandpa know where you are at?"

"Yes, I gave him the number in case I get a coroner call. Did you know that Karen and I are going to be working with Dave on sexual assault cases?"

"Yeah, he told me. Now there's a good man for you Liz. He's only five years older than I am."

"That makes him ten years older than me."

"I thought you liked older men."

"There is an age limit, you know. Does he have a girlfriend?"

"Not a steady one," Jon answered her. "I was thinking he would make a good match for Karen. About the same age."

"She and Doctor John are pretty tight."

"You'll like working with Dave. It's good that the Sheriff is putting this sexual assault thing together."

"Grampa has known Chuck for a long time. He was his family doctor for a long time."

"I heard Chuck talk about taking your Grampa in a horse drawn sled to make house calls when the snow was bad a long time ago."

"When would that have been?"

"Back before the Second World War. Chuck was in the Navy in the Pacific. His ship was hit bad, and they made it back to a harbor crippled. A bunch of sailors were dead in flooded compartments. When they got to port, Chuck and a bunch of the crew had to go in and get them out of the compartments. He told me about it one time."

"That would be terrible. My dad was in the Korean War. He worked in a MASH Unit. He was a Navy Corpsman. He never talked a lot about it. Just said it was really cold there in the winter."

"I'm going to bed. I'm tired. It's been a long day," Jon said.

"Are you allowed to shower?"

"Yeah, I took one at the hospital this morning."

"I'm going to take a shower and watch T.V."

Jon went to bed. Liz went through the bedroom into the bathroom, and he could hear her taking a shower. She came out wearing a robe and sat in a chair by his bed and started brushing her wet hair.

"Sorry. Am I tempting you again?" she asked.

"I can handle it."

"Good. I want to talk. I miss having someone young to talk to. Grampa likes to tell me stories and I enjoy them, but I miss talking to a young man like you."

"What you want to talk about?"

"Police work. Investigations. Tell me about some cases you've had."

"I'll tell you how I made some hippies police fans."

"Hippies, I didn't know there were any left."

"This was about four years ago, when I was a deputy. But there are still some around. Most are living on small farms, sorta like communes."

"So, what happened?"

"Well, I came in on day shift on Sunday by myself. The night shift deputy was getting ready to go home, and we were talking when the phone rang and the jailer took a call. He hung up and told me that there was a man and a woman out on Jisco Road that had parked their car along the road and back-packed into Buckeye Lake and spent the night, and when they hiked out, their car was missing its rear tires and wheels."

Liz was interested, he could tell. She was still brushing her long, dark hair. She was exciting to look at.

"The night shift deputy said he had seen that car sitting there about 3:00 A.M., and it still had the tires on it. He drove out the road aways and saw a car driving slowly down Cove Road, so he stopped it. There were two, young men in it. He got their names. He said they were up to no good and he bet that they were the ones who took the tires and wheels. He told me where they lived."

"Did you find them?" Liz said.

"I went out there, and here was this guy and his girlfriend, and it was obvious they were hippies. The kind that call cops pigs and oink at them. Anyway, the back of their car was sitting on the axle. I told them I would take them to town and find them another wheel and a used tire. They had a spare in the trunk. On the way to town, I told them I had to stop and check on something. I went over passed Oakland Church to these guys' house, and the car the night deputy told me they were driving was sitting there. I knocked on the door, and Mom told me they were upstairs in bed. I asked her to get them. About ten minutes went by, and I knocked again. Mom said she told them to get up. I asked her if I could get them up. She said I could, so I went upstairs and rousted them out."

"Did they give you a hard time?" she asked.

"No, they were too sleepy. I took them outside. The hippies were sitting in my car. I asked the guys to open the trunk of their car. They did, and there were the tires. I motioned for the hippies to get out of the car. They came over, and I asked them if that was their tires. It was. They smiled and you could tell they were really amazed. I had the boys load the tires in the back seat of the cruiser and made them take the lug nuts off their car as they had told me they had taken the hippies lug nuts and thrown them out in the cornfield. We all squeezed in the car. The hippies in the front. The boys and tires in the back. We went out and the boys put the tires back on the hippies' car. I had the hippies follow us to the jail, so I could get their statements. I locked up the boys. The hippies were really happy and said something about how I wasn't like the pigs they knew in the big city."

Liz laughed, "That's really neat. I bet they've told this story to their hippie friends more than you have told it."

"Probably."

"Did they ask you how you knew where their tires were?"

"Yeah, I told them some lie about how I knew who all the thieves were and where they lived at and what they liked to steal."

"So, Nurse Liz, tell me what you're lookin' for in a man," Jon asked.

"No, you're not fixin' me up."

"No. I just want to know."

"Well, no more than five or six years older than me. I don't want a guy younger than me. Tall and good looking. Smart. Employed in a good job. He doesn't have to make a lot of money. Church going is important. Faithful. One woman man. Likes the country."

"That shouldn't be a hard order to fill. Lots of guys around here meet them specs."

"Well, like I told you before, I'm not lookin' to get a husband. I just want a guy to go with steady and be good friends with."

"How long you been livin' down here?

"Eight months," she said.

"Well, you got plenty of time. You got the looks. You're nice and caring. It'll all work out."

She started sobbing. "Look at me. I'm sitting here in the bedroom of a guy who doesn't want me, wearing a bathrobe with just a tee shirt on underneath. I'm ridiculous."

"You're not ridiculous. You're helping your friend."

"I'm going to the couch," she said.

Jon was having the dream again. He was chasing someone down an alley. Flames in the background. Then he turned a corner. He followed. Around the corner. The guy was standing there pointing the gun at him. The gun went off. "NO, NO, NO!" he screamed. He woke up. Liz was sitting on the bed holding him, his head on her chest.

"Are you all right?" she said. He started to sob. "You're soaking wet with sweat," she said. She continued to hold him. It seemed like an hour went by. "Let's move you over to the chair," she said.

He sat in the chair. She pulled his wet tee shirt over his head. She found him a clean shirt in a drawer. He watched as she stripped the bed of the sheets and put clean ones on. She left the room and came back with her thermometer and blood pressure cuff. "You don't have a fever, but your blood pressure is high. One sixty-five over ninety-five. That's too high. It's probably high from the nightmare you were having."

"I've had the dream before. I've been having it for about two years."

"Get back in bed. I'm going to get you a glass of milk."

She returned with a glass of milk. It was then that he noticed that she was wearing a tee shirt that barely covered her butt. He could feel himself becoming aroused. She sat down on the edge of the bed. She had a cool washrag that she wiped across his forehead several times. She brushed her forearm across his arousal. She became embarrassed. "You're tempting me," he said.

"Sorry," she said, "I'm going back to the couch."

Jon was awakened by Rita and Liz talking in the living room. He got up and put on sweatpants and went out and sat down in a chair.

"You want bacon and eggs for breakfast?" Rita said.

"Okay," Jon replied.

"I'm going home to do chores," Liz told them both.

"Liz said you had a bad nightmare," Rita said after Liz had left.

"Yeah, I been having the same one for a couple of years, but I never woke up screaming like she said I did."

"I'll start breakfast."

Jon liked the smell of bacon frying. "Can we go for a walk this afternoon after you sleep?' he asked Rita.

"Sure."

By Friday Jon was able to walk three blocks without stopping to rest. He walked to the courthouse on Friday morning for the Grand Jury Hearing. He sat in the hallway with Dave, the BCI Agent, the EMT's that came to the scene and Jess. Liz walked in and sat down beside them. "I have to read the medical examiner's report," she told them.

"Did you go to the scene that night?" Jon asked her.

"Yes, I didn't tell you because I didn't think you wanted to talk about it, and I didn't want to tell you the details," she said.

"I've got your gun in the trunk of my car," the BCI guy said. "When we're done here this morning, I'll give it back to you. I even cleaned it for you."

"Thank you," Jon said.

Jon was the last witness to testify. He told the jury what had happened. It was the same jury that had indicted both Brown brothers. As they sat in the hallway waiting for the jury to come to a conclusion in walked the city police chief and sat down with them. "Hi Duane," Jon said.

"Got something for you Jon," Duane said, handing him a white paper. Duane Light had been police chief for three years. He had come up through the ranks to Sergeant and then Detective and then Captain and then Chief.

"You're shittin' me, Duane," Jon said. "A warrant for my arrest for not paying traffic tickets? I suppose this is the Mayor's doing?"

"Yeah, when you get done, come down and see him. He'll be in all day. See what you can work out," Duane said as he got and left.

"Bunch of bullshit," Dave said. "You been through enough the last couple of weeks. Couldn't he have just called you or sent you a letter."

The prosecutor came out of the judge's office and stood in front of them. "No bill. They ruled it was a justified homicide in self-defense."

"That's a relief," Dave said.

Jon stood up. Liz got up and hugged him. He shook hands with the prosecutor and Dave. Jon handed the prosecutor the warrant. He read it and laughed. "Politics," he said. "Democrat Mayor and Republican Sheriff. I think he's trying to start some kind of a feud."

"I better go turn myself in before he sends Duane looking for me," Jon said. He walked out of the courthouse with Dave and the BCI guy. The agent walked to his car and opened the trunk and brought Jon a bag with his gun in it. He then gave him a small box. Jon opened it. It contained a spent bullet.

"Twenty-two hollow point," the agent said as he handed Dave a clipboard. "Sign here, please."

"What about the gun that shot me?" Jon asked.

"The prosecutor has it. If you want it, you can ask him to get the judge to release it to you."

Jon walked down to the City Hall. The mayor was newly elected. He was in his late fifties and really a pretty nice guy, but this thing about parking behind the jail he didn't understand. He didn't think it was political. The sheriff had not gotten involved in supporting anyone for mayor. He walked into the mayor's office and sat down in front of his desk. The mayor looked up at him.

"Hello, Jon, how are you doing? I heard you were under the weather."

"I'm doin' all right," Jon said as he handed him the warrant. "How much money do I owe you?"

"Fifty dollars. Woulda only been twenty if you had paid them within twenty-four hours."

"I was in the hospital all week."

"That's what I heard. How'd things go in Grand Jury?"

"Justifiable."

"That's good."

"So, you gonna give me a break for being in the hospital?"

"Give me thirty dollars," he said as he picked up the phone and punched a button. "Mabel, write Jon Hamer a receipt for thirty dollars please."

"You're not the only one who has to pay. If you guys don't stop parking in those spaces, I'm going to have the signs taken down and meters put in place. I don't want to do that to the Sheriff."

"I don't want to cause him any trouble, either."

"I don't have any trouble with the highway patrol. They park in front of the courthouse."

"I ain't never seen them dropping dimes in the meters. I never heard tell of any of them getting a parking ticket either," Jon replied.

"Well, I'm glad you brought that to my attention. I'll have to tell the meter maid to start checking them."

Jon got his wallet out and put thirty dollars on the desk and got up and left, stopping to get his receipt.

When he got home, Rita was asleep in his bed. He loaded his gun and put it in his holster and put it in the closet. He went in the bedroom and got undressed and slid in bed beside Rita and spooned with her. She was sound asleep.

Soon he fell asleep. He awoke in a state of arousal. Rita was awake and looking at him smiling. "No, not till you talk to the doctor," she said as she gave him a kiss. "I have something to talk to you about."

"You pregnant again?" he asked her.

"No. Don't say that. I'm getting promoted to supervisor at the plant. It means a three dollar an hour raise."

"That's great."

"The only thing is they don't have an opening for a supervisor right now, so they want me to work at the plant in Logan."

"You going to drive back and forth?"

"No. I can't afford it with the price of gas the way it is. When they get an opening here at Jackson, I can transfer back here."

"So, what are you going to do?"

"I'm going to take it. I have a friend in Logan that used to work at the Jackson Plant. I'm going to live with her and share expenses. I'll come home on my days off. The only thing is that they just expanded the plant in Logan and they are working a lot of overtime. I am thinking about taking classes part time at Hocking. I want to be a nurse."

"That's good. I'll sure miss you, but we'll have your days off."

"Jon, I've been thinking a lot about us. Do you love me?"

"Well, no, but I think we have drawn a lot closer lately, and I care a lot about you. We're more than just good friends like we used to be."

"But don't you think your feelings toward me had a lot to do with the baby and your feelings of responsibility?"

"Well, it may not have happened if that hadn't happened."

"Exactly. We're not in love. We're lovers, but we're not in love."

"I know, but we have a lot in common you know. We always have. I don't want us to break up."

"I think we need to think about things. I know that Liz really likes you a lot."

"You and she been talking?" he asked.

"No, not about this, but I can tell how she feels about you."

"Are you wanting to break up?"

"No. Just cool it for a while. I'll be working a lot of hours up there. If you want to date around that's all right with me. I trust you. Maybe we're not meant to be together."

"Gosh darn. I been enjoying being with you."

"I've liked it to. I really have. You've been very good to me. I feel safe with you. We have something between us that a lot of folks don't have, but I'm not sure how long it's supposed to last."

"Okay, but let me down easy if you're going to."

"What do you want for supper?"

"Surprise me. Are you taking me to Huntington to the doctor on Monday?"

"I have to be in Logan Monday and every day next week for supervisor training. Eight to four-thirty."

"Okay. I'll find someone to take me. What's Liz working next week?"

"I don't know. I don't think she ever works anything but midnights."

"Yeah, but she's starting to work part time at the SO on this sex offense thing."

"She told me about it. She really wants to be a cop."

"I'm gonna take a shower while you cook."

On Monday Liz picked up Jon and took him to his doctor's appointment. The report was good, but he had to return to the hospital on Thursday to have the drain tube removed.

"Did you know that Rita is moving to Logan?" Jon asked Liz as they were driving back up Route 3.

"Yes, she told me a couple of weeks ago."

"She just told me a couple of days ago."

"Are you going to miss her?"

"Yes."

"When can you go back to work?"

"Next Monday. I need someone to drive me Thursday when they take the tube out."

"I can do it."

"And Rita is going to college to be a nurse," he said.

"Yes. We talked about that. She would do well in nursing."

"And what about you? You staying in nursing, or are you going to be a cop?"

"I don't know. Maybe this part time work on sex cases will satisfy my desire."

"Can we stop at the Highway in Oak Hill and eat?"

"Okay."

"It's getting close to Christmas. You going to your parents?"

"No, they're coming down to Grampa's for a few days at Christmas. What do you do?"

"Well, I always worked when I was a deputy. Last year I got called out on a fire that took me three days to investigate. Fatality on Christmas Day."

"Around here."

"Zanesville. I was in training then."

"Do you put up a tree?"

"No, I don't know where the folks that own the house I am sitting keep that kind of stuff, or if they even have one."

Reverend Evans was serving coffee when they went in the Highway to eat. He greeted them warmly and asked about Jon's health. "I haven't seen you in church for a couple of weeks, Liz," the reverend said.

"Been busy taking care of this guy. I'll be there Sunday."

"You want to go? You been kind of gloomy since you came home," she asked Jon.

"I should go."

"You have a lot to be thankful for," Liz told him.

"I'm still alive. A few inches and I would have gotten it in the heart."

"Maybe you need to continue your counseling."

"All we have is the public mental health place, and I don't care for them."

"Why don't you ask the reverend if you can see him? I think he would be just as helpful as a counselor, and he likes to make people laugh."

"Maybe so."

"Doesn't your agency provide that kind of service after traumatic events?"

"I don't know. They've never said anything about it. I suppose they'll probably have a review on the shooting like the last one. They don't understand police work. Commerce is a regulatory agency. The Arson Bureau is the only law enforcement agency in Commerce, and they don't know what to do with us."

"You ready to go? Do you want me to stay with you tonight?"

"No, I'll be all right. If you can take me down there Thursday, that would be fine."

"Okay."

Jon called his boss when he got home to tell him he would be back to work on Monday. "Did you get the new firearms policy in the mail?" Joe asked him.

"What are you talking about?" Jon asked him.

"The Friday before your shooting the new firearms policy went out in the mail. You should have gotten it either Saturday or Monday at the latest."

"I never check my post office box on Saturdays, and I don't think I checked it on Monday. I would have remembered something like that. I would have read it. Matter of fact, I forgot all about my mail. I need to go to the post office today and get it."

"They want to have a hearing sometime next week on your shooting. The policy prohibits shooting at or from a moving motor vehicle."

"Here we go again."

"They had a training class on the policy while you were off sick. You'll have to make it up. I'll make arrangements for you to do it. There were two others that missed it, too."

"I'll let you know. Go check your mail."

"Okay. See you sometime next week."

Jon went to the post office. He had to get his mail over the counter, as his box was full. He sat in his car and read the firearms policy. Of course, as he expected it prohibited warning shots and shooting at or from a moving vehicle. Well, here we go again. He looked at the postmark on the envelope. The Friday before his shooting. He had already told his boss that he didn't check his mail between Friday and the day of the shooting. He wasn't going to lie anyway. No sense in it. He had sworn to uphold the truth.

CHAPTER 24

Jon got up Saturday morning, looking forward to the day. There was the first snow of the year, about two inches. He thought about a hike in the woods and then a night at the disco. He was still sore from having the drain removed on Thursday. Liz had driven him back. They stopped at the Highway Grill in Oak Hill and ate supper. Reverend Evans was there and he asked him if he could come see him next week. He told him he could come to the Manse any evening, but to call ahead of time as he sometimes got called out to see those that were ill.

At ten in the morning, the phone rang. It was his boss, Joe. A fatality fire in Vinton County. In the small town of Dundas. Even though his official day back to work was not to be until Monday Joe asked if he could go on the call as he couldn't get ahold of anyone else within a reasonable distance. He told Joe that he would take of it.

When he arrived, he saw Liz. He had forgotten that she was doing Vinton County now. He also saw a guy running around with a pole with a loop on the end of it. He looked like he was probably the dog catcher.

"Hi Liz, what's going on?" he asked.

"I beat you here, so now I can brief you about what we know." She smiled. "Go ahead."

"Male victim, age eighty. Lived alone in this mobile home. Had about ten dogs that the dog catcher is trying to round up right now. Fire discovered by neighbor across the street who heard an explosion and woke up and saw bright light. Looked out and the trailer was heavily involved in fire. He called the fire department. Victim is laying on the floor beside the wood burning stove on his side. Badly burned."

"Very good. Any background on the victim?"

"Sheriff said he walked around town to go to the little store in town and the beer joint. Not a heavy drinker. Just went down there and drank a couple of beers and loafed. Retired from the dynamite factory at Zaleski. Never married. No family known in the area. Lived his whole life in Dundas. He smoked. Rolled his own."

Jon saw a scraggly dog go into the trailer. The trailer was an older one. About twelve feet wide by forty feet long. The roof was still intact. The exterior walls were burned through in the center of the home. The dog came out of the trailer with an arm in his mouth. "Get that dog," Jon said. The dog catcher, who had just returned with a dog and put it in his truck, reached out with his pole, but missed the dog. He took off after it down the road. The dog cut between two houses.

"Well, if he doesn't catch the dog and get the victim's arm back, then about a hundred years from now someone is going to be digging a hole and find an arm bone and create a big mystery that will never be solved," Jon said, laughing.

A hearse pulled in, and two men wearing suits got out. "Let's look at the body, so they can remove it," Liz said.

The body was badly burned. It laid on the floor between the wood burning stove and the couch. It appeared to Jon that the fire started on the couch. The body was touching both the remains of the couch and the stove. Jon rolled it over and took a sample of the clothing. Blue jeans and a flannel shirt. "You going to draw blood?" he asked Liz.

"Yes, but I've never done it on one this badly burned. Unless we find something suspicious the county doesn't have the money for an autopsy. The former coroner used to take bodies to a vet to have them x-rayed."

"You'll need a really long, heavy needle. You go through the chest into the heart."

Liz got her kit and found the right needle. Jon showed her about where to insert it. She shoved the needle in and stopped where he told her to. She drew the plunger back, and the syringe filled with a light brown watery liquid. "No blood. Got to move over a little bit and try it again," Jon said.

Liz pulled the needle out and ejected the liquid and tried another location. This time she drew blood.

"This doesn't work on babies. Their heart bakes so that there is no liquid blood in it because the body is so small," Jon said.

"I don't look forward to trying this on a baby," Liz said.

Jon hollered at the funeral home guys to bring a body bag and the cot. They came in the trailer in their nice suits. He never could figure out why these guys came to a fire to get a body dressed like this. He and Liz put the body in the bag and the two guys carried it out and put it on a cot. "You might ask them to hold on to the body a few days and not do anything to it till we get the blood work and my samples back," he told Liz. He then took some samples of fire debris from the frame work of the couch and the floor beneath the couch. He would have it tested for an accelerant.

"You going to the disco tonight?" he asked her.

"I'd like to," she said.

"Let's split up and do a door-to-door in the neighborhood and see what people have to say. You take the little store, and I'll do the beer joint. Maybe we can get done in time to go dancing."

"Okay," Liz said as she took off her fire boots and coveralls.

About two hours later, they met back at the scene. The dog catcher was gone. He must not have found the arm. "Well, he was at the beer joint till midnight. Nothing out of the ordinary happened there. He left by himself," Jon told Liz.

"He hasn't been to the store for two days. He cashes his social security check there. He has a charge account that he pays off when he cashes his check. Leaves him about three hundred cash left. Everyone likes him, except his dogs are a nuisance. He lets all the dogs inside at night. I wonder how they all got outside. There were only two dead dogs in the trailer," Liz said.

"Let's take a look at the door."

They found the door was burned off. The two hinges were in the open position. The door jamb had deep charring on it indicating to Jon that it was probably open during the fire.

"Well, that sheds a different light on things," Jon said to Liz.

"Maybe the dogs could have knocked the door open," Liz replied.

"Possible. Some of them looked to be pretty big. How about getting your blood to the hospital right away and put a rush on it. I'll get my samples to the lab Monday and put a rush on them. You put a hold on the body till we see what our labs find."

"Okay. Sounds good. I may be a little late getting to the lounge tonight."

"Me, too. I'll see you there." He said as he started his car. "I'll stop in McArthur and talk to the Sheriff and let him know what we found out." McArthur was the county seat of Vinton County. The Sheriff's Office was located next to the courthouse in the old jail building. The jail was no longer in that building. When a new courthouse was built in the thirties, the jail was put on the third floor of the courthouse.

Jon was late getting to the Lounge. The DJ was already playing. Everyone was dancing. Rita was there, as well as Liz and the rest of the gang.

Rita came over and sat next to him. "How are you feeling, Jon?"

"Pretty good. Got my drain out. Went back to work. Had a fire today. How was your week?"

"Classes all week on being a supervisor, safety, union stuff, grievances, that kind of stuff."

"You moved up there yet?"

"All my clothes I have. I need someone to help me move my bedroom set."

"Maybe we can borrow Liz's truck and I can help you move it," he said.

"That would be nice. Here she comes. I'll ask her."

"Hi, everyone," Liz said.

"Liz, could Jon and I borrow your truck next week to move my furniture to Logan?"

"Sure, and if you want more room you can borrow a trailer, too," Liz said.

"I think we can get it all on the truck," Rita said.

A slow song came up. "Let's dance, Jon," Rita said.

"I missed you this week," Jon said as they danced.

"I missed you, too. You get okayed for sex?"

"Yep."

"Want me to stay with you tonight?"

"Yep."

"I'll come over after we leave here. I'm living out of my suitcase."

Jon and Rita got to his house about one in the morning. He was tired and sore. He tried to fast dance once but had to stop. He shouldn't have tried it. He was anxious to get in bed with Rita. She showered first and came in the bedroom with a towel wrapped around her. She turned off the light and let the towel drop to the floor and got in next to him. He, too, was naked. They engaged almost at once, with little foreplay.

"Whew, that was good," he said, as she got off of him. She had insisted in being on top because of his injuries.

"Yes, it was good," she said as she snuggled up to him.

Within a few minutes, they were sound asleep.

On Monday, Jon took the evidence to the arson lab on the fatality fire at Zaleski. When he walked into the Arson Bureau, he saw his boss at his desk. "Hi, Chief. Brought up the evidence on the fatality in Vinton County."

"What happened down there?" Joe asked him.

Jon told him all about the case and that the body was on hold, pending the lab tests.

"Since you're here, you might as well spend the night," the boss said. "Tomorrow at nine is the hearing on your shooting."

"I'll find me a place somewhere around here and type my report on the fire I did yesterday."

About four in the afternoon, Jon called Liz to see if she had anything on the labs on the blood. "No carbon monoxide in the blood," she told him.

"It looked like a smoldering fire to me," Jon said.

"How can you tell?" Liz asked.

"The window glass had dark baked on smoke stains, which happened when a fire smolders for a long time, slowly building up heat. You need to send the blood to another lab that can test for Cyanide poisoning. When a couch or other things that have certain plastic materials in it burns slowly it can give off Cyanide gas that can kill a person before they inhale enough carbon monoxide to kill them."

"Where can I get the test done at?" she asked.

"Call the Franklin County Coroner, or if you want to talk to someone you already know, call the lady we met at the seminar from Toledo. She probably knows. She would be at the Lucas County Coroner's Office."

"Okay, I'll get on it."

"I won't be back till tomorrow afternoon. I got to stay here for a hearing on the shooting tomorrow at nine."

"I thought the Grand Jury cleared you."

"They did, but this is administrative."

"Good luck tomorrow."

In the morning, Jon found himself sitting before the same legal counsel he set before at the first hearing on his last incident. The same DD of Commerce was also in the room. Joe sat at the rear of the room.

The attorney asked him to tell what had happened and he told them.

"Have you read the new firearms policy that went into effect the Monday before the incident in question?" the attorney asked.

"I have read it since the incident, but I did not receive a copy of it until over a week after the incident," Jon answered.

"How did that occur?" the attorney asked.

"I have a post office box, and I don't check it every day. I never check it on Saturday, as that is not a work day. Monday and Tuesday things were moving too fast on this case. We had Grand Jury on Tuesday, and I just didn't have time. Then I was in the hospital for a week."

"Is the mail one of the regular ways that you communicate with this office and the way that this office communicates with you?" he asked Jon.

"Yes, it and the telephone," he answered.

"Then it is your duty to check your mail in a timely manner so as to receive important documents from this office."

"Yes, it is," he agreed.

"I am going to refer this matter to the Deputy Director here to make a decision on. He may hold another hearing if necessary. You have admitted that you fired at the moving vehicle. What was your purpose there?"

"To stop this fleeing murderer who may bring harm to some other innocent person down the road."

"I think the appropriate term is alleged murder suspect.," the attorney stated.

"Well, I had all the facts that the Grand Jury had when they indicted him."

"Are you implying that he is guilty of the crime?"

"We wouldn't have taken it to the Grand Jury if we didn't think so. I wasn't shooting to kill the suspect. I was shooting to stop the car that was carrying the suspect."

"You could have accidentally killed either of those persons in the car."

"No. I'm a good shot. I know my shotgun and the pattern it holds. I knew I was only going to hit the tires when I fired the shots."

"This is the second time that you have been here for this type of incident in the last three months. If you wouldn't have shot out the tires and caused the car to wreck then the guy wouldn't have shot at you, and you wouldn't have had to kill him."

"No, but he would have probably done the same thing to some other person or law enforcement officer. Better I nipped it in the bud than someone else had to get hurt or killed."

"This concludes today's investigative hearing. The matter is turned over to the Deputy Director."

Jon and Joe returned to his office. "They don't understand our work," Joe said. "If it weren't for the money that the Fire Marshal's office brings in to Commerce, they would get rid of us."

"Well, I'll probably get disciplinary action this time. I should have checked my mail. It probably wouldn't have changed what I did, though."

"You better be careful who you say that to," the chief told him.

"That guy killed that little old lady for a fifty-dollar T.V. and an old sewing machine and some pocket change. His own brother testified against him. The testimony was corroborated by the physical evidence that we had and the testimony of other witnesses. Not one person on that Grand Jury questioned me on what I did or shouldn't have done. Probably because they knew what the guy did to that woman. It was the same Grand Jury that indicted both brothers."

"You did the right thing, as far as I'm concerned. You're a good investigator. Now go back home and don't let these idiots get you riled up. You getting any counseling about the shooting?"

"I talked to a psychologist every day at the hospital, and I'm going to start meeting with the preacher this week. Probably once a week for a while," Jon said.

"That's good. Stay in touch. I'll try to get down to spend a day with you before Christmas."

"You better hurry up; it's almost here."

When Jon got home, he called Reverend Evans and made arrangements to meet him at the Manse at seven that evening. Growing up as a Baptist, he always heard the preachers home called the parsonage. He knew the Catholics called theirs a Rectory. He wondered if all Presbyterians called it the Manse, or just the Welsh.

"Do you like to play cards, Jon?" the reverend asked him as he entered into the study room of the old brick house, about a block from the church.

"I really don't know much about it. But I like to play checkers."

"Then we will play checkers," he said as he brought over a nice, wooden checkerboard and placed it on the table. "My great-great-grandfather made this in Wales and brought it to America with him."

"It's really nice," Jon said.

"You know, you have been through quite a bit over the last year or so, beginning with the loss of our mutual friend," he said as he placed the checkers in their places on the board.

"Yes, I know," Jon agreed.

"That was the hardest funeral I have ever done in my time in this parish. Such a fine young man gunned down by such a crud. In the prime of his life. People asked me to explain why, and I just could not find the words to say."

"Your job must be a hard one at times," Jon said. "Do you ever find the need to talk about it?"

"I think that our meeting like this will benefit us both."

They started moving their checkers. Jon right away jumped two of the preachers and took them.

"I was surprised when you left the Sheriff's Office and went to the Fire Marshal. I have on good authority been told that you were in line to run for sheriff someday."

"Yes, I was told that plan. After Chuck retires, I was to be the chief deputy for the next sheriff, and then when he had two terms, it would be my turn to run. I don't think I could do the politics, and I wasn't willing to work as a deputy all those years at such low pay. Guys like Chuck and Dave should get a medal for their dedication to serving the people of the county at great sacrifice to themselves and their families."

"Yes, I agree; it does not seem to pay much here in Southeast Ohio, does it?" The reverend jumped one of Jon's and took it.

"No, and I don't know if it will ever get any better especially in the smaller counties," Jon admitted.

"You have a great passion for the fire service, as well as law enforcement. I saw it when you served on the volunteer fire department."

"Thank you," Jon said, "I really think this is what I am supposed to be doing."

"I'm sure that our Heavenly Father has you where he wants you, at least for the present time. You must always be open to his plan for your life."

"I never really thought of it that way."

"It is good to seek his guidance, but even if you don't he may still guide you to do his will."

"I haven't gone to church much since I left home after high school."

"It is hard when you work shift work," the reverend agreed.

"Yes, once you quit going, it's hard to start back up."

"Yes, it is. Now Liz I have known for many years. She has attended here often over the years when they were down here on weekends. She is quite a remarkable young woman. I am glad to see that she is following in her grandfather's footsteps."

"She is doing a good job as the coroner's investigator. Everyone enjoys working with her. It's nice to have someone come out to the scene. Her grandpa is just too old to get out like that anymore. I'm glad that he came up with the idea of hiring her."

"I know that she considered police work instead of nursing, but chose nursing instead when she went to college."

"Yes, she told me about that," Jon said as he kinged one his checkers.

They spent well over an hour talking, and played several games of checkers.

On the way home, Jon thought he would drive by Doc's farm and see if Liz was there. He found her in the barn. "What are you doing?" he asked her.

"Getting the evening chores done. What are you doing out this way?"

"Been down to Oak Hill talking to Reverend Evans."

"How nice. Did you play cards?" she asked.

"No, we played checkers. He thinks a lot of you," Jon told her.

"He's really a nice man."

"Yes. I think I should start going to church regularly. I'm not comfortable with the Catholic Church. I just can't get used to the services. I've been there with Rita several times."

"We can set together, you know."

"That's good. Did you find a place to test the blood?" he asked.

"I sent it to the Hamilton County Coroner. I packed it in dry ice and sent it UPS overnight."

"I should know about my samples I took by Thursday. I don't expect them to find any accelerants."

"You want to go inside for a cup of hot chocolate?"

"Okay."

They went in to the kitchen. "Where's Doc?" he asked her.

"Oh, the neighbor picked him up and took him to a Grange meeting."

"I had to go to that hearing on the shooting up at the office this morning. I spent the night up there."

"How'd it go?"

"Seems they adopted a firearms policy and mailed it out the Friday before the shooting, and I didn't get around to checking my mail, so I didn't know anything about it."

"I suppose it has a prohibition against shooting at a moving vehicle."

"Exactly and they're making a big deal about it and the fact that I didn't get my mail when I should have they aren't going to buy as an excuse."

"Hey, *Dallas* is about to come on. You want to watch it?"

"Okay. I forgot all about it."

They went into the living room, and she turned on the T.V. The Christmas tree looked nice. They sat on the couch and finished their hot chocolate.

"So, you going to go to church with me this Sunday?" Liz asked Jon.

"If I don't get called out I will. I'll pick you up."

"Come about eight thirty for breakfast."

"Okay. I wanted to thank you for all your help when I was in the hospital and when I got home. You are very nice."

"Thank you," she said. "That's what friends are for."

When the show was over, Liz walked Jon out to his car. It was starting to snow. "Maybe we will have a white Christmas," she said.

"Be nice. I got enough snow the winter of '78."

"That was a bad one. I was in college then."

"I was driving around this county in a sheriff's car. Had to park and walk a long ways to get to calls. We delivered medicine to older folks who couldn't get out."

"I'll call you when I get the labs back," Liz said.

"Okay. See you later."

CHAPTER 24

As Jon was getting ready for bed about eleven, the phone rang. It was the Vinton County Sheriff's Office.

"Is this the Fire Marshal?" the man said.

"Yes, it is."

"This is the Vinton County Sheriff's Office. We have a house that blew up out at Wilkesville up behind the schoolhouse. They believe there is a man in the house. They can't find him anywhere. I got ahold of the coroner lady, and she's on the way."

"Okay, I'll be there in about thirty minutes."

Wilkesville is a small village in Southern Vinton County. There is portion of Vinton County that is like a peninsula that extends south of the Appalachian Highway. It is bordered by Meigs County on the east, Gallia County on the south and Jackson County on the west. It is somewhat isolated from the remainder of Vinton County. It is difficult for the Sheriff's Office to police as it is a long ways from the county seat of McArthur and the only highway that leads one there is very crooked.

When he arrived on the scene, he found that the house had completely burned down and was still smoking. The fire department was still cooling down the debris in the basement.

"What you got, Chief?" Jon said when he recognized the fire chief.

"Well, the neighbors heard an explosion, and when they came out, they saw the couch had been blown halfway out onto the front porch through the picture window. Heavy smoke was coming out everywhere, and fire was shooting out the basement windows on the right side of the house. When we got here it was fully involved."

"You think someone is in there?" Jon asked the chief.

"Eighty-year-old man lived by himself. Doesn't have a car as he quit driving about five years ago. His son lives in Athens. Neighbors said the son was here today. They called him, and he is on his way down. No one has seen the man since the fire. He didn't get around well. Used a walker. Lady across the street visited him several times a week. She also cleaned his house for him once a week. Her teenaged daughter came over every day about five and fixed his supper. He paid them for helping him."

"When you get things cooled off enough, we'll need to set up lights so we can go through the debris to see if we can find him. Don't let the firemen use straight streams. They destroy evidence and tear up a burned body," Jon advised the chief. He was referring to the stream of water coming from the hose nozzle.

Jon walked around to the back of the house and found that the back door, frame and all, had been blown away from the house and hit a tree about thirty-five feet away. He found a natural gas meter at the right front corner of the house. It was turned off. "You guys shut the gas off chief?"

"Yeah, one of my guys got here ahead of the trucks and shut it off."

Jon found clear glass blown out into the back and both side yards of the house. Clear glass blown out away from the house was an indicator that no or very little fire was burning before the explosion. If fire was burning the glass would have smoke stains on it. The back door that came to rest against the tree was not burned either. He took pictures as he moved about.

Liz pulled in and got out of her truck. She was wearing her nurse dress. She got into her coveralls and came over to him. "Well, we meet again so soon," she said.

"I take it you were going to work."

"I was at work. Had to wait for someone to come in and take my place."

He filled her in on what he knew. "It will be awhile before we can look for the body. Maybe a couple of hours. We can talk to the neighbors while we're waiting.

They talked to the mom and her daughter across the street who helped take care of the man. The daughter had been there from five till six that evening to fix supper. The victim always did the dishes himself. The mom had seen the man's son at the house earlier in the morning.

"Did the man seem to be acting normal?" Jon asked the girl.

"Yes, but he was kind of down. He said that his son wanted him to go to a nursing home and he didn't want to go," the girl answered.

"The fire call came in at 9:00 P.M. You called the fire department. Right?"

"Yes," the woman said. "I heard an explosion and looked out and the couch was halfway out the front window on the porch and smoke coming out the windows and fire coming out the basement windows on the right side of the house."

"What time did he go to bed?" Liz asked the ladies.

"Always ten o'clock. He would turn his living room light off at ten every night. He slept in the back bedroom."

'Have you ever smelled natural gas while you were inside of his house?" Jon asked them.

They both shook their heads to indicate no.

"Thank you for your help, ladies. We'll be back in touch."

When they got back outside, the chief came over and told them that the man's son was there. They had him sit in the front seat of Jon's car. Liz got in the back. Jon got the basic information from him that was needed, name, date of birth, nonsmoker, physical ailments, meds, moods, how often the son visited.

"You were here to see your dad this morning?" Jon asked him.

"Yes. I wanted to take him to Athens to look at a couple of nursing homes, but he refused to go."

"Did you argue?" Liz asked from the back seat where she was taking notes.

"No. I just left and went and looked at them myself and found one I liked and got him on the waiting list. I decided I was not going to tell Dad until it came time to move him there."

"Has he been suicidal ever?" Liz asked.

"No, not at all ever. He has been depressed about this nursing home business," the son answered.

"Has he ever complained about smelling gas in the house, have you every smelled natural gas in the house?" Jon asked him.

"No. Never."

"All right. It is going to take us some time to dig through the debris. It was likely that he would be in the living room this time of night according to the folks across the street."

"That's correct. He went to bed at ten," the son agreed. "I'm going to visit the neighbors while I wait," the son stated.

It was cold out. The neighbors opened their garage door and moved their cars out so the firemen would have a place to get out of the wind. They set up a kerosene heater in the middle of the room and the lady brought out a large pot of coffee and set it on the heater and set cups on a small table. Jon liked the way that people were always helpful on fires. In the summer, they brought out ice water and lemonade. It started to snow again. What a winter. Too many fatality fires. Winter was always worse than summer for fatals, as a lot of them were heating related. So many people were using wood now that the price of fuel oil and propane had increased so much. Some installed them in a crude way, not following manufacturer's instructions. Of course, there were no building or fire codes for homes and trailers in the rural areas and small towns. He had seen some really jury rigged set ups that had caused fires. But his one was a natural gas explosion he believed.

It was three o'clock in the morning before they started to look for the body in the basement. The first floor of the ranch-style house was completely burned through, as well as the walls. They found him below the living room leaning up against an outside block wall, like he was sitting there. It didn't make sense if he had been in the living room and dropped down into the basement. They put him on a back board and took him out into the back yard. He was burned very much. Arms burned off at elbows. Legs at knees. Head had exploded. Liz was able to get blood from the heart on the first draw.

Jon started following the gas line that came into the house from the meter on the right side of the house. It went over to the furnace and then to the hot water tank and then to the kitchen for the range. The furnace was laying on its side. He looked it over good and examined the piping. He found that the drip leg was missing from the gas pipe where it went into the furnace. The drip leg is a short piece of gas pipe that goes down toward the floor about six inches to catch dirt that may be in the gas. He examined it and found the pipe was not broken off. Threaded pipe usually breaks off at the threaded joints. It leaves the male threads inside the female threads. This is because cutting threads on pipe weakens the pipe.

"Chief, look at this here," he said, showing him the piping. "No drip leg, and it's not broken off. We need to carefully shovel this floor around the furnace and look for it."

They shoveled slow and carefully. One of the young fire fighters found it a few feet from the furnace. It had the male threads on one end and the cap on the other end.

"Now we need to look for a wrench. You thinking what I'm thinking, Chief?" Jon had told the chief about the nursing home business.

"Yeah."

The chief found a pipe wrench laying near where they had found the body. Liz was doing the photography. She had a better camera than Jon had.

"If he took the drip leg off and sat down over there against the wall, the gas probably ignited off the gas hot water heater. The furnace would not work with the gas disconnected. This may be what happened. He didn't want to go to the nursing home. The son was here today to discuss it. I doubt that the gas killed him before the explosion. It may have put him to sleep. Liz will have the blood checked for carbon monoxide and ask them if they can check for gas poisoning. The house filled up with gas. That's why the couch is on the front porch and the back door blown out in the yard. Natural gas is lighter than air and rises," Jon explained to those present in the basement with him.

Jon and Liz explained to the son what they thought happened. The official cause of death would be pending the lab test results. He did not dispute the fact that this is what could have happened.

It was six in the morning when they finished up at the scene. "We're saving the county some money on autopsies these last two fires," Jon said to Liz.

"The commissioners will appreciate it," she replied.

"You won't be going back to work, will you?"

"No, I have to go to the hospital to take this blood to the lab and then home."

"I'm going home and get some sleep and hope the phone doesn't ring again," Jon said.

It was noon when Jon got up. He walked up town and ate breakfast at the Diner. There were two inches of snow from overnight. He stopped at the barber shop and got a haircut. When he got home, he called Liz. She said that the carbon monoxide level in the blood of the old feller was sufficient to cause death. They had no way to test for natural gas. Her ruling on cause of death would be suicide. Actually, it would be Docs ruling to make. He was the coroner. Jon called his office and got a case number for the fire and sat at the typewriter and started on the report.

Later in the afternoon, Liz called Jon and said that she got the labs back from the Hamilton County Coroner's Office on the fatal fire at Zaleski. There was sufficient cyanide gas in the blood to more than cause death. "Corroborated by the signs of a smoldering fire and the fact that the arson lab did not find any accelerants in the samples we took at the fire scene and the lack of suspicious circumstances, then I think we can close that case out," Jon told Liz.

"What will you say that the cause of fire is?" Liz asked.

"It will be listed on the report as undetermined. In the narrative of the report it will state that it started in the couch, that it was a slow smoldering fire and that it could have been caused by a cigarette," Jon answered.

"Okay, then Grampa will put the cause of death as accidental," Liz said.

"That's good. We've closed out two cases today. That's pretty good," Jon told Liz.

"Why don't you come down to the house for supper tonight, Jon?" Liz asked.

"That sounds good. What time?"

"Six," she responded.

"I'll be there. Bye."

Jon arrived at the farm at six. He sat in the living room, talking to Doc, as Liz finished preparing supper. Doc was an interesting story teller. He had been coroner for almost forty-five years. He had doctored longer than that. When he first started making house calls in the rural areas, he often used a horse, as the roads in the early thirties were not good in the winter and spring time. When he did use a car, he often got stuck in the mud and had to get a farmer to pull him out with a team. He had long ago lost track of how many babies he had delivered. He recalled going for six years straight in the forties without a single murder case. The most murders he had ever had in one year had been five, but that was a rarity. He had never had opposition in any election, being reelected every four years the same year as the president and most of the county government officials. He had worked with five different sheriffs. He had arrested one sheriff who had been sent to prison. In Ohio, the coroner is the only person with the authority to arrest the sheriff. In the old days, he used to present cases to Coroners Juries who decided the cause of death. He had not done this for years, but the law still allowed for coroners to do this. He once was threatened by a man who was mad because his wife's death was ruled a homicide by the doctor. The man came to his house one night brandishing a pistol. Doc slipped out a side door and shot him with bird shot on the front porch as he was trying to kick the door in. When the neighbors arrived to help, they brought the man inside and laid him on the dining room table, where Doc removed the birdshot and had him bandaged in time for the sheriff to take to jail. Doc treated the man who tried to shoot him. The man confessed to killing his wife while in jail.

"Suppers ready," Liz hollered from the dining room. "I heard Grampa telling you that story about the guy he shot. I first heard it told by my daddy."

"Your daddy was in the eighth grade when that happened," Doc said.

"Would you offer grace, Grampa?" Liz asked.

Doc said a nice prayer before they started to eat.

"You've sure been getting yourself in some scrapes here lately, Jon," Doc said.

"I sure hope that's the last of them for a long time," he replied.

"Times have changed. Used to be you could go away all day and leave your house unlocked. Now days they break in your home in broad daylight while you're at work. Twenty years ago, that was never heard of," Doc commented.

"Yes, it is getting bad. Drugs have a lot to do with it I think," Jon said. "Some of these punks would kill their own grandma to get drug money."

"I hear they are starting up a fire department down in Hamilton Township. Back when I started as coroner, there were only four fire departments in the county: Jackson, Coalton, Wellston, and Oak Hill."

"That will only leave one township without fire protection now: Bloomfield," Jon responded.

"It's been good for folks to come together to do this in their communities," Doc said.

"Didn't you lose a barn to fire one time, Grampa?" Liz asked.

"Back during the Second World War. Franklin Township didn't have a fire contract with the city of Jackson back then. Only thing we could do was watch it burn down and wet down the side of the house to keep it from catching."

"What happened to cause it?" Jon asked.

"I don't know. We were all in bed asleep. The train was going by and they saw the fire and stopped and laid on the whistle to wake us up. We had a gasoline powered water pump on the cistern by the house that we ran once a day to fill a small water tank on the second floor of the house. I fired it up and hooked a hose to it to save the house.

"Not long after that," Doc continued, "we tried to start a fire department, but not enough interest. So many were away at war or working in defense factories.

Six families right in this community got together and built a trailer with a small water tank and pump on it and some hose. We kept it in the heated school bus garage over at the school. If we had a fire someone went and hooked their pickup truck to it and took it to the fire. We could pump out of a cistern or pond with it, too."

"Wow, that was neat," Jon said.

"It's still sitting out back in my machinery shed. Probably hasn't been run for twenty-five years."

"Not many trains come through here anymore," Jon said.

"Just a freight train comes down in the morning to Oak Hill and returns in the evening. Used to be three a day with a passenger car," Doc said. "When my wife and I first moved to this farm I took the train to Jackson to my office in the morning and back in the evening."

"One night I got a call from the doctor at Oak Hill. There was a lot of flu going on and he was covered up. There were several families sick down in Monroe Hollow. There was a deep snow on and roads were covered. I took a lantern over to the train tracks and flagged down the train. I got off on the Firebrick road and a man with a team and sled took me to the houses where they had sickness. I was down there two days. Stayed with the storekeeper in the holler."

"That sure was good fried chicken and mashed potatoes and gravy, Liz," Jon said.

"Thank you. Grampa is going to wash the dishes. I have barn chores to do."

"I'll help you with them," Jon told her.

They went out to the barn. It was cold.

"Can you go to the loft and throw down six bales of hay, Jon?" Liz asked.

"Sure."

After doing chores, they went back to the house and made hot chocolate and sat in the kitchen and drank it.

"Karen and I are enrolled at the Career Center next October for the Basic Police Academy class," Liz told Jon.

"That's good. Maybe you can start a mounted unit, too. A lot of sheriffs have mounted posses. They use them in parades and for patrolling at like the county fair and for looking for lost people in the forests. The deputies use their own horses and trucks and trailers."

"That's neat," Liz said. "Have you talked to Rita lately?"

"Talked to her on the phone once. She's working a lot of overtime up there," Jon answered.

"I thought you were going to move her furniture up to Logan?"

"As soon as she says so I will. You going to still let us use your truck?"

"Of course," Liz answered.

"Well, I'm going to have to be getting home," Jon said.

"I'll walk out with you." It was a clear and cold night. They had a friendly hug and parted. Jon drove up Franklin Valley Road. He wondered if Rita was losing interest in seeing him. She didn't come home often and she was hard to get ahold of by phone as she was always at work or asleep. Oh, well.

Chapter 26

A week before Christmas, Jon helped Rita move her bedroom furniture to Logan. She and her friend shared a nice, big, two-story house. It had three bedrooms and two baths. Her roommate was a nice young lady about Rita's age. They fixed a nice supper before he started back to Jackson in a heavy snow. Jon couldn't help but think that Rita had moved on to another phase of her life. She was enrolled in Hocking College taking one class per quarter until things slowed down at the plant and she could carry more classes.

Driving down State Route 93 through Vinton County, he thought about how busy it had been since early fall. A lot of fires to investigate. They solved one murder. Got convictions on several other cases. Had one case still pending in the courts, the old truck stop case. Waiting to see what happened between the prosecutor and the defense attorney on that one. Maybe they could turn the boyfriend against the owner and prosecute her. He always liked to get the owner on the fraud cases. It took the profit out of it.

Now it looked like things were going to be over with Rita. They'd probably remain friends, but not as closely as they had been at one time, before they slept together. He would miss that kind of friendship. Once you had slept together, it was kind of hard to go back to just being good friends.

He stopped at the one traffic light in McArthur. There were only two traffic lights in all of Vinton County. One in front of the courthouse in McArthur and one in the little village of Hamden just before you crossed into Jackson County at Wellston. As he sat at the light in McArthur, he looked at the courthouse. It was built during the Depression. There was a jail on the top floor, the third floor, but no elevator in the building. He had taken a few drunks up those stairs to the jail. Not an easy thing to do. The sheriff's office was in a brick house next to the courthouse. It at one time, had a jail attached to the rear of it until the new courthouse was built. It was another one of those old jails that the sheriff lived in.

His mind drifted to the killing of the Vinton County Sheriff in 1970. It was the year before he had started in law enforcement. He had heard the story many times. There was a huge manhunt that went on for over a week, and the suspect was finally found hiding in a field under a multi-floral rose bush. The officer that spotted him was on horseback. It was actually his horse that spotted the guys leg sticking out from under the bush. The horse had been trained to hunt deer and elk. The suspect gave up without a fight, though he was armed. He was sent to prison for life. He had shot the sheriff, who had been in office for many, many years. He only had two deputies. One of them was injured in the shooting that killed the sheriff.

By the time he pulled into Doc's farm to drop off Liz's truck, there was four inches of newly fallen snow. He was glad that her truck was four-wheel drive. He knocked on the door. Liz came to the door in her robe. "Grampa is at Grange. Come on in," she said.

"I filled up your truck with gas," Jon told her.

"You didn't have to do that," she said.

"Yeah, I did. You always do that when you borrow someone's vehicle."

"I'm just getting ready to shower. I work tonight. I'll put some hot chocolate on and you can watch it while I get cleaned up."

Jon was sitting at the kitchen table drinking hot chocolate when Liz came in and sat down in her robe and started brushing her long, dark hair. He poured her a cup of chocolate.

"I know I'm probably tempting you again," she smiled.

"I enjoy it," he said.

"I'll behave. Grampa will be home shortly. Did the moving go well?"

"Yeah. All done. She has a nice set up with her roommate."

"You aren't very talkative tonight. You been back to see Reverend Evans?" she asked him.

"I need to go again. Should go tomorrow evening."

"Sad about Rita?"

"Yeah. Kinda. I think our relationship is over."

"I'm sorry."

"What do you want for Christmas?" Jon asked her.

"I need to get a deputy's uniform. A gun belt and all that stuff. Where do you get them?"

"There is a place in downtown Columbus that has the franchise for them. It's a big men's store, but of course they have women's uniforms, too. You can call and order or go up there and get fitted."

"Would you take me?" she asked.

"Sure. I need to put together a class A uniform for funerals and special occasions, too. The fire marshal doesn't provide you with one. Most guys put one together themselves. It is more along the fire service line than law enforcement."

"Are they open on Saturdays?"

"Till three."

"I don't work Saturday. You want to go?" she asked him.

"Okay. "I'll buy you your gun belt for Christmas."

"That's nice of you," she said as she continued to brush her hair.

Jon got up and looked outside. It was still snowing. Must be almost six inches by now. He looked down the road and saw the lights of the train coming back from Oak Hill. It would be loaded with clay from the refractories and maybe charcoal from the kiln at Clay.

"Well, I better be getting home. You'll be getting ready for work soon," Jon said.

"Grampa should be home any minute now. I better go change. If he finds me sitting here in my housecoat with a man at the kitchen table, he won't like it."

"I'll get going then. We going to Columbus Saturday, then?"

"Yes. I get off at eight that morning. We can leave then. I'll come by your house, if that's all right."

"Okay. I'll see you Saturday morning." Jon said, giving her a small hug.

On Saturday, Jon and Liz left Jackson at eight-thirty and drove to downtown Columbus to purchase her uniforms. Jon got her a good holster to go with her leather belt. It was a new style of holster that keeps the pistol secure and prevents someone from taking the gun. It wasn't a good-looking holster, but it beats being shot with your own gun.

"What are you doing for Christmas? It's Monday, you know," Liz asked him on the way back down route twenty-three.

"I volunteer to work the desk at the SO eight to four Christmas Day, so the dispatcher can have the day off."

"Do you want to come out to Grampa's Christmas Eve? My parents and brother come down and spend the night. We go to church at eight o'clock Christmas Eve."

"Sounds nice. I would like that."

"We eat dinner at six before church."

"Okay. I'll be there. Should I bring gifts?"

"No. I'll have something for you to show my appreciation for all you have done for me helping me get started in my part-time job."

"You don't have to do that," he answered.

"Oh, I want to," she said.

Jon arrived at Doc Carter's Christmas Eve as it was beginning to snow again. Looked like it would be a fresh snow for Christmas. Mr. and Mrs. Carter were there, as well as Liz's younger brother, Robert. He was a student at Ohio State taking prelaw. He explained that he planned to go to Capital University for his law degree.

"Liz has told us about some of your recent experiences, Jon," Mrs. Carter commented.

"Yes. You seem to be somewhat of a local hero," Mr. Carter said.

"I usually don't get into that kind of stuff that often. I would just as leave it be the last time I have to draw my gun for the rest of my career."

"You plan to stay in law enforcement until you retire, then?" Mr. Carter asked.

"Yes. I like it. I can retire after thirty years on a good pension with good insurance."

"We were worried that Liz was going to go that route for some time, but I think that her work with her Grampa has satisfied her fascination for such things," Liz's mother explained.

"She is doing a good job. Her work at the Sheriff's Office in the new sex crimes unit is going to be very good," Jon explained to them.

"We weren't aware of that, Liz," Mrs. Carter said as she looked at Liz.

"I hadn't mentioned it yet, Mother. I know how you feel about me being involved in police work," Liz responded.

Jon felt a bit of tension. Mr. and Mrs. Carter seemed a little bit uppity and formal. Doc just sat there, listening to the conversation.

"More women are getting involved in police work, Mother. In the next ten years, you're going to see a lot of women in uniform," Robert said.

"Thank you, Robert," Liz said to her brother.

"We were rather hoping that Liz might consider medical school. Women seem to be taking to that field also and it is not nearly as dangerous," Mr. Carter said.

"I would have to go back to college for premed, Mother," Liz explained.

"She would make a good coroner for this county, and she would have to be a doctor to do that," Jon said, trying to agree somewhat with Liz's parents.

"Maybe she could run for sheriff someday," Doc said. "I think there has only been two women sheriffs in the state of Ohio."

"That's enough of that, Dad," Mr. Carter said to his father.

"Liz, help me check on supper and set the table," Mrs. Carter said as she got up from her chair in the living room.

"What kind of law do you plan to practice, Robert?" Jon asked Liz's brother.

"Criminal Law. Probably get me a job as an assistant prosecutor when I get out of law school."

"Good prosecutors are in high demand," Jon said.

"Our neighbor has offered him a position in his law firm when he passes the bar. They do mostly insurance work. Pays very well," Mr. Carter said.

"I'd rather cut my teeth prosecuting criminals," Robert said to his father.

"Dinner is served," Mrs. Carter said from the dining room.

"The best part of Christmas Eve," Doc replied.

"That was a good dinner, and I really like your parents," Jon said to Liz as they drove to church. They were in his car. The rest of the family went in Mr. Carter's Lincoln Towne Car. They were going to Oak Hill to the Presbyterian Church. Franklin Valley Methodist didn't have a Christmas Eve service.

"I'm sorry, it's so apparent that they don't want me involved in law enforcement, Liz replied.

"Sorry about letting it slip about the sexual assault detail."

"I was going to tell them anyway, but don't tell them that I was with you the day you saved the highway patrolman. They know about what happened to you, but not about me being there. I made Grampa promise not to tell them."

"Okay. They would probably write me off as a danger to your health and safety. I can see where you are coming from," Jon answered.

"Mother didn't want me helping Grampa as his assistant, but Daddy talked her into it. I think he thought it would satisfy me and keep me out of police work."

"My great-grandpa on my mother's side was a constable in Madison Township. I never met him. He was shot in a shootout when a couple of escaped prisoners from somewhere were holed up in a house out toward Thurman. He lost his arm because of it. Mother remembers it well. They lived next to each other on the farm when she was growing up."

"That probably explains her concerns," Jon said.

"I don't know. I think they just want me to do something more womanly like and not try to go into a job that has been mostly for men."

The church service was very good. At the end, they all lit candles and held them while singing *Silent Night*. Reverend Evans was pleased to see Liz's parents. It brought back pleasant memories of Jon's childhood, and he had a desire to return to the church. He had been absent for over ten years, and he knew deep inside that he needed this. He had two close calls with death in the last few months, and he had been thinking about that sort of thing. His talks with Reverend Evans had served to also whet his appetite for a return to his faith. He had spent the last ten years doing a lot of partying. It was time for a change.

"I would like to start going to church with you regularly, Liz, if you will permit me to accompany you," Jon told her as they drove up Route 93. It was still snowing, and about two inches had fallen since they were in church.

"I would like that very much. It's an important part of my life. I can't imagine life without it. When I was in college I attended every Sunday."

"That's where I went wrong. When I left for college, I left my religion at home."

"We'll open gifts when we get back to the house. You'll stay, won't you?" Liz asked.

"Yes. I put your belt, holster, handcuff case, and mag holder in a box and wrapped it up for you."

When they got back to Doc's, they all gathered around the tree in the living room. Mr. Carter passed out the gifts. Jon got two. One box from Liz and a box from her parents. Liz opened a box from her parents. It contained an old but good pair of handcuffs.

"Those were my grandfathers," Mrs. Carter explained. "I wanted you to have them. It's not an approval of your interest in that kind of work, but I think they should stay in the family. His initials are stamped in them."

"Oh, thank you so much, Mother. I didn't know you even had them," Liz said with excitement.

"Don't put them on because I don't have the key."

"I can find a key for them," Jon said. "There's a drawer full of old keys at the sheriff's office."

Jon opened his gift from Liz. It was a pair of brown cowboy boots. "Thank you, Liz, I really like them."

Jon had gotten Doc a pair of wool socks. He took his shoes and socks off and put them on. "Thank you, Jon." Doc said.

Liz's parents got Jon a nice pair of black leather gloves that were lined with rabbit fur. "Thank you, Mr. and Mrs. Carter. I really need these. I don't have any dress gloves."

Robert sat down at the piano and started playing a medley of Christmas songs. "My late wife played the piano," said Doc. "She used to play at the church regularly. Robert is the only one in the family who plays."

Jon felt a warm feeling sitting with this family. Mr. and Mrs. Carter had relaxed and became less formal in their talk. They were even laughing at a funny story what Doc was telling. Doc and Liz's dad looked very much alike. There was a good fire burning in the fireplace. Jon got up and put a couple more logs on.

As Jon was leaving, Mr. Carter said, "Come back out tomorrow, Jon. If the snow isn't too deep, Robert and I will go rabbit hunting, and you can join us."

"I'd love to, but I'm working the desk at the SO all day so the dispatcher can be at home with her family. I really enjoyed spending the evening with you."

Liz walked onto the big porch with Jon. "When will I see you again?" she asked him as she slipped her arms around his waist and he slipped his around hers.

"We have to quit meeting in the middle of the night on calls. Maybe we can do something some evening this week. Then there is New Year's Eve. We all go out to the disco that night and have a good time."

"That would be nice," she replied. Their eyes met and their lips moved toward each other's, and they embraced in a long kiss. He couldn't help but allow his hands to drop and grasp her rear end and pull her close to him.

"He turned and left. "See you, and thanks for sharing the evening with me."

"Bye," she said.

CHAPTER 27

The phone was ringing. Jon looked at the clock. It was four in the morning. He answered it. "This is the Jackson Co SO. We have a fatal fire on 279, west of Oak Hill, near Slab Hill," the dispatcher said.

"Okay. I'm on my way. What are the roads like?"

"Snow covered; about six inches and still snowing. The coroner and Dave are on their way," she said. He could hear Dave calling in on his radio in the background of the radio room. "Forty o three signal 33."

Forty o three was Dave's unit number. Forty meant county number forty in alphabetical order and 03 was his badge number. Three meant that he was next down the totem pole below the chief deputy, who was two and the sheriff being one.

It took Jon almost an hour for a drive that should have taken twenty minutes. The roads had not been plowed yet. At least the back roads that he drove. The state highways had been plowed. When he arrived, he saw Dave's car and Liz's truck. He found the fire chief. It looked like an older trailer, about twelve by fifty feet. It set on a hill side. The fire trucks had not been able to drive up the driveway and had stretched their hose about two hundred fifty feet in the deep snow. It looked like they did a good job on the fire. It was still standing, and they were ten miles from the fire station and the trucks would have been driving slow because of their tire chains and the snow. "What can you tell me chief?" Jon asked.

"When we got here, the fire was coming out the kitchen window. We went in and knocked it down real quick. The front door was not locked. We found a body on the living room sofa. DOA. Didn't move it. Dave and the coroner lady are looking at it now. The guy that delivers the newspapers out here discovered it and stopped at a house on down the road to have them call. All he saw was thick smoke at the time he went by."

This is what Jon liked to hear from a fire official. The facts as the chief knew them. It helped him to get started on his investigation.

The living room and kitchen was lit up with fire department lights. Liz and Dave were standing there, looking at the body and talking. "Morning, every-one," Jon said. "Nice way to spend Christmas Day."

"Yeah, look at this. We got another murder," Dave said. Liz was holding a pillow in her hand. The victim was lying face up on the couch. She placed the pillow on the victim's face and chest.

"This is how the FD found the body, with the pillow on it," Liz stated. She then removed the pillow. "Look at these marks on the chest."

Jon could see bloody marks on the chest. Probably a half-dozen of them.

"Looks like he's been hacked at with something. Not big enough marks for an axe," Dave added.

"No signs of a struggle," Liz said. "Like he was laying here asleep and someone attacked him."

"We'll need an autopsy on this one, for sure," Jon said.

Jon stood back and looked at the living room scene. There was some burn-ing around the couch and the floor next to it. Not much. Most of the damage in this room was from heat. He moved into the kitchen. There was a stuffed chair that was burned up. Only the metal springs and some of the wooden frame remained. He studied the kitchen and checked the range. No doubt the fire started on the chair. He took his flashlight and went back down the hallway and checked the two bedrooms and bath. Just heat and smoke from the kitchen fire. No signs of forcible entry to the rear door of the place. He found the breaker box in the master bedroom closet. No breakers were tripped. The fur-nace was electric and had no fire damage. The hot water tank was in a closet in the bath and was all right. It was important to eliminate all causes of a fire.

"Let me get a sample of the couch and the victims clothing before you bag him," Jon said to Liz. Jon cut up a piece of carpet next to the couch and smelled it. He held it to Liz and Dave's nose's.

"Gasoline," they both said.

Liz and Dave took photos of the body. Dave then went on to search the rest of the trailer. It might shed some light on the lifestyle of those that lived there.

"The guy lived here with his wife. No kids. Mid-twenties. Neighbors saw her leave yesterday afternoon with his father. Don't know where she is. A couple guys in a truck stopped and asked me what was going on when I first got here. I told them someone was killed. They knew his name. Said they were friends. I got their names. They need to be talked to again. They don't live too far away." Dave told them before he started down the hallway. "The victim's name is James Dean. Hers is Samantha Dean. They call her Sammy. He works at the frozen food factory at Wellston. She doesn't work."

Jon finished his fire scene investigation while they waited on the undertaker to come take the body to the Franklin County Morgue. Dave spent a lot of time in the rear of the trailer. When he came out, he was carrying a pump shotgun and a set of scales. "Found some residue that looks like cocaine and these scales. Looks like a dealer. Also, a twenty-gallon garbage bag with remainders of marijuana seeds and stems. No money. We need to search the kitchen and living room for cash. I'm going to talk to neighbors," Dave explained.

Jon and Liz tore apart the living room and kitchen and found no money. The undertaker arrived and they bagged the body and helped them take it down the hill to the transport van. Liz left to go find a phone and call the Franklin County Morgue.

"I just talked to the victim's father," Dave told them when he returned to the scene. "He showed up. Lives in Jackson. Said he was here Sunday late in the afternoon to visit his son. Everything was okay. No one else was around. The wife left on Saturday and went to Dayton to see her family. Her kids live there with a sister. He got ahold of her and someone is bringing her down right away."

"You know the father, Dave?" Jon asked.

"Yeah. He's a drug dealer. Been arrested and served time for it before. Moved down here about five years ago, from some big city in Ohio."

"You tell him we think he was killed?" Liz asked Dave.

"No. I think we should wait."

"We searched the living room and kitchen. No money or drugs. Nothing that looks like it could be the weapon that made those marks," Jon said.

It was still snowing when Liz returned from calling in her autopsy request. Jon and Dave were sitting in Dave's car talking. The neighbors had brought over some coffee and a Coke for Dave. Everyone in the county knew that Dave didn't drink coffee. "Get in the back. We're having a meeting," Dave hollered to Liz as she walked up the slippery hillside through the snow.

"So, what you guys thinking?" Liz said as she got in the back seat.

"Well, we got another murder. Probably drug related, but it's too soon to tell." Dave said.

"What's next?" Liz said.

"When the victim's wife gets back to town, we should learn some more by talking to her. She should know what's been going on around here and who her husband hangs out with," Jon told Liz.

"It's almost noon. What a way to spend Christmas Day," Dave said.

"You think I should go in and work the desk the rest of the day? I was supposed to sit all day so the dispatcher could stay home," Jon asked Dave.

"No, one of the special deputies came in and took care of it," Dave answered.

"You want to interview the wife today if she gets back or wait until tomorrow?" Jon asked.

"I think tomorrow would be better. Give her some time to get over the initial shock. I don't mean to shove you out Jon, but I think Liz and I should talk to her. I like this idea of having a woman around to help with interviews of ladies. It makes them more comfortable with a woman in the room."

"I agree. I'll be in your office at nine tomorrow. We can call Liz when we find out what time the wife will be available. That way she can get some sleep. Besides, she has to feed the horses," Jon said.

"The sheriff is on his way down to look at the scene before we leave," Dave told them.

"I'll stay round so I can tell him how the fire was set. We got two points of origin. The main one in the kitchen and one around the body that didn't burn very well."

"Do you need me any longer? Liz asked them.

"No. Thanks for coming out. It's nice to have someone come out to the scene and take care of the body," Dave said.

"My parents will still be at Grampa's. I left a note before I left," she told them.

"I'm glad your Grampa came up with this idea of you being his assistant," Dave said.

"Me, too," Jon agreed.

"Thank you, guys. I like what I am doing," Liz said as she got out of the car and fell on her rear end.

Jon got out and helped her out and fell on his rear end in the process. "It must be getting colder. The snows starting to freeze where it's packed down," he said.

"Stop by the house on your way home Jon," Liz said to him.

"Okay. I'd like that.," Jon said as he got back in the car to sit with Dave until the sheriff got there.

"You gettin' any of that, Jon?" Dave said chuckling.

"No. Haven't tried. I'm a gentleman, you know."

"You're a lady's man, you mean," Dave said. Cops seemed to talk like this all the time about women. Most of it was just talk. Some of the guys that were married even talked that way, but they didn't cheat on their wives. Some liked to make you think that they did, but they really didn't. On the other hand, the most common trouble that cops got into had to do with women. Most cops that took a fall took it over a woman.

"So, what did you do Christmas Eve?" Dave asked him.

"Went out to Liz and Doc's. Met her parents and brother. We went to church service."

"It's got be serious if she's got you going to church."

"I like going. I haven't gone much for ten years. You know that. I think it's time to start going again. I've had some close calls lately. Gets you to thinking about things."

"I met Liz's friend, Karen. She's going through the police academy next fall and help us on the sexual assault detail," Dave said.

"Now you'll be doin' her, Dave. Chuck always said he didn't want any female deputies cause the deputies would be screwing them."

"Well, I'm single, and she's single. Chuck is more worried about the married guys. I'll have to keep them away from her. Part of my duties," Dave said, grinning.

"What better way to keep her out of someone else's bed than to keep her in yours," Jon said, laughing.

"Whatever works. Looks like the Sheriff's here. I think he just wanted to try out his new Blazer. See how it goes in the snow."

They got out and Jon shook hands with the Sheriff. Dave filled him in on things as they walked up the hill to the trailer.

"Here's where the body was," Dave told the sheriff pointing to the sofa. "Face up. Had a pillow laying on the face and chest. Deep cuts in the chest from some kind of sharp instrument. Not wide enough for an axe. Too wide for a knife. Liz came up with the idea that it might be a splitting maul. He wasn't burned bad. The pillow protected his face and chest and the blanket that covered him protected the rest of him."

"What about the fire Jon?" Chuck asked.

"Over there in the kitchen, the big stuffed chair was set on fire. No accidental reason for it. Also, some gasoline poured on the sofa and a separate fire set, but it didn't burn very good."

"Any gas on the chair?" the sheriff asked him.

"Probably. Couldn't smell it like we could on the sofa, but I would say there was. I took samples to send to the lab."

"Didn't find the weapon?" the sheriff said.

"No. Must have took it with them when they left," Dave answered.

"Sounds like you got your work cut out for you. You guys done here for the day?"

"Yeah. The guy's wife should be back from Dayton by tomorrow and we'll start by talking to her," Dave explained.

"Okay. We been gettin' calls from the press. We'll do a press release in the morning," the sheriff said, shaking his head. "We're setting a record this year. This is the third murder we've had this year. I think it's the drugs these folks are using."

Jon drove back up the Four Mile Pike and crossed over to Franklin Valley and stopped at Liz's place. Her parents' car was in the driveway.

Liz's mom had hot chocolate sitting on the table in the kitchen for him. "Liz and her brother are out in the barn. Quite a way to spend Christmas Day for you two," she said to him.

"Yes. The county has had three murders now this year. More than ever before. Usually one a year. Sometimes two," Jon said to her.

"Yes, I know. Doc and I and my husband were just talking about how things have changed so much."

"Did you know the officer that was killed in Oak Hill last January?" Mrs. Carter asked Jon.

"Yes. He was my best friend."

"My mother taught him at the high school," she replied.

"Yes, Liz told me."

"I see that Liz is carrying around a gun now," Mrs. Carter said.

"I taught her to shoot. If she's going to work on these kind of things, she needs to be able to protect herself. She's a natural at shooting."

"I just hope she doesn't give up nursing and become a cop."

"I don't think she will. She likes this coroner business. The problem is when Doc gives it up will the next coroner hire her. He can hire whoever he wants to. More likely he will do away with her position because the county can't afford to pay both a coroner and his investigator."

"That's another reason for her to stay out of police work. It doesn't pay anything," she said as she refilled his cup with chocolate.

"Not around these parts, it doesn't," Jon agreed. "That's why I took a state job. Pays better."

"Now her brother wants to be a prosecutor. I bet they're out in the barn trying this case you were on right now."

Jon laughed. "Public service does tend to run in some families."

"Did it in yours? she asked him.

"My dad worked in an office at a large factory. Mom stayed home. My great-grandfather was one of the first fire marshal investigators in the state of Ohio. He worked from 1910 until 1945. Started on horseback and transitioned to automobile."

"I stayed home, too. That's interesting about your great-grandfather."

"Yes. I don't know a lot about him. He died before I was born."

Liz and her brother came in and brushed the snow off themselves. Mrs. Carter handed them hot chocolate. "Nice to see you so soon again, Jon," Liz said, smiling.

"We're done for the day down there. You have to work tonight?"

"Yes," Liz said. "I've got to get a few hours of sleep," she answered.

Jon looked at the clock on the wall. It was four o'clock. "When's it supposed to stop snowing?" he asked.

"It's supposed to snow all night. My husband and I are considering staying all night again," Mrs. Carter said.

"Well, I better get home and start on my report. I'll probably see you in the morning when you and Dave interview our victim's wife," Jon said as he looked at Liz.

"I've got to get some sleep so I can work tonight," Liz said.

"Honey do you have to be involved in that part of the investigation?" Mrs. Carter said to Liz. "You'll never get enough sleep to work your shift tomorrow night."

"I'm alright, Mother. The poor girl will want a woman present with her."

"I'll see you tomorrow, Liz," Jon said. "Nice to meet you and your family, Mrs. Carter. I hope to see you again some time."

"Be careful driving in the snow, Jon," Liz said as she took his hand and squeezed it.

The interview of Sammy Dean had been going on for about forty-five minutes. Jon had been watching from an adjacent room through the one-way mirror. They had gotten the preliminaries aside. Sam told them that her father-in-law had picked her up at the trailer Saturday afternoon and taken her to Dayton and dropped her off at her sister's house where she was going to spend a week visiting with her two children. The kids had been taken away from her by the court and placed in her sister's home. James was home when she left that afternoon. No one else was there.

"Sam," Dave said to her in a calm voice, "we found evidence at your place of selling cocaine and marijuana. Now, you're not in any trouble, but that might have something to do with why your husband was killed. We need you to tell us about this."

Liz handed Sam a tissue as she started to sob again.

"He was dealing. He has a good job, but he wanted to save up money so that we can build a house. His dad set him up in the business. His dad has several dealers working for him. He goes to Dayton every two weeks to get the stuff and distribute to his dealers. That's why I rode to Dayton with him. He was bringing back some coke."

"Do you know if he delivered to your husband when he came back?" Dave asked her.

"No. I've talked to him since I got back last night, but not about that," Sam said.

"How does he do his selling?" Dave asked.

"People come to the trailer. Users. I don't know all of them. I know some of them. They don't come when he isn't there."

"Do you know Mike Gore?"

"Yeah, he buys from him. He hangs out a lot at the trailer with my husband and sometimes they go places together."

"When was the last time you saw him?"

"He stopped by the day I left. He told Mike he would be getting some coke the next day."

"Has there ever been any trouble between your husband and Mike?"

"I think he thought me and Mike were having sex. Mike would come over when James was at work and we would smoke some weed, but I never had anything like that to do with him. He came onto me, but I wasn't interested."

"Tell us about Mike."

"He lives over toward South Webster with his parents and his woman. They got two little kids. He don't work anywhere. He runs the roads at night with different people. He never brings his woman over with him. James would go over to his house once in a while, and they would work on their cars."

"Who would you suspect would want to kill James?" Dave asked her.

"I don't know. A lot of people knows he is selling. They know he gets it every two weeks on Saturday or Sunday. He keeps it in the bedroom. He never takes them back there. They do the business in the kitchen. He stashes the money in the dresser drawer in the bedroom."

"How much cash did he have on hand?"

"Maybe a couple hundred. He puts it in a savings account. He would have given his dad cash the day his dad picked me up. I didn't see him give it to him, but he always does right before his dad goes to Dayton."

"We know that James' dad was there on Sunday. He told us he was. Of course, he didn't tell us why he was there. He didn't even tell us about taking you to Dayton."

"So, he would have given him the Coke on Sunday," Sam said.

"Has James ever been ripped off before?" Dave asked her as she continued to sob. Liz took the young girls hand in hers and patted it.

"No. He always carried a pistol at the house when he was sitting on the stuff to sell."

"We found a shotgun in the closet, but no pistol. What kind was it?"

"A big thing with a long barrel. A .44 something."

"Forty-four Magnum?" Dave asked.

"Yeah, I think so. He was afraid of getting ripped off. That's why he carried it."

The interview went on for another forty-five minutes with the young girl. Liz walked her out to the lobby where Sam's sister in law was waiting on her.

"Good job, Dave and Liz," Jon said as the three of them sat down in Dave's office. Jon had gotten him and Liz coffee from the kitchen and Dave a Coke from the machine.

"I think someone came there that night and ripped him off, took his coke. We didn't find it or any money. I wonder what happened to the gun. He wasn't wearing it," Dave told them.

"They may have taken the gun, too," Liz said.

"Did the bedroom look like it had been ransacked that night we were there?" Jon asked Dave.

"No. They knew where to look. They didn't tear things up," Dave replied.

"You think we can get much out of his dad, Dave?" Jon asked Dave.

"No. He's not going to admit to bringing him coke to sell. That may be necessary to prove motive if that is the reason he was killed. We'll just have to go with what Sam told us."

"Guess we'll just have to go out and beat the bushes. Talk to James friends. Some will tell us they buy from him if we promise they won't be in any kind of trouble. Some won't want to admit they do business with him," Jon said to them. Liz was taking all this in. It was obviously rather new to her, the drug business, that is.

"The snow is letting up. I don't like this Mike Gore. He was awful nervous when he stopped at the scene yesterday morning and asked what was going on. We need to have a serious talk with him," Dave said. He was good at getting the feel for a person.

"If you guys don't need me anymore, then I'm going home to get some sleep," Liz told them.

"Okay. Thanks for your help with the girl. It made a difference," Dave told her.

"See you later, Liz," Jon said.

Jon and Dave spent the rest of the day driving around finding James' friends and talking to them. As they expected, some were up front about buying from him and some denied using the stuff. They found no one that had contact with him that weekend. They left Mike Gore for last. They went to his home. His woman said he had left that morning and had not yet returned. She did not know where he went to.

Chapter 28

That evening, Liz came over to Jon's house about seven. She had to go to work at midnight at the hospital. "Want to go for a walk?" she said when she knocked on the door. "I like to walk in new snow. I haven't been getting enough exercise in this cold weather. Neither have you."

"Okay. Let me get my boots and coat on," he said.

They walked for over an hour. Most of the walks had been shoveled of snow. They went over to Parkview School and built a snowman on the ball field. Then they had a snow ball battle. They stopped at the sub shop and got subs and took them to Jon's and ate them while drinking hot chocolate.

"That was fun, wasn't it, Jon?" Liz said.

"I haven't been in a snow ball fight since I was in high school," he said.

"Are you going to the disco this Saturday night?"

"Yes. Can you go?" Jon asked Liz.

"I want to go, but I'll have to leave to go to work at midnight."

"So, I'll meet you there then."

"Yes. I'll drive so I can leave for work."

"It's time for our favorite show," Jon said.

"Oh. *Dallas* is tonight. I forgot about it." Liz said as she got up and turned on the T.V.

"I wonder what evil JR is going to get into tonight?"

"Probably going to put the screws to someone. I hope it's not poor Suellen again."

"Yeah. She needs to leave him," Jon said. They sat on the couch together. She took her socks off, and he rubbed her feet.

"Is it all right if I change here to go to work after a while? I have my bag out in the truck."

"Sure," Jon answered.

"Mother and Father like you," she said.

"Good. They're nice. They want the best for you."

"It's obvious they don't want me doing police work, isn't it?"

"Yeah, especially your mom."

"Dad thinks it's all about money. He wants my brother to join a law firm and make big bucks."

"I think he'd like to try prosecuting, wouldn't he?" Jon said.

"I think so. He would be good at it. He has several years to go to make up his mind."

Liz got her bag and went through the bedroom into the bathroom. Jon was sorting through fire scene photos and putting case numbers on the back of them and logging them into each case when she came out wearing her robe. She sat down next to him on the couch and started brushing her wet hair. Her robe came up above her knees and she crossed her shapely legs. She was very attractive. He wondered why she was here like this. He guessed she liked his company. He didn't mind hers. Especially now that things between him and Rita seemed to be cooled off.

"Do you mind having me around?" she asked him.

"I like it. Want to go hiking this Saturday. I've got two pairs of show shoes. We can go out to Lake Katherine and hike."

"That would be nice. I've never used snow shoes. I've skied. We used to go down in West Virginia every winter for a long weekend when my brother and I were growing up. We haven't been there since I left home to go to college."

"I've never been on skies," he replied.

"I think my parents still have a weekend reserved at a condo down there in late January. They kept the lease in case they wanted to start going again."

"I like it down there. Where is it?"

"Canaan Valley."

"That's a nice place. Near my favorite place. Blackwater Falls."

"We always stopped there on the way home and checked out the falls. One year I remember that they were frozen solid."

Jon could not keep his eyes off Liz's legs. Her robe had pulled up a little further. He was wondering if she had anything on under the robe.

"Jon," Liz smiled, "you're looking at my legs."

"Yes, I am. They look nice. You're tempting me again."

"I'm sorry," she said as she pulled her robe down toward her knees and continued to brush her hair dry.

"I'm enjoying it."

"How about we take a four-day weekend and go to the mountains? I'll see if Mother and Father will let us use the condo. I'll have to tell them that we're taking several friends with us."

"Are we?"

"Are we what?"

"Taking a bunch of friends with us."

"No, just you and me for four days," she said as she moved close to him on the couch. She took his face in her hands and kissed him passionately. He placed his hand on her thigh.

"Are we going to do things like this?" Jon asked her.

"Yes. We are practicing right now," she said as she kissed him again.

"Too bad you got to go to work. We could practice a lot."

"I guess I better get dressed."

"You got anything on under your robe?"

"What do you think?" she said.

"I don't know."

She took his hand and moved it up her thigh to her waist. He moved it around and found no underwear. "I don't think you do have anything on under your robe," he said.

She removed his hand and said, "That's enough practice for tonight." She then got up and went back into the bedroom. He was tempted to follow, but he decided not to. Don't want to rush things. She came out ten minutes later dressed for work. He walked her to her truck.

The next day, Jon got called to Gallia County on a mobile home fire. No one was hurt, but it took his whole day. He wanted to work with Dave on their new murder investigation. The trailer fire in the city of Gallipolis he determined started underneath the home where the water pipe came up through the ground and into a closet in the bathroom where the hot water tank was at. He found the remains of a heat tape that had been wrapped around the pipe. He knew that if these things were not installed properly according to the directions that came with them, that they could overheat and cause a fire. He checked on the insurance. It was a rental trailer that was not rented out at the time of the fire. The insurance was minimal. There was no mortgage. The owner had no previous fires. He owned several rental units in the area and they were all decent properties. No reason to suspect that the fire was set.

It looked like it was going to be the next week before he and Dave could work together again. Jon had to go to the office in Reynoldsburg for a day to take the class on the new firearms policy. The class that he missed when he was in the hospital after the shooting. He wondered on the way back when the hearing on his shooting was going to be held. His boss was not in the office that day, so he had no one to ask about it. He called Dave from the office. He had been out beating the bushes, but had not been able to find their only person of interest, Mike Gore. His woman had not seen him for several days.

His mind wondered to Liz. A weekend in the mountains with her sounded good. He almost forgot about their snow shoeing hike on Saturday. Maybe it would snow a few more inches. There was over six inches in most places and eight some places. He had no idea how much was on the ground in the mountains. Probably over a foot or more. It hadn't been cold long enough for Lake Katherine to be frozen enough to walk on. They would have to stay on the trails Saturday.

Saturday morning was cold. There had not been any new snow, but what there was would be good for snow shoeing. Jon went out to Liz's place at eight-thirty and helped her with the chores in the barn. By ten-thirty they were headed to Lake Katherine. Liz made sandwiches and hot chocolate to take.

It took Liz a while to get used to the big snow shoes. They made you work hard to get where you were going, but it was better than trying to walk in deep snow which really wore you out and was very slow. Jon had gotten his snowshoes the winter of '78 between the first blizzard and the second blizzard when he was a deputy. He kept them in his cruiser trunk and used them when he had to walk a long way through deep snow to go on a call. Most of the calls during that time were to check on people who could not get out and had lost phone service or had no phone.

They hiked for about two hours and found a small overhang cave where they built a small fire and ate. They had shed their coats and put them in his backpack as they hiked. Even though it was cold, they were working up a sweat with the snow shoes.

"You ever cross country ski?" Jon asked Liz as they sat near the fire.

"No. Just downhill skiing," she responded.

"I haven't either. They say it's easier than snow shoeing. I'd like to try it."

"How about next weekend? I've got the condo Friday through Monday. Can you get off work?"

"I don't see why not. Let's plan on it."

"I don't have any skis."

"I'll borrow my brothers for you. If we cross country ski, we'll have to each rent a pair as they're a lot different kind of ski," she explained to him.

"Are you going to Chillicothe to visit your parents?"

"No. They're coming down on Monday, New Year's Day. I'll ask them to bring two sets of skis for us to use."

"The lake looks nice with the snow on it. The ice isn't thick enough to walk on, though."

"You never did take me canoeing on the lake."

"Yeah. Too many things happened this fall. We'll do it this spring."

"We have a big dinner at one at Grampa's on New Year's Day. You want to come out?"

"I'd like to, but I'll work so I can take Friday off. Dave never takes that day off, so we'll probably work together on that murder case."

"Got anything new on it?"

"No. The guy Dave has a feeling about has made himself scarce. When Dave has a feeling about someone then it's usually right. He's good about smelling these things out."

"Do you have anything on him?"

"No, not really. Just Dave's hunch."

They snow shoed back to Liz's truck and drove out to her place. Jon helped her with her barn chores, so she could get some sleep. He headed home. He hoped this murder didn't drag itself out a long time. He had never been involved in a murder case that was not solved. Some investigators say that the first forty-eight hours on a case are the most critical. The first forty-eight on his one did not yield much except to establish that they had a murder with an arson set to cover it up. They hadn't gotten the autopsy results back yet. Must be busy at the Franklin County Morgue. They did a lot of work for the smaller counties.

Sunday night, New Year's Eve, they all met at the disco in Jackson at eight-thirty. Jon sat next to Liz. The whole gang was there except for Rita. Since it was Sunday they could not serve hard liquor so everyone was either drinking beer or soft drinks. Some had their favorite mixed drink minus the liquor. The DJ started playing at nine. The party would go until one when the place closed.

"What time do you have to leave?" Dave asked Liz as they slow danced.

"About 11:15. I'll change in the locker room at the hospital."

"Looks like Rita's here," Jon said. "Looks like she brought a date."

"Does that bother you?" Liz asked.

"No. Not at all."

They went over to the table as Rita was introducing her guy to everyone. "This is Robert. He works at the plant with me at Logan. He lives in McArthur," Rita said.

"Glad to meet you, Robert," Jon said to him as they shook hands. Rita then approached Jon and they hugged.

"Are you staying the night in town?" Liz asked Rita.

"No, we have to drive back tonight. We both go to work at eight in the morning," Rita answered.

"You used to work at the Jackson Plant, didn't you?" Jess asked Robert.

"Yeah, I transferred to Logan two years ago," Robert said.

"Didn't you have your car broken into in the parking lot a few years ago?" Jess asked.

"Yeah, I remember you. You were the cop that came out. You got my eight-track player back for me and arrested the guys."

"That was me," Jess said.

"I always wondered how you caught them," Robert said.

"Well, a couple of weeks later, I caught them breaking into a car at the hospital. They confessed to a bunch of car B&E's. We searched their place and found a bunch of tape players and CB radios. They were just getting ready to make a trip to Columbus to sell them," Jess explained.

"I got restitution for the damage they did to my car. Thanks for what you did."

"Just old fashioned police work. Actually, someone from the hospital called and reported some suspicious activity in the lot, and I parked my car and walked around to the lot and crept up on them while they were busy."

"I remember that," Jon said. "That was good work, Jess."

When it was time for Liz to leave to go to work, Jon walked out with her and they sat in her truck as she warmed the engine up and talked.

"Remember we got a date this weekend," Liz told him. "Four days in the mountains. I sure could use the break."

"I'm looking forward to it," Jon said. He kissed her good night and returned to the disco.

CHAPTER 29

On New Year's Day, Jon went to the SO, and he and Dave reviewed everything they had done on their most recent murder case. The SO was pretty quiet as it was a holiday. Just them and the dispatcher and one deputy working.

"I think we need to talk to Mike Gores woman," Dave said, "and see if she provides him with an alibi for that night."

"What do we know about her?" Jon asked Dave.

"She's about twenty years old. Has two kids by him. One is only a few months old. They live with Mike's mom."

"Let's go see if we can find her, then," Jon said.

On the drive down to find her, Jon asked Dave, "You know why this part of the county is called the Redbrush?"

"No. I heard it called that. I know they have a red brush festival of some sorts over around Minford."

"It's cause of the leaves of the sumac trees. In the fall, they turn real red. Back in the days of the old iron furnaces they used to make charcoal for the furnaces. They would clear cut a bunch of timber and cut it up and take it to the charcoal furnace. The first thing that grew back was the sumac. They grow real fast. In the fall the hillsides turned red. That's why they call it the Redbrush."

"That's a pretty good history lesson. You been readin' history?" Dave asked him.

"Some, but Chuck told me about it first. Then I read a book that some guy around here wrote about the Redbrush."

"Those old kilns over on 279 are charcoal kilns, aren't they?"

"Yeah, they are. Been there a long time."

"You know we got to find the murder weapon. We don't have enough to get a search warrant for Mikes place, but we could ask for a consent to search. I suppose we need to wait for the autopsy report. That might give us a better idea of what we are looking for," Dave said.

"Maybe he threw it out of his truck somewhere between the scene and his house."

"That's about six miles or more. A lot of looking to do."

"I remember the old sheriff made us walk along Pine Ridge for three miles looking for a pair of boots that a guy used to stomp a woman to death with. He told the sheriff he threw them out of the car after he killed her. It was cold and snowing. We walked that road and didn't find them. We walked it again that afternoon and found them. Had blood on them," Jon told Dave.

"I didn't know that. That was a couple of years before I got on the SO."

They pulled in the driveway at the Gore residence. Mike's truck was not there. There was an old single car garage next to the house. It didn't have a door on it. Dave stopped in front of it and they got out.

"You see what I see in that garage, Jon?" Dave asked.

Dave looked in the garage door. "No, not really."

"Look over there in the corner. A splitting maul. We ought to get that."

They knocked on the door, and a woman came to the door who said she was Mike Gore's mom. They asked her if they could look in the garage. She didn't like that idea that they suspected her son of killing this guy. "My boy was home all night, I tell you. He didn't leave all night," she told them. She signed a consent to search.

Jon and Dave went in the garage and looked around. Dave picked up the splitting maul. No blood on it. The blade on it was about the right width of the marks on the victim's chest. The wooden handle had been replaced with a steel pipe handle that was welded to the head. Dave put it in a plastic bag and gave the woman a receipt for it.

"Is Mike's woman here?" Dave asked the lady.

"Diane," she hollered into the house, "the cops want to talk to you. Don't you be fibbin' to them. You know, Mike was here all night."

Diane came to the door. "Can you go with us to the sheriff's office, Diane? We'd like to talk to you. We'll bring you back," Dave asked her.

"Let me see if she'll watch the kids."

She came back out about ten minutes later with her coat on and got in the back of the car. They were quiet on the way to the office.

"Diane, how long you and Mike been together?" Dave asked her as the three of them were seated in his office.

"Three years. We got a two-year-old and a four-month-old baby."

"Have you always lived with his mom since you been together?"

"Yeah. We can't afford no place of our own. Mike don't get much work cuttin' timber."

"Do you know the guy who was killed over by Slab Hill?" Dave asked her.

"I met him a couple of times. I been over there with Mike. I never been in the trailer. I always sit in the car."

"When was the last time you seen the guy?"

"About a month ago or longer. He stopped by our place one day and helped Mike work on his truck."

"Did you know his woman?"

"No. Never met her."

"Diane, I want you to know that you're not in any trouble here. We just want to figure out what happened that night. When did Mike leave your place Christmas Eve?"

"He left about eleven that night. We had a fight. I wanted to go out and he didn't want to so he up and left and didn't come home till about four in the morning."

"Are sure about that? His mom says he was home all night," Jon asked her.

"I'm not going to lie about it. She told me to tell you that, but I can't."

"Are you sure what time he got home?" Dave asked her.

"Yeah, cause he woke me up, and I looked at the clock and the baby woke up, and I got up and fed her."

"Did he tell who he was with that night?"

"All he said was that he had been over to that guy's place. The guy that was killed."

"Was he over there all that time?" Jon asked.

"I don't know."

Jon and Dave both looked at each other. They could tell that this girl was getting nervous, that maybe she knew something.

Dave scooted his chair closer to hers and looked directly in her eyes. "Do you know who killed him?"

She looked down at the floor and started to sob. They knew she was on the verge of telling them something important. They had to be careful of what they said or she wouldn't tell them.

"You can tell us. You aren't going to be in any trouble. We won't let anyone hurt you," Dave said.

"When Mike came home that night and got in bed with me, he told me he killed a guy," she told them.

"Did he say who the guy was?" Dave asked her.

"James, the guy in the trailer over there by Slab Hill," she said.

"Did he say how he did it?"

"He beat him with an axe is what he told me."

"Why did he do it?" Jon asked.

"I don't know. He didn't say."

After taking a tape-recorded statement from Diane with all the details that she could supply, they took her back home. Dave told her not to tell anyone what she told them. They were not ready to arrest Mike yet.

On the way back to the SO, Dave and Jon talked about what was next.

"We need to get the autopsy results back," Jon said.

"I'll take the splitting maul to BCI first thing in the morning and put a rush on it. Have you got anything back from the arson lab yet?" Dave asked Jon.

"No. I'll call them in the morning and see if I can speed it up. I can testify about smelling gasoline on the sample near the couch. It would be nice if they found gasoline on the chair that burned up in the kitchen. There won't be any problem proving the fire was set with two points of origin and the elimination of accidental causes." Jon explained.

"Let's get some supper. This has been a long day," Dave said as he pulled into the K & L Parking lot. There were a couple of Jackson PD cops eating at a table. They joined them.

"You guys have a busy day?" Dave asked them.

"Day shift didn't have a single call. We came on at three this afternoon and haven't had anything," the sergeant told them.

"How about New Year's Eve?" Dave asked.

"No bar calls. One drunk driver. One car crash with a drunk driver that was a hit and run. They had a good description of the car and found it at a house on David Ave. The guy fessed up," the patrolman told them as the sergeant. was cutting his steak.

"What are you guys workin' on this holiday?" the sergeant. asked.

"That murder down on 279 that happened Christmas Morning," Dave said.

"Gettin' anywhere?"

"I think we about got it solved. Waitin' on the autopsy report then we can put things together and take it to the prosecutor."

"Well, boys," the sergeant said. "I turned in my paper work at the retirement board last week. I got nine more months to work and I'm hangin' it up."

"Doggone," Dave said. "Hate to see you go. How long you been on?"

"It'll be thirty-five years. I started in 1946 when I got back from the war."

"Tell us about them old days," Jon said. He liked to hear the sergeant tell tales.

"We didn't have radios then. When you called the police number if no one answered at the station on the second ring then the operator answered. If we had a call the operator flipped a switch that turned on a red light on the pole at Broadway and Main and three other places in town. When we saw the lite was on we went to a call box and called the operator and got the call. We had to check the lights every twenty minutes while we were on patrol, either on foot or in the car."

"That's really neat," Jon said.

"We only had one officer on duty on midnights. On Friday and Saturday nights, we had a guy who worked 8:00 P.M. to 4:00 A.M., so we had extra help. They were always the busy nights."

"Where was the police station back then?" Jon asked.

"Above the old fire station," the sergeant said.

"You going to keep on painting houses, Sarge?" Dave asked, referring to the sergeant's house painting business that he did on his time off.

"No, I'm hangin' that up, too. I'm lookin' for a job somewhere to give me something to do."

"I'll never forget that kidnapping and rape you and the sheriff solved back when I was a dispatcher at the SO. It was the first time I ever saw anything like that take place. It was really neat how you knew who did it when the woman described the guy to you," Jon said.

The sergeant. laughed. "That was a long night. I saw the suspect walking up town about an hour before he abducted her. I knew he was up to no good.

On Tuesday morning, Liz called and said that she got the report on the autopsy. No carbon monoxide in the blood. An artery in the chest was cut in one of the six hits with the sharp instrument. The cuts all went deep. That was the cause of death. She was going to drop off the report at the SO in a few minutes. Jon called the Arson Lab and they had found gasoline in the sample he had taken from the couch but found nothing in the samples from the chair in the kitchen. He called the SO, but Dave had already left for BCI with the splitting maul. He then typed out all his reports on the murder bringing it up to date.

Jon went up to the SO when Dave got back from BCI. Dave said that they would be able to compare the cuts on the body with the blade on the splitting maul as well as process it for latent fingerprints and blood. "You think our man will take off?" Jon asked Dave.

"I don't think so. At least as long as his woman keeps her mouth shut," Dave answered.

"So, we're going to wait on the lab work on the maul before we arrest the guy."

"I think we should," Dave said, "then we'll decide if we want to get a warrant for an arrest or take it to the Grand Jury for a secret indictment. That will be up to the prosecutor. We'll talk to him after we get all the lab stuff done."

"Did you read the autopsy report?" Jon asked.

"Yeah, it's good. And your lab report. We've got a pretty good case. If they find anything on the maul it will be great."

"Yeah," Jon said.

"You know we're missing the .44 Magnum revolver from the crime scene and the cocaine and probably some amount of cash."

"What do you think about talking to the victim's dad again and asking him about his son's little business?" Jon asked.

"We could give it a try. I doubt that he will tell us. He's probably feeling pretty bad that he got his kid in a business that got him killed."

"We could offer him immunity from prosecution on any drug related charges if he tells us."

"I'll call the prosecutor in the morning and ask him if we can do that," Dave said.

"I'll be off Friday. Taking a four-day weekend and going to the mountains to learn to ski," Jon announced.

"Why do I have the feeling that this involves our coroner investigator?"

"It might," Jon said, smiling.

That evening, Jon called Reverend Evans and went to the Manse and had another session with him. The reverend was teaching him how to play chess as they talked. He enjoyed talking to the guy. He was interesting to talk to and very nice. This time the reverend asked Jon if he could pray with him before he left the Manse. It was a short and to the point prayer, and Jon left there feeling good.

CHAPTER 30

On Friday morning, Liz picked up Jon at his house in her truck and they headed east on the Appalachian Highway. They drove to Belpre and crossed the Ohio River into Parkersburg, West Virginia. They continued on U.S. Highway 50 over into the mountains.

It was a nice sunny day with snow still on the ground. "What's the weather like in the mountains?" Jon asked Liz.

"About like it is here except with about two more feet of snow on the ground," she answered.

He told her about the recent developments in the murder investigation that they were now referring to as "the axe murder."

"So, you'll be making an arrest soon," Liz said.

"Yeah. When we get the lab results on the splitting maul. We'll go talk to the prosecutor and see which way he wants to go. Through Municipal Court or take it directly to the Grand Jury. Prosecutors like to go direct to the Grand Jury so they can avoid having a preliminary hearing in Municipal Court. The hearing takes more time and they have to reveal a lot of their evidence in it."

They stayed on US 50 and stopped in Clarksburg, West Virginia, for lunch. The highway from Clarksburg the rest of the way was two-laned and crooked. They started going up higher into the mountains after they went through Grafton and the snow on the ground got deeper as they got up higher. The roads were dry as it hadn't snowed any for several days. Liz had put a big trunk in the back of the truck to put their luggage in and keep it dry. He noticed several bags of sand back near the tailgate to give the truck traction in case they had to drive in snow.

Canaan Valley is a big wide area in the mountains. It is surrounded by mountain peaks and is the home to two state parks and two ski resorts. There were a lot of nice vacation homes in the area. Liz told him their place was a condo in a little vacation community. It had a restaurant in the middle of it and was just a half mile off the main highway that ran down the valley.

"We have to stop at the restaurant and get the key to the house, but first we have to stop at the grocery store in Davis and get us some food for the weekend," she told him as they were entering the little town of Davis.

The condo was nice. Three bedrooms and two baths. A garage in the basement for the truck. A big stone fireplace in the living room which had French Doors that went out onto a deck that looked out over the valley. They carried in the groceries and their luggage.

"Can you bring in firewood and start a fire in the fireplace Jon?" Liz asked him.

"Sure. Where's the wood at?"

"In that little shed in the back yard."

Jon got the fire going and brought in what he thought was enough wood to last through the night. Liz turned the furnace up when they got there and it was starting to get comfortable. He could smell something cooking. He went into the kitchen.

"How's steak and salad and a baked potato sound?" she said.

"Good. This place is really nice. How far are we from the ski resort?"

"About two miles."

After supper, they sat in front of the fireplace and played checkers and after Jon told Liz that Rev. Evans was teaching him to play chess, they played chess. Liz had bought Jon a six pack of Miller Lite. She was drinking 7-Up.

"So, what is on for tomorrow?" Jon asked her.

"I'm teaching you to downhill ski," she replied.

"I can't afford to break a leg."

"They have a beginner's slope. You'll get the hang of it."

Liz put away the chess board and they got comfortable on the couch. They kissed several times and it became very passionate. Liz took Jon's hand and placed it underneath her sweater. He began to caress her breasts.

"Can we sleep together?" Jon asked her.

"I would like that very much," she said. "I'm going to take a shower. I'll meet you in bed."

"Okay. I'll bank the fire with some hickory so it'll last a while."

Jon waited about a half hour and went in the bedroom, and Liz was sitting in bed with the sheet up around her and brushing her hair.

"You are sexy when you do that," he told her. He went in the bathroom and took a shower. When he returned to the bedroom, Liz had finished brushing her hair. He turned off the light and dropped the towel he had wrapped around him and slide in beside her. They turned to each other. She was naked. He was naked.

Jon woke up and looked at the clock. It was one in the morning. Liz was asleep with her head on his chest. He gently got up and put the towel around his waist and went to the living room and put more wood in the fireplace. When he got back in bed Liz woke up and kissed him passionately. He immediately became aroused. "You were a virgin," he said to her.

"I was, but I'm not now," she said.

"I never thought to ask if you were on the pill."

"I have been on it for several months. Ever since we first met. I knew you were going to be the one," she said as she ran her hand across his chest.

I'm glad I got to be the one. You're the most beautiful woman I have ever laid eyes on."

They made love again and went back to sleep. They woke at daylight and did it again and then took a shower together.

Jon helped Liz fix breakfast. "I may be too tired to ski after last night," Jon said as they ate.

Liz smiled. He helped her with the dishes and they got dressed for a day at the ski slope.

Liz was very patient with Jon in teaching him to ski. She brought a pair of her brother's ski boots that were exactly his size and of course she brought the skis from home. They spent all morning on the beginner's slope, and after lunch, they took the lift up the mountain and skied down one of the slopes. Jon took a couple of falls but didn't hurt anything. By dark they were worn out and returned to the condo. Jon got the fire going again while Liz finished supper. She had put chili in a slow cooker before they left that morning and they roasted hot dogs in the fireplace.

"Do you want to cross country ski tomorrow, Jon?" Liz asked him as they ate.

"Yes, I would. I know a good place we can go. It's called Canaan Loop Road over at Davis. They don't plow it so it's good for cross country. I brought a backpack and we can take our lunch."

"We'll have to rent some cross-country skis," she said.

"One thing I learned is to layer your clothes, so you can take some off as you get warmed up."

"Would you like to go to church services in the morning at the Lodge at the park?"

"Sure, what time?"

"Nine. The pastor from the Lutheran Church in Davis does the service. It's very informal. We always go to it when we are down here."

Being out in the fresh cold air all day caused them to go to bed early that night. After making love, they both slept through the night without waking. When they got up, the fire in the fireplace was out. Jon didn't rebuild it as they were going to be gone all day, to church and then skiing. The next day was Monday, and they would have to leave. Jon wished they had the whole week together. Liz was a lot of fun to be with and very easy to get along with. She had an endless amount of energy.

After church service, they rented cross country skis and drove over to Davis and got on the Loop Road. There were plenty of ski tracks on it from others. They went several miles out the road and then off on a side trail about a half mile to a backpack shelter where they ate their lunch.

"Have you ever backpacked Liz?" Jon asked her.

"No, but I would like to try it. I have trail camped with horses a lot. We used to bring our horses down here to Spruce Knob and trail ride and camp."

"We'll have to do it this spring. Spring and fall are the best times. The middle of the winter is too cold and the snow is too deep."

"I'm glad we came down here this weekend. We seem to have a lot in common. We like doing things outdoors. I wish we didn't have to go back home tomorrow."

"Me, too. I enjoy being with you."

After cross country skiing they drove out to Blackwater Falls State Park at Davis and walked down the steps to the big waterfall. It was flowing pretty good but not frozen, although the rocks at the foot of the falls were coated with ice from the spray. They returned to the condo, and Jon got the fireplace going again while Liz fixed supper.

"I am really tired," Liz said. "We don't have to be in a hurry to get back home tomorrow, do we?"

"No. I was hoping that you were going to suggest that we sleep in tomorrow."

"That's what I had in mind. We can go over to the lodge for breakfast. We'll have to clean the condo. I brought clean bed linens so we won't have to do laundry. I'll take the dirty one's home."

They awoke at nine in the morning. They had both fallen asleep as soon as they got in bed about ten the night before.

"Jon, can we make love before we get up? We're too young to not do it every night," she said.

"Okay. I'm sorry. Too much fresh air and exercise. I fell asleep and didn't wake up all night."

"That's all right. I just can't get enough of you. What are we going to do when we get back home?"

"We'll have to just make time for us," he told her as they embraced and kissed.

"Well, how was your trip to the mountains with our pretty coroner investigator?" Dave asked Jon as they sat at the kitchen table in the jail eating pancakes for breakfast.

"I learned to ski and didn't break anything."

"Wish I could get away like that."

"You just got to take the time. For years, I never took much time off. Now I realize there is more than just the job."

"Grand Jury is Friday on the axe murder. I got subpoenas for you and Liz. I'll give you Liz's to serve her. The prosecutor is going for Aggravated Murder with Death Penalty, Aggravated Burglary, and Abuse of a Corpse," Dave told him.

"Is our suspect still around?" Jon asked.

"I talked to his woman over the weekend. He tells her we don't have anything on him. He's been cutting firewood for some folks on Gieke Ridge."

"What's the plan for the arrest?" Jon asked.

"I hope it's not as exciting as the last one we did together."

"Yeah, me, too"

"She's going to call me on Saturday and let me know when he is going to be at home. She is going to try to keep him home Saturday night, so we can go down and get him at the house."

"Has he got the .44 Magnum that is missing from the crime scene?"

"She hasn't seen it. He may have sold it. They have a couple of shot guns in the house, but I don't expect any trouble from the guy. I thought about just calling and asking him to come in to the office, but he might take off."

Jon got up and filled his coffee cup again and put his plate in the sink. "Those were really good pancakes Millie," he said to the cook.

"I made them from scratch. No store-bought stuff made in this kitchen," Millie said.

"Oh, yeah, I forgot to tell you; we got the lab results on the splitting maul back. They found blood down in a crack where that pipe handle was welded to the maul head. It matched the type of the victim. We really got lucky there."

"Yeah that is a good break. How about finger prints?"

"None," Dave told Jon.

"Well, his woman and his mom both told us that the suspect used the maul to split firewood with."

"Yeah, we got a good case, but we still need to get a confession. I think we can get one."

"Let's hope so," Jon agreed.

It was starting to snow as Jon drove out to Liz's place to give her the subpoena. He had expected to have a fire or two waiting on him when he called in after having four days off, but there were none. He found Liz in the barn working. They embraced and kissed.

"Here's your subpoena on the axe murder for Grand Jury Friday morning," Jon told her.

"Great," she said, "anything new?"

"They found blood on the splitting maul that matched the victim's blood type."

"I have to go back out on midnight shift tonight," Liz said.

"You want to stop by the house before you go to work," Jon asked Liz, smiling, suggesting some repetition of the weekends nightly events.

"I'd like that," she said, smiling, suggesting the same thing he had on his mind.

Liz came over to Jon's every night that week about nine and stayed until time to go to work at the hospital. Each night they took a short walk through the neighborhood and then spent time in bed together before she showered and got ready for work. Jon wondered if the newness of this would wear off, or if this was going to be a lasting relationship. He could tell that Liz was in love with him and his feelings for her were growing.

On Friday morning, Jon, Liz, and Dave met in the kitchen of the jail before Grand Jury. Fried eggs, bacon, and toast for breakfast. As in the last Grand Jury they did, Liz would read the medical examiner's report on the autopsy and talk about examining the body at the scene. Jon would talk about the cause of the fire and Dave would give a summary of the investigation, tell about the suspects interview and read the test results on the splitting maul. The suspect's wife would testify. So, the suspect would not know who told on him, the suspect's mother and two of his friends were subpoenaed to testify, also.

The courthouse hallway was crowded that morning. Several police officers, deputies and others testifying on other cases. The axe murder was on first. Dave was the first witness. He had the splitting maul wrapped up in brown wrapping paper. It would make a good impression on the jury. Juries like to look at things and handle things.

Jon entered the courtroom when it was his turn. He was sworn in by the court reporter. He took his seat in the witness box. The jury was seated in the jury box. He looked at the jury members and saw several that he knew. He smiled at them. One man asked him if he was ready for spring trout fishing. Grand Juries are informal. It is the Grand Jury's job to investigate and determine if there is probable cause to send the case to a jury trial. The prosecutor briefly asked Jon his experience and qualifications and then had him tell about the fire and what caused it. That was it. He was in there about fifteen minutes' total.

The case took a little over an hour. The suspect's woman and mother and two friends testified as planned. The woman's testimony was crucial. They were hoping that she would not change her story. The prosecutor came out in the hall and sat with them as the jury deliberated. After about fifteen minutes, a juror opened the door and motioned for the prosecutor. He went back in and then came back out and gave Dave a thumbs up signal, meaning they had gotten the indictment. It would be late afternoon before the warrant was typed up and sent over to the Sheriff's Office.

Dave, Jon, Liz, and the Sheriff were all sitting at the kitchen table in the jail eating lunch. Baked ham, fried potatoes, baked beans, and coleslaw was to-days menu.

"Chuck, tell Liz why you feed the prisoners so well in your jail," Jon said to the Sheriff as they sat at the big table.

"Well, it all goes back several years to an old sheriff we had. He had been a prisoner of war and they about starved him to death, so when he became Sheriff he said he would eat the same meals that the prisoners ate and they would be decent meals. So, that's how it got started and it has never changed," Chuck told them.

They all decided to come back to the Sheriff's Office about five that af-ternoon to make the arrest on the indictment. Liz was going to go with them. Dave was going to stay in the office all afternoon waiting on the suspect's lady to call him and tell him when the guy would be home that evening.

Liz and Jon went over to Jon's house to wait. Liz needed to get some sleep as she had to work that night.

"You go to bed and sleep. I got some reports to type up," Jon said.

"I thought maybe we could take a nap together," Liz said to Jon as she put her arms around him and drew him close to her as they stood in the living room.

"You know, we wouldn't get any sleep doing that," Jon said, smiling, "And you been up all night working. If you're going to go with us, you need to be awake."

"Okay, but we need some sex time soon. I like it."

"I do, too. When are you off work again?" he asked her.

"I get a three-day weekend coming up."

"We can spend a night together here if you want to."

"You know I want to. I don't think Grampa minds. I don't think he'll say anything to Mom and Dad about it."

"What did your mom say about our trip to the mountains?"

"I told her we took Karen with us. She doesn't ask personal questions. I haven't told her I'm in love with you yet, but she will probably figure it out before I tell her."

"Will she approve?" he asked Liz.

"Yes, I think she will. Of course, she doesn't like the cop part too well, but she'll get used to it."

Liz walked into the bedroom and started taking off her clothes to go to bed. "You better shut that door. You're distracting me," Jon said.

"Maybe you'll change your mind about joining me."

The phone rang. Jon answered it. It was his boss.

At four-thirty, Jon woke Liz up so they could go meet Dave at the SO. "My boss called while you were asleep. I have to go to the office next Tuesday for a hearing on that shooting. He says they are going to make a big deal out of me shooting the tires off the car when the guy was trying to get away."

"Are you worried?" she asked.

"No, not really. I've got a good, clean record. They won't fire me, but they might suspend me or something else. They don't understand police work. We're the only law enforcement agency in the Commerce Department. They don't like people that carry guns. It's not what they're used to dealing with."

"I'm hungry," Liz said.

"I just talked to Dave. He wants us to go through McDonald's and get him a Big Mac. We'll get us something, too, and eat with Dave."

"His woman called me," Dave said to them as they sat in his office, eating Big Mac's. "He's going to be home until about nine. They are both going out together tonight over to the Swamps to party. They're leaving about nine. We'll go down about eight to the house and get him. Chucks going with us. Jon, you and I will go to the front door. Liz and Chuck will go to the back door. Should just be him and her and the kids and his mom in the house."

"Sounds good," Jon said. "You got radios for us?"

"Only got two. Each team will have to share one so if something happens each team needs to stay together. You got your gun, Liz?"

Liz pulled her parka back and showed her .45 on one side and her spare mags on the other side. "I've got my handcuffs in my pants pocket and my flashlight in my coat pocket," she said.

"All right," Dave said. "You're all ready."

"Actually, I helped her get ready," Jon said, smiling.

"What's the suspect saying? He knew about Grand Jury. Is he worried?" Jon asked Dave.

"She said he hasn't said a word about it. Didn't ask her or his mom any questions about what they did in Grand Jury or anything."

"What are we driving?" Jon asked.

"Chucks unmarked and your unmarked."

"What are we supposed to do if he comes out the back door?" Liz asked.

"If he's armed, then shoot him. If he isn't then grab him. Chuck will tell you what to do. Stay right with him," Dave told her.

"You all right, Liz?" Jon asked her.

"Kind of nervous. I've never done anything like this before," she said.

"Just listen to Chuck. He's done it hundreds of times," Jon told her.

"By the way, I've got the dates for you and Karen to start your basic class in April. You'll go every evening Monday through Friday from Five until Ten and every other Saturday from eight until four," Dave told her.

"How long does it take?" she asked Dave.

"April, May, and the first two weeks of June, and you'll be done."

"Guess I won't be getting much sleep for a while, then," she said to them.

"We all had to work the midnight shift when we took ours. Didn't we, Jon?" Dave said.

"Yeah. Left the school at ten and went and ate supper and then on patrol all night. Back then I was painting houses, too, so I worked four hours after I got off in the morning painting and then got about four hours' sleep."

"I was driving a wrecker when I was off duty back then. I was on call on the wrecker," Dave told them.

They left the SO about six-thirty and drove down route 139. Jon and Dave were leading and Chuck and Liz were following. They went over toward South Webster and turned up the holler. They were still in Jackson County, but not far from Scioto County. It was dark and cold. They pulled up in front of the house. Mike's truck was there. There was a man in the front yard who looked a lot like the guy they were after, Mike. Dave hollered at him, "Where's Mike at?"

"In the bathroom, taking a shower. I'm his brother. Go on in. We been expecting you," the guy said.

Chuck and Liz went around the back of the house, and Jon and Dave went up on the porch and opened the door and went in. Mike's woman was sitting in the living room with a baby on her lap. The room was hot. There was a wood burning stove going full blast in the living room.

"Where is he?" Dave asked her.

"In the shower," she said and pointed down a hallway.

Jon went down the hallway with his gun drawn. At the end of the hallway he could hear a shower running in the bathroom. The door was closed. There was a bedroom on each side of the bathroom. Dave stepped in the door of one of the bedrooms and Jon stepped in the door of the other one. Jon reached out and knocked on the door of the bathroom. "Mike, it's the Sheriff; you in there?" he said.

"Yeah," came the reply," I'm taking a shower."

"We're here to arrest you; come out with your hands on your head," Jon said through the door.

"I ain't got any clothes on," Mike replied.

"Put your hands on your head, and come out anyway," Jon said.

The shower quit running. The door opened slowly. Jon and Dave had their pistols trained on the door. Mike appeared in the doorway, buck naked, with his hands over his private parts.

"Get your hands on your head, or I'll shoot your cock off," Jon said.

Mike complied. He put his hands on his head.

"Turn around and face the wall," Jon said.

"Where's your clothes?" Dave asked.

"Behind you, on the bed," Mike replied.

Dave handed him his underwear, then his jeans, after checking the pockets, then a shirt. Mike got dressed.

"Now put your hands behind your back," Jon said.

He put his hands behind his back and they took him out into the living room. They let him sit in a chair. His mother started crying. Dave looked at Mike's woman and asked her to get Mikes shoes and put them on him. She did. She got him a jacket. Dave checked it and Jon had Mike stand up and Dave put the coat over his shoulders. "We have him and we're coming out the front door," Dave said into his walkie talkie.

"Okay," Chuck replied. They put him in the back of Jon's car on the passenger side. Dave got in the back on the driver's side. Liz and Chuck came around from behind the house. They went in the house to talk to the women for a few minutes and assure them that Mike would be treated right.

"You go ahead and go back to the jail. We're going to stay and talk a few minutes," Chuck said on the radio. "We need to have a tow truck sent down here to get his truck and have BCI process it."

"Okay," Dave said, "4003 to County, we're headed 25 with one 21."

"Clear 4003," the dispatcher answered.

Twenty-five was the code for "office" and 21 was the code for "prisoner."

At the office, they took Mike into an interview room and changed his handcuffs from the back to the front so he would be more comfortable. Dave read him his rights and explained them to him. He agreed to talk and signed the waiver saying that he was willing to talk at the time and did not want a lawyer, but that he understood that he could stop at any time and request and attorney.

"The charges against you are serious, Mike," Dave said as he and Jon started the interview. "You are charged with Aggravated Murder with the Death Penalty specification which means that if you are convicted you could be executed. You are also charged with Burglary and Abuse of a Corpse and Aggravated Arson."

"I didn't kill him. I wasn't even there when it happened," Mike said.

"You know, Mike, things would go better for you if you told us the truth. We have a good case on you. We have the murder weapon that we found in your garage with the victim's blood on it. We have the testimony of persons who you told that you killed the guy," Dave said.

"Man, I didn't do it. That guy was my friend."

"So, if you didn't do it, then who do you think did it?" Jon asked.

"I don't have any idea. I was home all night. You know that. You talked to my woman. She told you that."

"No, Mike, she told us the truth. She told us you were gone. She told us you came home very late, after the fire had happened," Jon said.

Mike looked at the floor. He didn't say anything. He started to cry a little. Dave and Jon both thought that he was going to come clean.

"Tell us, Mike, what really happened that night. You can get the death penalty dropped. You'll have to go to prison," Dave said as he looked directly at Mike.

"Man, I didn't do it," Mike said as he continued to shed some tears. "Why would she say those things about me?"

"She's telling the truth," said Dave.

"I want a lawyer," Mike said.

"Okay," Dave said. He and Jon knew that they could go no further once those words were stated. They took him back to the jail and had him strip and gave him jail clothes, a blanket and a sheet, a towel, and a washcloth. They put him in the main cell block. The next day he would be photographed and fingerprinted.

Dave Jon, Chuck, and Liz sat in the deputy's room. Dave had just told them about the results of the interview.

"He'll get an attorney. Hopefully it will be one that will make a deal to drop the death penalty and maybe a couple of the other charges and plead to the murder," Chuck said. "I can't see any good attorney taking a chance of getting him executed by going to trial. We'll just wait and let the lawyers work it out. You guys did a good job. Girls, too."

"So, how did you like your first arrest, Liz?" Dave said.

"Well, we didn't have to do much out back there. We could hear you inside the house," she said.

"Did you hear what Jon told him about putting his hands on his head," Dave said.

"No," Liz said.

Dave started laughing. "Mike was in the shower. Jon told him to come out with his hands on his head. He came out with his hands covering his privates. Jon told him to put his hands on his head or he would shoot his cock off."

Chuck laughed. Liz was embarrassed.

"I'm goin' home," Chuck said. "I got to feed some calves yet tonight."

"See you tomorrow," Dave said.

"Well, I've got to go home, too. Grampa will be wanting to hear about this. I told him what I was doing tonight. He promised not to tell Mom or Dad."

CHAPTER 31

Jon was driving back from the Reynoldsburg Office. He had just had his hearing on the shooting where he had killed the guy who had shot him in the lung. The Department of Commerce made a big deal of the fact that he had shot out the two tires on the suspects' vehicle as they tried to flee. They said it was a violation of the firearms policy even though he had not yet received a copy of that new policy and had not yet attended any training on it. Jon's attorney had hit hard on that fact, and also on the fact that Ohio Law permitted deadly force used to stop a fleeing violent felon. The Department argued that if he had not shot at the vehicle then they would have gotten away and there would not have been a fatal shooting. His attorney argued that it would just have meant that someone else would have been shot by the suspect, officer or civilian, on down the road, that night or over the next few days as the search went on for the suspect.

Jon didn't have a good feeling about the whole thing. He knew what he did was right. The truth is that he would have shot the tires out anyway if he had gotten the firearms policy. He didn't say that when he testified in the hearing. It just didn't make sense to let someone get away that had killed an innocent old lady who would have given them guys money if they had just asked her. He was afraid he was going to get fired over it. As far as anyone knew, he was the first fire marshal to ever shoot anyone. It didn't matter that the Grand Jury had cleared him. There had even been an editorial in the newspaper commending him for his actions. No one had voiced any objection to his actions except for Commerce. The Fire Marshal's Office and the Arson Bureau had been established in the first decade of the twentieth century. His great-grandfather had been one of the first investigators. He knew very little about his work. There were no records existing from back then. There were no stories passed down through the family.

If he got fired for this, it would probably end his career in law enforcement. No one would hire him with a bad shooting on his record. Oh, Chuck would probably hire him back on to the SO. He forgot about that. Maybe he should never have left the SO. At one time, the county commissioners had tried to stir the deputies up against the sheriff over pay raises. They had summoned the deputies to one of their meetings. Jon had been the only one to refuse to go. He had called the sheriff once he got the call to attend. The Sheriff didn't tell him not to go, but he knew that if he went he would be disloyal to the sheriff as the commissioners had no right to be doing what they were doing. When it was over, with the sheriff had called Jon in to his office and thanked him for his loyalty.

He needed cheered up. He stopped at a payphone on the way home and called Liz and asked her if she wanted to go out to eat this evening. No, she couldn't go out because the hired hand was sick so she had to do farm chores. However, she had potato soup simmering on the stove, and she invited Jon to come out. Doc was going to his Grange Meeting.

Jon got to Liz's place about five and found her in the barn. "Need help?" he asked.

"Sure," she replied. "You can get some hay from the loft for the horses while I fill their water buckets."

"How did things go at the office today?" she asked him.

"Not very good. They might fire me. They say I violated the firearms policy by shooting at a moving motor vehicle. They have fourteen days to decide and notify me by letter of their decision."

"Why do you think they might fire you?"

"I've just got a bad feeling about it. But, you know, even if I was aware of the policy, I would have still shot at the tires. I wouldn't have let him get away. I didn't say that in the hearing, but that is how I feel about it."

"I don't know what to say. I'm new at this stuff. I agree that you did the right thing."

"The worst part is the waiting for the decision."

"Just keep busy and don't worry about it."

"I know, but I have a tendency to think about things at night, and I lose sleep."

"I know a cure for that," she said as she put her arms around his waist.

"What would that be?" he said.

"You should sleep with me. I'll wear you out, and you'll sleep good. If you wake up in the middle of the night, we'll have sex again."

"That sounds fun, but you're on night shift."

"I know. We can do it before I go to work. It'll help you sleep."

"Okay."

"Let's go inside and eat. I made cornbread, too."

"That goes good with potato soup."

After they had eaten and washed the dishes, Liz took Jon's hand and led him down the hallway to her bedroom.

"Grampa won't be home until eleven. We have plenty of time," she said as she started to unbutton his shirt.

"What if he comes home early?" Jon asked.

"He won't. They have some kind of a special program tonight."

Jon pulled her sweater over her head. She had on a black bra. They finished undressing each other and got between the sheets. Liz turned off the light and lit a candle.

"Wake up, Jon, it's ten-thirty; Grampa will be home in a half hour," Liz said as she sat in a chair, wearing a white robe and brushing her wet hair.

"You're right about sex putting me to sleep."

"I like what we do together," she said, smiling.

"Me, too," he said.

"Jon, I'm in love with you. I have been for a long time."

"I feel the same way about you."

"Really?"

"Yeah, I do. I've been thinking about it for a long time now. You're a good woman. You're nice. You're beautiful. You have good character. You're everything a man would want in a woman."

"Thank you," she said and got up and laid down beside him and put her lips to his. He slipped his hand beneath her robe and took her breast in it.

"No," she said, smiling. "I have to get ready for work, and Grampa will be here soon. You need to get dressed and go to the living room before he gets here."

"Okay," he said as he rolled out of bed and started getting dressed. Liz went into the bathroom, and he watched as she removed her robe, revealing her perfect body. She put on black panties and a black bra. He had to get out of here and into the living room before he went after her again.

Jon had a nice visit with Doc as he waited for Liz to finish getting ready for work. Doc was pleased that Liz was doing a good job as his investigator, and he was glad that she was getting involved in working at the SO. Liz came out, and they talked about the arrest Liz helped them with on the axe murder case.

"I think it would be best if you don't tell your parents about that, Liz," Doc said.

"I'm not. At least not for a long time. Not till after I finish my basic police class and get some more experience."

"By the way, the Sheriff called me and asked me if I wanted to go fox hunting with him this Saturday. I told him I would. I don't have a dog anymore. I used to hunt with him when I had a dog."

"That's great, Grampa," Liz said. "You haven't been fox hunting for years."

"We're goin' with the sheriff from over in Pike County and one of the county commissioners over there. Chuck is going to pick me up."

"You be sure to dress warm," Liz said.

"I will. They'll have a big fire going, and if it gets too cold, I'll just sit in the car."

"Well, I got to be going home," Jon said.

"And I have to go to work," Liz said.

"You come back anytime, Jon," Doc said. "You're welcome anytime."

"Thanks, Doc; you got an awful nice granddaughter."

Jon and Liz walked out together. They kissed goodbye, and Liz headed up the road with Jon following behind.

The next few days were quiet for Jon. He spent some time helping Dave on some burglaries. He really wasn't supposed to do that sort of thing on state time, but he couldn't solve any arson cases in the county without Dave's help. Since he still held a deputy's commission it was perfectly legal, just against State Fire Marshal Policy. They got a bunch of guns back from a house burglary just outside of Jackson. They found them down at Eifort, a small community down on Route 140 just across the line in Scioto County. They made two arrests for burglary. They gave one guy a break for receiving stolen property, as long as he agreed to testify about buying the guns from the burglars. He bought six guns from them for the price of just one gun. That is what they call "Prima Facia" evidence that he knew that they were stolen. One of the burglars confessed, but the other one was a hard-nosed case and refused to talk. If they had to, they would offer the one that confessed a deal if he testified against his partner. Dave had been after the hard-nosed one for a couple of years. He had been breaking into a lot of houses.

On Saturday morning when Jon got his mail, there was a letter from the Commerce Department. It was signed by the Director of Commerce. It told him that he was being suspended without pay for two weeks, starting that Monday, for violating the firearms policy. He was glad it was over. He didn't like having this in his personnel file. It wouldn't go good if something like this happened again. He was going to have to be careful.

"Being too careful is what gets a lot of officers killed," Dave said as they discussed the letter in his office on Saturday morning. "You hesitate to think about how you're going to get in trouble, and in that second or two, you get shot."

"I know," Jon agreed.

"What you going to do for two weeks?" Dave asked.

"I think I'll ask Liz if I can help out there on the farm. They need to put a new roof on the barn, and the hired hand can't do it by himself. I won't take any pay for it."

"Yeah, you'll take it out in trade with Liz," Dave said as he laughed. "If Doc wasn't out there, you'd be moving in soon."

"She's a good cook and a hard worker. Her parents are afraid she is going to quit nursing and go into police work."

"You think she will?" Dave asked.

"No, I don't think so. She's making good money at the hospital. She's got an expensive hobby in those horses."

"Well, if she married a guy with a good-paying state job, she could afford to quit the hospital. Too bad she's not a doctor. She could run for coroner when Doc hangs it up."

"I don't think she's looking for a husband. Not right now," Jon said.

"How about you. You looking for a wife?"

"Might be if the right one comes along. Gettin' close to thirty years old. Most people my age are married. Some been married and divorced and married again."

"That Liz would be the right one, if you ask me."

"We got to get to know each other better before thinking about that sort of thing."

What's the longest time you ever dated a girl?" Dave asked.

"A year. Two times. The old sheriff we had before Chuck told me that a man could do better in police work if he stayed single. Said it was hard on a marriage."

"I can't find one that would put up with the hours that I put into this job."

Printed and bound by PG in the USA